THE
ROBIN'S
GREETING

Amish Greenhouse Mystery
Book 3

THE
ROBIN'S
GREETING

WANDA E
BRUNSTETTER

SHILOH RUN PRESS
An Imprint of Barbour Publishing, Inc.

© 2021 by Wanda E. Brunstetter

Print ISBN 978-1-64352-479-5

eBook Editions:
Adobe Digital Edition (.epub) 978-1-64352-481-8
Kindle and MobiPocket Edition (.prc) 978-1-64352-480-1

All scripture quotations, unless otherwise noted, are taken from the King James Version of the Bible.

All German-Dutch words are taken from the *Revised Pennsylvania German Dictionary* found in Lancaster County, Pennsylvania.

This book is a work of fiction. Names, characters, places, and incidents are either products of the author's imagination or used fictitiously. Any similarity to actual people, organizations, and/or events is purely coincidental.

For more information about Wanda E. Brunstetter, please visit the author's website at the following internet address: www.wandabrunstetter.com

Cover Photograph: © Jill Battaglia / Trevillion Images
Cover Design: Buffy Cooper
Model Photography: Richard Brunstetter III

Published by Barbour Publishing, Inc., 1810 Barbour Drive, Uhrichsville, OH 44683, www.barbourbooks.com

Our mission is to inspire the world with the life-changing message of the Bible.

Member of the
Evangelical Christian
Publishers Association

Printed in the United States of America.

Dedication

To my Pennsylvania friends, Diane and Phil,
who are avid bird-watchers.

I will say of the LORD,
He is my refuge and my fortress:
my God; in him will I trust.

PSALM 91:2

Chapter 1

Strasburg, Pennsylvania

Belinda. . .Belinda. . .Belinda. . .

She opened her eyes, still heavy with sleep, sure that the voice she'd heard was her beloved husband, Vernon, calling out to her. But that couldn't be. He'd been gone nearly two years—killed in a tragic accident that had also taken the lives of her son Abe and son-in-law, Toby. The voice Belinda heard must have been a dream, or just the howling November wind outside her bedroom window.

Belinda lay there, with the quilt on her bed pulled up to her chin. The lovely covering with the Wedding Ring pattern had been made by her mother and given to Belinda and Vernon the day they'd gotten married. To her, it was a priceless treasure.

Belinda remained still as she reminisced about days gone by. While there'd been some tough times over the years, nothing she had faced compared to the agony of losing three family members in the same day. Her struggles had increased with the responsibility of running the greenhouse without Vernon's help. Belinda didn't know what she would have done without the help of her daughters and teenage son. They'd needed the greenhouse for financial support, and even more they'd needed each other for emotional support.

Now that Amy was married to Jared, and Sylvia was in a relationship with Dennis, things had changed once again. Belinda was okay with all of that. What she wasn't okay with was the senseless vandalism on her property, most recently the barn. Seeing the building her husband built go up in flames had pierced her heart like a dagger. No one knew how the fire had started. It may have been arson, but if someone had been smoking in or near the barn, the fire could have been an accident.

Unable to resume her sleep, Belinda fluffed her pillows and sat up in bed. How grateful she was for all the help they'd received a few weeks ago when they built a replacement barn. English and Amish friends, neighbors, and family members came together and gave of their time. Now Belinda and her family were ready to begin again, with the hope and prayer that things would settle down and there'd be no more vandalism or tragedy. Given all the needless attacks they'd experienced, Belinda felt certain someone wanted to put them out of business, and perhaps do enough harmful things so Belinda would become discouraged and move somewhere else.

She swiped her tongue across her parched lips and swallowed. At one time, Belinda had believed that her youngest son might have been responsible for the vandalism that had occurred in and around the greenhouse. After his father and brother died, Henry had let it be known that he did not want to take over the beekeeping job Abe used to do. Nor did Henry wish to help in the greenhouse. But he'd assured Belinda that he was not responsible for any of the destruction to their property. She had no reason to doubt him. Henry had proved himself many times with all the help he'd done around here. If the greenhouse folded, Henry would have as much to lose as Belinda and her daughters, since it was the sole means of their livelihood.

Belinda's eldest son, Ezekiel, a minister who lived in Clymer, New York, had offered to give up his bee-raising supply business and move back to Strasburg to help in the greenhouse. But Belinda insisted that he and his family stay put in the community that had become their home.

Bringing her thoughts to a halt, she turned on the battery-operated light resting on the nightstand beside her bed and looked at the alarm clock. It was almost 5:00 a.m. She turned off the alarm, pulled the covers back, and climbed out of bed. It was time to begin another day.

When Belinda entered the kitchen, she found her eldest daughter in front of the stove. The light from the gas lamp hanging on a ceiling hook illuminated the room, and except for the whistle of the wind outside, all was quiet.

"*Guder mariye*, Sylvia." Belinda placed a hand on her daughter's shoulder. "You're up early this morning."

"Good morning, Mom." Sylvia turned the propane gas burner on under the tea kettle. "The howling wind woke me, and I couldn't get back to sleep."

Belinda nodded. "Same here." She moved across the room and lifted the dark green shade that covered the kitchen window. It would be another hour or so before the light of day replaced the darkness in their yard.

Once the water heated, Sylvia made a small pot of tea. "Why don't we get out our favorite teacups and sit until it's time to fix breakfast?" she suggested.

"Good idea. A cup of warm tea is what I need right now." Belinda got out the cups and joined Sylvia at the table. A few minutes later, she poured tea for both of them. It was nice to have some uninterrupted time with her daughter. With Belinda running the greenhouse, and Sylvia taking care of her two children, they didn't get many moments alone.

"It's hard to believe November is here already," Sylvia commented. "Seems like just yesterday when Amy and Jared got married."

Belinda smiled. "Thanksgiving will be here in a few weeks, and next thing we know, it'll be Christmas."

"*Jah*. Too bad Ezekiel and his family won't be coming down for Christmas like they did last year."

"But we're all planning to go to their place to celebrate the holiday this year, and that will be nice."

Sylvia picked up her spoon and swirled the amber liquid in her cup. "I had hoped they would come here instead."

"How come? I figured you and the *kinner* would enjoy getting out of Strasburg for a few days and seeing where your brother lives."

Sylvia drank some tea and blotted her lips with a napkin. "At first I wanted to go, but now that I'm seeing Dennis regularly, I'll feel bad about leaving him to celebrate the holiday alone."

"I would think he'd want to spend Christmas with his mother and siblings."

"I'm sure he would enjoy that, but if Dennis leaves the area for the holiday, he will have to get someone to watch his dog, not to mention the horses he's recently bought for breeding purposes."

Belinda tipped her head. "So what are you saying, Daughter—that you would like to stay here so you can spend the holiday with Dennis and cook him Christmas dinner?"

Sylvia smiled wistfully. "If the children and I went to New York with you, I wouldn't enjoy myself knowing Dennis was all by himself."

Belinda stared into her cup of tea, evaluating her daughter's last statement. She couldn't blame Sylvia for wanting to be with Dennis, especially since they were courting. She had a hunch that it wouldn't be long before Dennis asked Sylvia to marry him. Things would surely be different around here, if and when that event occurred. Sylvia, along with her daughter, Rachel, and son, Allen, had been living with Belinda since the tragic accident that took her husband's life. It was hard to think of how things would be if they moved out of the house to begin a new life with Dennis Weaver.

"Would you mind if the children and I don't go with you to Ezekiel's for Christmas?"

Sylvia's question pushed Belinda's thoughts aside. "If you feel you should stay here to spend Christmas with Dennis, it's fine with me. I'm sure Ezekiel and Michelle will be disappointed, but they'll also understand." The words didn't come easy for Belinda, but it was the correct thing to say. She had no right to interfere in Sylvia and Dennis's relationship. If Belinda were in her daughter's place, she'd no doubt make the same choice.

"*Danki*, Mom, for understanding." Sylvia took another sip of tea.

The two women spent the next hour talking about other things. When a ray of sun shone through the kitchen window, Belinda got up. "Guess we ought to get busy and fix breakfast before the kinner wake up." She glanced toward the hallway door. "I'm surprised Henry isn't up already and outside doing his morning chores."

"He came in pretty late last night, after spending time with some of his friends. Maybe he forgot to set the alarm and overslept."

"That could be." Belinda glanced at the clock on the far wall. "I would call up the stairs to see if he's up, but I don't want to wake your children."

"If you like, I'll go upstairs and knock on his door. It's about time to get Rachel and Allen up anyway."

"That might be a good idea," Belinda said. "He needs to get the chores done so we can eat breakfast and get the greenhouse open on time."

After Sylvia left the room, Belinda cleared the table and put their cups in the sink. As she glanced out the window, she was taken by surprise when a male robin flew out of a tree in the yard and bumped the kitchen window. Believing it was just a fluke, and that the bird would return to the tree, Belinda merely shrugged and turned on the water. She'd no more than filled each cup when the robin was back again. This time he bumped the window a little harder.

Belinda shook her head. "What in the world?" She assumed with cooler weather setting in, most of the robins in their yard would have moved on to warmer territory by now.

As Belinda stood watching, the robin kept hitting the window, then returning to the tree.

She shook her head. "What a silly *voggel.*"

"What bird are you talking about?" Henry asked when he sauntered into the room.

"That one." Belinda pointed to the robin as it made another pass at the window. "The crazy thing acts like it wants to get into our house."

"He probably sees his reflection in the window and thinks it's another bird." Henry moved closer to the window and looked out.

"Well, I can think of a better way to be greeted this morning than watching that poor bird beat himself up." Belinda rolled her eyes. "Wouldn't you think with the colder weather we've been having that Mr. Robin would have moved on to a warmer climate by now?"

Henry shook his head. "Not necessarily, Mom. Robins can withstand very cold temperatures. It's not that unusual to see some of 'em in the wintertime, although they survive off a different kind of food than the worms and seeds they eat during the warmer months," he added.

Belinda stared at Henry with her mouth slightly open. "I had no idea you knew that much about robins. How'd you gain such wisdom?"

With a single raised eyebrow, he cocked his head. "Do I have to remind you that I've been bird-watching for some time, not to mention reading up in that bird book of mine. I can tell you a lot more about robins if you're interested."

"Maybe another time." Belinda pointed to Henry's hat and jacket, hanging on a wall peg near the back door. "Right now you need to get out to the barn to do your chores, and I need to get breakfast ready so we can eat when you come back in."

"Jah. I'll go right now." Henry slipped into his jacket and slapped the straw hat on his head. Once the weather got colder, he'd no doubt wear his knitted stocking cap instead.

Henry had no more than gone out the door when the robin smacked against the window again.

Belinda reached up and pulled the shade down. If the crazy bird was determined to keep that up, at least she didn't have to watch it.

After Sylvia got Rachel in her high chair and Allen on a booster seat, she joined Belinda and Henry at the kitchen table. Belinda took hold of her grandson's hand as they all bowed their heads for silent prayer.

Heavenly Father, she prayed, *please guide and direct our lives today. We ask that You would provide for our needs and help us to set a good example for others. Bless this food and bless all who are seated at my table. In Jesus' name I ask it. Amen.*

Once Sylvia and Henry raised their heads and opened their eyes, Belinda forked a pancake from the platter in front of her and put it on Allen's plate. After passing the platter on to Henry, she poured a small amount of maple syrup over Allen's pancake.

The young boy looked over at her and grinned. *"Gut pannekuche."*

"Jah," she replied, "The pancakes are good."

"Think I'll have some *hunnich* on mine instead of *sirrop.*" Henry passed the bottle of syrup to Sylvia and reached for the jar of honey. "Since I work so hard at beekeeping, I deserve the fruits of my labor."

Belinda couldn't argue with that. In spite of the fact that beekeeping was not her son's favorite thing to do, he'd been expected to take over the job after his older brother was killed. He still complained about it at times, but not as much as he had at first.

As they ate their meal, the conversation centered mostly around the sale they would be having at the greenhouse next week. In addition to fall plants and flowers, many other things they sold in the greenhouse, like honey, jam, solar lights, and several outdoor decorative items, would be on sale. Belinda hoped they would do well and make enough to put some money away for the winter months when the greenhouse would be closed.

They were getting close to finishing their meal when a knock sounded on the back door. Belinda went to answer it. Monroe Esh stood on the porch, holding a bakery box.

"I brought you some glazed *faasnachtkuche*." He grinned and held the box out to her. "Figured you might like them for breakfast."

"It was kind of you to think of us, but we're already in the middle of eating." Belinda paused, unable to maintain eye contact with this attractive fifty-two-year-old Amish man. When they had been teenagers, Monroe had been interested in Belinda. She'd been flattered by his attention but chose Vernon instead. Monroe had moved away from Strasburg and returned to the area several months ago. He had been coming around ever since, offering to help out if needed. He clearly wanted to renew a relationship with Belinda, but she was unsure of her feelings for him and not nearly ready to make any kind of commitment.

Belinda took the offered doughnuts. "Danki. If you haven't eaten this morning, why don't you come in and have some pancakes with us? Or you could eat one of your doughnuts."

Monroe offered her a wide smile. "Don't mind if I do."

Belinda led the way to the kitchen, and Monroe kept in step with her. When they entered the room, he walked up to the table and greeted Sylvia and Henry.

Sylvia said hello, but Henry just sat with his arms folded. This was not the first time Belinda's son had given Monroe the cold shoulder. He clearly did not care for the man.

"Please, take a seat, and I'll get you a plate." Belinda set the box of doughnuts on the table, and then gestured to an empty chair.

"Sure thing." He hung up his jacket and hat on the wall peg next to Henry's.

Monroe bowed his head for a few seconds, then opened his eyes and forked three pancakes onto his plate and covered them with plenty of syrup. After his first bite, he grinned at Belinda. "These are sure tasty. You're a good cook, Belinda."

"I can't take all the credit," she responded. "Sylvia mixed the batter.

I'm only responsible for making sure the pancakes cooked all the way through and didn't get too brown."

"Well, all that being said, they're delicious." He smacked his lips.

When Belinda glanced at Henry, she couldn't miss his look of disapproval. *What was I supposed to do?* she asked herself. *I couldn't take the box of doughnuts from Monroe and shut the door in his face. I'm not trying to encourage this man, but I won't be unkind to him either. Henry needs to get over his irritation whenever Monroe comes around. I may have to remind him that the man was very helpful during our barn raising. That ought to count for something.*

Chapter 2

The greenhouse had only been open a few minutes when their first customer showed up. Belinda smiled as Herschel Fisher came in and stepped up to the counter. "Good morning, Herschel. Is there something I can help you with today?" she asked.

"Not particularly." He shifted his weight from one leg to the other. "I was in the area and thought I'd stop by to see how you're doing. There's been no more problems around here I hope."

Belinda shook her head. "Not since the barn burned, but then we don't know if that was a deliberate attack or an accident caused by someone's carelessness. We appreciated your help the day of the barn raising." She fidgeted with the pen beside her notepad on the counter, wondering why she felt so nervous in this man's presence. It made no sense, really, since Herschel had never done or said anything to cause Belinda to be tense or apprehensive. He was one of the kindest men she knew—not to mention good looking for a man approaching his sixties. Herschel's silver hair and striking blue eyes made him quite attractive, in fact.

Clasping the brim of his straw hat, Herschel tipped his head slightly. "I was glad to do it. If there's anything else you need to have done around here, don't hesitate to let me know."

"Danki, I will." Herschel's offer of help was the second one Belinda had received today. Before Monroe left, after consuming half a dozen pancakes, he'd mentioned once again that if Belinda needed anything she should give him a call. While Belinda appreciated both men's offers, she would only call upon them as a last resort. Henry was able to do many things around the place, and both Dennis and Jared came by to help out as often as they could. Of course, Dennis kept busy most days with horse training, and Jared had his roofing business, which took up a good many of their weekly hours.

Herschel stood near the counter a few more seconds, with his head tipped down. There was no doubt about it—this mild-mannered man was most definitely shy. At least he seemed to be whenever he spoke to Belinda. She'd observed him talking to other people before, like Jared or Amy, and he'd never appeared to be timid. It seemed a bit odd that he would be shy around her, but Belinda shrugged it off. She had too much to do today without trying to analyze Herschel's response to her.

Belinda felt relieved when he moved away from the counter and mumbled a quick, "Have a good day."

"Goodbye, Herschel. It was nice of you to stop in."

Shuffling his feet and with head down, Herschel went out the door.

A few minutes later, Amy showed up. "I saw Herschel Fisher get into his buggy, but he had nothing in his hands. Are we out of whatever he came here to buy?" she asked, joining Belinda behind the counter.

Belinda shook her head. "Herschel said he didn't need anything, just came by to see how we're doing and offer his help if we needed anything done."

"Ah-ha! I see how it is." Amy's eyes widened.

"You see how what is?"

"My *mamm* has two suitors."

Belinda lifted her gaze toward the ceiling and gave a little huff. "Don't be silly, Daughter. I have no suitors."

"I believe you're wrong about that. We've all known for some time that Monroe's set his cap for you. And now Herschel has shown interest too."

Belinda waved the thought aside. "That's not true. Where did you get such an idea anyway?"

"I've seen the way Herschel looks at you—kind of shy-like and with a crimson blush on his face. Also he seems to have trouble finding the right words whenever he's talking with you." Amy offered Belinda a dimpled grin. "I recognize all the signs, because that's how Jared acted when he was getting up the nerve to ask if I would let him court me."

Belinda clicked her tongue against the roof of her mouth. "That's *lecherich*. Herschel has no interest in me beyond a casual friendship, and

I'm sure he has no intention of asking if he can court me."

"I don't think it's ridiculous at all." Amy shook her head. "And I'm gonna say, 'I told you so,' when he finally gets the courage to ask if he can begin seeing you on a regular basis."

"We're done with this nonsensical conversation, so let's get to work." Belinda pointed to the hose across the room. "Would you please water all the plants while I set out some fresh jars of honey?"

"No problem, Mom." Amy stepped out from behind the counter and paused. "Oh, I almost forgot. When I rode in on my scooter a short time ago, Henry was heading into the phone shed—no doubt to check messages. He hollered at me and asked if I would tell you that he'll be here in the greenhouse soon."

"Danki for relaying that message."

"You're welcome. There's something else I was going to mention."

"What's that?"

"Before coming here, I stopped at the house to drop off some banana bread I made last night. While I was in the kitchen, I noticed that the shade on the window was pulled down. When I opened it up, you'll never guess what happened."

"A robin flew out of the tree and smacked the window?"

Amy's eyes opened wide. "Well, jah. How did you know?"

"Because the silly voggel was doing that while I was in front of the sink. He kept at it so hard that I finally closed the window shade, thinking it might dissuade him."

Amy shook her head. "Well, for goodness' sake. I wonder what flying into the kitchen window is all about."

Belinda repeated Henry's explanation of the strange occurrence. "I was impressed with how much your *bruder* knows about robins."

"Well we've both noticed his fascination with birds ever since that pesky crow showed up in our yard back when. . ." Amy's voice trailed off. "Sorry, Mom. I didn't mean to open up old wounds by mentioning what occurred after the death of our loved ones."

"Don't worry about it. The accident happened, and we can't change the past, so there's no point in trying to avoid mentioning it."

Amy nodded. "That's true, but I always feel bad for bringing up a topic that still hurts whenever we talk about it."

Belinda had to admit that it was painful to talk, or even think about, but not nearly as much as it had been when the accident first happened—and on her birthday, no less. What had started out to be a happy celebration with their whole family had turned out to be one of the saddest days of Belinda's life. Since that dreadful evening, she'd done her best to maintain a positive attitude, put her trust in the Lord, and make the best of every situation. No one's life was free of trials, but it was important not to give in to self-pity or succumb to depression, the way Sylvia had done until she met Dennis. Both of Belinda's daughters had found love since the tragic day that changed their lives so dramatically. But Belinda remained certain that love and romance were not in her future, for no one could ever replace dear Vernon.

Sylvia sat at the kitchen table, adding to the grocery list her mother had started last evening. This was a good time to do it, as the house was basically quiet, since Rachel was taking her nap and Allen played happily by himself in the living room across the hall.

"Let's see now. . ." Sylvia tapped her pen against the table as she studied the list. Toothpaste, mouthwash, deodorant, facial tissues. . . Those were all necessities, but it would be nice to buy something that was not particularly needed. She tapped the pen again. "Think I'll add some ice cream to the list. We haven't had any frozen dessert in quite some time."

Thoughts of ice cream drew Sylvia's thoughts back to the day they'd been celebrating her mother's birthday. Everything had been going along fine until the topic was brought up that they had no ice cream to go with Mom's cake. Mom had insisted that she didn't need ice cream, but Dad had been equally determined to go to the store and get some. When he asked who would like to go with him, Sylvia's brother Abe and her husband, Toby, had agreed to accompany him, never guessing that they would only make it a few feet past the driveway.

Tears welled in Sylvia's eyes as she remembered with clarity how the accident had occurred. A vehicle coming down the road rammed into the back of her father's buggy so hard that the impact killed all three passengers, as well as Dad's horse. What a shock it had been for the whole family to lose their dear loved ones in such an unexpected, tragic way.

As more tears came, Sylvia's vision blurred so that she could no longer read the grocery list. Just when she'd thought she had put it all behind her, a little thing like adding ice cream to the list had brought back the pain of that day.

Sylvia got up from the table and went across the room to get a tissue from the box sitting on the desk. "I need to get a hold of myself," she murmured. "I can't change the past or bring back my loved ones with a simple wish—as much as I would like it to be so. I need to keep my focus on the here and now and be thankful for the wonderful man God has brought into my life." Although there would always be a place in Sylvia's heart for the memories she held of Toby, there'd be lots of new memories to make with Dennis.

Sylvia dried her eyes and blew her nose before going back to the shopping list. No one knew what the future held, but they should live every day as if it were their last. This is what Sylvia had decided to do. She appreciated each member of her family and felt a sense of peace and joy when she spent time with Dennis. How grateful Sylvia was that she and Henry had met Dennis when they'd been out bird-watching one day. They'd made an instant connection, and each opportunity Sylvia had to spend time with Dennis caused her fondness for him to grow. It was probably too soon for him to propose marriage, but she knew that if and when he did, her answer would be yes.

A thump against the window halted Sylvia's contemplations. She turned and was surprised to see the robin Mom had mentioned earlier, smacking its little body against the glass.

Although she knew a little about robins from what she'd read in the bird book Henry owned, Sylvia had never seen one do this kind of thing before. Could the bird be trying to get in the house, or was it simply trying to say hello?

Unsure of what else to do, Sylvia reached up and closed the shade. *That ought to take care of the bird. At least for now.*

Chapter 3

Amy turned the gas burner down on the stove and went outside to call Jared for supper. Seeing that he was chopping wood across the yard, she cupped her hands around her mouth and shouted, "Supper's ready, Jared!"

Apparently he hadn't heard, for he made no response.

Amy stepped off the porch and made her way across the yard. A chilly wind had come up, causing her to shiver. *If I'd known I was going to have to walk all the way out to the woodpile, I would have put on a sweater.*

She paused by the woodshed and waited for him to finish with the piece of wood he'd placed on the chopping block. "Supper's ready, Jared."

He grinned. "That's good, 'cause I've worked up quite an appetite out here with all this." Jared gestured to the pile of wood he'd already cut.

Amy smiled. "We'll certainly stay warm during the coming months. It'll be nice to have a cozy fire in the fireplace during the cold winter evenings."

Jared put the axe away and swiped his hand across his sweaty forehead. "Just think, Amy, Thanksgiving and Christmas will be here soon, and we'll get to spend them together as husband and wife." He slipped his arm around her waist and pulled her close to his side.

"Are you wishing we could spend the holidays alone, without either of our families?"

Jared shook his head. "Although in some ways, it would be nice to have a quiet Thanksgiving and Christmas with just the two of us, it'll be nice to share a meal with your mother and siblings on Thanksgiving."

"Are you still willing to spend Christmas at Ezekiel's place in New

York?" Amy asked as they made their way to the house.

"Sure. It'll be nice to see where they live, and the change of scenery will probably do us all some good."

"I hope your parents won't mind."

"I'm sure they'll miss us, but we can celebrate with them when we come back to Strasburg."

Amy thought this was a good idea. She would never want to leave her husband's family out.

As they entered the house, Amy's sense of smell was filled with the delicious aroma coming from the kettle of chicken and dumplings simmering on the stove. How thankful she felt to be married to a wonderful man like Jared. She looked forward to spending the rest of her life with him and growing old together. Amy also felt thankful for the opportunity they'd been given to rent this cozy home from Herschel Fisher. While it might not be big enough to raise a large family, it was a place to call home for the immediate future. When they'd saved up enough money, they would either buy or build their own home.

A third thing Amy felt thankful for was Jared's willingness to allow her to work every other day at the greenhouse. In addition to the extra money it gave them, Mom needed the help. On Amy's off day, she watched her sister's children so that Sylvia could assist their mother and Henry in the greenhouse. Until Amy and Jared became parents, this arrangement should work well. After that, Sylvia might have to consider hiring someone else to watch the children while she helped Mom in the business.

Jared tapped Amy's shoulder. "Is there any reason we're standing in the middle of the kitchen when there's good-smelling food on the stove waiting to be dished up?"

Amy jerked her head. "Sorry. I was just thinking."

He tipped his head in her direction. "Mind if I ask what you were thinking?"

"For one thing, I was thinking about how lucky I am to have married you."

"I'm the lucky one." Jared pulled Amy into his arms and gave her a kiss. *"Ich liebt du unauserschprechlich."*

"I love you beyond measure too."

Virginia Martin curled up on the couch with a glass of apple cider and her cat, Goldie. All day long she had listened to cars going by and horse and buggies making ruts in the road, while stinking up the crispy fall air with their manure droppings. Living across the street from an Amish family was bad enough, but the excess traffic due to their greenhouse customers made it seem even worse. Virginia hated living here in Amish country, a feeling she'd had ever since she and her husband, Earl, had moved here. She wished he'd never gotten the bright idea to apply for a job as a sales representative at one of the large car dealerships in Lancaster.

Virginia had been perfectly happy living in Chicago near her friend Stella. She hadn't made any new friends here and had very little to do other than clean house and putter around in the yard. She had taken up bird-watching, plus neighbor-watching, using Earl's binoculars, but that didn't compare to sitting down with a cup of coffee and enjoying a long chat with a close friend. Neither she nor Earl had any family living in the area, so it was just the two of them for holidays, and they never went to any social gatherings like they'd done in Chicago.

Goldie purred and nuzzled Virginia's hand, pulling her thoughts aside. She set the glass of cider down and gave the cat's head a few gentle strokes. "Are you feelin' lazy today, girl? Are ya content to just lie here with me?"

The cat's purr increased in volume.

"Okay, I get it. You want me to keep petting you, right?"

Goldie licked Virginia's finger with her sandpapery tongue.

Virginia had chosen the female feline from the local animal shelter a few months ago. It wasn't like having Stella to talk to, but at times Virginia carried on a conversation with Goldie. It was better than talking to herself and foolishly answering in response.

She relaxed and thought about how she'd gone through her closet yesterday, pulling out the summer things and replacing them with all fall/winter items. It wasn't too hard for Virginia to make the transition since she'd stored them in a tote in the guest-room closet.

Today she'd chosen to wear a peach blouse with a rust-colored cardigan. Virginia liked it because she'd gotten some compliments in the past while living in Chicago, so she hoped Earl would like it this evening.

As she looked down at her shirt, the cat moved away for a moment. Virginia noticed a lot of loose fur clinging up and down the front of her sweater. *Oh Goldie, look what you're doing to my nice clothes.* Virginia tried to brush off the hairs while the cat nuzzled into her. "Look you." She picked Goldie up and placed the feline at the end of the couch. But the animal was insistent and headed right back to her.

"Come on, kitty." Virginia placed the cat back in the same spot. This wasn't working, for the animal seemed determined to seek attention. Virginia chuckled in defeat and let Goldie have her way.

"Guess I'll have to resort to using the lint roller that's in the kitchen drawer." Virginia patted the cat's head as it laid down in a contented manner.

She picked up the magazine lying nearby and thumbed through the pages until she spotted a young model with bold red hair. "Well that's a fancy color that pretty woman's wearing. I'd sure like to give that shade of red a try. Since I've got nothing better to do tomorrow, maybe I'll go shopping and see if I can find the right color to try on myself."

A few minutes later, she went to the kitchen to check on the chicken baking in the oven. Earl would be home soon, and he'd no doubt be hungry.

Virginia glanced toward the kitchen door to see if Goldie had followed her in, like she often did, but apparently the lazy cat had chosen to remain on the couch. That was fine with Virginia. At least she could fix the rest of the meal in peace, without Goldie begging for food or rubbing against Virginia's leg.

Seeing that the chicken was done, Virginia turned the oven to low. Instead of mashed or baked potatoes, she'd made a cold potato salad earlier today and put it in the refrigerator to serve with the meal. She had also baked an apple pie for dessert, which she would serve with vanilla ice cream. She hoped by fixing Earl's favorite pie, he'd be willing to listen to her request about spending Thanksgiving in Chicago. She hadn't mentioned it to Stella yet, but Virginia felt sure her good friend would be open to the idea and welcome her and Earl to join her family for the holiday meal.

After she set the table, she headed back to the living room. Since

Goldie was still sleeping soundly, she picked up Earl's binoculars and went to the front window to look out. Traffic had slowed on the road—probably because the greenhouse was closed for the day. Virginia caught sight of Henry King out in the yard. He appeared to be searching for something.

"Probably looking for his dog," she muttered. "I hope the mutt doesn't come over here and start trampling my bushes."

"Who's looking for his dog?"

At the sound of Earl's voice, Virginia whirled around. "For heaven's sake, Earl, you shouldn't sneak up on me like that. I didn't know you were home."

"If you'd quit spying on the neighbors you might have more awareness of what's going on around you." He stepped up beside her. "Is supper ready? I didn't take time to eat lunch today, so I'm starving."

"Yes, everything's ready. I just need to set it on the table."

He gave her a peck on the cheek. "Okay, then I'll go wash up and meet you at the table."

"Sounds good." Virginia put the binoculars away and returned to the kitchen.

A short time later, she and Earl were enjoying their meal. "I made your favorite apple pie for dessert." She smiled at him from across the table.

He nodded. "That's good, but I may want to wait awhile to eat it, 'cause I'm gonna be plenty full from this meal."

"Is the chicken done to your liking?"

"Yep, sure is. The potato salad's good too."

Virginia wiped her mouth with the napkin and decided not to wait till they'd had dessert to ask her question.

"Say Earl, I've been thinking how nice it would be if we had Thanksgiving at Stella and Joe's place this year."

His brows rose. "You mean drive all the way to Illinois just to eat dinner?"

"Actually, I thought we could go a few days early, or until the day after Thanksgiving. I haven't seen Stella since she came here to visit all those months ago, so. . ."

Earl held up his hand. "Not gonna happen, Virginia."

"How come?" Her spine stiffened.

"Because I have to work."

"On Thanksgiving?"

"No, the day after. You should know by now that the day after Thanksgiving is one of the biggest shopping days of the year. If it goes anything like it did last year, there'll be lots of people coming in to the dealership to buy a new car at our sales prices." He glanced at her, then back at his food. "So going anywhere for Thanksgiving is out."

Virginia swallowed around the constriction that had formed in her throat. She'd lost her appetite for the food on her plate and didn't think she could eat another bite.

My life stinks—it's boring and it's not fair that I can't spend time with my best friend anymore. I feel like getting on a bus and going to Chicago for Thanksgiving without Earl. I wonder how he'd like that.

She released a sigh. *Guess I won't do it, but I will go into town tomorrow to find a brighter red hair color. Maybe that will make me feel a little better about myself.*

Belinda stepped out the back door and rang the dinner bell to let Henry know that supper was ready. He'd been in the barn for some time, and she figured he must be done with his chores by now.

I'll give him a few more minutes and then ring the bell again. Belinda stepped back inside and went to the stove to stir the pot of stew that was plenty done and just keeping warm.

"Where's Henry?" Sylvia asked when she entered the kitchen a few minutes later. "With his voracious appetite, I figured he'd be in here by now asking if supper was ready."

"I rang the dinner bell, so hopefully he will be in shortly." Belinda pointed to the kitchen table. "You may as well bring the kinner in and get them seated. Then we can eat as soon as Henry comes in and washes his hands."

"Okay." Sylvia went out of the room and returned a few minutes later with Allen and Rachel. After getting them situated—Rachel in her high chair and Allen on his booster seat, she filled a pitcher with water and placed it on the table.

Belinda glanced up at the clock. "Still no sign of Henry, so I guess

I'd better ring that old bell again." She moved toward the door, but as she was about to reach for the nob, the door opened and Henry rushed in. A sheen of sweat covered his forehead, and his cheeks were bright red. Belinda had a hunch it was not from the cold.

"What's wrong, Son? You look *umgerrent*."

"I'm very upset." He swiped a hand across his forehead. "Two of our best laying hens are gone. I can't find them anywhere, Mom. They just vanished from the coop." He scrunched up his face. "I bet the vandalism's started up again."

"Now calm down, Henry. The chickens may have found a way out of the pen. Did you check to see if there were any holes or tears in the chicken wire?" Belinda spoke quietly, so as not to rile him more. The last thing she wanted was for her son to start shouting and upset the children who'd been waiting patiently at the table for their supper.

"Of course I checked, and everything was fine. Someone let themselves into the pen and took those hens." Henry pulled his fingers through his sandy brown hair repeatedly. "We need those chickens for the eggs they produce, and I aim to find out who took them. The bad stuff that's been going on around here ever since Dad, Abe, and Toby died has gone on long enough. And by the way. . .I ain't hungry!" He whirled around and stomped down the hall.

Belinda turned to look at Sylvia to gauge her reaction, but her daughter merely shrugged and said, "Should we start eating supper without him?"

"I suppose so." Belinda drew a quick breath and blew it out. There had to be some explanation for the missing hens. But if someone had come into the yard today and taken the chickens, they may never learn who that person was. She hoped Henry wouldn't go around the neighborhood and start accusing people. *My boy's making a big deal out of nothing. I'm sure there's a perfectly reasonable explanation for the missing chickens.*

Chapter 4

With his binoculars in position, Henry sat cross-legged inside the large open window near the top of the barn. He'd done this every morning and evening since two of their hens had vanished. So far he'd seen nothing suspicious, nor had any more chickens disappeared. Even so, Henry felt sure the hens had been stolen, because if they'd been eaten by some critter, he should have seen some feathers left as evidence.

Today was Thanksgiving, and except for Ezekiel and his family, all the Kings would be together. Mom had also invited Jared's parents to join them, but Ava and Emanuel had made plans to visit one of their daughters.

Thankfully, Monroe had not been included in their Thanksgiving plans. Henry had no tolerance for the irritating man. He hoped Monroe would never succeed at worming his way into Mom's heart, because Henry couldn't imagine her being married to anyone but Dad. Just the thought of Monroe becoming his stepfather left a bitter taste in Henry's mouth. If that ever happened he didn't know what he would do. He sure couldn't live in the same house with Monroe.

Maybe Jared and Amy would take me in. Henry lowered the binoculars into his lap.

"What are ya doin' up there with those field glasses—looking for birds?"

Henry looked down and spotted Dennis on the ground below, pointing up at him. "Not the kind of birds I normally watch," he called in return. "I'm watchin' my chickens."

"Can't you do that from down here?"

"I'll be right there." Henry moved away from the window and

climbed down the ladder. Before he could make it to the barn door, Dennis stepped in.

"So what's this about you watching chickens?" he asked with a grin.

Henry explained about the missing hens and said that in addition to making sure no others disappeared, he was on the lookout for the thief who stole the chickens.

Dennis pulled a stubble of hay from one of the bales close by. "Are you certain they were stolen?"

"Jah. I looked the chicken wire over really good, and there was no way those hens could've gotten out by themselves." Henry frowned. "I think whoever set our barn on fire and did all those other acts of vandalism to our property ripped off our *hinkel*, and they might try to take more of them again."

Dennis placed his hand on Henry's shoulder. "You can't sit up in the hayloft like a security guard twenty-four hours a day, so why don't you come out in the yard with me, and we'll do a little bird-watching until dinner is ready."

Henry hesitated but finally nodded. He wasn't sure if Dennis agreed with his theory or not, but since Blackie was roaming freely in the yard today, he figured the dog would bark out a warning if anyone who shouldn't be there came onto their property.

Clymer, New York

Ezekiel left the phone shed where he'd called his family in Strasburg. Even though it didn't happen very often, he'd hoped someone might be nearby to speak with directly, but all he got was the message machine, so he'd recorded his Thanksgiving greetings.

Ezekiel wished he and Michelle could have taken their son and daughter to Strasburg for the holiday, but it was nice that Michelle's brothers could be here. Because she and her siblings had been taken from their parents and put in foster care when they were children, Michelle, Jack, and Ernie had missed out on so much. Being reunited a few years ago had seemed a miracle, and Ezekiel was pleased whenever Michelle and her brothers could get together. Besides, his side of the family would be here for Christmas, and he looked forward to that.

I wonder how my little brother is doing these days, Ezekiel thought as he made his way back toward the house. *Sure hope he's not giving our mamm any trouble like he did for so many months after Dad, Abe, and Toby were killed.*

Ezekiel stopped walking long enough to throw a stick for Michelle's dog, Val, and watched as the mutt chased after it, barking all the way. He still remembered the joy he had seen on Michelle's face when he'd presented the dog to her on Valentine's Day, back when they were courting. Ezekiel enjoyed every opportunity to bring a smile to his wife's pretty face.

After tossing the stick to Val a second time, Ezekiel reflected a bit more. Michelle had grown up in an English environment, and he still marveled at how well she had adapted to the Amish way of life. In fact, she seemed to flourish—as if she'd been destined to live as one of the Plain people.

He reached under his hat and scratched his head. *It's hard for me to believe sometimes that I once had it in my head to go English so I could drive a motorized vehicle and own modern things. Michelle was a good influence on me in that regard. She helped me realize that material things are not important. It's the relationship I have with God and my family—those are the things that count the most for me now.*

Ezekiel still couldn't believe he'd been chosen by lots to be one of the ministers in their church district. He felt humbled and unworthy but also blessed to be able to minister to others through the preaching of God's Word. Sometimes, like last week, Ezekiel was called upon to counsel a couple who were struggling in their faith. In his younger days, he would never have imagined being put in a position where he'd have to preach, teach, and counsel. But with total commitment and reliance on God, Ezekiel's calling had become a blessing to him as well as to others.

"Ernie and Jack have arrived with their wives," Michelle called from the back porch. "Are you coming inside to greet them?"

"I'll be right there." Ezekiel tossed the stick to Val one last time and hurried up the steps to the back porch. A day of good food and fellowship was about to begin, and he looked forward to every moment.

Virginia stood in front of the hallway mirror, staring at her reflection. She had colored her hair days ago, and the red was far more vibrant than ever before.

Earl had noticed her hair as soon as he'd come through the door and hadn't seemed to mind it. In fact he gave Virginia a compliment about the newer, brighter shade. Virginia felt good and was delighted that she had gone to the trouble to do it. Her crooked bangs, which she'd cut herself some time ago, had grown out, but it was time for another haircut. This time, though, she wouldn't tackle it herself. She'd tried making an appointment at the styling salon in town, but couldn't get in until Tuesday of next week. Virginia could have tried some of the other salons outside of her area, but didn't want to start over with a new stylist. Since she and Earl were going to a nice restaurant in Lancaster for Thanksgiving dinner, Virginia wanted to look her best.

"You look great, honey, so stop fretting and get away from that mirror." Earl stepped up behind Virginia and put his hands on her shoulders. "You've got the prettiest red hair in all of Lancaster County."

She rolled her eyes. "Yeah, right."

"It's true. Your carrot top is one of the reasons I married you, didn't ya know?"

He nuzzled the back of Virginia's neck. "The perfume you're wearing is real nice too. You smell like a rosebush in full bloom."

"Thanks, Earl. Now we'd better get going before we miss our reservation."

"Yep. I'll get our coats right now."

Virginia felt relieved that Earl hadn't asked if she'd quit smoking, like she had promised. The truth was, she hadn't quit and had used the perfume to cover up any telltale odor from the cigarette she'd snuck this morning. She'd also brushed her teeth twice and swished plenty of mouthwash around in her mouth before getting dressed. Virginia wanted to quit smoking because it wasn't good for her health, but her nerves were frazzled, and having a cigarette was one of the few things that helped. Hopefully she could keep Earl from finding out that she'd started up again, because Virginia couldn't tolerate it when he began nagging.

"That was sure a good dinner, Belinda. Danki for all your hard work." Jared patted his stomach. "I ate so much I don't think I'll have to eat again for at least a week."

Amy poked her husband's arm. "I've heard you say that before. Why, I bet by tomorrow you'll be saying, What's for *friehschtick, fraa?*"

He chuckled. "You're probably right. I can't see going through tomorrow without my supper."

"I'm glad you enjoyed the meal," Belinda said, "but I can't take all the credit. Sylvia helped with most of the cooking, and as you know, your wife brought two pumpkin pies."

"I stand—or should I say, sit—corrected." Jared's gaze traveled from Amy to Sylvia and then back to Belinda. "I appreciate each one of your efforts."

"Same here," Dennis spoke up. "We men would have gone without food if it weren't for you kind ladies today."

Smiling, Sylvia gave him a sidelong glance. "I'm sure you would have managed to fix yourself something to eat."

"True, but it wouldn't have been near as tasty as this Thanksgiving treat."

Belinda glanced at Henry to see if he would comment, but he sat fiddling with the knife beside his empty plate. Except for a bit of conversation with Dennis, when he told him about the robin that had kept hitting their kitchen window for several days in a row, her son hadn't joined in much of the conversation going on around the table. She hoped he wasn't still sulking about the missing chickens. None of the other hens had turned up missing, so he ought to just leave it alone. She wouldn't force Henry to be more verbal today. Sometimes he simply needed time to think about and deal with things in his own way. She couldn't deny that the hens weren't important to the family, since they provided eggs, but two missing chickens did not signal the end of the world.

Perhaps, she thought, *Maude, the homeless woman, took the hens so*

*she would have something to eat for her Thanksgiving meal and beyond.
We have plenty of hens out in the coop laying eggs, and with the cost of
their feed bill each month, it wouldn't hurt to have a few less chickens to
feed.*

Belinda sipped the rest of her water. *If the poor woman felt the need to
snitch cookies that had been set out in the greenhouse, and take produce from
our garden last summer, then she could very well be the reason the chickens
went missing.* Of course, Belinda was not about to offer this suggestion
to her son. He would no doubt get right on his scooter and head over
to the shanty where Maude stayed most of the year and confront her
with his suspicions.

Amy stood and began clearing the table. "Should we bring out the
pies for dessert or wait till we've done the dishes?"

"I'm too full to eat anything more right now," Jared said. "But I'll
watch the rest of you eat dessert now if that's what you want to do."

Dennis shook his head. "I'd rather wait too."

Belinda looked at Henry. "What do you think, Son?"

He shrugged and mumbled, "It ain't up to me."

Rather than correcting his English, Belinda looked at Sylvia and
then Amy. "Are you two in agreement with waiting awhile to bring out
the pies?"

They both said yes.

"All right then, let's get the table cleared and the dishes done. Then
we can all relax in the living room with the warmth of the fireplace
while we watch Rachel and Allen play." Belinda rose from her seat,
and was about to pick up the first plate when a knock sounded on the
front door. "Now I wonder who that could be. We weren't expecting
more company today." She glanced over at Henry, slouched in his chair.
"Would you please answer the door?"

"Okay." Henry pushed back his chair and shuffled out of the room.

Belinda stacked several plates but decided not to take them out to
the kitchen until she found out who was at the door. A few seconds
later, Henry came back with Monroe at his side.

Her son's narrowed eyes and tightly pressed lips said it all. He was
not happy to see Monroe.

"Sorry for the intrusion." Monroe looked at Belinda and smiled.
"I bought a mincemeat pie at the bakery yesterday, and since it's one

of your favorites, I wanted you to have it." He handed the dessert to Belinda.

"Oh, well. . .um. . .danki, Monroe. It was nice of you to think of me." She placed the pie in the center of the table. "We just finished our dinner and won't be eating dessert until the dishes are done, but you're welcome to join us if you like."

A wide grin spread across Monroe's clean-shaven face. "I'd be pleased to join you. That'd be real nice."

Belinda glanced at Henry and wasn't surprised to see the whitening of his knuckles as he clasped his hands tightly at his sides. Her son had never made it a secret how he felt about Monroe. But that didn't excuse his rude behavior whenever the man came around.

Belinda gestured to the adjoining living room. "Monroe, why don't you make yourself comfortable with the other men while we women do the dishes? Afterward, we'll bring out the rest of the pies."

Monroe didn't have to be asked twice. Following another big smile in Belinda's direction, he headed to the living room with Jared, Dennis, and the children.

Belinda picked up the stack of plates but paused to see what Henry would do. True to form, wearing a frown, he left the dining room and clomped up the stairs. She figured they wouldn't see him again until Monroe went home. It was too bad Henry couldn't be a little more cordial to the man. If he gave Monroe half a chance, he might discover that he wasn't so bad—a little pushy, perhaps, but with some good qualities too.

Chapter 5

Virginia limped out to the kitchen to pour herself a cup of coffee. She'd slept later than usual this morning and barely remembered Earl telling her goodbye when he left for work. With colder weather setting in, her bum leg hurt more than usual. She was fairly sure that arthritis had set into her old leg injury where several bones had been broken. Other parts of Virginia's body felt stiff too, but none as bad as the pain she felt nearly every day in her leg.

After filling her coffee cup, she opened a can of cat food and called for Goldie.

"Here, kitty, kitty. . . Come get your breakfast."

When there was no immediate response, Virginia went to the living room to see if the cat might be sleeping on the couch. But there was no sign of Goldie.

"Goldie. . .where are you, kitty?" Virginia stood still and listened. Normally when she called for Goldie, the feline would come running, no doubt believing she was going to be fed or cuddled.

"That's sure strange." Virginia limped her way through the house, calling the cat's name, but Goldie could not be found.

Puzzled and more than a bit frustrated, Virginia returned to the other side of the house. The only place she hadn't checked was the utility room. When she stepped in there it felt chillier than usual.

"Oh no." Seeing the back door was open a crack, Virginia groaned. *Earl must not have closed it tightly when he left for work this morning.* Her muscles tightened. *If Goldie got outside and ran off, Earl will never hear the last of it!*

With no thought of fixing herself something to eat, Virginia went to her room to get dressed. She would start by going across the street in search of her cat. Since the King family had cats, Goldie may have gone there to bond with them.

A short time later, Virginia found herself limping up the Kings' driveway with her cane as she scanned their property in search of Goldie. She hobbled along with a watchful eye, not wanting to step in a fresh pile of horse droppings.

Virginia thought back to that fall evening when she'd lost her binoculars in the grass, trying to spy on the wedding she hadn't been invited to at the Kings' place. "I think I should've gotten an invite to Jared and Amy's ceremony—or at least the meal following the nuptials," Virginia mumbled as she looked ahead.

Two horse and buggies, along with one car, were parked near the greenhouse, but there was no sign of Virginia's cat.

She kept going until she entered the Kings' yard, where many plain clothes, towels, and sheets flapped in the chilly breeze on the clothesline. Virginia shook her head. *I could never hang my laundry outside in cold weather like this. How thankful I am for an electric washer and dryer. Sure wouldn't want to hang my clean clothes outdoors all the time.*

As Virginia approached the barn, she saw two black-and-white cats run from the building. *Hmm. . .I wonder if Goldie went in there.*

She paused and looked up at the new structure. It sure didn't take those Amish folks long to build a new barn after the old one burned down. From what Virginia had seen through Earl's binoculars on the day of the barn raising, it looked like every Amish person living in Strasburg had come to help construct the new building. *Must be nice to have so many people who care about you. Wish I could say the same.*

Redirecting her thoughts, Virginia stepped inside and called the cat's name. No response from Goldie, but a few seconds later, a voice called down from the hayloft: "Who's there?"

"It's Virginia, your neighbor from across the street. My cat's missing, and I came over to see if she wandered in here."

"I don't think so, but I'll come down and take a look."

Virginia watched as young Henry descended the ladder from above.

When he stepped off the last rung, he turned and brushed some straw off his trousers.

"What's your cat look like?" Henry questioned.

"She's kind of orangeish-yellowish. Her name is Goldie. She's an inside cat, but my husband left the back door partway open when he left for work this morning, so I'm sure she got out."

"I haven't seen any cats that color around here, but I'll have a look-see." Henry began moving about the barn, looking behind boxes and calling for the feline.

Virginia followed, but there was no sign of Goldie.

Henry tipped his hat off his forehead. "Guess your cat didn't come in here, 'cause there's sure no sign of her."

Virginia sighed. "Okay, I'll head back home for now, and then go out looking for her again after I've rested awhile."

"I'll let you know if I see a cat that looks like the one you described," Henry said.

"Thanks." Virginia shuffled out the door and made her way slowly down the driveway toward home. She hated the thought of never seeing Goldie again, but if she didn't find the cat soon, it might end up that way.

"My only friend, and now she's gone," Virginia lamented as she entered her house.

She sat at the kitchen table several minutes, drinking a second cup of coffee and eating a glazed doughnut Earl had brought home from the bakery yesterday. Although the coffee warmed her insides, and the doughnut tasted good, neither did anything to lift Virginia's spirits. *Think I'll go get my cigarette stash.*

Virginia left the kitchen and headed down the hall to the linen closet. She'd found a new hiding place for her cigarettes—under a small box inside the closet.

Virginia was almost to the closet when she heard a slight *meow*. She tipped her head and listened. The sound seemed to be coming from the closet where they kept their coats. The desire to find Goldie took precedence over smoking, so Virginia turned back and opened the door of the hall closet. There sat Goldie inside a box filled with gloves and scarves for wearing in cold weather. The poor feline looked up at Virginia and gave a pathetic *meow*.

"Oh Goldie, I'm so glad I found you." Virginia leaned down and scooped the cat into her arms. "Why didn't you meow when I called for you earlier? If you had, it would have saved me the trouble of going over to that smelly farm across the road."

Goldie's only response was another *meow*, followed by plenty of purring.

At noon, Belinda left the greenhouse and headed down the driveway to get the mail and check for any phone messages that may have come in. As she approached the mailbox, she spotted her neighbor across the road, standing in front of her living-room window. It looked like Virginia held a pair of binoculars up to her face.

I wonder what she is looking at. Could Virginia be watching me? Belinda smiled and lifted her hand in a wave. The red-haired woman lowered the binoculars and moved away from the window.

Belinda opened her mailbox and sighed. She'd tried on several occasions to strike up a conversation with her neighbor, but Virginia had never been very receptive. Belinda could only assume the woman either didn't like her or wasn't the friendly type. Either way, Belinda would pray for Virginia and keep trying to be a good neighbor.

After retrieving the mail, Belinda walked halfway up the driveway and entered the phone shack. She found two messages from customers asking if they had any poinsettias left in the greenhouse, and another message from Ezekiel, wondering if Belinda knew what time she and the family might arrive the day before Christmas.

Belinda responded to all three messages, and was about to leave the shed when the telephone rang. Pleased that she was here and the caller would not have to leave a message, Belinda picked up the receiver. "Hello."

A cold chill swept over her as a muffled voice said: "I've warned you before—you need to close up the greenhouse and move. If you don't heed my advice, you'll be sorry."

Belinda sat in stunned silence. This was the second time an unidentified person had called and demanded that she close the greenhouse and move.

"Who is this?" Her voice quavered.

Click! Whoever the caller was, they'd hung up.

Belinda's grip tightened on the phone. *Who would make such a threat as this, and why? Could the muffled-voice caller be the one responsible for starting the fire in our barn? Did they think that would be enough to get us to move?*

Belinda closed her eyes and lowered her head. *Heavenly Father, please protect my family, as well as every bit of the property our home and greenhouse sit upon. Convict the person responsible for all the vandalism and threats that have been done so they will see the error of their ways and stop doing it. In Jesus' name I ask this, amen.*

As Belinda remained in the phone shed, trying to compose herself, she made a decision. She didn't want to frighten her family, so in addition to not telling Ezekiel, she wouldn't mention the muffled phone call to any of them at this point. She would, however, continue to pray about this matter and also ask her good friend Mary Ruth Lapp to join her in prayer.

"In fact," she murmured, "I'm going to call and leave a message for her right now."

"Hey, Mom, since there are no customers in the greenhouse right now, is it okay if I quit for the day?" Henry asked, stepping up to the counter where Belinda stood.

She shook her head. "We still have another hour before closing, so there could be more people coming in, looking for things on their Christmas list." She gestured toward the shelves where they sold honey, jams, and some other gift items. "Would you please set a few more things out? The next week will no doubt be busy, since we'll be closing soon for Christmas and the remainder of the year."

"Jah, okay. I'll go to the storage room and get out some more jars." Henry glanced around. "Where's Amy? I haven't seen her for a while."

"She's not done with her Christmas shopping yet, so since we've been slow this afternoon, I said she could leave a little early today."

He frowned. "If she got to leave early, then why can't I?"

"Because someone needs to be here with me, in case we do get busy."

Henry mumbled something Belinda didn't understand, before he headed to the storage room.

Belinda took a seat behind the counter and rubbed her forehead. Ever since the phone call that had upset her this morning, she'd been struggling with a headache. It was ever so difficult to hold this inside and not tell someone.

She glanced up at the clock. It would be closing time soon, and then she could go up to the house and lie down for a while before it was time to start supper. Maybe while she rested, Sylvia might cook the meal, which she often did on the days when she didn't work in the greenhouse.

A short time later, with only a few minutes left before it was time to put the CLOSED sign on the front door, Belinda told Henry he could do his chores in the barn and that she would lock up the building.

"Okay, Mom. I got everything put on the shelves, like you asked me to do," Henry said before he went out the door.

Belinda remained in the greenhouse and spent the next half hour straightening a few items and going over some paperwork. She was about to leave the building when a horse and buggy pulled in. Opening the door, she saw Mary Ruth and her granddaughter, Lenore, get down from their buggy.

"I got your phone message saying you wanted to talk to me." Mary Ruth stepped up to Belinda. "Lenore volunteered to come along with me, while Jesse watches their kinner."

Belinda wasn't sure what to say. As much as she wanted to talk with her friend, she didn't want Lenore to hear it, because she might repeat it to Sylvia. The young women had been friends since they were children, and Lenore might feel that Sylvia had the right to know.

Belinda felt relief when Lenore said she would go up to the house and visit with Sylvia while her grandmother and Belinda talked.

"Danki, dear one." Mary Ruth gave Lenore's shoulder a pat. "I hope you two will have a nice visit."

As Lenore headed for the house, Mary Ruth entered the greenhouse with Belinda. Once inside, she turned to Belinda and said, "I could tell by the tone of your voice that something was troubling you. The fact that you asked me to pray but didn't say why, made me wonder if something might be seriously wrong."

Belinda drew a quick breath and released it slowly. "I don't know if it's serious or not, but something is definitely wrong. If you'd like to take a seat on the stool behind the counter, I'll tell you about it."

Mary Ruth did as she suggested and sat quietly waiting.

Belinda rubbed her forehead as she leaned against the front of the counter. "I received a disturbing phone call this morning while I was in the shed."

"Oh?"

"The voice was muffled, so I have no idea who the caller was, but they said. . ." Belinda paused and swallowed hard. "The person said we should close up the greenhouse and move, and if we don't, we'll be sorry."

Mary Ruth's fingers touched her parted lips. "Oh my. Did you call the sheriff?"

"No, I did not, and I haven't told any of my family about it." Belinda shifted her weight. "This is the second time I've received such a message, and I have to wonder if the person who called isn't the one who's done all the vandalism to our property."

"This is very disconcerting, Belinda. I really think you should call the sheriff."

She shook her head. "I don't want the law involved. For that matter, if word gets out and too many people know what's been happening around here, they might say something to Ezekiel. I'm sure he still keeps contact with some of his friends from our area."

"Are you still worried that if he were to find out, he'd move back to Strasburg in order to help out in the greenhouse and make sure that you and the rest of the family are okay?"

"Jah, and I don't want him to make that kind of sacrifice for us. My son has established a good life there in New York, and I won't take that away from him."

"It's your decision, but if it were me, I'd want my son to know what's been going on."

Belinda shook her head vigorously. "Promise you won't tell anyone what I've shared with you today? I just need your prayers, that's all."

Mary Ruth got off the stool and came around to give Belinda a hug. "I will definitely be praying for all of you, as well as the person behind the senseless, destructive acts. In fact if it's all right, I'd like to pray with you now since we're alone in the shop."

Belinda murmured her agreement.

Although most Amish didn't pray out loud, Mary Ruth took hold of Belinda's hands and prayed out loud with an understanding that touched Belinda's heart. She felt comforted by what was said as her dear friend asked the Lord to give Belinda and her family strength and protection. When she finished, Mary Ruth expressed her willingness to help out in any way she could.

A few tears escaped from under Belinda's lashes and she reached up to wipe them away. "Danki, Mary Ruth. You're such a good friend."

Chapter 6

The next day after enjoying a visit with Sylvia's children and Amy during lunch, Belinda returned to the greenhouse with a plate of Amy's cookies.

"Are those peanut butter *kichlin*?" Henry asked after she placed the plate on the counter.

"Yes, you're welcome to have a couple, but don't eat too many. Amy and I sampled a couple right after lunch. She did a good job, because they're sure tasty. I brought them out to share with our customers."

Henry's brows lifted as he looked around. "What customers, Mom? There's only been a handful of people come into the greenhouse this morning, and I doubt we'll see many more this afternoon either."

"You never know." Belinda stepped around behind the counter where Sylvia sat. "You're free to go up to the house and eat lunch now. And no doubt you'll want to check on the *kinner*."

Sylvia smiled. "I'm sure Amy has everything under control, but I am getting hungry, so I'd better go fix something to eat."

Belinda smiled. "Your sister has things all ready to go. You just need to show up with an appetite."

"That sounds good to me." Sylvia stood up and walked toward the exit.

After she left the building, Henry grabbed a cookie and took a bite. "Yum! This is sure tasty. You and my sisters make the best cookies, Mom."

"I'm glad you like it." Belinda pointed to a row of Christmas cactus and poinsettias. "Could you please make sure those got watered this morning?"

"I think they did, but I'll check just in case." He took another cookie and shuffled down the row.

Belinda shook her head. *That boy! Seems like he's always hungry.*

A short while later, Maude entered the greenhouse, wearing a heavy black coat with a hood. It looked almost new, and Belinda wondered where the woman had gotten it, since she'd never seen her wear it before.

Pushing the hood off her head, Maude stepped up to the counter and snatched a cookie from the plate without asking.

"Would you like me to put the rest of the cookies in a plastic sack so you can take them with you?" Belinda asked.

Maude bobbed her head with an eager expression.

Belinda reached under the counter, took out a plastic sack, and put the cookies inside. "Your coat looks nice and warm. Is it new?"

"It's new to me. Got it at the thrift store in town." Maude wiped her mouth on her coat sleeve. "I wear it in my cabin when I have no wood for heat."

"Do you have any wood now?"

"Nope, sure don't. Haven't got enough money to buy any either—not till the dinky pension I get comes, but the next won't be for several weeks."

"Do you have any family living in the area? Perhaps they could help with your needs."

Maude shook her head. "Nope. I'll manage on my own—least till winter."

Belinda's heart went out to the poor woman. They needed to do something to help her—especially now, with colder weather setting in. *I should have asked Maude more questions sooner. I really know so little about her.*

"I'll ask my son to bring you some wood as soon as the greenhouse closes today."

Keeping her gaze toward the floor, Maude said, "Okay."

Although the older woman had not offered any words of thanks, Belinda was certain that Maude appreciated the gesture. Considering she had so little and lived in a shanty, surely she would see any offer of help as kindness.

"Think I'll take a look around before I head back to my hovel," Maude mumbled. Still holding the bag of cookies, she turned and shuffled down the aisle where Belinda had sent Henry to check on the plants.

Several minutes elapsed before the woman returned to the counter. "Does your boy know where I live?"

"Yes, I'm certain he does. You can expect to see him there in a few hours."

Maude put her hood back on and shuffled out the door.

"Think I know who stole our chickens, Mom." With narrowed eyes, Henry stepped up to Belinda.

"Oh?"

"It was Maude."

"How do you know? Did she admit that she took the hens?"

He shook his head. "Nope, but I saw the evidence."

"Really? And what evidence would that be?"

"There was chicken manure on her shoes."

"Maybe she stepped in some as she walked up our driveway."

Henry slapped both hands against his hips. "My hinkel do not roam around our yard, Mom. You know I always keep them in their pen."

"Good point, but I suppose she could have picked up the manure from someone else's yard, or even along the side of the road, where she's often seen walking."

"I haven't seen anyone else with chickens in our area, and we are the only ones that are close enough to Maude."

Belinda tilted her head. "That's true, Son. You've made a good point."

Henry moved his hands from his hips to his pockets. "As soon as we close the greenhouse today, I'm gonna head over to her place and see if she has my chickens. Okay?"

"As a matter of fact, I planned to ask you to go over there anyway."

"How come?"

"Maude has no firewood, and I'd like you to fill up our wheelbarrow and take her some."

Henry's brows lowered. "If that woman has our hinkel, she doesn't deserve any firewood."

"This is not about deserving, Son." Belinda shook her head. "It's about being kind and helping out a neighbor in need."

Henry pulled his hands out of his pockets and turned them

palm-side up. "Okay, I'll do whatever you say."

"And Son, please don't accuse poor Maude of stealing our chickens."

He shrugged, before heading toward the back of the greenhouse.

Half an hour after Maude left, Monroe entered the greenhouse. He sauntered toward Belinda, steeped in heavy cologne and wearing a big smile. "How are things going? Have you been busy today?" He stepped up to the counter where she sat.

Why does Monroe think he needs to splash on so much of that overpowering fragrance? He wears enough for himself and at least one other man. "A little slower than I expected," she replied, looking at Monroe. "With Christmas only a few weeks away, we normally have more customers coming in to buy gift items and indoor plants."

"Maybe people are shopping at the new greenhouse across town." He gave his left earlobe a tug. "They do have a lot more available there."

Belinda cringed inwardly. She didn't need the reminder of their competition. Before the new greenhouse opened, their family business was the only one in the area that sold plants and flowers, and they'd been doing so well. They were still managing, despite all the vandalism that had taken place, but things could be a lot better.

"What are your plans for Christmas?" Monroe asked, detouring Belinda's thoughts.

I wonder if he wants to spend the holiday with us. Surely Monroe would enjoy spending Christmas with his parents and siblings. "We're all going to New York to see Ezekiel and his family," she replied.

His brows furrowed. "For how long?"

"Three or four days. We'll leave here on Christmas Eve day."

"Who's gonna feed the livestock and watch the place while you're gone?"

"We'll probably ask our neighbors to the right of us, or maybe see if our friend Jesse Smucker would come by."

Monroe shook his head. "There's no need for that. I'd be more than happy to come by every day and do whatever you need to have done."

Belinda shifted on her stool. "Oh, I couldn't ask you to do that."

"You're not asking. I'm volunteering." He leaned a bit closer. "I'd like to do this for you, Belinda, so please don't say no."

She tried not to choke on the strong musky odor as it wafted her way. "Well, since you put it that way. . .I don't have much choice but to accept your kind offer."

Monroe's clean-shaven chin jutted out a bit as he gave her a wide smile. "I'll come by the day before you leave to get a *schlissel*."

Belinda tipped her head. "For what, Monroe? Why would you need a key?"

"So I can put your mail in the house."

"Our mailbox is the locking kind, so any mail we get should be fine in there until we get home." *I really wouldn't feel comfortable with him looking through our letters, but I'm sure Monroe only means well and is just trying to be helpful.*

"Oh, I see." He folded his arms. "What about any plants you might have in the greenhouse or inside your home? Those might need to be watered, don't you think?"

Belinda tapped her knuckles gently on the counter as she thought through Monroe's request. "If we have any plants that don't sell before Christmas, those will need to be watered, so we'll put our houseplants in the greenhouse, and you can check on those too."

"I'll need a schlissel for the greenhouse then."

"Jah, and when you come by for the key, I'll have Henry show you what needs to be done with his *hund*, and also the *katze* and *gaul* in the barn."

"Don't you worry about anything, Belinda." Monroe looked directly into her eyes. "I'll make sure the dog, cats, and horses are well taken care of while you're away."

Belinda hoped allowing Monroe to check on things while they were gone was the right decision, and that the rest of her family would be okay with it.

Pushing a wheelbarrow full of split wood, Henry headed in the direction of Maude's run-down cabin. When he arrived, he looked on all sides of the small building, but there was no sign of any chickens on the overgrown property. *Could I have been mistaken?*

Henry stacked the wood on the dilapidated, uneven porch and then knocked on the door. When Maude didn't answer, he knocked again. After a few more tries, with no response, Henry was about to give up until he heard a familiar, *Bawk! Bawk! Bawk!*

Scooting over to the only window in the front of the cabin, he peered through the dirty-looking glass. Henry couldn't see anything until a chicken startled him by jumping up on what looked like a wooden box and began pecking at the window. He felt sure it was one of his hens, but couldn't figure out what it would be doing inside Maude's old cabin. Was it possible that Maude let them run all over the place, and that's why she had chicken manure on her shoes?

Henry knocked one more time then tried the knob, but the door appeared to be locked. Could the eccentric old woman be inside, choosing to ignore him?

He tried two more times but finally gave up. If Maude was at home, she obviously wasn't going to let him in.

Henry's facial muscles tightened. *I need to get home and tell Mom about this.*

Belinda stood at the stove, stirring a pot of chicken noodle soup, while Sylvia made a tossed salad. Dennis would be coming over soon to join them for supper, which Belinda felt sure was the reason for the radiant smile on her daughter's face.

Although she hadn't approved of Sylvia and Dennis's relationship in the beginning, Belinda had come to realize that Dennis was exactly the man her daughter needed. He was kind, polite, a hard worker, attentive, and good with Sylvia's children, who both seemed to like him. Belinda hoped in time Dennis would feel ready to marry Sylvia and become part of their family.

"Are you looking forward to spending Christmas with Ezekiel and his family?" Sylvia asked.

Belinda turned toward her daughter and smiled. "Jah. I can hardly wait to see them all again, and hold those cute little grandchildren in my arms."

"It was nice of Ezekiel to leave a message the other day, inviting

Dennis to join us. It'll give him a chance to get to know Dennis better. I'm sure my boyfriend would like to become better acquainted with my brother and his family, so it was good he asked a neighbor to feed his dog and horses, in addition to keeping an eye on the place while he's gone."

Belinda was about to respond when Henry stepped into the kitchen. His nostrils flared as he breathed noisily through his nose and mouth, as though he'd been running.

"Did you get the wood delivered to Maude?" Belinda questioned.

"Sure did, and you'll never guess what I discovered."

Belinda tipped her head in question.

"Our missing hinkel. They're in that old shack where she's been livin'. I heard 'em cackling, and then when I looked in the window, I saw one of the hens." His lips pressed into a white slash. "I knocked on the door, but Maude either wasn't at home or she was hidin' in there—probably afraid I'd take those chickens away from her."

"Oh dear." Belinda's fingers touched her parted lips.

Henry tromped across the room and stopped in front of her. "I was right all along about the manure on her shoes. Figured for sure that she had our chickens."

"When did you see manure on Maude's shoes?" Sylvia asked.

"Today, when she was in the greenhouse. I told Mom that I thought Maude was the one who took our hens." Henry shook his head. "That *verrickt* old woman's not to be trusted, and I think we should notify the *schrief*."

Belinda shook her head. "No, Son. We will not report this to the sheriff, and I don't think Maude is crazy. That was not a nice thing to say."

"Okay, but let's go get the chickens. It wasn't right for Maude to take them. She's a thief."

"Henry has a point, Mom," Sylvia interjected. "This is not the first time that woman has taken things from us without asking."

"Maybe if we'd been more giving and helpful to her, she would not have been desperate enough to steal."

"Taking things that ain't yours is wrong, plain and simple," Henry said.

"That is true, and I will have a talk with Maude."

"When?"

"Tomorrow morning, when I take her a sack of groceries," Belinda replied.

Henry's brows shot up. "You would give her groceries after she's stolen from us?"

"Yes, because it's the charitable thing to do."

Pink spots erupted on Henry's cheeks before he whirled around and headed for the back door.

"Where are you going?" Belinda called.

"Out to feed my hund." He swung the door open, and it clicked shut behind him before she could say anything more.

Belinda looked at Sylvia and released a sigh. "That bruder of yours has a lot to learn about forgiveness and being a good neighbor."

Chapter 7

New York State Line

"I still don't see why you asked Monroe to take care of things while we're gone," Henry mumbled as their driver's van left Pennsylvania and entered New York.

"I did not ask him," Belinda replied. "He volunteered."

Henry grunted. "I don't trust that fellow. I bet the only reason he offered was so he could snoop around."

Belinda turned her head to look at him in the seat behind her and frowned. "We've been over this before, Son, and I don't want to discuss it now."

"Jah, well, I think you're too nice sometimes, Mom." Henry shook his head. "I still can't believe after Maude stole our chickens that you went over there and gave her a sack of groceries."

"Our mamm did what she felt was right," Sylvia interjected.

"Maybe so, but I bet that old woman didn't even say thank you."

"That's not true," Belinda said. "When I handed Maude the paper sack, she said thank you."

"She shoulda said more than that." Henry's gaze flicked upward. "Maude should have apologized for stealing those hens and been willing to give them back. But no—you let her keep 'em."

"This discussion is over." Belinda turned back around and stared out the front window of their driver's van. She hoped her son's disposition would improve once they got to Ezekiel's. Otherwise it could ruin everyone's Christmas.

Clymer

As their driver pulled into Ezekiel's yard and parked his van, the doors opened. Everyone piled out, and they were almost immediately joined by Ezekiel and Michelle, who rushed out the front door to greet them.

Belinda's heart swelled with joy. It was so good to see this part of her family again.

After everyone had received a welcome hug or handshake and their luggage had been taken from the van, they all headed for the house. Belinda went straight for her grandchildren. Vernon stood in his playpen, and Angela Mary sat on a blanket nearby. Bending down and swooping the little girl into her arms, she gave her granddaughter a kiss. Angela Mary giggled as she wrapped her arms around Belinda's neck.

"I've missed you, little one," Belinda said in Pennsylvania Dutch.

"Can I hold my niece now?" Amy stepped forward and held out her arms.

"Of course." Belinda handed the child to Amy and lifted Vernon out of the playpen. "Oh, my sweet grandson, I can't believe how much you've grown." She lowered herself into the rocking chair and held the little guy in her lap. His smile reminded her of Ezekiel when he was a young boy. She felt warm inside as memories stirred from within to a time when she and Vernon had held their own children when they were about the age of her sweet grandchildren. *I'm so glad to have those images saved from a long while ago to reflect on. I am even more grateful for new opportunities with my loved ones here and now.*

Everyone else took a seat, and as they visited with each other, contentment filled Belinda's soul. How wonderful it was to have family together to celebrate this special holiday remembrance of Jesus' birth.

"Can I talk with you in private?" Henry whispered to Ezekiel, who sat beside him on the living-room sofa.

Ezekiel glanced around the room, where the rest of the family and Dennis sat visiting. "Can it wait awhile?" he quietly asked. "You've only been here a short time, and I don't want to be rude by leaving the room."

Henry leaned closer to his brother. "I need to talk with you now. Can't we go outside or someplace else? Everyone's talking a mile a minute, so I bet we won't even be missed."

"Okay, if you insist." Ezekiel gave another quick glance around the room, and then he stood. Michelle looked at him and smiled before she continued to share with his mother about what baby Vernon had done the other day.

Henry was immediately on his feet and followed his brother to the utility room, where everyone's outer garments had been hung. After putting on their jackets they stepped out the back door.

"It's too cold out here to stand around and talk. Let's go out to my shop," Ezekiel suggested. "You might enjoy seeing all the *iem* supplies that I sell."

Henry wasn't the least bit interested in looking at bee supplies, but he gave an agreeable nod. At least they'd be out of the cold and away from listening ears.

When they entered the building a short time later, Ezekiel lit one of the gas lamps and motioned toward his supplies. "I'm sure happy with the amount of interest the bee stuff generates. I've added more hives outside and have been able to keep up with the amount of honey needed to sell to the tourists as well as the locals. Even Michelle likes to help out when she can, and she often shares the feedback she gets from our customers."

"That's nice." Henry's impartial tone fell from his lips as he waited.

Ezekiel told Henry to take a wooden stool near his desk. "I sense you want to get something off your chest. So what's on your mind?" He seated himself behind the desk.

Henry took a deep breath and released it slowly. *I'm hoping since Ezekiel is a minister it won't influence his thoughts about this situation. I want my brother to agree with me and nip in the bud any chance of Monroe winning our mother over.*

Henry folded his arms and looked directly at Ezekiel. "You're not gonna believe this, but Mom gave Monroe permission to feed our animals, water the plants, and keep an eye on our house while we're here." He uncrossed his arms and gave his jacket collar a tug. "He even had the nerve to ask her for a key to the house so he could bring the mail inside and check on things."

Ezekiel leaned forward, with his arms resting on the desk. "How did Mom respond to that?"

"She said since the mailbox locks, whatever mail we may get while we're gone should be fine in there till we return." Henry paused and swiped his hand across his forehead. "And she said there wasn't anything in the house that needed to be checked, so all he has to do is take care of the animals, water everything in the greenhouse, and make sure everything on the property looks okay."

Ezekiel tapped his fingers against the surface of his desk. "I don't understand how this took place. It was my understanding that Monroe had quit coming around, so why would our mamm ask him to do anything while you're gone?"

Henry felt a sense of tightness in his jaw and facial muscles. "She didn't ask him. He suggested it. And even though Mom did not encourage him, he's started coming around again, asking how we're all doing and if there's anything he can do to help out."

"I see."

Henry frowned. "Is that all you have to say about this, Brother? Can't you see what that irritating man is up to?"

"I suspect he's still trying to win Mom's *hend*."

"Jah, well, if I have anything to say about it, Monroe's not gonna win Mom's hand." Henry got up from the stool and stood in front of Ezekiel's desk. "I don't trust that man; *Er is en missdrauischer mensch.*"

"How do you see him as a suspicious person?"

"I can't put my finger on it, but Monroe's not to be trusted. In fact, he's on my list of suspects."

Ezekiel's brows lifted. "Suspects for what?"

With eyes closed, Henry pinched the bridge of his nose. *What am I thinking? I almost blurted out the fact that we've had some vandalism at our place since Dad, Abe, and Toby were killed. If I let it slip to my brother, he'll ask Mom about it, and then I'll be in trouble with her for blabbing what she doesn't want him to know.*

"What is your list of suspects for?" Ezekiel asked again.

Henry opened his eyes and pulled his fingers through the back of his hair. He had to think quick and come up with some kind of believable explanation. "Umm. . .I guess suspects isn't really the word I shoulda used. What I meant was the list of men I believe might be interested in our mamm."

Ezekiel's eyes widened. "There are others, besides Monroe?"

Henry nodded.

"Have some other men been hanging around, asking Mom if they can court her?"

"Well, not exactly."

"What then?"

Henry shuffled his feet on the concrete floor. "I've seen a couple of widowed men in our church district eye-balling Mom lately. And then there's Herschel Fisher, who drops by sometimes too. He was there to help raise the new barn, and. . ."

Ezekiel held up his hand. "Even if there are some men who are interested in Mom, it's none of your *gscheft*."

"Why isn't it my business?"

"Because it's up to our mother to decide if she's interested in a relationship with another man."

"You've sure changed your tune. I thought you didn't care much for Monroe."

"He did come across as a bit irritating, but if Mom should decide to let Monroe, Herschel, or any other man court her, then we need to accept it and do nothing to stand in the way of her happiness."

Henry's face warmed. "I cannot stand by and do nothing if Mom chooses Monroe, or even Herschel. She still loves Dad and no one can ever replace him, plain and simple!"

He turned and stomped out the door.

I shoulda never brought this up to Ezekiel. He didn't care for Monroe when he met him before, but apparently he's changed his mind. Henry moved briskly through the path leading back to the house. *Sure am glad I didn't say what was really on my mind concerning Monroe. He's definitely high on my list of suspects and could only be showing interest in Mom to get his hands on our greenhouse.*

Strasburg

Virginia stood in front of her living-room window looking through

Earl's binoculars again. Sometimes it was to get a closer look at the birds in their yard, but most often she used the field glasses to spy on the neighbors across the road. *I wonder what those Amish folks are up to today. They're always busy, and I'm sure I'll see something going on over at the Kings' place.*

The first thing she'd noticed early this morning was when an over-sized passenger van drove into the yard. She had watched with interest as the King family came out of the house with suitcases and piled into the van. She had no idea where they were all going but figured it was probably somewhere to spend the Christmas holiday. Why else would they have loaded suitcases into the back of the vehicle?

As Virginia continued to stand there, her bum leg began to throb—a sure sign that she'd been on it too long. She took a seat in the recliner and tried to rub the pain out, but it did little to help the discomfort.

Goldie leaped onto of the arm of Virginia's chair. "You silly cat—come here." She scratched behind the animal's ear while a chorus of purring began. Virginia tried to relax in the recliner with Goldie, but her leg continued to ache. "I'm sorry to disturb you, sweet kitty, but your mommy needs to take care of something." Virginia moved the cat to the carpeted floor.

Rising from the chair, she limped into the kitchen. After pouring herself a cup of coffee, Virginia took an ice pack from the freezer compartment of the refrigerator, then back to the living room she went.

She was about to take a seat when her ears perked up at the sound of a horse and buggy coming down the road. *Well, at least it's not heading to the greenhouse, because thankfully, it's closed for the winter season.*

As the sound grew closer, Virginia glanced out the window and caught sight of the horse and buggy turning up the Kings' driveway. *Hmm. . .that's strange. The sign out by the road says the greenhouse is closed for the winter, so who would be going there today?*

Virginia sat her coffee mug on the end table, along with the ice pack, and then she picked up the binoculars and stood in front of the window, ignoring the pain in her leg.

Her interest piqued when she watched an Amish man with no beard get out of the buggy and tie his horse to the hitching rail near the house. Virginia had seen this same man come to the greenhouse on several occasions, but she didn't know his name, or if he had any kind of relationship to the King family. Since the man was here now, she figured he either hadn't seen the sign or, if he knew the Kings personally, didn't know they were leaving.

Virginia continued to observe until the Amish man disappeared around the side of the house where the new barn had been built to replace the old one. *He's not heading to the greenhouse, or the Kings' home, so I wonder what he's up to.*

She was tempted to put on her warm jacket and go over there to see what the man was up to, but in addition to the colder weather that had set in, her leg hurt too bad to walk that far. She returned to her recliner and put the ice pack against her leg again. She wished Earl could have stayed home from work today. It wasn't fair that he had to show up at the car dealership this morning. After all, who would be looking at new vehicles on Christmas Eve day?

Maybe some rich guy wanting to buy a new car for his wife or spoiled teenager, she thought. *But then why would anyone wait till the last minute to get a big Christmas gift like that? And who has that kind of money anyway?*

She reached for her cup of coffee and took a drink. While she and Earl were getting by financially, they were far from rich and never would be. It was hard not to be envious of people who could afford the finer things in life.

Virginia glanced at the small Christmas tree on the other side of the room. *Big deal! What's a holiday without a family to spend it with? As usual, Christmas Day will be just me and Earl, watching TV and eating a meal by ourselves. Oh, how I wish we were back in Chicago and could get together with Stella and her husband for at least a part of the holiday. We could visit, eat snacks, and play one of our favorite card games, like we did in the past.*

The longer Virginia stewed about this, the worse she felt. And the worse she felt, the more tempted she was to light up a cigarette.

Virginia's thoughts were pulled aside when she heard a horse whinny. She got up and made her way over to the window again, in time to see the Amish man undo his horse and climb into the buggy. Whatever he'd come over to the Kings' place for, he'd obviously figured out that they weren't home.

"Good riddance," she mumbled. "I hope I don't see or hear anymore

Amish buggies on our road the rest of the day." Of course, Virginia knew that was not likely to be the case. Like every other day since she and Earl had moved to this area, she was sure to see horses and buggies. The only good thing was that now, with the greenhouse closed until spring, there would be a lot less traffic on this road. At least she had something to be thankful for on this boring Christmas Eve.

Chapter 8

Clymer

Christmas morning, after breakfast and a time of devotions, the women did the dishes while the men went outside to look at Ezekiel's shop and tour the property.

Jared took a sip from his cup of coffee and then looked over at his brother-in-law. "Thank you for leading us in the devotion after the meal earlier."

"Jah," Dennis agreed. "It was a timely reminder of how God sent His Son to earth as a baby, in order to later die and rise again so that those who believe on His name will be saved from their sins."

"I remember when my *daed* was the one leading our morning devotionals in the past," Ezekiel said. "Then after his death, Mom took over for him to keep the family who lived in her home moving on the right path."

Jared's gaze drifted toward the floor of the shop. "It's important to spend time in God's Word, and I'm thankful that He helps us through the good and bad times."

The men agreed, and Ezekiel continued showing them around the shop.

"This is quite an operation you've got going here," Dennis commented after Ezekiel described some of the supplies he either made in the shop or sold from where he purchased them at wholesale prices. "Do you also raise bees and sell honey?"

"While beekeeping is not my primary business, we do make some extra money by selling jars of honey to several local stores." Ezekiel smiled. "Growing up in Strasburg, I became interested in raising bees for honey when I was a teenager. Although I helped in my parents' greenhouse, it was never my favorite occupation. I preferred selling the honey my bees made, and jumped at the chance to move here when I learned of this business that was for sale. Let's go outside now so I can give you a tour around the property."

With eager expressions, the men headed out the door.

"I've always thought it was important to work at a job I enjoyed," Jared interjected. "When my uncle Maylon taught me the roofing business, I knew I'd found my niche."

"I feel the same way about training horses," Dennis put in. "Even when I was a young boy, I was interested in them. When I got my own horse after turning sixteen, I could get him to do most anything." He chuckled. "My older brother always teased me and said the only reason my gaul did what I wanted was because he knew there'd be a lump of sugar as a reward."

"Makes sense to me." Ezekiel smiled. "Everyone—even a horse— needs a little incentive to get certain things done."

"True." Dennis glanced from where he stood facing the backside of the house. "Guess I'd better go find Henry. He's supposed to be in the front yard waiting for me. There's a little project the two of us need to work on." Dennis looked at Ezekiel, and then Jared. "I'll see you two back at the house."

After Dennis left the shop, Ezekiel looked over at Jared. "I can't figure out what kind of project those two would need to do in my yard."

Jared lifted his broad shoulders in a shrug. "I have no idea, but one thing I can tell you is that your young brother has sure taken a shine to Dennis."

"Since I can't be there for Henry, I'm glad he's found a friend in Sylvia's new boyfriend. From what I can tell, Dennis has been good for my sister as well as my brother." There was a part of Ezekiel that wished he could be the person to help his brother. But the Lord had provided Dennis, and Ezekiel would trust him to take good care of Henry.

Soon after the men came inside, the family gathered in the living room to open gifts. The room seemed to be filled with excitement and anticipation. The pretty red-and-green wrapping on some of the gifts added to the expectancy.

Sylvia smiled, seeing the look of joy on Henry's face when Dennis presented him with a gift subscription to a well-known birding magazine.

"Danki, Dennis." Henry grinned as he thumbed through the first issue, which accompanied the subscription notice. "Bet I'll learn a lot while looking at this magazine when a new issue arrives in our mailbox every month."

"You're welcome, Henry." Dennis turned to Sylvia and handed her a package. "I hope you like what I got for you."

The present had been wrapped nicely, and Sylvia wondered if Dennis had done the work or asked someone else to wrap it for him. The package felt a little weighty. She couldn't begin to guess what was inside. Curious to see what it was, she hurriedly opened the gift and discovered a pair of binoculars.

She looked at Dennis and smiled. "Danki. It's nice to finally have a pair I can call my own." Sylvia inspected the field glasses and placed the leather strap over her head to try them out.

"They have a stronger power than many of the binoculars I looked at," Dennis explained. "Looking through these, you should be able to see most birds easily, even from quite a distance."

Sylvia held them close to her chest. "I can hardly wait to go birding again so I can put these to good use."

"Why wait till then? Let's go over to the front window and you can try them out now." He winked at her. "You never know. . .there might be something in the front yard worth looking at."

Sylvia wasn't sure there would be any birds in Ezekiel's yard to look at, but she didn't want to disappoint Dennis, so she left her seat and followed him to the window. When she held the field glasses up to her face, Dennis said, "Scan the whole front yard now, and look for anything interesting that might catch your eye."

Sylvia did as he asked, and nearly dropped the binoculars when a large heart-shaped sign came into view. Painted in bright red letters was a surprising message: "WILL YOU MARRY ME?"

Sylvia had never seen nor heard of such an unusual marriage proposal, but then she'd never met a man quite like Dennis before. Happy tears pricked the back of her eyes, as she turned to him and said: "Jah, Dennis, I will marry you."

Sylvia had no sooner said the words, when her whole family clapped and gathered around them, offering hearty congratulations.

Sylvia felt a sense of weightlessness as she shed more tears of joy. It had been a long time since she'd felt so happy. Oh, how she looked forward to becoming Dennis's wife, but first they'd need to set a wedding date and do a lot of planning in the days ahead.

After everyone gathered around the tables Ezekiel had set up in the dining room, all heads bowed for silent prayer. Although Belinda missed her husband, son, and son-in-law's presence at this meal, she felt a sense of calm being here with the rest of her family. As the platters and bowls of food were passed around, she studied each person's face, committing their happy expressions to memory. Even Henry, who looked like he'd been forced to eat a bowl of sour grapes on the trip to Clymer, wore a pleasant expression on his face. No doubt the happiness he felt was because of his friendship with Dennis. Belinda felt pleased that Sylvia's future husband had taken her son under his wing. Since Ezekiel lived too far away to spend much time with Henry, it was good that he had a special bond with Dennis.

Belinda's attention turned to Sylvia. The transformation in her eldest daughter since Dennis had come into her life was wonderful to witness. Sylvia seemed more sure of herself these days, and Belinda noticed a spring in her step and a brightness in her eyes that hadn't been there since Toby died.

She looked across the table, where Amy and Jared sat. Both wore happy smiles as they dished up their food and made conversation with Michelle and Ezekiel.

My eldest son and youngest daughter are both happily married, and soon my eldest daughter will be too, Belinda mused. *I'm happy for them, but I can't help thinking that it'll only be me and Henry running the greenhouse by ourselves once Sylvia and Dennis are married. After Amy has a baby and perhaps Sylvia has more children, neither will want to work away from their homes.* Belinda helped herself to some gravy, which she ladled over the mashed potatoes on her plate. *I've reflected on all of this too many times, and I need to focus on the treasured moments I'm making with my family today. My thoughts should be on the present, not the future, which is out of my hands, for only God knows what lies ahead for each of us.*

Strasburg

Virginia frowned as she watched her husband sleeping in his recliner a few feet from where she sat on the couch. "Merry Christmas," she mumbled. "What a quiet, boring day."

Earl didn't open his eyes or move a muscle, but his snoring increased. He'd fallen asleep soon after they'd finished eating the ham and baked potatoes Virginia had fixed for their holiday meal. She'd even gone to the trouble of making a green bean casserole and sweet potatoes with melted marshmallows on top. Earl had eaten more than his share, which had no doubt contributed to his sleepy state.

The television blared with some action movie playing in the background. This sort of thing happened more often than not in the evenings after dinner. *How in the world can that man of mine sleep through all the noise?*

Virginia went over quick enough to turn down the volume on the set and return to her seat without disturbing Earl. *That's better, even though I'd rather be watching something else that has to do with Christmas today.*

She looked around the room for the cat, but Goldie wasn't in sight. *I'm sure she's asleep on our bed. It's one of her favorite spots, especially on top of my pillow.*

Hearing a horse and buggy coming down the road, Virginia rose from her seat and went over to the front window to look out. The buggy looked the same as most of those she'd previously seen, but she recognized the horse as it turned up the Kings' driveway.

Virginia picked up Earl's binoculars for a better look and watched as the same Amish man she'd seen before got out of his rig and secured the horse. *I wonder what he's doing back here again.*

She couldn't help watching as the man walked in the direction of the barn and disappeared from her sight. *Drats! Sure wish I could see what he's up to. If some of those trees weren't blocking my view, I'd have a front row seat into their yard.*

"Hey, why'd ya turn the volume down?" Earl sputtered. "And what are ya doin' with those binoculars, Virginia?"

She whirled around. "Earl, you about scared me to death. I thought you were sleeping."

"Nope. I was listening to the TV while resting my eyes."

"Puh!" She flapped her hand in his direction. "People don't snore unless they're sound asleep. I don't see how anyone can rest their eyes the way you do with the volume up so loud."

"It doesn't bother me." Earl let out a yawn and pointed at the binoculars Virginia still held in her hands. "Who are you spyin' on this time?"

"If you're really interested, there's an Amish man who's been over at the Kings' place since they left to go somewhere yesterday morning."

"Maybe he doesn't know they're not home." Earl got up and moved over to the window. "Or maybe he's checking on the place while they're gone. They do have some critters that would need to be fed and watered, you know." He took the binoculars from her and motioned to the couch. "Why don't you sit down and relax, before your leg starts to hurt from standing so long?"

Virginia gave a huff. "I am tired of sitting, and on top of that, I'm bored. Except for our scrawny little tree, and the few lights you put up outside, it doesn't even feel like Christmas to me."

"Didn't you make a chocolate mint cake for our dessert?"

She put a hand on her hip. "Is that a hint that you have room for more after eating our big meal?"

"I could handle a piece of your delicious cake. Also a cup of hot coffee would go real good with it too."

"Okay, whatever you want." Virginia headed for the kitchen.

Once there, she got out some holiday plates and a couple of matching mugs. At least the dessert would add a little cheer to the hum-drum day. *I wouldn't mind having a few grandchildren to spoil today, or at least some family around to make the season brighter.*

Virginia grabbed a tray to set the plated desserts and coffee mugs on. She returned to the living room and served Earl his dessert. With an eager expression, he gobbled it down, while Virgina ate hers slowly.

"Let's watch one of those sappy Christmas movies." Earl remained in the recliner as he picked up the remote. "That oughta be enough to put you in the holiday spirit."

Virginia took a sip of her coffee and wrinkled her nose. "Yeah, right."

After she returned to the couch, another thought popped into her mind. *If the Kings are away on a trip, I wonder why they didn't ask me and Earl to keep an eye on the place instead of some fellow who lives so far that he has to travel over there by horse and buggy. I bet they don't think we're trustworthy enough to take care of their place while they are gone. Amy, and probably Mrs. King too, must not care much for us, or we'd have gotten an invitation to Amy and Jared's wedding.*

Dwelling on this topic for too long caused Virginia's stomach to knot up. She still held a grudge and didn't think she could get past the feeling of rejection she'd felt.

"How 'bout some more cake and coffee?"

Earl's question halted Virginia's negative thoughts. "Sure, why not? Your wish is my command, Earl." She pulled herself up from the couch and limped out to the kitchen. Maybe another piece of cake would make her feel better too. At least for a little while it might squelch her self-pity.

Chapter 9

Virginia watched out the living-room window as a van pulled onto the Kings' driveway. As near as she could tell, it was the same one that had left the place with the King family the day before Christmas. Now, here they were, two days after the holiday, returning home.

Earlier this morning, shortly after Earl left for work, Virginia had seen the old woman, Maude, standing near the mailboxes across the road. She'd been about to open the front door and holler out, asking Maude to move along, when the scraggly-looking woman finally ambled on down the road. With the way her mouth moved as she shook her head, Virginia figured Maude must have been talking to herself.

She's probably senile, or maybe has some kind of mental problem, Virginia told herself. *A person like her can't be trusted. I wonder if she went onto the Kings' property while they were gone. I wouldn't be surprised if she took something.*

Purring like a motor boat, Goldie rubbed against Virginia's leg, swishing her fluffy tail.

"Okay, okay, you determined cat. Let's go out to the kitchen, and I'll get you some food." As Virginia made her way to the kitchen, Goldie pranced beside her. While the cat couldn't converse with Virginia, at least she was good company.

She grabbed a can of food from one of the lower drawers and opened it. The aroma of fish and chicken permeated the room. "This stuff doesn't smell too bad." Virginia lowered her glance at Goldie as she plopped the food into the cat's dish. "Here you go. Enjoy your breakfast."

Virginia noticed a bit of the food had remained in the can. *I wonder what this stuff tastes like. What would it hurt to sample a bit?* She took her finger and ran it around the inside of the can. But before she could retrieve it some blood began dripping from her finger.

"Oh no! That wasn't a good idea." Virginia went to the sink, rinsed off her hand, and took a closer look at the wound. It was still bleeding, but at least it wasn't a deep cut that might require stitches.

She went to pull off a paper towel, but the way she'd yanked it, with only one hand, sent the roll from the counter onto the floor. Goldie jumped when the towels landed near her, and Virginia moaned. "This is turning out to be a bad morning." She left the mess where it lay and grabbed a damp dish rag from the sink to wrap her finger in. Then Virginia limped off to the bathroom to find the right bandage to tape the cut closed.

She fumbled about, working to get her finger taped up, and when she finished she brought back the stained rag to the kitchen. Goldie had eaten all of her food and now lay on the throw rug, bathing herself. "At least you are satisfied and happy."

Virginia picked up the unwound roll of paper towels and tore off the long tail from it. She hung up what was left and threw away the rest in the garbage. Her finger hurt and some blood seeped through the bandage. The can of cat food remained on the counter, along with traces of blood. Virginia, still curious after everything that occurred, picked a spoon from the utensil drawer and gave the cat food a taste. It didn't linger long in her mouth before she rushed to the sink and spit it out. "This stuff tastes nasty! How can it smell one way and taste so bad? Well, at least no one but me will know I gave Goldie's food a try."

Virginia picked up the can and tossed it in the garbage on top of the wad of paper towels. Then she retrieved the used blood-stained rag and tried to rinse it out. It wouldn't come clean, so she used it to wipe away the rest of the blood droplets and threw it away too. *At least Earl won't find out what happened, since I did a good job of taking care of things.*

After Henry helped bring everyone's luggage inside, he said goodbye to Dennis, Jared, and Amy before they climbed back into the van to be driven to their homes.

"Want me to check for phone messages?" he asked his mother.

"That would be helpful. And please get the mail too." She handed him the key.

"Sure, I'll do that first, and then after I leave the phone shed I'm gonna let my hund out of his dog run for a bit while I make sure the horses and chickens are okay."

"I'm confident that they're all fine. Monroe knew we'd be home today, so he probably came over early this morning to take care of things."

Henry resisted the urge to say something negative about Mom's would-be suitor. She didn't like it when he bad-mouthed someone—even Monroe, who no one in the family particularly cared for, except maybe Mom. Henry couldn't be sure how she really felt about her old boyfriend, since she treated him kindly whenever he came around. But she had stated on more than one occasion that she had no romantic interest in Monroe Esh. While that might be true, Henry was concerned that the persistent man might keep trying to charm his mother until she finally gave in and allowed him to court her. That, of course, could lead to a possible marriage proposal, which Henry could not stand for.

He gripped the mailbox key in his hand so hard it dug into his palm. *Don't know what I'd do if Mom ended up marrying that irritating fellow. I couldn't live in the same house with him, that's for sure.*

Forcing his thoughts aside, while shivering against the harsh wind that had begun to blow tree branches about, Henry hurried through some scattered leaves the heavy breeze had pushed down along the driveway. When he came to their mailbox and opened it, Henry discovered only a few advertising pamphlets inside, along with a couple of bills.

Holding tight to the mail in one hand, he made his way back up the driveway to the phone shed. Upon entering the small building, Henry shut the door, took a seat, and clicked on the answering machine. It was good to get out of the wind even if it had to be in the tiny, cold cubical. The first message was from Herschel Fisher's daughter, Sara, saying she wanted to wish the King family a Merry Christmas because she didn't have time to send out cards this year. The next message was from Mary

Ruth Lapp, inviting Mom to join her and some other ladies in their church district to a quilting party that would take place next week in Mary Ruth's home.

Henry paused the answering machine and wrote both messages on the tablet beside the phone. When he finished, he clicked the button again to see if anyone else had called.

The third and final message caused Henry to freeze in place. He was so stunned in fact that he had to replay it again, to be sure of what he'd heard.

The voice sounded muffled, but the message was clear: "You've been warned before, but chose to ignore. You need to sell your place and move before it's too late."

Henry's ears rang as a knot formed in his stomach. Warned before? Had there been a similar message he didn't know about? If so, who'd listened to the muffled voice, and why hadn't they said anything? Whenever the earlier threatening message had come in, it had obviously been deleted because there were no other muffled voices left on the answering machine.

Why didn't anyone tell me about this? I'm not a child. I can't help but feel hurt by being left out of what is going on around here. Henry needed to let go of the disappointment and focus on the matter of his family being threatened. He listened to the message one more time, trying to decipher who the person was, but to no avail. The man or woman who'd made the call had done a good job masking their voice.

He remained in the phone shack a few more minutes, mulling things over. The frightening message made him even more determined to find out who was responsible for the damage that had been done to their property. He felt sure that whoever had made the call was the person who'd done it, and might even be responsible for their barn burning down.

Henry saved the message so his mother could listen to it, and then he left the phone shed. He would go inside and talk to her once he'd let Blackie out for a run and gone out to the barn to check on the horses. Henry needed the extra time to think things through before talking to Mom.

After letting Blackie out of his pen, Henry started for the barn. The dog, however, had other ideas. Barking and nipping at Henry's heels,

Blackie continued to carry on until Henry stopped walking. "Knock it off you crazy hund. I know ya missed me, but I don't have time for this right now."

When the dog continued to bark, Henry picked up a stick and gave it a toss. Blackie gave another excited *woof*, and took off after the stick. Henry took advantage of this brief reprieve and made a dash for the barn.

He'd barely entered the building when he spotted a note tacked up on the wall near the double doors. It said: *"Sell Out or Face the Consequences!"*

Henry's heart pounded as he grabbed a bright-beamed flashlight to check every area of the barn. He hoped he would find some sort of evidence as to who had hung that sign. Someone who wanted them gone had not only left the muffled message, but they'd been in the barn.

Henry couldn't shake the uneasy feeling. He wanted to catch this person so his family could have peace again. After his father, brother, and brother-in-law passed away, he and the rest of the family had enough to deal with. They certainly did not need this type of problem on top of everything else.

After looking in the horses' stalls and all the other areas in the lower half of the barn, Henry felt defeated because he'd found no clues. *I'd like to see this person be held accountable for his or her actions.*

With jaw clenched, he climbed up the ladder to the loft. There had to be a clue somewhere that would let him know who had come to the barn and hung that sign. The only person Henry knew for sure had been in the barn while they were gone was Monroe, since he was supposed to feed and water the animals.

Henry snapped his fingers. *That's it! Why am I looking for clues when the answer's so clear? That aggravating man has been up to no good ever since he came back to Strasburg and started hangin' around Mom. Monroe needs to be confronted, and I aim to do it as soon as possible.*

With her suitcase lying on the bed, Belinda was busy unpacking when Henry stepped into the room. "Was there any mail or phone messages waiting?" she asked, barely glancing his way.

"Jah, there was some mail, and. . ."

"Where'd you put it?"

"Umm. . .I must have left it in the phone shed."

"Could you go back and get it, please?"

Henry's gaze darted around the room as he blew out a series of short breaths.

"What's wrong, Son? Is something bothering you?"

"Jah, and I am very *verlegge*."

"What is it? What has you so troubled?"

"There was a muffled message on our answering machine and a threatening note tacked to the barn wall near the double doors."

A rush of adrenaline passed through Belinda's body as she listened to Henry explain what both messages said.

Henry moved closer to the bed. "This has happened before, hasn't it, Mom?"

She nodded. "Not the note on the barn, but the muffled voice on the phone."

"Why didn't you say something about it?"

"I didn't want to upset you."

"Well, it's too late for that. I'm umgerennt now, and I woulda liked to have known about this sooner."

"How would that have done any good, Son? We don't have a clue who's behind all of this, and the truth is, we may never know."

Henry planted his feet in a wide stance and stared at her. "There's only one person who could've done it, Mom."

"Oh? And who would that be?"

"Monroe. He went in the barn to feed the horses and cats while we were gone."

"I realize that, Henry, but it doesn't mean Monroe is responsible for the note you discovered." Belinda put both hands on her hips. "Monroe's never given me any reason to believe that he would want us to sell and move out. In fact, he's been kind enough to drop by regularly to see how we're doing and ask if there's anything he can do to help out."

Henry's eyes narrowed as he reached up to rub the back of his neck. "He's pretending to care about us, Mom. Can't you see that? For some reason that man has been trying to frighten us so we'll move out."

"What reason would he have for doing that?"

"Maybe he wants the greenhouse for himself, and since he hasn't been able to win you over, he's changed tactics and decided to use threating messages to get what he wants. He could also be the one responsible for all the vandalism that's been done around here."

Belinda held up her hand as she lowered herself to the bed. "That's enough, Henry. I don't want to hear any more of your *narrisch* theories."

"It's not foolish." Henry shook his head vigorously. "That man is not to be trusted, and I aim to prove it. Right now, though, I'm goin' back out to the phone shed to get the mail."

Henry turned and tromped out of the room before Belinda could form a response. Monroe might be a lot of things, but she couldn't believe he would stoop so low as to frighten them so he could get his hands on the greenhouse. After all, what did he need it for? He had his own furniture business to run. *It sounds like my son wants to find out who's behind this and so do I. I'm sure Monroe isn't the person but that still leaves my family in a precarious situation.*

Belinda picked up the dresses from the suitcase and hung them in her closet. She did not want to move from her home. *Dear Lord, please help me to have the faith that You will take care of all this.*

"You look umgerrent, Mom. Is something wrong?" Sylvia asked when she entered the kitchen where Belinda paced the floor.

She stopped pacing and turned to face her daughter. "As a matter of fact, I'm very upset." Belinda relayed everything Henry had told her before he'd rushed back outside in a huff. She also told Sylvia about the muffled phone call she'd received previously and apologized for keeping quiet about it.

Sylvia's brows drew together as she lowered herself into a chair. "Oh dear. That's so frightening. Do you think Henry could be right about Monroe? Is it possible that he's the one responsible for the muffled phone calls and all the other negative things that have happened around here?"

Belinda took a chair across from her daughter. "I can't imagine why he would do such a thing. Monroe claims to care for me, so I wouldn't think. . ." Her voice trailed off as she placed her fingers across her forehead and massaged the pulsating parts.

"Are you going to talk to Monroe about this?"

"I. . .I don't know what I would say, other than to come right out and ask if he's responsible for any of what's been done."

"If he is, he'd probably deny it."

"Maybe it would be better if I tell Monroe about the phone message and note tacked to the barn wall. Then I'll wait and see how he reacts."

Sylvia bobbed her head. "That might be the best approach."

At the sound of a horse and buggy coming up the driveway, Belinda got up from her chair and stepped into the hallway to look out the small window on the front door. *I guess there's no time like the present, because Monroe just pulled in. I need to speak with him right away, before Henry sees him and makes an accusation that is most likely false and could make things worse.*

Chapter 10

Belinda waited until Monroe stepped onto the porch before she opened the door. "I saw you coming, so—"

"It's good to see you. When did you get home?" he interrupted.

She glanced in the entry where Henry's suitcase sat. Belinda slid it against the wall to be out of the way. Her face warmed, feeling a little embarrassed. "A few hours ago. I was going to call and leave a message for you, but now I won't have to." Belinda opened the door wider. "Would you like to come in and join me for a cup of *kaffi* and some kichlin?"

A wide smile stretched across his face. "Coffee and cookies sounds good to me." He stepped inside and joined her in the hallway. Monroe seemed to be in good spirits, and his gaze never left Belinda as he slipped off his shoes by the door.

"Sylvia's in the living room with her kinner, so let's go in the kitchen where we talk in private." Belinda gestured in that direction.

"Okay, that's fine with me." Monroe followed Belinda to the kitchen and took a seat at the table. "Everything went fine here while you were gone." He grinned at her. "I had no problems with any of the animals, and I remembered to water all the plants." He reached into his pants pocket and handed Belinda the key to the greenhouse.

"Danki." Belinda poured them both a cup of coffee, set a plate of ginger cookies on the table, and took a seat across from him. "There's something I'd like to talk to you about, Monroe."

"Sure, no problem. I always enjoy talking to you." He reached for a cookie and gobbled it down, then followed it with a drink from his cup. A look of contentment showed on Monroe's face as he stared at her. As usual, his appearance was neat as a pin, and his hair had been combed back from his face. The aftershave or men's cologne he wore had a light musky odor. She caught his boyish grin before he took another sip of coffee. "Belinda, your place is kept up nice, but I don't know how you manage to run your business and keep up with this big house."

"I have a lot of help. My children pitch in; especially when things get hectic around here." She dropped her gaze. *I've known this man for a good many years and he's never shown any signs of contempt. In fact, since Vernon's death Monroe has been nothing but supportive.*

She added some cream to the hot liquid and gave it a stir. *But my children haven't warmed up to him and have expressed their lack of fondness toward Monroe many times. Are the negative things they've complained about enough reason to think he would be capable of vandalizing, leaving threatening notes, or making muffled phone calls?*

Belinda sat a little straighter in her chair. She cleared her throat, and was about to ask if he knew anything about the note tacked up in the barn, when Henry came into the kitchen with a stack of mail in his hand. A sheen of sweat formed on Henry's face as he glared at Monroe. "You're just the person I wanna see."

"Oh?" Monroe tipped his head. "I'm glad to see you too."

Henry dropped the mail on the counter and pulled a folded piece of paper out from the stack of envelopes. Then he marched across the room, unfolded the paper, and placed it on the table in front of Monroe. "What do ya know about this?"

Belinda held her breath as she waited to hear Monroe's response. While this wasn't the way she would have brought up the topic, at least now they would know whether her ex-boyfriend had written the note, and if so, what made him do it.

Monroe stared at the piece of paper several seconds before he spoke. "Where did you get this?" He looked right at Henry.

"In the barn. It was tacked up on the wall near the double doors."

A muscle on the side of Monroe's neck twitched. "That's sure strange." He tapped the piece of paper with his index finger. "I never saw this while I was in the barn feeding the horses and cats."

"So you didn't put it there?" Henry's eyes narrowed as he continued to stare at the man.

"Of course not! Are you suggesting that I wrote the note?" Monroe's mouth slackened.

"That's how it seems to me," Henry stated.

Monroe looked over at Belinda. "Surely you don't believe I would do something like this. I mean, why would I, for goodness' sake?"

Belinda opened her mouth to respond, but Henry cut her off. "Did you leave a muffled message on our answering machine?"

"What? No!" Monroe's cheeks colored. "I have no idea what you're talking about."

"Someone left a threatening message while we were gone, and we couldn't tell who it was because their voice sounded strange—barely audible," Belinda explained.

"And you think I did that?"

Belinda blinked rapidly. "Well, I—"

"I can't believe you would even suggest that I'd be capable of doing such a thing. I care about you, Belinda, and would not do anything to hurt or upset you. I've never been anything but helpful and kind where you and your family are concerned." Monroe's jaw clenched, causing his lips to form into a white slash. He stared at Belinda and then pushed his chair away from the table. "Think I'd better go."

As he walked briskly toward the door, Belinda called out to him. "I'm sorry, Monroe. We didn't mean to offend you. It's just that. . ."

"Enough said. I guess our friendship is purely one-sided." He rushed out the door before Belinda could try to stop him.

She turned to Henry and said, "I wish you hadn't accused him, Son. I was only going to ask if he had seen the note or might know if anyone besides him had been on our property while we were gone." She heaved a sigh. "Now he's offended and will probably never come around here again."

"That's good." Henry gave a shrug. "Maybe now that I've confronted him with what I've suspected, he'll finally leave us alone."

Monroe snapped the reins and got his horse moving at a good pace down the road. "I can't believe the way Belinda talked to me. And that son of hers—well, he should be seen and not heard. If he were my boy, he'd get a good tongue-lashing and plenty of extra chores to do for being so disrespectful to me."

Every muscle in Monroe's body tensed. "At this rate I'll never convince Belinda to marry me." He pressed one fist against his mouth and puffed out his cheeks. "And just when I thought I was gaining ground with her. Now I'm not sure what to do. Should I wait a few days and then go back over there—try to make her listen to reason and convince her that I'm not the enemy? Or would it be better to stay away longer and hope that she'll make contact with me? I lost Belinda once to Vernon. I won't lose her again."

As he headed down the road, Monroe got to thinking about what Henry had said. *I can't allow them to believe I had anything to do with the things that have happened to them.*

Sylvia got up off the living-room floor where she'd been rebraiding Rachel's hair and went to the kitchen. She found her mother sitting at the table with her head bowed and hands folded, as though praying. She waited quietly until Mom lifted her head.

"Is everything okay?" Sylvia asked. "I heard you talking to someone awhile ago, and it sounded like Monroe."

Mom moved her head slowly up and down. "He was here all right, and he may never be back."

"How come?"

Sylvia took a chair and listened as her mother repeated everything that had been said between her and Monroe, as well as what Henry had accused the man of.

"Monroe denied knowing anything about the note or threatening phone calls." Mom's chin quivered. "He seemed sincere, not to mention deeply hurt by the accusations. Monroe's final words were that he thought our friendship has been one-sided."

"That's good in a way, Mom. He obviously realizes now that you don't care for him."

Mom shook her head. "I never said that, Daughter. While I don't think of Monroe in a romantic sort of way, he has been a good friend, who I felt sure cared for me."

Sylvia sat quietly for a few moments, carefully forming her next words. "I'll admit that I don't care much for Monroe, but he doesn't seem the type who would do anything malicious to you or anyone in our family."

"I agree. But I doubt we could convince Henry of that. He's sure Monroe is the one responsible for the phone message and note left in the barn, and for that matter, all the rest of the things that have happened to us since your daed, Abe, and Toby were killed."

"And you think it's not *meechlich*?"

"Anything's possible, but I've known Monroe since we were youngsters, and if he cares for me the way he's often stated, then I am quite certain he would not do anything to knowingly hurt or upset me."

"So now what?" Sylvia asked.

"The first thing I'm going to do is have a talk with Henry." Mom rapped her knuckles on the table. "Then I am going to call Monroe and say that I'm sorry for anything we said that may have hurt his feelings." She looked at Sylvia and smiled. "And you, my dear daughter, don't need to worry about this. After that very original marriage proposal you received from Dennis on Christmas Day, all you should be thinking about is planning for and looking forward to your wedding."

"Oh, I am looking forward to the day I become Dennis's fraa, but we haven't set a date yet, so I can't do much planning." Sylvia spoke in a subdued tone.

"I understand. It would have been difficult for you to do much planning with all the commotion we had during the few short days spent at Ezekiel and Michelle's place."

"We had a nice time though, and I was pleased that my bruder and his fraa welcomed Dennis into their home and everyone got along so well. I was a little worried about Henry at first because he seemed kind of sullen when we arrived." Sylvia took a cookie from the plate in the center of the table. "After he opened his Christmas gift from Dennis, Henry's attitude improved."

"Jah. Henry looks up to Dennis, there's no doubt about it. His coming into your life has been good for both you and your young brother."

Sylvia couldn't deny it. The part of her soul that she never thought would heal had been brought to life again. She looked forward to seeing what God had in store for her, Dennis, and the children in the days ahead. She'd continue to pray for the protection of her family. And if, for some unimaginable reason, Monroe was to blame, her prayer would be that God would convict him of his wrongdoings and the attacks and threats would end.

"I enjoyed our trip to your brother's place in New York, but it's good to be home," Jared commented as Amy got out some bread to make them both a sandwich.

She nodded. "I was glad for the opportunity to finally see where he and Michelle live, and having our whole family together for Christmas made it even more special."

"True." Jared joined her at the counter. "Is there anything I can do to help?"

"You can get out the lunch meat and cheese while I slice the bread and spread some butter."

"Not a problem." Jared opened the refrigerator and took out what Amy had asked for. "Would you want some *sellaat*, a *tomaets*, or the jar of *bickels*?"

"Lettuce and tomato might be nice, but I don't care for a pickle on mine. Feel free to get them out if you want one though," Amy responded.

"Naw, I don't need a bickle either."

After the sandwiches were made, and they took seats at the table, Amy and Jared bowed their heads for silent prayer.

Heavenly Father, Amy prayed, *thank You for keeping us safe on our trip home from Clymer, and for giving us such a wonderful Christmas with our family. Bless this food we are about to eat, and please bless and protect each member of our family in the days ahead so we may better serve You. Amen.*

Amy kept her eyes closed and head bowed until she heard the rustle of Jared's napkin. When she opened her eyes and looked at him from across the table, she smiled. "After all the commotion that went on at Ezekiel's place the last few days, it seems kind of quiet in here with just the two of us."

Jared bobbed his head before taking a bite of sandwich. "Someday, when the Lord blesses us with kinner, it won't be so quiet in this home."

Amy placed one hand against her stomach. She hoped it wouldn't be long before they were expecting their first child. While it was nice to spend time with her nieces and nephews, it wasn't the same as having children of their own.

"Getting back to our conversation about the time we spent with your brother and his family"—Jared paused for a drink of milk—"I enjoyed seeing Ezekiel's shop and listening to him talk about all the bee supplies. From some of the things Ezekiel said, I'd guess he's quite *zufridde* living in Clymer."

"You're right, but my brother wouldn't be so contented if he knew about all the vandalism that's been done at Mom's place." Amy blotted her mouth with a napkin. "I still think he has the right to know, and it's getting harder to keep it a secret. I'm surprised Henry hasn't blurted it out already."

"Nothing's happened recently though, right?" Jared asked.

Amy shook her head. "Not that I'm aware of. I'm sure Mom would have said something to us if anything new had occurred, if for no other reason than to ask for our prayers."

Chapter 11

"Is that another *amschel* I see in the yard?" Belinda turned to face Henry, who'd come into the kitchen after doing his outside chores.

He stepped up to the window next to her and peered out. "Yep. That's a robin, all right."

"But it's cold outside and heavy frost is on the ground. I wouldn't expect to see any robins in the middle of February. They usually don't greet us until the beginning of spring," Belinda commented.

"That's true, Mom, but as I've mentioned before, not all robins are the same."

She pointed into the yard. "At least this one isn't banging against our window, like that poor one did a few months ago. I found that to be quite stressful."

"Guess the amschel got tired of abusing himself. Either that or he finally realized no matter how many times he hit the window, he wasn't gonna get in." Henry continued to watch out the window. "Even though robins are considered migratory, some of them stick around and move about in northern locations."

"But what do they eat? I doubt they'd be able to find many worms or insects this time of the year."

"You're right, but they can survive off fruit and berries that are still on trees and bushes."

"Another interesting fact."

"That's not all. Robins can handle very cold temperatures. To keep warm, they fluff up their feathers, which makes 'em look really big. I read about this in the latest birding magazine." Henry sounded enthusiastic.

Belinda was glad to see this side of her son. She smiled and gave his shoulder a tap. "You certainly know a lot about birds."

"Wouldn't know near so much if it weren't for the birding magazine I'm getting thanks to Dennis. I've gotten two issues already."

"It was a thoughtful gift. Your sister's future husband is a good man."

"Jah, not like Monroe." Henry's mouth turned down at the corners. "Sure am glad he quit coming around. Even though he said he wasn't the one responsible for the note on the barn wall or the muffled phone message, I don't believe him."

"Do you really think he would lie about it?" she asked.

Henry shrugged. "If he is the guilty one, I doubt that he'd admit it."

"Maybe not, but he said he didn't do it, so we need to give him the benefit of the doubt."

"You can if you want to, Mom, but I'm gonna keep an eye on things. If Monroe Esh shows up here again I'll watch him like a hawk."

Belinda rolled her eyes. *Does my boy think he's a detective now?* "I don't believe you have to worry about Monroe coming around again," she said. "When he stormed out of here after hearing your accusations, I called and left him a message, apologizing for both of our comments. I also said I appreciated him looking after things while we were gone." Belinda released a heavy sigh. "That was a month and a half ago, and Monroe hasn't come around since. He didn't even call me back to say he accepted my apology."

Henry sagged against the counter. "It's just as well. Even if Monroe isn't responsible for any of the bad things that have been done around here, he's had his eye on you, and I don't like it one bit. If Dad was still here, he wouldn't like it either."

Belinda pressed a hand against her chest. "If your daed was alive, this wouldn't be an issue. We'd still be happily married and Monroe wouldn't even be in the picture."

Henry lowered his gaze. "I wish that was the case. I'd give anything to have Dad, Abe, and Toby back in our lives."

Belinda slipped her arms around Henry and gave him a hug. "I would too, Son, but since that's not possible, we need to move on with our lives and look to the future. We can't change the past."

"It figures you'd say somethin' like that." Henry turned toward the door. "Want me to go out and check for the mail? Nobody got it yesterday, so there's bound to be some."

"That would be most appreciated."

"I'll be back soon."

When Henry went out the door, Belinda's thoughts returned to Monroe. It bothered her that he hadn't returned her call, and she couldn't help wondering if Monroe would ever talk to her again.

Belinda's thoughts switched to Herschel. At least he was an easy-going person, although a little shy. And from what she had witnessed whenever he'd come into the greenhouse with his mother, Herschel appeared to be an attentive son.

Belinda opened the pantry door and took out a box of oatmeal. On a chilly morning such as this, a hot breakfast would be most welcome.

"That Monroe fellow really gets under my skin," Henry fumed as he tromped down the driveway to get their mail. "I can't believe Mom apologized to him for asking questions that needed truthful answers."

Regardless of Monroe's denials, Henry felt sure the man was up to no good. He hoped for everyone's sake that Mr. Esh would never come around their place again. Since they hadn't seen or heard from him since they'd gotten home from Ezekiel's, Henry took it as a good sign that he'd finally gotten the message and wouldn't bother them again. There had been no more muffled phone messages or threatening notes since then either, so maybe things would be normal again.

As normal as they can be, Henry thought.

When Henry stepped up to the mailbox, he nearly collided with the redheaded neighbor lady from across the street. Apparently Virginia had been unaware of his presence and stepped in front of his family's mailbox at the same moment he did.

"Excuse me." Virginia's cheeks reddened and she took a step back. "I should've been watching where I was going instead of looking at my mail." Virginia held up a stack of envelopes. "Turns out they're mostly advertisements."

"It's okay. No harm done." Henry unlocked their mailbox and pulled the flap down. There were only a few pieces of mail, which he didn't bother to identify. After taking the envelopes out, Henry closed the box and turned to face her again. "Say, do you mind if I ask you a question?"

"I guess not." Virginia shifted her weight from one foot to the other. "What is it you want to know?"

"I was wondering if you or your husband noticed anyone hanging around our place while we were gone over the Christmas holiday."

Her forehead wrinkled. "You're asking me about something that happened almost two months ago?"

"Yes, well. . ." Henry gave his earlobe a tug. "I hadn't thought to ask you before." *Duh, stupid me. Why didn't I think to ask any of our neighbors that question?*

"I doubt that Earl saw anything out of the ordinary, since he works most days and spends his evenings in front of the TV. But now that I think about it, I did see someone at your place while you were gone."

Henry blinked. "Did you recognize the person? What'd they look like?"

Virginia shook her head. "It was an Amish man, but I didn't recognize him. He came over by horse and buggy a couple of times while you were gone. I figured he was either being snoopy or had been asked to check on your place."

"His name is Monroe, and my mom asked him to feed our animals and water plants while we were visiting my brother and his family in New York. Well, actually," Henry corrected, "she didn't ask—he volunteered and she agreed."

"I see."

"Was Monroe the only person you saw on our property while we were away from home?"

"Yeah, except for that old woman, Maude. I didn't see her in your yard, but she walked by a couple of times and even stopped once at the entrance of your driveway." Virginia frowned. "That unkempt woman is strange."

Henry thought so too, but he chose not to respond. "Well, I'd best get back to the house with the mail."

"Sure, okay."

When Henry said goodbye, the red-haired neighbor mumbled something he couldn't understand and limped her way across the road.

More than once Henry had been on the verge of asking about the leg she favored, but he figured it was none of his business and she might take offense. If he and the rest of the family knew her better, it might be okay to ask, but Virginia and her husband pretty much kept to themselves. Since they weren't Amish, they probably wouldn't have much in common to talk about anyway, so the least said the better.

Henry started back up the driveway, pausing briefly to admire a ruffed grouse. The brown, chicken-like bird with a long, squared tail had a tuft of feathers on its head that stood up like a crown. The black ruffs on the bird's neck were what it had been named for. Since the grouse was nonmigratory, it wasn't uncommon to see one or more of them during the winter months.

Once the bird skittered into the bushes along the left side of the driveway, Henry moved on. When he entered the house a short time later, he went to the kitchen and handed his mother the mail.

"You can put it over there." She gestured to the desk on the other side of the room. "I'll look at it while we're eating breakfast."

"Okay." Henry did as she asked, then he went down the hall to wash his hands in the bathroom. When he returned, Sylvia, along with his niece and nephew, were in the kitchen. Rachel had been put in her high chair, and Allen was seated on his booster seat up at the table.

"The oatmeal is ready, and we can eat now." Mom pointed to the chair where Dad used to be seated. "Henry, why don't you sit there this morning?"

He swallowed hard as he did what she suggested. Sitting in Dad's chair was an honor for Henry, but at the same time he felt humbled. Even though Henry was almost a man, he could never measure up to his father.

Once Mom and Sylvia were seated, it was time for silent prayers to be said. Henry bowed his head and closed his eyes, but the words he wanted to say to God wouldn't come. He sat quietly until his mother cleared her throat, indicating that she'd finished her prayer.

Using a large metal spoon, Mom put oatmeal in everyone's bowls, while Sylvia gave her son and daughter each a piece of toast with some of Mom's special strawberry-rhubarb jam.

Henry took a piece of toast and put plenty of honey on it. The tasty but gooey amber treat was the best part of raising bees. In fact, it was the only thing Henry liked about it.

As they ate, the little ones chattered and made a mess with their food, and his mother and sister talked about Sylvia's engagement to Dennis.

Henry really liked his sister's fiancé. He had no problem with Sylvia marrying Dennis. He thought it would be great to have a brother-in-law who shared his interest in birds. Henry still missed his father and Abe being around to talk to and learn things from. But as of late, spending time with Sylvia's boyfriend had filled in some of those empty places in his life, and Henry felt like he and Dennis had become good friends.

Henry swallowed the spoonful of oatmeal he'd put in his mouth. *I wonder where Sylvia and Dennis will live after they're married. Would she be comfortable moving back into the house she used to share with Toby, or will they buy a new place somewhere in the area and start over? Guess it wouldn't be right to bring up the topic. It's something Sylvia and Dennis must decide upon themselves.*

"Want me to bring the mail over to you?" Henry asked, pushing his contemplations to the back of his mind. "When I brought it in, you said you'd look at it while you ate breakfast, and you're about done now, so. . ."

"You're right, Son. I almost forgot about the mail." She looked over at him and winked. "Who knows? There could be a big check in one of those envelopes."

Sylvia laughed. "Now wouldn't that be a nice surprise?"

Henry got up and went over to the desk. When he returned, he placed the letters next to his mother's bowl. "Here you go."

Mom picked up the first envelope and opened it. "Just another advertisement." She set it aside. The second piece of mail was a larger envelope—the kind a person would use if they were sending someone a card.

Henry watched as Mom opened it.

"Well, for goodness' sake. This is sure unexpected. I'd forgotten that today is Valentine's Day, and I certainly never expected this."

"What is it, Mom?" Sylvia leaned to the right as she moved her chair a bit closer.

"It's a Valentine card from Herschel Fisher."

"This certainly is a surprise," Sylvia commented. "I wonder why he sent you a card."

"I wonder that too," Henry interjected.

Their mother blinked tears from her eyes, while staring at the card. "I don't know, but it was a thoughtful gesture."

Henry couldn't help noticing the blotches of red that had erupted on his mother's cheeks. This had clearly come as a surprise to her, and no doubt she felt embarrassed.

The more Henry thought about it, the more confused he became. *Herschel doesn't know Mom very well. So what reason would he have for sending her a Valentine card?* Henry squinted as he rubbed his forehead. *At least it wasn't from Monroe. If it had been, I hope Mom would've thrown it out. Think I'd better keep a closer watch on the mail from now on.*

Chapter 12

After the breakfast dishes had been washed, dried, and put away, Belinda picked up the Valentine she'd received from Herschel and read it again. In addition to a picture of a pretty red rose and red heart on the outside of the card, inside, after a Valentine's greeting, was a hand-written note. Belinda read it silently for the third time.

Dear Belinda:
I hope you and your family are doing well. I'd meant to stop by the greenhouse before you closed for the winter, but things got really busy for me at the bulk-food store before Christmas, and I couldn't seem to get away. In addition to seeing how you are doing, I'd wanted to buy a nice indoor plant for my mamm's Christmas gift. I ended up giving her a set of towels for the bathroom instead, which I found at the variety store not far from where I live.

Things have slowed up at my store now, so if there's anything I can do to help you, please let me know.

Most sincerely,
Herschel Fisher

Belinda put the card aside. It seemed a bit odd that Herschel would send her a Valentine card. Even his note was a surprise, because whenever she'd seen him in person, he'd been a man of few words. She remembered the meal she and Herschel had shared when Amy and Jared were courting and they'd moved into the small home Herschel owned and offered to rent to him and Amy. Herschel had been friendly but kind of quiet the first part of the evening. He'd become a bit more vocal during the meal while talking with Jared, although some of his conversation had been directed at her. Once Herschel seemed to relax, Belinda had too, and she'd enjoyed the rest of the evening.

Belinda glanced at the battery-operated clock on the kitchen wall and mumbled, "I'd better get started on mopping this floor. It could sure use a good cleaning."

A knock sounded on the front door, and Belinda went to answer it since Henry had gone bird-watching and Sylvia was upstairs with the children.

Monroe stood on the porch holding a box of chocolates in one hand and a big red balloon in the other. "Happy Valentine's Day, Belinda." His smile stretched wide. "I hope you don't mind me dropping by without calling first, but I wanted it to be a surprise." He held the balloon and chocolates out to her.

Belinda was almost too dumbfounded to think of what to say. After all these weeks of hearing nothing from him, now he was here with Valentine's Day gifts? She wondered what was behind his sudden appearance.

"You. . .umm. . .caught me by surprise," she murmured. "I wasn't expecting you to come by today—much less with gifts."

He continued to look at her, still smiling. "I couldn't let Valentine's Day go by without letting you know how much I care. Also I wanted to clear the air with you regarding the insinuations that I might be responsible for the threatening phone message and note on the barn wall."

"Didn't you get my message, apologizing for the things that were said?"

"Jah, but I thought it best to let some time pass before I came over here again." He took a step toward her. "I really hope you don't believe I had anything to do with what happened. I'd never intentionally hurt you or any of your family, Belinda. I've always had your best interest at heart."

Seeing his sincere expression caused Belinda to weaken a bit. "Why don't you come in out of the cold and have a cup of coffee or tea with me?" She was glad to be able to clear the air in person. Despite Henry's disapproval of Monroe, Belinda remembered back to the days when she was young and had been fond of him.

"That'd be real nice," Monroe said. "I'd appreciate a warm cup of kaffi."

When they entered the kitchen, Belinda placed the candy on the counter and attached the string on the balloon to the back of a chair. Since it had been filled with helium, it floated up, nearly touching the ceiling. It reminded Belinda of her childhood days, when her parents took her and her siblings to various activities in the area where balloons and souvenirs had been sold. At one event a man dressed in a clown costume made animal figures by twisting long, skinny balloons. Those were carefree days when she had so little to worry about. If only her life could be simpler now.

Monroe pulled off his hat and coat and hung them up. Then he took a seat at the table while Belinda poured coffee for both of them. He looked well-groomed, as usual, and smelled of that same musky-scented cologne he'd worn when he'd been to her place on other occasions. "It's a little chilly out there, but it feels nice and comfortable here in your kitchen," he commented.

Belinda stepped over to the cupboard and retrieved a mug. "It will be nice when spring arrives and we can enjoy the warmer weather. Here you go." She placed Monroe's cup in front of him and set a plate of peanut butter cookies within his reach. He wasted no time in helping himself to two of the biggest ones.

"You're sure a good cook," Monroe said after he'd eaten the first cookie. "It's no wonder Vernon wanted to marry you."

A warm flush spread across Belinda's cheeks. "Vernon often said he appreciated my cooking, but his desire to marry me came from the close friendship we developed during our days of courting. Not only that, but Vernon and I both loved flowers, and that gave us a common bond that eventually prompted the opening of our greenhouse."

"Yes, yes, I understand. I just meant. . ." Monroe sputtered, as though trying to find the right words. Instead of finishing his sentence, however, he reached for his cup and drank some coffee.

Barely hearing Monroe speak again, Belinda glanced at the clock, wondering how long he planned to remain at her table and hoping Sylvia wouldn't come into the kitchen. It would be even worse if Henry got home and saw her visiting with Monroe.

Monroe cleared his throat. "Belinda, did ya hear what I said?"

"Uh. . .no, sorry. . .my mind had wandered a bit. What did you say?"

"I asked when you would be opening the greenhouse."

"Not until the middle of March," she replied.

"Just another month then, huh?"

"Jah, but I have a lot of planning to do in order to get the business ready to open, and time can get away from me in a hurry." She rose from her chair. "I don't mean to be unhospitable, Monroe, but I have some things I need to get done yet today. So if you'll excuse me. . ."

Monroe snatched two more cookies and pushed back his chair. "No problem. I should be on my way anyhow. I have some errands to do before going back to the house. Just wanted to drop by to wish you a Happy Valentine's Day and make sure there are no hard feelings between us."

"None on my part." Belinda offered him what she hoped was a reassuring smile. *I'm glad we are back on good terms again. I would've disliked it if I'd spoiled a friendship because of an assumption.*

Monroe hesitated a moment, then moved toward the back door. He put on his coat and grabbed the straw hat from the wall peg. "I'll stop by again once the greenhouse opens and check things out. You might have something for sale that would look good in my yard."

"Do you mean your parents' yard, or are you expecting to get a place of your own now that you've settled back here in Strasburg again?"

"Actually, since my plans are to remain in the area, I've been thinking about either buying a house or getting some land and having my own place built." Monroe wiggled his brows. "I'm not a kid anymore, so I can't remain at my mamm and daed's home indefinitely. One way or the other, I plan to make Strasburg my home, and if things go well, I'd like to own another business or two."

"Are you wanting to open a second furniture store?" Belinda questioned.

He shrugged. "Maybe, if it was located someplace other than this town. It would be rather foolish of me to compete with myself." He plopped his hat back on his head. "Have a good rest of your day, Belinda, and I hope you'll enjoy the *schochlaad* candy I brought."

She gave a heartfelt smile. "Danki, I'm sure I will. However, since everyone in my family likes chocolate candy as much as I do, I'll willingly share some with them."

"Tell 'em I said hello." He lifted his hand in a wave before going out the back door.

She waved back, and then watched out the window as Monroe headed to his buggy. In a small way he reminded her of Vernon, but she wasn't sure how. Even though some time had passed since Belinda lost her husband, something stirred within her as she remembered how she and Vernon had spent some of their Valentine's Days together. *You and I made sure to make the time for romance, didn't we? Even though I remember the ups and downs in our marriage, I wouldn't trade one moment of them for anything.* She brushed a tear from her cheek, and it landed on her dress sleeve.

Belinda looked toward the entrance of the kitchen, hoping she had this private moment alone. She collected herself quickly, not wanting to trouble her daughter or son by acting sappy.

Her gaze went to the box of candy and then the red balloon. When Sylvia and Henry saw the gifts, they were bound to ask questions. *Would it be wrong to say nothing and just take them to my room?* Belinda pursed her lips. *Guess I'll have to tell them, because I certainly don't want to eat all that candy by myself.*

Henry had been out bird-watching for over an hour when he spotted his friend Seth's car through his binoculars. With this close-up view he was able to see a couple other fellows in the vehicle too.

Henry waved, but apparently no one saw him, for the car sped on down the road.

I wonder what they're up to today. Henry lowered his binoculars and frowned. *Wouldn't be surprised if Seth and the other fellows are stinkin' up his car with cigarette smoke. Sure am glad I never got hooked on any kind of tobacco.*

Henry thought about the package of cigarettes that had been found outside the barn after it burned. He hoped Seth wasn't the one responsible for the fire or any of the vandalism that had been done at their place. Henry's friend would remain on his list of suspects until the mystery had been solved and the person responsible was punished. "Monroe, Seth, Maude, Virginia, or the owner of the new greenhouse across town." Henry counted with his fingers. "I'm sure it's gotta be one of those people—unless I've missed someone. I really oughta start lookin' for more clues."

When Henry returned home a short time later, he entered the kitchen to get a glass of water. Despite the cold weather, he'd worked up a sweat walking to and from the meadow where he'd gone to search for birds.

None of his family was in the room, but he noticed a box of candy sitting on the counter, plus a red balloon tied to the back of a chair and floating toward the ceiling. Henry assumed Dennis must have come by while he was gone and given the gifts to Sylvia for Valentine's Day.

Henry was on the verge of opening the heart-shaped box when Sylvia entered the room.

"Oh, you're back." She smiled at him. "How'd the bird-watching go?"

"It went okay, but I didn't see anything special today. Just a couple of bobwhites, and one hawk. Nothing I haven't seen before." Henry gestured to the box of candy. "Looks like Dennis must have been by with a gift for you, huh?"

Sylvia shook her head. "I won't be seeing Dennis until this evening. He's taking me out for supper."

Henry's brows squished together. "That's nice, but then where did these come from?" He pointed to the candy and then the balloon.

"Mr. Esh."

Henry's head jerked back. "Monroe was here?"

"Jah. He came by awhile ago, when I was upstairs with the kinner," Sylvia replied. "Mom told me about it when I came down and found her in here with the gifts."

"Oh, great! I thought we'd seen the last of him." Henry smacked the side of his head. "So now the determined fellow comes back with gifts, hopin' to win Mom over with his fake smile, heavy cologne, and sickening comments." He shook his head. "Wish I'd been here when he showed up. I would have told him that Mom's not interested in any of his gifts."

Sylvia placed her hand on Henry's shoulder. "You need to calm down. I don't care for Monroe any more than you do, but it's Mom's place to decide if she wants to accept a gift from him. My advice is to keep quiet and let our mamm handle things with Monroe however she thinks is best."

"I'm having a hard time doing that, Sylvia." Henry folded his arms and gave a huff. "If Mom was handling things right, Monroe wouldn't still be comin' around."

Henry's mother came into the kitchen. "Oh good, Son, I'm glad you're home. I was hoping you might hitch my horse to the buggy and go to town to get a few things I need at the store."

"Okay, yeah, I can do that. Is your list ready?" he asked.

"Not quite, but I'll finish it while you get the buggy out of the shed and prepare the horse for travel." She moved over to the counter and opened the heart-shaped box, revealing a layer of chocolates. "Would you like one before you go?"

Henry shook his head. "I heard they're from Monroe."

"That's right. He came by to clear the air with me and—"

"So does that mean he'll be comin' around all the time, like he used to?" Henry's face tightened.

She shook her head. "It just means there are no hard feelings between us."

Henry felt some relief. He glanced at Sylvia as she pressed a hand against her chest. No doubt she felt a sense of relief too. Maybe their mom hadn't been taken in by Monroe's sappy gifts after all.

Chapter 13

"I see you've started *nachtesse* already," Jared commented when he arrived home from work that evening and joined Amy in the kitchen.

"Jah, there's a ham and two nice-sized potatoes baking in the oven for our supper." She lifted her face toward him and waited for the expected kiss.

Jared lifted Amy's chin and caressed her lips with his own. "If I'd known you were going to cook this evening, I would have told you before I left for work this morning that I was planning to take you out for supper." He kissed her again. "I'd hoped it would be a nice Valentine's Day surprise."

Amy put her arms around Jared's waist and gave him a hug. "I have an even bigger surprise for you, and I don't want to share it in a public place."

Jared tipped his head to one side. "Oh? And what surprise do you have for me, Fraa?" Amy placed both hands against her stomach and smiled up at him. "I'm expecting a *boppli*. The doctor confirmed it today when I went in for an appointment."

Jared's mouth opened slightly. "Oh Amy, that's *wunderbaar*!" He put his hands on her shoulders. "I didn't know you had a doctor's appointment. Why didn't you say something?"

"Because if what I'd suspected wasn't true, I didn't want to disappoint you. And if it was true, then I wanted it to be a surprise."

He pulled Amy even closer and gently rubbed her back. "So when will we become *elder*?"

"According to the doctor's calculations, and mine, we should take on the role of parents the first or second week of September."

"This is such good news. I can hardly wait to tell both of our families."

"I'm sure they'll be happy for us," Amy said, "but can we wait until later in the week? I'd like us to savor this information awhile—at least for tonight."

"I have no problem with that. Maybe tomorrow evening, if the weather holds, we can visit our parents' homes and share the good news."

Tears sprang to Amy's eyes and she blinked to keep them from escaping onto her cheeks. "If only my daed and brother were still alive. I know they would be happy to hear our good news. For that matter, Toby would have been pleased too, since he would have been the boppli's uncle.

"I can't pretend to know what goes on in heaven, but maybe our loved ones who have passed and entered the pearly gates are allowed to see or even hear about some of the good things that happen on earth."

Amy took comfort in her husband's words. *Whether my father, brother, and brother-in-law are aware of anything that's happened down here, the one thing I feel confident in is that they were true believers and had accepted Christ as their Savior, which means they had the promise of heaven.*

Virginia sat on the living-room couch with her arms folded across her chest. If it weren't for the nice card and note she'd received in the mail earlier today from her friend, Stella, it would hardly seem like Valentine's Day. Earl hadn't sent her flowers, like he had in years past, nor had he made any mention of what day it was before he left for work this morning.

He must have forgotten. Virginia shifted her position on the couch. *Either that or he's too cheap to buy me anything this year. Maybe he's still irritated because I bought a new outfit for Christmas, which he said was pretty, but not something I needed.*

Virginia thought about the horse and buggy she'd seen drive onto the Kings' property earlier today. She'd noticed a big red balloon poking out of the back of the rig, where the flap had been open. It appeared as if someone might be getting a gift for Valentine's Day.

Virginia speculated on who the lucky recipient had been. She couldn't help feeling envious.

Goldie purred like a motorboat as she came up and nuzzled Virginia's chin.

"I'm upset right now, so this isn't a good time for you to try and butter me up." Virginia remained rigid, but her cat seemed determined to melt away any resistance. Each time Goldie cuddled she released a soft *meow*, and Virginia couldn't help smiling.

"Okay, you win. I can't stay mad anyways with you being so sweet to me."

Virginia uncrossed her arms to pet Goldie after the feline curled up in her lap. "At least you still love me, don't ya, pretty girl?"

The cat's response was another *meow*, followed by rhythmic purring. The pleasing sound calmed Virginia's nerves for a bit, until she observed an advertisement on TV where a handsome man presented a lovely young woman a heart-shaped box of chocolates. Another ad followed, showing an older woman receiving a beautiful necklace with matching earrings from a gentleman with silver hair.

"Must be nice to know that someone besides your cat cares about you." Virginia glanced at the card lying on the coffee table from her Chicago friend. "I guess Stella cares about me too, or she wouldn't have sent the note. Of course," Virginia reasoned, "I sent her a card with a letter, so maybe she was only reciprocating."

Virginia grinned despite her melancholy mood. Reciprocating was not the kind of word she would normally use, but because of the crossword puzzles she often did, she'd discovered the word in the thesaurus while trying to find an answer to the question: *To do for someone after they've done something for you.*"

Virginia stopped petting Goldie and lifted both hands over her head as she yawned. It would be time to start supper soon, but she had no desire to cook even a simple meal this evening. After all, why should she fix a nice supper for Earl when he couldn't even remember to get her something for Valentine's Day?

She suppressed another yawn then she put Goldie on the floor and reclined on the couch. It wasn't long before the cat jumped back up and curled into a ball on Virginia's chest. The vibration of the cat's purring put Virginia into a drowsy state. She soon closed her eyes and gave in to slumber.

"Hey, wake up, sleepyhead."

Virginia's eyes snapped open and she sat up so quickly Goldie jumped down. "Wh–what are you doing here, Earl?"

He lifted his gaze toward the ceiling. "I live here—remember?"

"Don't be funny." She flapped her hand. "I mean, what are you doing here when you should be at work?"

"It's five thirty, and I'm done for the day." Earl leaned over and placed his hand on her shoulder, giving it a little shake. "I figured you'd be all dressed up and ready to go by now, but since you're not, it'll give me enough time to shower and change my clothes into something more presentable."

"Presentable for what?"

"For supper."

"Since when do you worry about looking presentable for any of our meals?"

"I do when we're going out to eat."

She gave a bark of laughter. "We're going out to a restaurant?"

"Yep. Thought I told ya that this morning when I kissed you good-bye. Said a meal out would be your Valentine's gift from me this year."

Virginia shook her head. "If you said it, I must have been asleep because I have no memory of it at all." She pulled herself up off the couch. "While you're taking your shower I'll look through my closet for something nice to wear."

"Sounds good. I'll meet you back here in half an hour." Earl kissed Virginia's cheek and sauntered out of the room.

Virginia couldn't take the smile from her face. It was nice to know Earl hadn't forgotten about Valentine's Day after all, and wanted to surprise her, no less.

Bird-in-Hand, Pennsylvania

"I still can't believe you agreed to marry me." Dennis reached over and took Sylvia's hand, as they sat beside each other in a booth at the

Bird-in-Hand Family Restaurant. "Every day since you accepted my proposal I've had to pinch myself to make sure I'm not dreaming."

Sylvia smiled. "I feel the same way, and I'm truly looking forward to becoming your wife."

He grinned back at her. "We still haven't set a date, and we need to do that soon."

"Agreed."

"I don't see any reason to wait till fall, when many other Amish couples will be getting married."

Sylvia nodded. "Since this is a second marriage for me, there's no reason to wait that long." She paused for a drink of water. "We do have some planning to do that will involve the wedding, though, and it will take some time. Would the first Thursday in August work for you?"

"I'd like it to be sooner, but the time between now and then will probably go fast." Dennis added a spoonful of sugar to his coffee and stirred it around. "Speaking of planning. . . We haven't discussed where we're going to live after we're married. Even though it's become like home to me, I would understand if you didn't want to live in the house you once shared with your first husband."

Sylvia's throat constricted. "Can I pray about it for a few days before I decide?"

"Of course. In the meantime, though, can we tell our families that we've set a date for the wedding?"

"That's fine. Why don't you come over to my mamm's place tomorrow evening? We'll tell her and Henry, and then I will call Amy the following day to let her and Jared know about our plans."

"Sounds good. I'll call my mamm tomorrow too. She can relay the information to the rest of my family there in Dauphin County. I'm sure everyone will be happy for us." Dennis took hold of Sylvia's hand again and gave her fingers a gentle squeeze.

Sylvia looked down at her unfinished plate of food. It would be difficult to share a home with Dennis that had once been meant for her and Toby. However, the land and even the outbuildings were perfect for Dennis's horse training business as well as for raising horses, which he'd already begun to do. It might be difficult and time consuming to find another place for them to live—not to mention expensive. Then there would be the chore of selling Sylvia's home, and it could take time to find the right buyer. If she and Dennis were going to be married by August, it might be best for her and the children to move into her old home with him after the wedding. Maybe it wouldn't be as hard as she imagined. And if it was too difficult an adjustment, they could look for another home with plenty of acreage that would work well for Dennis's business.

Sylvia would pray about it, of course, and do whatever God laid on her heart. One thing she had learned over the last several months was that everything went better when decisions were made following prayer.

"We're eating here? I thought we'd be going to Miller's Smorgy." Virginia couldn't hide her disappointment when Earl pulled into the parking lot at the Bird-in-Hand Family Restaurant.

"What's wrong with this place?" Earl turned off the engine. "They serve good food."

Virginia wrinkled her nose as an Amish couple walked past and entered the restaurant. "Those Plain folks like to eat here. Don't think I've ever seen any Amish or Mennonite people eating at Miller's."

"I'm sure some of them do." Earl reached across the seat and gave Virginia's arm a poke. "Are you ever going to get over your prejudice against people who don't look, dress, or think the way you do?"

Virginia gave the collar of her heavy jacket a tug. "I'm not prejudiced. I am just not comfortable around people who—"

"Are different than you? Is that what you were going to say?"

She sighed. "Those old-fashioned people are so different than you and me. The way they live is strange, and to me it makes no sense."

"Maybe not, but it's the way they choose to live, and as far as I know, we're still living in a free country." He tapped the steering wheel. "Now are we going inside, or would you rather go home and throw something in the microwave for supper?"

Virginia's shoulders slumped as she gave a dejected sigh. "Okay, have it your way." She opened the car door and stepped out. *Happy Valentine's Day, Earl.*

When they entered the restaurant and had been seated at a table, a young waitress came and handed them a menu. Then she asked each of them what they'd like to drink with their meals and wrote it down on her tablet. "The buffet is also available, if you'd rather choose from that. There are many items to choose from there," she stated.

"I'll have the buffet." Earl handed the menu back to the waitress then he looked at Virginia. "How 'bout you?"

She perused the menu briefly before handing it to the young woman. "Guess I'll go with the buffet as well."

The waitress smiled. "Feel free to go up whenever you're ready. I'll bring your beverages to the table while you're getting your food."

Earl looked over at Virginia. "Are you ready?"

"I guess so, but I wish we would've been seated in a booth instead of a table."

"What's wrong with this spot? It isn't so bad." He grinned. "We're close to the buffet, so it won't be too far of a walk for you."

"Okay, let's get in line for the food." Virginia waited until Earl got up from his chair, and when she did the same, she bumped her bad knee into the table leg. "Ouch."

"Are you okay?"

She remained beside the table, massaging the sore spot and hoping to relieve the pain. "I'll be all right. Let's go on up so we can eat."

This is not the way I'd hoped to spend the evening. Virginia pursed her lips as she followed Earl over to the buffet. On the way there, they passed an Amish couple sitting in a booth. When Virginia realized it was her neighbor Sylvia sitting with an Amish man she'd seen at the Kings' several times, she hastened to look away. No way did she want to engage them in conversation. They had nothing in common, and as far as Virginia was concerned, her Amish neighbors were rude. She still hadn't forgiven them for not inviting her and Earl to Amy and Jared's wedding last fall. At this point, Virginia didn't care about going across the street for anything except to get her mail.

Chapter 14

Strasburg

Fully intending to leave a message, Dennis punched in his mother's number. He waited as the phone rang several times, meanwhile, picking at a sliver embedded in his thumb. Dennis was surprised when Mom answered the phone. She was obviously in the phone shed either making calls or checking for messages.

"Hi, Mom. It's Dennis."

"Well hello, Son. How are you doing?" Her tone sounded upbeat.

"I'm doing okay. How about you and the rest of the family?"

"Everyone's fine here, although the weather's cold, so we're all eager for spring to arrive."

"Same here." Dennis reached for his cup of coffee and took a drink. "The reason I'm calling is to let you know that Sylvia and I have set a date for our wedding. It's going to be the first Thursday of August. I wanted to give you advance notice so you could make plans to come down here for our big day."

"We wouldn't miss it for the world, and I'm happy you've found someone you care about, Son. My only concern is the responsibility you'll be taking on by marrying a widow with two kinner."

Dennis blew out a noisy breath. "Not this again, Mom. You've brought this topic up to me a few times already, and my answer is still the same. I love Sylvia and her children, and I'm not concerned about becoming their stepfather. In fact, I'm looking forward to my new role."

"But can you financially afford to provide for a readymade family?"

Dennis reached up with his free hand and rubbed the back of his tight neck muscles. "Can't you just be *hallich* that I've found the woman of my dreams and I'm eager to make her my fraa?"

"Of course I'm happy. I'm just afraid you might be taking on more than you can handle."

Dennis clenched his teeth. If he didn't hang up now, he might say something he'd later regret. "It'll be fine, Mom. You'll see. Listen, I'm sorry for cutting this short, but I need to go. In addition to grooming the horses in my barn, I have several errands to run yet today. I'll talk to you again soon, though, okay?"

"Jah, sure. Tell your intended I said hello."

"I'll do that when I see her this evening. Bye, Mom."

When Dennis hung up, he closed his eyes and said a quick prayer. *Lord, please give my mother a sense of peace about me marrying Sylvia. Also guide and direct me and Sylvia in the days ahead as we make decisions about our future together.*

Amy's pulse quickened as Jared's horse and buggy approached her mother's house. They'd just come from telling his parents their good news. Jared's mother and father, Ava and Emanuel, had expressed their happiness at becoming grandparents and said they'd be praying for an easy, healthy pregnancy for Amy. She felt thankful to have loving, caring in-laws. Some people, like a young woman she knew in their church district, weren't so fortunate. Kara's mother-in-law had never approved of her, and sometimes said hurtful things to her. Amy wondered if Kara's husband, Ronald, had ever spoken up and put his mother in her place.

She glanced over at Jared as he gripped the horse's reins securely in his hands. *I'm sure my man would stand up for me if his mother ever said hurtful things. I bet Jared would even put my own mom in her place if she spoke out of turn and caused me grief.*

When he guided the horse up her mother's driveway, Jared looked over at Amy and smiled. "Are you ready to relay our good news a second time?"

She reached across the seat and squeezed his arm. "Definitely."

When a knock sounded on the front door, Sylvia got up from her seat on the couch in such a hurry that Belinda had to laugh. No doubt it was Dennis on the porch, since Sylvia had mentioned during supper that he'd be dropping by this evening. It was a joy to see her daughter so enthused about her future husband coming for a visit.

Belinda remembered how eager she'd always been when she and Vernon were courting and he'd come to her parents' house to see her.

Those were such happy days, she mused while patting Rachel's back as she attempted to rock the fussy girl to sleep. Allen sat on the couch, next to where his mother had been, engrossed in a picture book.

Sylvia returned to the living room, but not with Dennis. Belinda smiled as Jared and Amy came fully into the room. "Well, this is a nice surprise. We didn't know you two would be dropping by this evening."

Amy chuckled. "That's what Sylvia said when she answered the door. Apparently she'd been expecting Dennis." She looked over at Jared. "Should we wait till he gets here to tell them why we came by?"

"That's a good idea."

Sylvia took their outer garments and said she'd hang them on the coatrack in the hall. "Would anyone like a cup of hot chocolate or some warm apple cider," she called from the hallway.

"Hot chocolate sounds good to me, if it's not too much trouble." Jared looked at Amy. "Does that appeal to you?"

"I think I'd rather have the cider," she replied. "I'll go out to the kitchen and help Sylvia with that. But first, what would you like, Mom?"

"Cider for me." Belinda looked at Henry, who had just entered the room. "How about you, Son? Would you like to join us for hot chocolate or apple cider?"

"Sure." Henry meandered over to the couch and sat down beside Allen.

"Sure what?" Amy asked. "Do you want cider or hot chocolate?"

"I like them both, but if I'm given a choice, guess I'll take a cup of hot chocolate." Henry patted Allen's knee. "I bet he'd like some too."

"Okay, I'll go put in our orders, and then Sylvia and I will bring the beverages out to you soon."

Belinda stroked Rachel's soft cheek. Her precious granddaughter had finally settled down and fallen asleep. "Think I'd better put this little one to bed," she whispered.

"Would you like me to do it?" Jared offered.

She hesitated but then nodded. Amy and Jared would no doubt

have children of their own someday, so this would be good practice for him.

After Jared took the child in his arms, Belinda got up from her chair. "I'm going out to the kitchen to help Amy and Sylvia," she told Henry, who'd picked up one of his birding magazines. "Would you please keep an eye on Allen? I don't want him going upstairs and waking his sister."

"Sure, Mom. I'll make certain he stays put while you're gone."

"It might be good for you to remain on the couch beside him." Belinda had spoken all this in English so Allen wouldn't understand. She didn't want the little fellow to know they were talking about him or what was being said.

Henry's eyebrows lowered and pinched together. "Don't see why I have to stay next to him if I decide to sit someplace else." He gestured to one of the recliners. "I can see him just fine from over there."

"Not with your nose in that magazine. If you're sitting right beside Allen you'll be more aware if he decides to get up."

"Okay, whatever." Henry reached over and tousled Allen's thick crop of hair.

The young boy looked at him and grinned. Then he pointed to the page he had opened in his children's book. *"Bussli."*

"Jah, that's a kitten," Henry responded in Pennsylvania Dutch.

Belinda figured Allen would keep Henry busy for a while, showing him pictures and pointing to each one, so she hurried out of the room. Belinda was almost to the kitchen when another knock sounded on the door. She went to answer it and found Dennis on the porch.

"Good evening." Stepping into the hallway, he smiled. "Looks like I'm not the only visitor you have here this evening." He turned and pointed at the other horse and buggy parked next to his horse and carriage at the rail.

"Amy and Jared stopped by." Belinda took his hat and jacket. "My daughters are in the kitchen getting ready to serve warm apple cider and hot chocolate. "If you'll tell me which one you'd like, I'll let the girls know."

"Cider sounds delicious."

"Okay. Henry's in the living room with Allen, and Jared's putting Rachel to bed. I'm sure he will join them soon, so why don't you go in and make yourself comfortable?"

"I will, danki."

As Dennis headed for the living room, Belinda entered the kitchen. "Dennis is here," she announced, stepping up to the counter where Sylvia stood, cutting slices of banana bread.

"Oh, good. Did you ask if he'd like something hot to drink?"

"Jah. He'd like warm cider. Why don't you take the bread to the dining-room table and ask the men to join us there?" Belinda suggested. "I'll help Amy bring in the beverages."

Sylvia smiled. "Okay, Mom." She picked up the plate of bread and hurried from the room.

Amy looked at Belinda and chuckled. "I do believe my sister is eager to see her future husband."

Belinda gave a deep, gratified sigh. "Jah, and I'm ever so happy for her." She felt joy in seeing one daughter married, and the eldest with a suitor who was a good man. Her loved ones were all healthy and doing well in their lives, so there was much to be thankful for.

I wonder what the future holds for me. I have suitors of my own, or so my daughters believe, even though I don't have any notion at this point of letting things get serious with either man. Belinda slid the tray closer to the stove and began loading it with the hot beverages. *I could use some help with Henry though. I can't help feeling concern because my son doesn't have a true, constant male figure in his life. Over the next few years, while he's still living at home under my care and guidance, I need to do what is right by him.*

When Belinda followed Amy into the dining room, both carrying trays with everyone's beverages, she noticed Dennis and Sylvia standing close together in one corner of the room. He appeared to be whispering something in her ear. They made such a nice couple, and Belinda felt good about their relationship.

Now I'm curious. What could Dennis have to say to my daughter that he doesn't want us to hear? Belinda pondered this question for a few seconds. *Is he telling Sylvia how much he loves her?*

She remembered how things had been between her and Vernon during their courting days. Belinda couldn't imagine anyone as handsome or grounded in his faith as her special man had been. She reflected on the way Vernon used to plan their dates to go places, and how special he had treated her. He would often whisper tender words of love, sometimes even when they weren't alone. She'd thought his sweet actions were endearing. Once again, Belinda felt a pang of regret at losing her dear husband.

Refocusing, she invited everyone to take a seat at the table. Once they were all seated, the hot beverages were handed out and Sylvia passed the nice-sized plate of freshly made banana bread around.

They chatted for a bit about the weather, with Dennis bringing up how strange it was that they'd only had a few light dustings of snow so far this winter.

"You're right," Belinda agreed. "Usually by the middle of February we've had a foot or two—sometimes more—of snow on the ground."

Everyone but Allen agreed. He was busy poking at the marshmallow in his cup of hot chocolate.

Dennis looked at Sylvia, and when she smiled at him, he cleared his throat real loud. "Sylvia and I have an announcement to make."

All heads turned in their direction.

"We've decided to get married on the first Thursday of August."

Everyone clapped—even Allen with his sticky fingers.

"Can you get all your plans made and everything put together by then?" Belinda asked. She'd really thought after Dennis proposed to Sylvia on Christmas that they would have set their wedding date right away so it would give them plenty of time to plan everything out.

"I'm sure it can be done," Sylvia replied. "It won't need to be a big occasion, since it's a second marriage for me."

She heard in her daughter's voice the determination driving their decision. "But it's Dennis's first marriage." Belinda looked over at him. "Are you okay with keeping things small?"

"All I care about is marrying your daughter," he said. "Nothing else matters to me."

Belinda saw sincerity in the young man's expression and heard it in the tone of his voice. She took another sip of her beverage. *At this point I can tell their minds are made up, so I'll let that subject rest.*

"We'll all help out as needed," Amy said.

All heads bobbed in agreement.

"Now it's our turn to share some news." Amy looked at Jared.

"Would you like to tell them, or shall I?"

His smile was directed at her. "Why don't you go ahead?"

Amy's cheeks colored as she placed one hand against her belly. "Jared and I are expecting our first child. He or she is due to make an appearance in early September."

More hand clapping ensued and everyone, including Henry, extended hearty congratulations.

Belinda closed her eyes briefly and lifted a heartfelt prayer. *Things are swinging to the positive side for our family, Lord. Amy and Jared are expecting their first child, and I'm ever so happy for them. Sylvia and Dennis have set their wedding date, and I look forward to having him as my son-in-law. Also there's been no more vandalism, threatening notes, or muffled voice messages aimed at us this winter, and I thank You for that as well. Please continue to be with us in the days ahead. Amen.*

Belinda opened her eyes, looking fondly at each of her family members. She hoped all of their lives had turned the corner toward a happier life.

Her gaze landed on Henry. *Now if my youngest boy would just let go of his negative attitude, and turn his worries over to God, the future will look even brighter.*

Chapter 15

Today was the first day of spring, and the greenhouse had been open for a week. The weather was chilly, and the sky seemed full of gray clouds. Belinda wondered how this umbrella-type day would impact the number of customers they'd see. Although mid- to late-March was never as busy as April through November, they'd had some customers last week, so she felt sure things would pick up. They needed money coming in to pay bills, not to mention the expense of her oldest daughter's upcoming wedding.

Belinda carried a small lunch with her, just half a sandwich and an orange. The baked oatmeal she'd eaten for breakfast had filled her up good. Besides, she needed to reorganize some of the seed packets on the rack, since they'd gotten in some new ones. Belinda figured she'd stay put and eat her lunch in the greenhouse today.

As she entered the building and put the OPEN sign in the window, an image of Sylvia's smiling face at breakfast came to mind. It did Belinda's heart good to see the change that had come over Sylvia since she'd met Dennis. She was more positive and less fearful. Last week she and Dennis had taken her horse and buggy out, and for the first time since Toby's death, Sylvia had been in the driver's seat, taking control of her mare. She'd admitted to being nervous, but with Dennis by her side, patiently coaxing and guiding along the way, the experience went surprisingly well. They drove several miles down the road to a fabric store, where Sylvia had purchased thread and material for her wedding dress. She'd also purchased some scraps of colorful fabric to make potholders to sell in the gift side of the greenhouse.

Henry had painted and decorated some horseshoes to put in there too, and on the shelves sat jars of amber honey, along with apple butter Belinda and Sylvia had put up last fall.

I wish there was enough money in my bank account so we could add on to the greenhouse, Belinda thought as she put her insulated lunch bag behind the counter. She looked over at the seed rack. *I need to take care of those, but first I should check on the plants to make sure they're well-watered.* Belinda turned on the hose and uncoiled it as she went down the first aisle to water all the plants and shrubs. *Even a separate building where we could sell only gift items would be nice.*

While home-canned jams, jugs of cider, and honey were not traditionally sold in most greenhouses, they made a nice addition to offer their customers—especially the tourists who often came in by the busloads. Those people were usually interested in potholders, solar lights, and other small items her family had come up with to sell. Every sale, big or small, helped. She'd even gotten some cute birdhouses in a couple of sizes and styles to sell that she'd ordered last month.

"A delivery truck came up to the house with a big box filled with bags of potting soil," Henry said when he entered the greenhouse.

Belinda saw by her son's squinted eyes and the slight tilt of his head, that he was unhappy about this. And rightly so. The man who delivered their planting supplies always brought the boxes and packages to the greenhouse and dropped them off. "Was someone new driving the truck?" she questioned.

Henry shrugged. "Beats me. I was in the barn when the vehicle pulled in and didn't see the driver."

Belinda gave a weary sigh. This was only the second time it had happened. Apparently it had been a new driver today, and he didn't know to bring the packages out to the greenhouse.

"You'll need to open the boxes and then haul all the bags of potting soil down here in the wheelbarrow."

Henry groaned. "Aw, Mom, that's gonna take me several trips, and who's gonna be here to help you while I'm doin' that?"

"I'll be fine when Sylvia gets here. She needs to wait until Amy comes to watch the kinner."

"I wonder how long she'll be able to keep doin' that. With her bein' in a family way, I'd think she would need to stay home and rest."

Belinda gave his shoulder a few pats. "It's nice of you to be concerned about your sister, but Amy's feeling fine, and she's agreed to watch Allen and Rachel as long as she's doing well."

"But not after she has the boppli, right?"

"Correct. And by then Sylvia and Dennis will be married, so neither one of your sisters will be working here in the greenhouse."

Henry's pinched expression made it appear as if he'd eaten something distasteful. No doubt he felt some bitterness about being stuck helping here and doing the kind of work he'd often said was not what he wanted to be doing for the rest of his life.

Ezekiel felt that way once too, Belinda reminded herself. *That's why I'll never say anything that would encourage him to move back.*

"Look, Son. . ." Belinda spoke quietly, in a reassuring tone, "When you are old enough to move out on your own and you wish to find some other means of employment, then I'll either learn to manage by myself or hire someone else. But for now, and until you're at least eighteen years of age, you are my responsibility, and you'll be expected to do as I say. Is that understood?"

Henry's posture slumped as he lowered his head. "Jah, Mom, I get it." He turned and shuffled out the door.

Belinda walked with slow, heavy steps up the next aisle. This work day had not begun well.

She'd finished watering all the plants and headed for the front counter when a middle-aged English man entered the building. "May I help you?" she asked as he approached.

"Are you the owner of this establishment?"

"Yes, I am." Belinda smiled. "Are you looking for anything particular today?"

"Actually, I need a lot of things." The man opened his jacket and pulled out a card from an inside pocket, which he handed to her. "My name is Brian Rawlings, and I own Rawlings' Landscaping Service. We're located about halfway between here and Lancaster, and our business has been growing by leaps and bounds."

Belinda moved to the front counter, where she studied his card. While she'd had no contact with his business previously, a few customers had mentioned having some work on their property done by Mr. Rawlings's company.

"The thing is," Brian continued, "I've been looking for a local supplier, and someone suggested you. If you have the time right now, could we talk about what you have available here, and then discuss the cost?"

Belinda felt a sense of excitement over the prospect of being able to sell more plants, shrubs, and trees. If things worked out, this would make up for them having lost the contract with the flower shop in town after Sara Fuller sold it. She was about to respond to Mr. Rawlings when Henry came in with one of their shopping wagons piled high with bags of potting soil. He looked her way, pulled the wagon off to one side, and joined her behind the counter.

"Everything okay?" Henry leaned close to Belinda's ear.

"It's fine." She introduced the man to Henry and explained why he was there.

Henry asked Brian several questions.

A pleasant warmth spread through Belinda's chest. It pleased her to see Henry taking the initiative to ask pertinent questions, but she hoped the man would not be put off by them. He didn't appear to be, as the three of them discussed a suitable arrangement for providing the landscaping service with many items they would need. Before the man left, she gave him her business card.

"Thanks, I'll give you a call when I'm ready to place my first order." He gave them a wide smile before heading out the door.

"Danki for your input." Belinda placed her hand on Henry's shoulder. "For a young man who doesn't want to take part in this business, you sure know what you're talking about. Also the questions you asked were things I may not have thought to ask."

"Sure you would, Mom. You and Dad began running this greenhouse a long time before I became involved."

"That's true, but you've caught on fast in regard to the business end of things, not to mention your knowledge of the plants, flowers, shrubs, and trees we have available here. I'm proud of you, Son."

A crimson flush spread across Henry's cheeks. "Aw, Mom, it ain't nothin'."

Belinda was tempted to correct his English, but instead, she put her arm around him and gave him a hug.

Henry didn't pull away until a customer came in. Then he stepped out from behind the counter, grabbed the handle of the shopping wagon, and pulled it toward the area where potting soil and fertilizer were sold.

"Before you head out to bid on some roofing jobs today, could I ask you a question?" Amy asked Jared when he came into the kitchen to get his lunch pail.

"Sure, ask away."

"I was wondering what you would think about us having a bonfire supper here this Friday evening, with hot dogs and marshmallows."

He tipped his head. "Just the two of us?"

"Actually, I would like to invite my family, as well as Herschel Fisher, to join us."

"It's a nice idea, Amy, but I'm worried about you doing too much. You're already watching Sylvia's kinner so she can help your mamm in the greenhouse, and that can be quite tiring for you."

Amy shook her head. "It's not really. I rest when they're napping, and I'm doing fine physically. And remember, we had your folks over for a meal last week, and I didn't overdo." She moved over to where he stood leaning against the counter and placed her hand on Jared's arm. "I promise to keep things simple for the bonfire meal. It would be so nice to sit outside under the moon and stars while we enjoy a time of eating and fellowshipping with my family."

Jared quirked an eyebrow. "But Herschel isn't part of your family."

Amy bit on her lower lip, then released it and smiled. "No, but he might make a nice addition."

Jared's eyes widened. "Are you hoping your mamm and Herschel will get married someday?"

"Mom needs a man in her life. After Sylvia and the kinner move out, it'll just be her and my bruder living in that big house and trying to run the greenhouse by themselves."

"I think you're forgetting something, Amy." Jared held up one finger. "First and foremost, your mother may have no desire to get married again." He lifted a second finger. "And even if she were thinking about remarrying someday, she might have no interest in Herschel."

"Are you finished, or do you have another point to mention before

I make a comment?"

"Just one more." A third finger came up. "If your mamm, with Henry's help, is not able to manage the greenhouse, she can always hire someone to work full-time or even part-time."

"That might be okay for a while, but eventually, Henry will reach the age where he'll be looking to find a wife and get married. Then my dear mother will be completely on her own."

Jared leaned away from the counter and crossed his arms. "She may decide to sell the greenhouse and move in with us or Sylvia and her family. I'm sure we'll have a bigger house by then, and hopefully, the home Sylvia and Dennis choose to live in will have plenty of bedrooms. Another option would be for a *daadihaus* to be added on to one of our places."

"While those ideas are all possible—that is, if Mom wanted them—I truly believe she would be happier if she got married again." For emphasis, Amy tapped the edge of the counter where she'd been making Jared's sandwich. "I think Herschel is the right man for her."

"There's a fourth thing to consider," Jared was quick to say. "Herschel may have no romantic interest in your mom, or even want to get married again. As you know, he's been a widower for a good many years, and if he wanted to get remarried, he'd have most likely done so by now."

"Maybe he was waiting for the right woman to come along."

Jared snickered and tweaked the end of Amy's nose. "Such a little matchmaker I married."

She swatted at his hand playfully. "Neither Herschel nor Mom will know if they're meant for each other if we don't get them together more often." She wiggled her brows. "Besides, I think he is interested in her. He sent her a Valentine's Day card, remember?"

Jared's shoulders rose as he lifted both hands in obvious defeat. "Okay, okay, feel free to invite Herschel to join us for the bonfire meal. "If he doesn't want to come, he can always say no."

"Do we need to tell him that my mamm is going to be here?"

"I think that would only be fair, don't you? The last time you invited your mother and Herschel to join us for supper, without either knowing the other would be here, it seemed a bit awkward for both of them."

"Only for a short time though," Amy argued. "As the evening

progressed they seemed to relax, and I'm sure they enjoyed themselves."

Jared bent to kiss Amy's forehead, then her cheeks, and finally his lips touched hers. "You have my blessing to do whatever you like, but please let both parties know that the other person has been invited."

Amy grinned up at him. "Danki, Jared. I have a good feeling about this."

He kissed her again, and then placed his hand against her stomach. "And I have a good feeling about you and our boppli. I can't wait to take part in raising this child."

She finished putting his sandwich together, placed it inside the lunch pail next to the apple she'd put there earlier, and handed it to him. "I feel real good about it too."

Chapter 16

Gordonville, Pennsylvania

Herschel stood in front of the bathroom mirror inspecting his face. He'd finished shaving above his upper lip, which Amish men always kept free of hair. Now it was time to do something with those unruly hairs sticking out at odd angles from his beard.

Picking up the comb, Herschel ran it down the length of his nearly gray beard a couple of times. He paused. "Hmm... I have to say my hair could use a good trimming too. I might as well speak to Mom about givin' me a quick haircut. She and Dad have been after me to get it taken care of anyways."

Until recently, he hadn't thought too much about his appearance, since he wasn't married and no longer had a wife to come home to each evening. When Mattie was alive, Herschel had always made sure he smelled nice and looked well-groomed. Before leaving his bulk-food store, he would wash up good and put on fresh deodorant so that when he came into his house and greeted his dear wife, she would find him appealing. But until recently, he'd let himself go, mostly worrying about his appearance on church Sundays, and if he attended a wedding, funeral, or some other special event.

Things were different now. While Herschel had not admitted it to anyone, he'd become interested in Belinda King. The first time he'd seen her in a different light was last year, when Jared and Amy invited them both for a meal. He'd been surprised when, soon after he arrived, Belinda showed up. However, what had surprised Herschel even more was how much he'd enjoyed her company, despite feeling a bit shy in her presence.

Is she interested in me at all? Herschel asked himself. Although Belinda had always been friendly to Herschel, she'd never given him any indication that she might see him as anything other than a casual friend.

Word had it on the Amish grapevine that Monroe Esh had set his cap for Belinda King. Herschel's mother had mentioned recently that while attending a Mud Sale, she'd overhead two women talking, and Monroe's name was brought up. One of the women said he'd been actively seeking to court the Amish woman who owned the greenhouse in Strasburg. Since the only greenhouse in Strasburg run by an Amish woman belonged to Belinda, Herschel knew exactly who that woman had been talking about.

He snipped off some of the stray hairs on his beard, then stopped and mused. *It has been awhile since my wife passed away, and I had a hard time letting her go. But the change that's been coming over me is like an awakening of sorts. It might be time to start over with someone I can share my life with.*

Herschel gave his facial hair some combing. *I'm only a couple of years older than Belinda, and truth be told, most people guess me to be younger than I look. But that's not a bad thing. I kinda like it.*

He grinned at his reflection in the mirror, but his smile faded as the reality of competing against another man for Belinda sank in. Herschel wondered how crafty Monroe would be if he made it known that his hat was set on Belinda too. The awful doubt that crept in seemed to yank at Herschel's confidence.

"What chance do I have against him?" Herschel spoke out loud. "Monroe's younger than me, and his furniture store is always busy, so he's probably doing well financially. Not only that, but he's quite a talker. I bet it wouldn't take much for him to win Belinda over."

Herschel reached around and scratched the back of his head. "Maybe she would think I'm too old for her anyway."

He picked up the scissors and made a few snips. *I need to quit worrying about all this and just relax and enjoy my time at Jared and Amy's this evening. If it's meant for me and Belinda to have a connection, then it will happen in God's time, not mine.*

Strasburg

When Herschel guided his horse and buggy up the driveway leading to the home he'd rented to Jared and Amy, he saw two other carriages parked there.

Everyone must be here already. I hope I'm not late. Herschel stepped down from the buggy and hurried to get his horse secured to the hitching rail. Once that chore was done, he reached inside the carriage and pulled out a paper bag. Even though Jared had said Herschel didn't need to bring anything, he wanted to do his part, so he'd purchased a bag of chips to contribute to the meal.

Herschel was glad his mother had taken the time to cut his hair. It really needed it, and Dad had even gotten Mom to trim a little on his hair too. Herschel hoped he would make a nice impression on Belinda and her family by having taken more interest in his appearance.

He looked down, making certain that his attire was in order and his dark trousers were free of any dust or smudges from the buggy. *If I'm going to the trouble of making sure my hair and beard look good, then everything else should too.*

Hearing voices coming from the backyard, Herschel headed in that direction. Upon rounding the corner of the house, he spotted a glowing bonfire in the pit he'd made a year after he'd bought the house as a rental. Jared, Amy, Belinda, and Sylvia, holding Rachel on her lap, sat on folding chairs. On the other side of the yard Dennis and Henry played catch with Allen, using a large rubber ball. Everyone appeared to be content, and he almost hated to interrupt. A pang of envy shot through him. How nice it would be to have a large family. For Herschel, it was just him and his parents living in the same area. When they got together, things were pretty quiet.

Jared must have seen Herschel coming, for he looked his way and motioned him over.

"*Guder owed,*" Herschel said when he joined the group.

"Good evening," came their responses.

"I brought some chips." Herschel placed the paper sack on the picnic table.

"Danki, that was nice of you." Amy smiled. "In addition to the hot dogs we'll soon be roasting, we have a tray of cut-up veggies. Oh, and there's also a big pot of savory baked beans. I'm sure you'll enjoy those as much as we all do."

Herschel's chin dipped slightly as he glanced in Belinda's direction.

Her cheeks looked a little pink, but then that could have just been from the glow of the fire. "It's a recipe my *mudder* used to make."

Herschel's mouth felt awfully dry all of a sudden. He didn't understand why he felt so nervous or at a loss of words in Belinda's presence.

"Why don't you take a seat over there?" Amy pointed to the empty chair beside Belinda.

Herschel waited to see if Belinda would object, and when she gave a little nod, he quickly sat down. "Nice evening, jah?"

She turned to him and smiled. "It certainly is. And I'm glad you could join us."

"I appreciate the invite." Herschel undid the top button of his shirt. It felt like it was choking him.

"How's your mother getting along these days? I haven't seen her in some time."

"She's getting by okay. Same with my daed." Herschel held his hands out toward the warmth of the fire. *Sure wish I could think of something interesting to talk about—a topic that might be of interest to Belinda.* He cleared his throat a couple of times. "How are things going at the greenhouse?"

"It's been kind of slow since we reopened, but as the weather improves, people normally start thinking about gardening and spending more time in their yards." Belinda glanced at her granddaughter, still sitting contently on Sylvia's lap, and then she turned her attention to Herschel again. "A man who owns a local landscaping business came to the greenhouse earlier this week. He talked with me about supplying some of the plants, trees, and flowers he would like to offer his customers."

Herschel scratched an itch behind his left ear. "Sounds like it could be a good thing for both of you then."

"Jah. I hope it works out."

"Okay, everyone, the fire's died down enough so we can roast our hot dogs," Jared announced. "Let's gather around to offer thanks, and then I'll pass out the roasting sticks."

Dennis, Henry, and Allen stopped playing ball and ran over to join the group. Dennis shook Herschel's hand. "It's nice you could join us."

"Danki. I'm glad I was invited."

At Jared's lead, all heads bowed for silent prayer. In addition to thanking God for the food they'd be eating soon, Herschel said a prayer on Belinda's behalf. *Lord, please bless Belinda and her family. Provide for them through the money the greenhouse brings in. And if it's meant for me to develop a deeper friendship with Belinda, then please give me some sign that she's interested so I won't barge ahead and make a fool of myself.*

Henry held his stick with a hot dog on it close to the embers and listened to the conversation between his mother and Herschel. They'd been sitting by each other since Herschel arrived, and now the man was roasting a hot dog for Mom. *She knows how to roast her own wiener, for goodness' sake. She's had plenty of practice over the years and doesn't need anyone's help.*

Henry angled his stick in a different direction so the hot dog wouldn't burn on one side. *I wonder why Mom didn't tell Herschel that she could manage on her own.* He glanced at Amy and noticed a big smile on her face. *What in the world is my sister so happy about? Is it because she's expecting a boppli? Maybe she just enjoys having our family together.*

Henry rotated his stick again. The hot dog had begun to brown quite nicely. *Or maybe Amy's glad to have Herschel visiting. He was nice enough to rent them this house at a reasonable price. Amy might feel beholden to him.*

Then another thought crossed Henry's mind. He'd heard his sister tell Mom on more than one occasion what a nice man Herschel was and that she was surprised he'd never remarried. *Is it possible that Amy invited Herschel here tonight so he and Mom could get better acquainted?* He looked in Mom's direction. She too wore a smile as she leaned closer to Herschel, while pointing at the two wieners on the stick he held close to the glowing embers. *Could my sister be plotting to get Mom and Herschel together? If so, is she succeeding?*

"Look out, Brother! One side of your hot dog is turning black." Sylvia pointed.

"You may have been holding it in one position too long," Dennis interjected.

Henry flipped the stick over and grimaced. Sure enough, part of the meat looked like charcoal. "It's okay," he mumbled. "I like it well done." He grabbed a bun from the table, put the hot dog inside, and then squeezed on plenty of ketchup and mustard. *There, that should make it taste better.*

"Who made the *gebackne buhne*?" Herschel asked after he'd finished roasting his and Mom's wieners.

Before Mom could respond, Amy and Sylvia both pointed to her. "You should try some," Amy said. "Our mamm makes the best baked beans of any I've ever tasted."

"That's right," Sylvia agreed. "I always have more than one helping."

No wonder she mentioned they were a recipe of her mamm's. "I'll be eager to try them." Herschel got their hot dogs ready, and then he spooned some baked beans onto his plate.

Meanwhile, Henry watched, while he chomped on a handful of chips.

Herschel ate the beans in short order, then helped himself to more. "I have to say, your daughters are right, Belinda. Your gebackne buhne are *appeditlich*. If there's enough to go around, I may have to eat three helpings."

Mom tilted her head to one side. "Why thank you, Herschel. I'm glad you think the baked beans are delicious."

Henry glanced at Dennis. Allen sat beside him, chattering away like a magpie. Every once in a while, Rachel, while sitting on her mother's lap, reached over, giggled, and touched Dennis with her grubby little ketchup-stained hand. Those two kids had really taken a shine to Dennis, but as far as Henry was concerned, they monopolized too much of his time. He had wanted to talk to Dennis about some unusual birds he'd seen the other day, but it didn't look like he'd get the chance.

At the sound of Mom's laughter, Henry looked her way again. Apparently Herschel had said something she thought was funny, because she'd just thanked him for sharing such a humorous story.

What story? Henry's hand tightened around his bun so hard that part of it crumbled and fell apart. He picked up the hot dog with his bare fingers and gobbled the rest of it down.

Henry remembered the Valentine card Herschel had sent to his mother last month and wondered once again if he had a personal interest in Mom. *Even though Herschel isn't nearly as irritating as Monroe, he should not be makin' a play for my mamm. He's been a widower for a good many years, and apparently remained content, so why the sudden interest in Mom?*

Henry spooned some baked beans onto his plate. *I'd better get 'em while the gettin' is good.* He ate the beans quickly, barely able to enjoy the savory flavor, while his thoughts remained on Herschel. *Hopefully Mom will say something to let the man know that she's not interested in a relationship with him. If she doesn't, then at some point, I may need to let him know that fact myself. I'll just tell Herschel that my mamm's still in love with my daed and has no plans of ever remarrying.*

Henry nearly choked on the forkful of beans he'd put into his mouth. *At least I don't think she does. Maybe Mom is looking to get married again and hasn't said anything to me.* The thought of it put a sick feeling in the pit of Henry's stomach, diminishing his appetite. Unless he got it back at some point this evening, he probably wouldn't bother roasting any marshmallows. What would be the point? If his mother and Herschel kept talking and laughing with each other, anything Henry ate from here on wouldn't have much of an exciting taste. Not even the chocolate brownies Sylvia had made for dessert.

Chapter 17

Monroe sat at his mother's kitchen table, eating a late supper after his folks had gone to bed. He'd worked later than usual on some paperwork at his furniture store and then gone over to the Kings' place to see Belinda. He had anticipated visiting for a while with the special woman he admired, but that didn't work out the way he'd planned.

Monroe wouldn't have minded being in Belinda's presence this evening and possibly getting to eat some of her delicious and hearty cooking. To his disappointment, she wasn't at home, and apparently neither was anyone else in her family, because nobody had answered the door. He'd been tempted to stop at Belinda's neighbors across the street and ask if they knew where she was, but decided against it. Belinda probably didn't keep her English neighbors informed of her whereabouts, and he couldn't fault her for that. On more than one occasion when Monroe had dropped by the greenhouse or up to Belinda's house, he'd caught sight of the red-haired English woman on her front porch, looking across the street with a pair of binoculars.

That woman is a snoop, he told himself. *She's probably a big gossip too.* Monroe had met plenty of people like her—busybodies who liked to stick their noses in someone else's business.

"Whatever goes on at Belinda's place should be my business," Monroe muttered, reaching for his glass of milk to wash down the sandwich he'd eaten a few minutes ago. He felt reassured that there wasn't anyone else to compete with to win Belinda's heart—at least not so far. He hadn't seen or heard about any of the other single men his age from their Amish community going over to her place or asking her out.

As his body relaxed, he muttered some more. "I'm the fella for

Belinda, and in time I'll win her and we'll be setting the date for our big day." If there was one thing Monroe wanted more than anything, it was to become Belinda's husband. He'd wanted it when they were young people, and his desire to have her as his wife had never died, not even after she'd married Vernon. Dejected and hurt by her betrayal, Monroe had left the area. He'd hoped to start a new life and put the pain of losing her aside. But when he heard from his mother that Vernon had been killed, Monroe couldn't wait to move back to Strasburg. Fortunately he'd had enough money saved up to start his new business, which had turned out to be a good investment. Many people living in the area and even from other places wanted expertly crafted furniture built by the Amish. So Monroe made sure everything his employees turned out was top-notch. Through some good advertising strategies and word of mouth, it hadn't taken long for Monroe's business to become successful.

Monroe felt a tingling sensation on his arms and the nape of his neck. *Now if I can just get Belinda to see that we're meant to be together, everything will be as it should, and my life will finally be complete.*

"What's for dessert?" Earl asked from his easy chair across the room. He'd come home from his job at the dealership sounding a little defeated. But before he'd changed from his nicer clothes into the comfy attire he had on, he'd shared the details of what had happened. Earl and another salesman had been trying to sell the same vehicle to make a potential sale. He admitted that they were both after their commissions. Unfortunately, the customer Earl dealt with didn't have enough money up front to purchase the car, like the other patron did. Rebounding from his wound, Earl seemed to be craving extra attention, and what helped him through it was being waited on. However, Virginia wasn't sure if her patience at this point could accommodate his mood.

Virginia groaned. She and Goldie had just gotten comfortable on the couch, and the thought of getting up so soon to get dessert held no appeal. *I know he's the breadwinner, but I've been busy today with ongoing chores here at the house. And things haven't been perfect around here either— especially when Goldie threw up on my pillow after I got up this morning.* Virginia petted the cat. *It's not your fault I gave you a new brand of cat food that was cheaper than the normal stuff.*

Virginia felt annoyed, and her limbs were growing rigid as she looked over at her husband. "Why didn't ya say something before I sat down, Earl?"

"Didn't think about it till now."

"Can't you go out to the kitchen and get something yourself?"

He shook his head and pouted. "Besides having a lousy day, I'm in the middle of my favorite show right now, and I don't want to miss the ending. Come on, honey. . .pretty please."

Wow! He is sure being a big baby. I suppose he'll keep it up if I remain here on the couch with Goldie.

Virginia set the cat aside and rose from the couch. "All right, Your Majesty, your wish is my command," she mumbled on the way to the kitchen.

Virginia pulled out the cookie jar and set several on a plate. *It's a good thing I made the time to bake these earlier today.* She replaced the lid and slid the jar back to its spot. *That ought to last Earl awhile, at least till the end of his show.*

She took the plate out to the living room and set it on the TV tray beside his chair. "Here you go—chocolate-chip—your favorite kind."

"Thanks, hon. Do we have any coffee in the pot?" He gave her a sheepish grin. "That would go real good with these yummy cookies."

Virginia stepped back. "Yes there's plenty in the carafe. I'll get you a cup." Before she had moved a step from his recliner he spoke again. "How about a bowl of ice cream to go with the cookies?"

Virginia poked her tongue into the side of her cheek and inhaled a long breath. "Won't the cookies and the hot cup of coffee be enough? You don't wanna get fat, ya know."

He swatted the air with his hand. "I am not overweight, Virginia, and a little ice cream won't tip the scales." Earl glanced up at her, and then looked quickly back at the TV. "You ought to have some too. Maybe a bowl of ice cream will cool you down."

"I am not hot. If anything, this room is a bit chilly."

"I didn't mean physically warm. I was talking about your disposition. You've been hot under the collar ever since I came home from work today." Earl raised his eyebrows. "And if anyone should be hot, it's me, because I'm the one who had a rough day."

She clenched her teeth.

"Could you please get me some ice cream? It'll help me feel better, my pretty red-headed doll."

Ignoring his compliment, Virginia couldn't deny her crankiness. She'd spent a good portion of her day cleaning and baking, as well as listening to and watching the traffic out front. And most of it was because of that stupid greenhouse across the road. But of course, Earl probably wouldn't care about any of that.

"You know what, Earl? I have good reason to be irritated this evening. You should know by now that all those horses and buggies on our road really get on my nerves. Not to mention all the messes those smelly horses create and leave behind." Virginia looked toward the front window. "It'll be another year just like the last one we had. You'll have to hang those sticky fly catchers outside near the exterior doors. And I have to say that we never had flies in the big city of Chicago like we have out here in this rural country." She turned to see if her husband was involved in the conversation.

Earl made no comment as he leaned forward with his elbows on his knees, looking intently at the TV.

Shaking her head and muttering to herself, Virginia returned to the kitchen for Earl's coffee and a bowl of ice cream. *That man doesn't give a hoot about my feelings. He has no problem with our neighbors and all the noise and icky smelling road apples on the road, because he's not here all day.*

Virginia felt a sense of tightness in her chest. *I wish there was something I could do to put a stop to it once and for all!*

From the passenger seat of her buggy, with her horse being driven by Henry, Belinda reflected on the wonderful evening they'd had at Jared and Amy's. She couldn't get over how enjoyable it had been—especially spending time with Herschel and getting to know him better. Although at first he'd seemed slow in taking part in a conversation, once he had opened up and become more talkative, Herschel had proved to be quite an interesting man. He'd told Belinda, as well as those who sat nearby, some humorous stories about when he was a boy. One in particular caused Belinda to laugh out loud. According to the story, when

Herschel was about six years old, he'd begged his mother to let him eat some of her baking chocolate. She had told him that it was quite bitter, not sweet like the chocolate bars sold in a candy shop. After Herschel's insistence and lots more begging, she finally gave in and cut off a chunk for him. One bite and Herschel raced for the garbage can to spit out the bitter-tasting chocolate. He told Belinda that it had taken him a long time until he could eat anything made with chocolate.

"What are you thinking about, Mom?"

Henry's question pushed Belinda's thoughts aside.

"Just reflecting on what a nice time we had this evening sitting around the bonfire. I'm glad Amy and Jared planned the event and invited Herschel too."

Henry didn't comment as they headed down the road toward home, with Dennis's horse and buggy following not too far behind. Sylvia and the children had ridden with him, and since it would have been a bit crowded with four adults and two children in one buggy, Belinda opted to take her own horse and carriage, allowing Henry to take charge as the official chauffeur. Her son was a careful driver and had good night vision, so she felt comfortable letting him take control of her horse.

"Did you have fun tonight?" Belinda asked, looking over at Henry.

"It was okay, I guess. Didn't get to talk to Dennis much though."

"He was kept pretty busy with your niece and nephew. He'll make a good father for Sylvia's children. I've even heard Allen call him 'Papa' a few times."

"But he's not their daed, and if you got married again, your new husband would not be my daed either."

Belinda couldn't mistake the angry tone in her son's voice. "Now what brought on that statement, Son?"

"Just saying, is all."

"If you're worried about Monroe—"

"Seems to me you might have two suitors vying for your hand in marriage."

"What suitors?"

"I saw how cozy Herschel was with you tonight, Mom. He monopolized all your time, making it hard for you to talk to anyone else. He even roasted a hot dog for you."

"For goodness' sake, Henry, Herschel was just being friendly and polite. I enjoyed his company, yes, but I am not thinking our friendship could end in marriage."

"You might not think so, but I bet he does. And it don't take no genius to figure out what Monroe has on his mind."

Belinda reached across the seat and placed her hand on Henry's knee. "You may be right about Monroe, but I seriously doubt that Herschel has anything more than a casual friendship with me on his mind. And you needn't worry about me getting married again, because I have no desire for that at this time."

"Well that's good."

Belinda sighed as she crossed her arms over her chest. *I don't think my girls would have a problem if I should ever decide to remarry. Why does Henry have to be so opposed to the idea? Doesn't he realize that someday he'll get married and leave home? Would he not care that I'd be in my big old house all alone and would most likely try to keep the greenhouse running by myself?*

Maybe by then, she consoled herself, *he will have changed his mind about me getting married again. And perhaps by that time I'll be ready to consider it as well.*

A short time later, Henry turned the horse and buggy up their driveway. The moon was out fully tonight, and Belinda thought she saw something dangling from one of the trees in their front yard. She didn't think too much about it until they were out of the buggy and Henry made a comment just moments after she'd heard the hoot of an owl.

"Look, Mom, there's something up in that tree." Henry reached into the buggy and grabbed his flashlight. When he shined the light on the spot, where the *hoo-hoo* had come from, Belinda gasped.

"Oh no. . . Someone draped toilet paper from the branches, and maybe other trees in our yard as well."

Henry shined the light around. Sure enough, the rest of the trees had also been done.

About that time, Dennis's horse and carriage pulled in. Belinda waited until Sylvia and Dennis got out with the children, and then she pointed to the white streamers, clearly seen under the beam of light from Henry's powerful flashlight. "Someone came onto our property and did this while we were gone," she exclaimed. "Just when we thought the acts of vandalism were behind us, now we're faced with this."

"It's so frustrating." Sylvia's voice quivered a bit. "Why would someone want to do such a thing?"

"It gets worse. Look there." Henry moved closer to the house, shining the light back and forth across the front living-room windows.

Belinda cringed when she saw that raw eggs had been thrown at the glass, creating a real mess on both windows.

Dennis stepped forward, holding Rachel in his arms. "This kind of thing needs to be stopped. Belinda, you really need to call the sheriff."

"What good would that do?" she asked. "Unless someone saw the person who did this, we have no witnesses, and how likely is that? It was probably just some rowdy kids going through their *rumschpringe*. I'm sure they meant no harm, and most likely our home wasn't the only one they targeted." She looked at Henry. "We'll clean up this mess in the morning when we have better light. Right now, we need to get the kinner inside and ready for bed."

As they approached the front door, Belinda's heart pounded. A note had been taped on the door. It read: *When are you going to give up and move?*"

Chapter 18

What kind of clues should I be looking for? Henry asked himself while he cleaned off the windows early the following morning. *Almost every time we've had an incident at our place, we were away for a while. That would mean someone is casing the property and knows when we're not here.*

Henry sprayed more cleaner on the window and rubbed at the dried egg yolk stuck to the glass. *I shoulda cleaned this mess off last night.* He'd already taken down all the toilet paper. "What a waste," he'd said when he threw it away.

He scowled at the eggshells beneath his feet. *This could have been done by anyone who decided to come in here last night.*

Henry gritted his teeth and squatted down to pick up the cracked shells. *I'm sure gettin' sick and tired of all this. It's gone on too long, and if Mom won't call the sheriff or even tell Ezekiel about it, then I have no choice but to find out who is responsible.*

Henry continued to fume and analyze things as he finished cleaning up the windows. So far he'd seen no evidence near the house that would give him any clues, but after breakfast, before it was time to help out in the greenhouse, he would do a more thorough search around the property. Surely there had to be a clue somewhere.

Belinda had a difficult time keeping her mind on the business of running the greenhouse. *I should be fertilizing some of the plants. I'll have to go back and grab the watering can and the mix.* She looked out toward the parking lot. *I'll take care of it after Sylvia returns, because Henry is*

already busy in the back. Besides, someone should be up front. I don't want the customers coming in and it appearing as if we're not here.

They'd been open about an hour, and a few customers had come in, but it had been a challenge for Belinda to converse with any of them. Sylvia came to work with her today, and she seemed quieter than usual as well. If only their lives could be peaceful again, without having to worry about if or when another act of vandalism may occur.

Henry had been out looking for clues earlier but found nothing out of the ordinary. Since part of last night's mess involved eggs, he'd mentioned the prospect of Maude being the culprit. "After all," Henry had told Belinda shortly before she'd opened the greenhouse, "the old woman probably has eggs now, since she stole two of our hens. Maude is one strange lady, and I wouldn't put anything past her."

Belinda looked toward the storage room, where Henry had gone to get a broom to sweep up some dirt that had been spilled in aisle 1. *My son is really concerned about this, and I am too, but I don't know how to put an end to it.*

Belinda fingered the tablet lying on the counter where she sat. *Would it help if I wrote a note and tacked it up someplace where the person doing the vandalism might see it if they came back again? I could ask what they have against us and suggest that we meet in person to discuss the situation.*

She tapped her pen against the tablet. *I suppose that wouldn't work if the person feels vindictive toward us for some reason. They obviously don't want us to know or they would have come to me and spoken their feelings face-to-face.*

Belinda closed her eyes and said a prayer for the man or woman who had made it clear that they wanted her to close the greenhouse and leave the area.

Her eyes snapped open when she heard footsteps approach. Thinking it was Sylvia, returning to the greenhouse after going to the house to check on Amy and the children, Belinda was surprised to see Herschel standing on the other side of the counter. She'd been so engrossed in her prayer that she hadn't even heard the bell above the door jingle, indicating that someone had entered the building.

"Guder mariye, Herschel." She offered him what she hoped was a welcoming smile.

"Good morning, Belinda." Grinning back at her, he removed his straw hat and held it by the brim. Herschel appeared to be less shy than usual. "I sure enjoyed myself last night at Jared and Amy's."

"I did too." *At least until we got home and found a mess, along with a note, waiting for us.* She wanted to tell him about the vandalism but decided it was best not to mention it. Herschel might say something to his parents or someone else, and then the news could travel quickly around their community.

Herschel shifted his weight and leaned against his side of the counter. "I came by to ask you a question."

"Oh?" She tipped her head slightly.

He glanced toward the front door, then back at her. "I. . .umm. . .was wondering if you might be free to go out to supper with me one evening next week. It would give us a chance to get better acquainted."

She touched her cheeks, which felt quite warm. "Well, yes, that would be nice. What night did you have in mind?"

"Would Friday work for you?"

"I think it would. In fact, I'm sure nothing else is going on that evening, so jah, I'd enjoy going out to supper with you, Herschel."

"Okay, good. Should I come by to get you around five thirty, or would that be too early?"

"The greenhouse closes at five, so could we make it six? The extra half hour would give me a little more time to get ready."

"Six it is. I'll see you then. Have a nice rest of your day, Belinda." Herschel put his hat back on his head and went out the door.

The corners of Belinda's lips twitched. *Did I just agree to go out on a date with Herschel? I'm surprised he came right out and asked me to go out with him. Herschel wasn't being shy at all and I'm glad.* She touched her ever-warming cheeks again. *Oh my. . .I wonder what my children will say when I tell them—especially Henry. This might not set well with him. It's a good thing my son wasn't here when Herschel extended the invitation. He may have spoken on my behalf and said no to Herschel, and that would have been most embarrassing.*

Monroe pulled his horse and buggy into the greenhouse parking lot in time to see Herschel Fisher come out of the building and approach his own rig. The man wore the biggest grin. Monroe had never seen the fellow look so happy.

"How are things with you these days?" Monroe asked, stepping down from his buggy.

Herschel gave his mostly gray beard a tug. "Fine and dandy. How about you?"

"Can't complain." *Things would be better if Belinda would let me court her though.* Monroe kept his thoughts to himself. Whatever happened or didn't happen between him and Belinda was none of Herschel's business.

Monroe scrutinized Herschel, noticing that he was empty handed. "You came from the greenhouse, but it doesn't look like you bought anything," he commented in a nonchalant tone.

Herschel shook his head. "Didn't come to buy anything. Came to talk to Belinda."

"Mind if I ask about what?"

"Oh, just wanted to see how she's doing this morning and ask if she'd like to go out to supper with me next week."

Monroe blinked rapidly, and his mouth nearly fell open. Until this moment, he'd had no idea Herschel was interested in Belinda. "Uh, what'd she say?"

"She agreed to go." Herschel pulled his shoulders back a bit and gave a crisp nod. "I'll be taking her out Friday evening."

A burning sensation traveled across Monroe's chest and all the way up to his neck. *Belinda's agreed to go out with Herschel but not me? What's going on here anyway? I'd bet Herschel's at least eight or ten years older than her. What in the world would she see in him?*

Struggling to keep his composure, Monroe forced himself to offer what he hoped was a pleasant smile. "Well, I need to head into the greenhouse and state my business, and then I'll be on my way."

"Have a good rest of your day." Herschel released his horse from the hitching rail, climbed into his carriage, and backed away.

As Herschel's horse and carriage started down the driveway, Monroe made a beeline for the greenhouse, ready to give Belinda a piece of his mind.

He stopped short, just outside the front door and sucked in several breaths of air. It wouldn't do to go charging in there like a jealous fool.

He needed to use some common sense and try to stay on her good side. The last thing Monroe wanted to do was rile her up. Then she'd never agree to let him court her.

So while he collected himself, Monroe assessed the situation. *It's obvious I'm not the only eligible man interested in Belinda. I'd thought this would be easy and that I had her all to myself. That's all right though. I'll just have to use my wit and come up with a way to win my gal. To start with, I'm younger and more financially sound than Herschel, so that could be to my advantage.*

Belinda was about to leave her place behind the counter and see what was taking Henry so long, when he showed up.

"Things were gettin' disarranged in there," he told Belinda. "So I took some time to straighten all the items on the shelves and make sure all the boxes were set so we can easily see the labels on what's inside each one."

"That's good. I appreciate it, Son." Belinda gave his shoulder a squeeze. This was the first time he'd seemed worried about disorganization. Maybe it was a sign that he had gained some maturity.

"I swept up the dirt you asked me to, so now what do ya want done?"

She was about to respond to Henry's question when Monroe entered the shop and stepped between them. "Can I talk to you for a few minutes, Belinda?"

"Well yes, I suppose, but. . ."

"Before you do, I'd like to ask a question." Henry looked right at Monroe, narrowing his eyes.

"About what?" Monroe asked.

"I was wondering what you were doing last night."

"I did several things. For one, I dropped by here to see your mamm, but no one was home." Monroe looked right back at Henry. "Do you have a problem with that, young man?"

"It all depends."

"On what?" A muscle on the side of Monroe's cleanly shaven face twitched.

"On how you answer my next question."

"And that would be?"

"What'd you do when you found out we weren't home?"

"Henry, please. . ." Belinda's elbow connected with his arm. Her son's behavior was embarrassing. She couldn't imagine what Monroe must be thinking. It seemed as though Henry thought Monroe might be guilty of something. Did he believe this man was responsible for hanging toilet paper from the trees in their yard, egging the front windows, and leaving the note on the door? If so, Belinda felt certain her son was wrong. Besides, it wasn't right to make accusations with no evidence whatsoever. She hoped Henry would not say anything more, because things were already uncomfortable.

"It's okay. I don't mind answering," Monroe said. "I went home. Why do you ask, son?"

Henry folded his arms and grunted. "I ain't your son."

"It was only a figure of speech." Monroe took a step closer to Henry. "Why did you ask?" he repeated.

"Did ya see anything out of place in our yard or anyone hangin' around the house while you were here?"

Monroe gave a hearty shake of his head. "The only person I saw at all is your red-headed neighbor lady across the road."

"Virginia came over here?" Belinda questioned.

"No, I saw her standing on her front porch. It looked like she had a pair of binoculars in her hands."

"That's no big deal." Henry shook his head. "Sylvia and I are bird-watchers, and we use our binoculars a lot."

Monroe shrugged. "Well, you asked if I'd seen anyone, and that woman is the only person I saw."

"Okay, whatever." Henry moved toward the front door. "I'm goin' out to check on the beehives, Mom. Give a holler if you need me." Henry was out the door before Belinda could respond.

"Well, good. I'm glad we have a few minutes to talk while there's no one else in the building."

"What did you wish to speak with me about, Monroe?" Belinda moved back toward the counter and stood behind it. She needed to be ready in case another customer came in.

Monroe followed. "I would like to take you out for supper one night next week. Are you free on Friday?"

Belinda's face warmed and she swallowed hard. "Um. . .well. . .I've already made plans."

"What kind of plans?"

Trapped. Now what should I say? Belinda glanced at the door, hoping Sylvia or a customer would come in. *What is taking my daughter so long in the house? She must know her help could be needed out here.*

"Belinda, are you going to answer my question?" Monroe looked at her pointedly.

She moistened her lips, feeling ever so anxious. "If you must know, I agreed to have supper with Herschel Fisher that evening."

His facial features tightened. "Oh, so that's how it is. You'll go out with that man, who has so little to offer, but not with me." Monroe tapped his foot and glared at her. "You know how much I care for you, Belinda, and yet you're choosing an older man who hasn't much of a personality, over me." He pressed one fist against his chest. "Do you have any idea how badly my feelings have been hurt?"

Belinda dropped her gaze to the floor. She hadn't meant to upset him. She felt pain in the back of her throat as she tried to come up with the right thing to say to Monroe. Somehow Belinda had to make it better.

"How about Saturday night? Would that be okay?"

He placed both hands on the counter and leaned in closer to her. "Are you saying that you'd be willing to go out for supper with me on Saturday?"

"Jah."

With a wide smile, Monroe clapped his hands. "All right then, it's a date. What time would you like me to pick you up?"

"Would six o'clock work for you?"

His head bobbed quickly up and down. "I'll see you then, Belinda, and be prepared to have a wunderbaar evening."

When Monroe went out the door, with a spring in his step, Belinda sank to the wooden stool behind the counter. *Oh my! What have I gotten myself into? Two meals out with two very different men, and all in the same week? What in the world was I thinking?*

Chapter 19

"Do I have any stray hairs sticking out of my bun or the sides of my head covering?" Belinda asked Sylvia when she entered the living room Friday evening to wait for Herschel.

Sylvia left the chair where she'd been sitting with a notepad and pen. She stepped behind Belinda and walked around to check both sides and the front. "Everything looks fine. You did a good job with your hair, but then you usually do. And you'll have a nice time, so please relax, Mom, because you seem a little nervous for your date."

"Jah, guess I am. It's because I'm a little rusty since my courting days, so I'm not sure how to act."

Sylvia took hold of Belinda's hand. "I have the best mamm a daughter could want, and I'm sure you'll get along fine with Herschel this evening."

Belinda's face warmed. "In some ways it feels like I'm a young woman again, until I look in the mirror." She laughed. "It's funny how, after all this time, those feelings can be stirred up again."

"Here, let me fix your apron tie. It's a little crooked." Sylvia leaned in and took care of the problem. "There you go—now you're ready."

"Danki." Belinda motioned to the writing tablet Sylvia still held. "Have you been working on your wedding plans?"

"Yes, and just when I'm sure all the details are covered, I think of something else to add."

Belinda chuckled. "It'll all come together. It has to, since you only have four-and-a-half months till the big day."

"True." The gleam in Sylvia's eyes couldn't be missed. No doubt, she'd been counting the days until she would become Mrs. Dennis Weaver.

Belinda glanced at Henry, slouched on the couch with one of his bird magazines. He hadn't said more than a few words to her all day. Her son had said plenty earlier in the week, however, when she'd let him and her daughters know about her two supper dates. Amy seemed pleased about Belinda going out with Herschel, but said nothing concerning Monroe. Sylvia's only comments were she hoped Belinda would enjoy herself and that she deserved an evening out now and then, giving her a break from having to help cook a meal. Belinda, however, couldn't miss her son's look of displeasure when he had said, "I can't believe you'd agree to go for supper with either of them, Mom."

Belinda had defended her right to spend time with anyone she chose and told Henry it was not his concern. All he needed to worry about was staying out of trouble and setting a good example for his impressionable niece and nephew.

She smiled when Rachel climbed up on the couch with a picture book and sat close to Henry, leaning her head against his side. Not to be outdone, Allen pranced across the room and took a seat on the other side of Henry.

Someday my youngest son will get married and have children of his own, Belinda thought. *So it's nice to see how well he gets along with Sylvia's kinner, and Ezekiel's too on the occasions we get to see my eldest son and his family. I could be happy and feel blessed if our entire family lived close by so I could see them more often.*

Belinda moved to the front windows and looked out. *No sign of Herschel's rig yet. Maybe he left his bulk-food store later than he'd planned.*

Herschel gripped the reins a little tighter as he urged his horse to move faster. He'd left the store later than he wanted and then taken a few extra minutes at home cleaning up and making sure he looked respectable. He had not taken a woman out to supper since Mattie died and rarely went out to eat alone. He had, on a few occasions, eaten at a restaurant with his mom and dad, but most of the time his meals were eaten at home or his folk's house.

What if I can't think of anything sensible to talk about? He lamented. *Maybe if I keep my mouth full of food, I won't have to say much of anything while we're at the restaurant.*

Herschel's lips pressed together in a slight grimace. *But I won't be eating any food on the ride to and from Dienner's Country Restaurant. I sure can't travel all the way to Ronks and back without talking to Belinda. She'd probably wonder why I even bothered to ask her out.*

Herschel let go of the reins with one hand and thumped the side of his head just below his straw hat. *Why am I thinking like this, anyhow? Last week at Jared and Amy's I conversed with Belinda without too much problem. And even when I went into the greenhouse the following day, things were okay. I just need to relax and enjoy my time spent this evening in the company of a very pleasant woman. I'm sure if I stop fretting about it, the words will come.*

"Supper's ready, Henry!" Sylvia called from the kitchen. "Would you make sure the kinners' hands have been washed before you bring them in to eat?"

"Already done. We've just come from the bathroom." Henry led the children down the hall and into the kitchen. He lifted Rachel into her high chair and made sure Allen sat securely on his stool, before taking his own seat.

Sylvia seated herself in her normal chair, and when she instructed the children, they all bowed for silent prayer.

Henry often wondered why he bothered to say any prayers. It seemed that God hadn't answered many of them, which was discouraging. He'd heard their bishop and the ministers from their church district say that God hears everyone's prayers and answers according to His will.

Henry curled his fingers into the palms of his hands. *Am I supposed to believe it was God's will for Dad, Abe, and Toby to be killed? Is God okay with someone vandalizing our place and makin' us worry?* Henry struggled to understand why God would allow any of those things. It didn't seem fair.

Henry figured Sylvia should be done praying by now so he opened his eyes. He found her staring at him with a strange expression.

"What's the matter?" he asked.

"Nothing. I've just never seen you pray at the supper table so long before."

Henry shrugged. No way would he admit to his sister that he hadn't been praying—just trying to figure out why God didn't always answer like he wanted Him to. For that matter, Henry wondered why the Lord allowed so much suffering to go on in the world.

Sylvia spooned some macaroni and cheese onto her children's plates, while Henry helped himself to one of the plump Polish sausage links she'd baked in the oven. There was also a fruit salad to accompany the meal.

Henry looked over at the chair where Mom normally sat and grimaced. It didn't seem right for her place to be empty, much less that she would be out on a supper date.

"What's wrong, Brother?" Sylvia questioned. "Isn't the sausage cooked to your liking?"

"It ain't that." Henry shook his head. "I was just thinkin' that our mamm oughta be here."

"She's entitled to an evening out, don't you think?"

"I suppose, but not with Herschel."

"Why would you say that? Herschel is a nice man, and I'm sure he's quite lonely."

"I don't see why he should be. His folks don't live too far from him, and his English daughter, along with her husband and baby, are in Lancaster, so he could visit any of them whenever he wanted." Henry's neck and shoulders tensed up. "I don't understand why he'd need to spend time with our mudder. He's quite a bit older than her, you know. They don't have much in common either, and there's probably very little for them to talk about."

Sylvia's voice lowered as she spoke. "Did you ever stop to think that Mom might be happier if she got married again? It's not fair to expect her to live alone for the rest of her life."

With forced restraint, Henry spoke through his teeth. "You know what? I didn't expect you to understand. All you ever think about is your upcoming wedding and how happy you're gonna be being married to Dennis."

Sylvia glanced at the children, then back at Henry, and put her finger against her lips. "Let's not talk about this anymore."

"Okay, sure. . .whatever you say." Henry looked down at his plate. He had enough on his mind trying to figure out who'd been threatening them without having to worry about their mother falling for one of the men in their community and getting married.

Amy and Jared stood at the kitchen sink doing their supper dishes. Jared had volunteered to wash, stating that Amy could dry and put them away, since she knew exactly where she wanted everything to go.

"I'm pleased that my mamm agreed to go out to supper with Herschel this evening." Amy looked over at Jared and smiled. "It must mean there's an attraction on both of their parts. Otherwise Herschel wouldn't have asked Mom out." She paused for a quick breath. "And if my mamm hadn't wanted to go, she would have politely said no."

"I'm sure you're right, but please don't meddle. You've already plotted to get them together on two occasions, so it's time now to sit back and see what happens. If it's meant for your mother and Herschel to be together, it will happen, all in good time."

"You're right," Amy agreed. "All in God's good time." *But that doesn't mean I can't be on the sidelines to encourage things along. With Herschel being kind of shy, and Mom not sure she wants to get married again, one or both of them might need a little nudge now and then to keep things moving in the right direction.*

Amy finished drying another dish and placed it in the cupboard. *One thing's for sure—Herschel would make a better husband than Monroe ever would. I doubt there's a woman in our community who'd want to be married to a man like him.*

Ronks

Belinda sat across from Herschel at a table inside Dienner's, enjoying every bite of food on her plate. She tried not to stare at how nice his periwinkle-blue shirt brought out the color in his eyes.

"The buffet here certainly has plenty to offer, doesn't it?" Herschel asked.

"I was just going to say the same thing."

He offered her a cute, almost boyish smile. As attractive as he was at the age of fifty-eight, she could only imagine what a handsome fellow he must have been in his twenties.

Belinda hadn't known Herschel back then. Besides their age difference, they'd both attended different schools as well as different church districts. Although she'd learned a few years ago that Herschel had fathered a child out of wedlock, Belinda had never cast judgment on him. From what her friend, Mary Ruth Lapp had told her, Herschel and Mary Ruth's daughter, Rhoda, used to go with each other when they were teenagers. Rhoda had run away from home when she realized she was pregnant, and didn't tell Herschel about the baby because she believed he was going to break up with her because he had another girlfriend. So the Lapps' daughter had taken off one day, leaving a brief note for her parents stating that she was leaving, but without a truthful explanation. From that day on, Mary Ruth and her husband, Willis, never heard from their wayward daughter again. It wasn't until Rhoda passed away that her daughter, Sara, read a note in her mother's Bible, telling of her grandparents from Strasburg and providing their address. Sara had been stunned when she arrived at her grandparents' home and found out that Michelle had impersonated her and wormed her way into the Lapps' lives. What a transformation in Michelle's life since then. It was hard to believe she'd once been a deceitful English girl, who later committed her life to the Lord, joined the Amish church, and married Belinda's son Ezekiel. It just went to show that no matter what sins had occurred in people's pasts, if they accepted Jesus as their Savior and turned from their sinful ways, they could become a new person in Christ.

Belinda watched Herschel eat the drumstick on his plate and thought about how he'd discovered that Sara was his daughter because of a note in an old jar found hidden at Mary Ruth's. It was a surprise to everyone to learn of this—Herschel most of all.

Our Lord works in mysterious ways, she thought. *And now, here I sit, having supper and enjoying myself with Sara's biological father.*

Belinda's musings were halted when Herschel pointed to her plate. "I'm guessing by what I see still there that you must be full and won't have room for dessert."

Belinda snapped to attention and picked up her fork. "I am getting full, but not so much that I can't finish the food I took from the buffet." No way would she ever admit that she'd stopped eating because her mind had wandered toward the past, and that most of her thinking had involved information about him and the child he'd fathered. If Herschel ever decided to talk about that time in his life, it would be his decision, not come about because she'd brought it up or asked for explanations. The truth was, Belinda had done a few things during her running-around years as a young woman that she wasn't proud of. But she'd sought forgiveness, and God had set her feet on a solid path in the direction of wanting to say and do things that pleased Him.

"If you're willing, I'd like to do this again sometime," Herschel stated. "And next time we can go to the restaurant of your choice."

"That sounds nice, but I was thinking maybe you'd like to come to my house for a home-cooked meal. There won't be nearly as much food as we've had here this evening, but if you'll tell me what you'd like, I'd be happy to fix it for you." Belinda could hardly believe her boldness in inviting him to supper.

Herschel rested both elbows on the table and leaned forward. "That suits me just fine, Belinda. Just name the day and time, and I'll be there." He paused and gave his beard a tug. "As far as what to fix, it doesn't really matter, because when it comes to food I'm pretty easy to please."

Belinda smiled. "How about a week from tonight? I'll invite Amy and Jared to join us too. Would that be all right with you?"

"Of course. It'll give me the opportunity of getting to know your whole family better."

"All but Ezekiel, his wife, and their two kinner," Belinda interjected. "It's not likely that they could come down from New York on such short notice. Maybe some other time it'll work out for them to join us."

"I'll look forward to that." Herschel pushed back his chair. "Now, if you don't mind, I'm goin' up to the dessert buffet and choose something sweet. Want me to get you a piece of cake or some pie?"

Belinda looked down at her plate. "Think I'd better finish what I have here and skip dessert this evening. You go ahead though. I'll enjoy watching you eat whatever you choose."

"Okay then, I'll be back soon."

As Belinda watched him walk away, her thoughts went to Monroe. *I seriously doubt that I'll have as good a time with Monroe tomorrow night as I'm having with Herschel this evening. But I said I would go out to supper with him, and I won't go back on my word.*

Chapter 20

"I went out to the phone shed and checked for phone messages," Henry said when he entered the kitchen Saturday morning.

Belinda turned from the stove. "Danki for doing that, Son. Were there any?"

"Only one. It was from that man who owns the landscaping business. He said he'd be by sometime today to see what we have in stock and to place an order."

She smiled. "That's good news. I'd hoped we would hear something from him soon."

"How long till breakfast?" Henry asked. "Just wondered if I have time to feed the chickens."

Belinda's brows lowered. "You haven't done that yet?"

"Huh-uh. Wanted to check for phone messages first."

"I see. Well, I've just started the bacon and still have eggs to fry, so if you hurry, I should have breakfast on the table by the time you get done tending the chickens."

"Okay, I'll snap to it." Henry hurried out the back door.

Belinda had a hunch that Henry went to the phone shed first in case there had been another muffled threatening message. She was well aware that he hoped to discover who was behind all the vandalism but doubted he'd have much success. Up to this point the person responsible had been clever enough not to leave any clues. Of course, there was the cigarette pack they'd found outside the barn after it caught fire, but that could have been accidentally dropped there by someone who'd attended Amy and Jared's wedding.

"Both of my kinner are up and dressed now, so can I help with breakfast?" Sylvia asked when she entered the kitchen.

"Let me see now. . . Would you mind setting the table?"

"Of course not." Sylvia moved closer to the stove and pointed to the bacon Belinda had been cooking. "That looks about done. Would you like me to take over at the stove and fry the eggs after I've set the table? You seem a little preoccupied this morning."

"I am a little," Belinda admitted. "Guess I have too much on my mind."

"Are you reflecting on your date with Herschel last night, or thinking about going out with Monroe this evening?"

Belinda's face filled with warmth. "I was actually thinking about your bruder when you came in."

"Which brother—Henry or Ezekiel?"

"Henry, but I won't go into that right now." Belinda removed the bacon strips from the frying pan and placed them on paper towels to absorb some of the grease. "If you don't mind frying the *oier*, I'll set the table."

"Okay. I'll scramble the children's eggs though. They like them best that way."

While Sylvia took over at the stove, Belinda got out the dishes and silverware.

"Did you enjoy yourself with Herschel last night?" Sylvia asked, glancing over her shoulder.

"Jah, we had a pleasant evening."

"I'm glad. You deserved some time away from your responsibilities here."

"I've never minded cooking. In fact, I invited Herschel to join us for supper next Friday evening, and he said yes."

"Oh did he now?" Sylvia looked at Belinda again, only this time with a smirk.

"Please don't read anything into it. Herschel and I are just friends."

"How about Monroe? Do you consider him a friend too?"

"Well yes, I do—although not in the way Monroe would like me to."

Sylvia cracked three eggs into a bowl and stirred them with a fork. "Do you suppose that Herschel would like you to be more than a friend?"

Belinda blinked. "I doubt it very much. I'm sure he's just lonely and in need of companionship."

Sylvia kept stirring the eggs.

Belinda finished setting the table and was about to take some apple juice from the refrigerator when Henry came in with a basket of eggs.

"If you need any oier for our breakfast, here's some fresh." He set the basket on the counter.

"We already have eggs out for this morning, so the ones you got can be washed and put in the refrigerator." Belinda placed the pitcher of juice on the table. "Sylvia will have the eggs fried soon, so why don't you go wash up and bring Rachel and Allen in from the living room?"

"Will do."

When Henry left the kitchen, Belinda heard his boots clomping down the hall. "Well, wouldn't you know? He forgot to remove his *schtiffel* and should have left them in the utility room. Guess he's got other things on his mind this morning."

Sylvia laughed. "What else is new?"

That evening, when Belinda heard a *clippity-clop* sound, followed by a horse's whinny, she went to the front window and peered out. As expected, her escort to supper had arrived with his well-groomed prancing horse and an equally nice buggy.

Belinda couldn't help smiling. Even back when they were young people, Monroe had taken pride in his horse and carriage. When he had brought her home from some of their youth singings, the inside of his rig had always been spotless.

"Guess some things never change," she murmured.

"What was that, Mom?" Sylvia asked from her chair across the room where she sat with Rachel in her lap. Sylvia and the children, along with Henry, had eaten an early supper this evening. This gave Sylvia an opportunity to enjoy doing something with Allen and Rachel before it was time to put them to bed.

"I was just thinking out loud," Belinda responded to her daughter's question. "But now I need to quit musing, because Monroe is outside."

"I figured as much, with the horse noises going on out there." Sylvia pointed to the clock on the mantel. "And he's right on time."

"Jah, Monroe's always been the punctual type. There's no need for him to come up to the house, so I'll just grab my shawl and outer bonnet, then head outside." Belinda came over and kissed Rachel's soft cheek. "Be good for your mamma now." She looked at Allen, sitting on the floor with his wooden horse and a small cardboard box he'd been using as a barn for the horse. "You be good too, little man."

Belinda had spoken in Pennsylvania Dutch so the children would understand what she said. They both grinned and bobbed their heads.

"Have a pleasant evening, Sylvia."

"I will, Mom. I hope you have a nice one too."

Belinda put on her outer wrappings and was almost to the door when she paused and turned back around. "Henry went out to the barn after you four finished eating supper. When he comes back in, would you tell him I said goodbye?"

"Jah, Mom, I'll do that." Sylvia pointed at the door. "Now don't keep your date waiting."

Belinda rolled her eyes. "Monroe's not really my date. We're just two old friends going out for supper."

"Okay, Mom. Whatever you say."

Belinda stepped outside and hurried out to Monroe's buggy.

He'd just gotten out and said he wanted to assist her, but Belinda insisted that she could get in by herself. "After all, I've been doing it for a good many years." She gave a small laugh.

"I suppose you have." Monroe climbed in and backed his horse up. Soon they were heading down the driveway. Before turning onto the main road, he looked over at her and smiled. "You look very nice this evening, Belinda. Seeing you sitting here in my buggy makes me think back to when you were a young woman and we were heading out on our first date."

Belinda's face burned with the heat of embarrassment. *He would have to bring up the past.*

Henry sat cross-legged in front of the open double doors of the hayloft overlooking their front yard. He'd seen Monroe pull up with his well-maintained rig and needed something to take his mind off the dislike he felt for this man.

Henry looked away and pondered where someone or, more to the point, the vandal could watch his family from. Henry's desire to figure out who the culprit was grew more intense each day, even though he didn't always talk about it with anyone. There seemed to be many spots where a person could observe his mother's home as well as the greenhouse.

Tapping his chin with his finger, he thought about a few of his suspects. *If it were say Seth or one of his buddies, it wouldn't be hard for one of 'em to hide behind a tree on our property. If it's old Maude, she's always walking by out front of our place, but of course she's too old to be climbing any of our big trees.*

Henry snickered a little over the idea, and then tensed up as he looked back at Monroe. *I'm leaning toward him, 'cause I believe he's hiding something. Just wish I could prove my theory. It don't help that Mom's in his corner. Apparently she thinks highly of him, because now she's lettin' Monroe into our lives again.*

He watched in disgust as his mother got into Monroe's buggy and struggled with the urge to shout down at her, "Please stay home!"

But what good would that do? he asked himself. *Mom promised she would go out to supper with Monroe, and she's always tried to keep her promises.*

It was wrong of Henry to think this way, but he couldn't help it. *Maybe Mom will have a bad experience with him while they're out to supper, and then she won't go on any more outings with Monroe. I wonder how he'd react to that. Would the persistent fellow finally give up, or would he keep comin' around, trying to worm his way into Mom's life?*

Henry's heart felt heavy as he watched Monroe's buggy lurch out onto the pavement with Mom in the seat beside him. *It's hard to see her being courted by anyone—especially Mr. Esh.*

Henry stood up and closed the doors. It would be dark soon, so there was no point in staying up here any longer. The problem was, he didn't feel like going back in the house.

"I sure miss Abe," Henry muttered as he made his way down the ladder. "If my brother was still alive, I bet he'd help me figure out who's behind the vandalism, threatening phone messages, and notes." Abe had been smart, and Henry had looked up to him ever since he was a boy. Henry had no doubt about his older brother's ability to search for important clues.

Once again, Henry ran over the list of suspects he'd come up with. *The red-haired woman across the road; Maude the chicken stealer; my friend Seth or one of his friends; the owner of the other greenhouse; and last, but certainly not least, Monroe Esh.* For the time being, at least, Mom's old boyfriend was at the top of Henry's list. The irritating man might pretend to be nice, but Henry felt sure that Monroe was only after the greenhouse.

Before leaving the barn, Henry stopped to pet Mom's horse. "I believe the fellow my mamm's out with tonight wants one of two things. Monroe would be happy if Mom agreed to marry him. That would make it easy for him to take over her business." He scratched the mare behind her ears and gave her neck a few pats. "And in case being nice to Mom doesn't work out the way he planned, then he will rely on the pranks he's been doing, hoping we'll all get so scared that we'll pack up and move." He shook his head. "Well, that's never gonna happen."

Bird-in-Hand

"How'd your day go, Belinda?" Monroe asked after they were seated in a booth at the Bird-in-Hand Family Restaurant.

"It went quite well," she responded, fidgeting with her silverware.

Monroe wished he could reach over and take her hand, but that would be too bold—especially here in a public place. "Lots of customers then?"

"Yes, we did have a fairly good turnout, but the best part of the day was when one of the local landscapers came in and placed a large order of bedding plants for several of his customers. He also bought a selection of our smaller fruit trees." A pleasant smile spread across Belinda's face. It was good to see her relax in his presence. On the trip here, she'd seemed preoccupied and hadn't contributed much to his conversation.

There has to be something I can say or do to win her over. Monroe pretended to study his menu, which was a waste of time, since he planned to choose his food items from the buffet. *If we were married, there isn't anything I wouldn't do for Belinda. I'd take her anywhere she wanted to go and buy her whatever she asked for.*

"How was your day?" Belinda asked, pushing Monroe's thoughts aside.

He looked away from the menu and put his focus on her. "It went well in the store during the morning hours when I was there. I didn't go in this afternoon, though, because I had some important things to do in town."

Their waitress came to take their orders, and Monroe told her he'd be going to the buffet. "How about you, Belinda?"

"I'll do the same."

After the waitress took their beverage orders, Monroe looked at Belinda and posed another question. "How'd your Friday evening plans go?"

Belinda tipped her head as she gave several rapid blinks. "My plans?"

"Jah. When I asked you to go out to supper with me, I mentioned doing it on Friday, remember?"

She nodded.

"Then when you said you had plans to have supper with Herschel that night, I suggested Saturday."

A rosy blush erupted on Belinda's cheeks. "Oh, umm. . .yes. . .my plans went okay."

Monroe balled his fingers into the palms of his hands beneath the table. *She's not going to tell me how her date went yesterday with Herschel. I'm thinking maybe it didn't go so well and she'll have a better time with me.*

"Shall we pray before we go to the buffet or would you prefer we wait until we come back to the table?" Belinda's question halted Monroe's contemplations.

"We can do it when we return to the table."

Belinda slid over and got up from the bench, and Monroe did the same. He decided not to say anything more about Friday night, because he didn't want her to know how jealous he felt.

Monroe smoothed the front of his black vest. *I will, however, whenever the opportunity affords itself, let it be known to my competitor that I'm the better man for Belinda. Herschel just needs to step aside.*

Chapter 21

Strasburg

The following Friday, Belinda woke up to the sound of a rooster crowing as daylight approached. Tonight Herschel would be coming over for supper, and she hoped things would go well. Jared and Amy planned to come over as well. Of course, since Amy would be watching Allen and Rachel while Sylvia helped in the greenhouse today, she'd already be at the house, so Jared would join her once he finished working for the day.

Belinda looked forward to having most of her family for a meal. Her only concern was whether she'd done the right thing by being so bold and inviting Herschel. He might take it wrong and think she was interested in him, which was ridiculous. Or was it? She had enjoyed his company last week—more so than she was willing to admit.

Belinda climbed out of bed and ambled over to the window to lift the shade. The sun peeked through the clouds, signaling a new day was about to begin.

Belinda remained at the window for a few minutes, reflecting on her supper date with Monroe. The evening had gone better than expected, and she had no complaints. The only thing that concerned her about seeing Monroe socially was the fact that he'd made it clear he had a personal interest in her. By agreeing to go out with him, he may have seen it as an encouragement on her part.

She touched her warm cheeks. *Oh dear, what have I done? There's no way I can go back and undo it, so I may as well put the matter aside and go forward from here.* The only problem was that part of going forward involved cooking and sharing another meal with Herschel. *After tonight, though, I won't take things any further by going anywhere socially with either of the men.* She bobbed her head. *That definitely seems like the smartest thing to do.*

Around noon, before Belinda went up to the house to get lunch, she made a trek down the driveway to the mailbox. She'd no more than retrieved a pile of envelopes from the box when she saw her neighbor preparing to cross the street.

Belinda waved, before thumbing through her mail, and was reminded that she still hadn't invited Virginia and Earl to their home for a meal. It wasn't like Belinda to make a promise and not follow through, and she felt guilty about it.

I need to extend an invitation to them now. Belinda waited for Virginia to cross the road, and then she approached her. "Good morning, Virginia. How are you and your husband doing?"

"We're gettin' along okay." Her dangling butterfly earrings twinkled in the sunlight while she pulled each envelope from her mailbox.

"Are you enjoying the beautiful spring weather we've been blessed with this week?"

"It's all right. Better than harsh winds, rain, or cold snow of winter. Makes me shiver just to think about it."

"I agree. I've always preferred warmer weather." Belinda took a few steps closer. "I was wondering if you and your husband might be free to come to our house for supper one evening next week."

Virginia looked at her with an incredulous stare. "Seriously?"

"Yes. I've wanted us to get together ever since you moved here, but our life gets so busy, and I've kept putting it off. Is there an evening that might work for you?"

Virginia dropped her gaze to the mail in her hands. "I. . .uh. . . would need to talk to my husband about it, so I can't give you an answer right now."

"That's perfectly understandable. Once you've had a chance to discuss it with him, would you please let me know?"

"Yeah, sure, I'll be in touch." Virginia looked both ways and made her way back across the street.

Belinda shut and locked her mailbox door and headed up the

driveway. Now that she'd finally extended an invitation to supper, she hoped her neighbors would be able to come.

"Well, if that don't beat all," Virginia muttered. "Sure never expected to get an invite to the Kings' for a meal. I wonder what brought that on anyway. If they didn't care enough about me and Earl to invite us to their daughter's wedding last fall, why would Belinda want us to eat a meal with them now?"

Virginia looked down at Goldie, curled up on the throw rug in front of the sink. The cat had followed Virginia to the kitchen after she'd come back with the mail.

Virginia put the stack of envelopes and advertising flyers on the counter and took a seat at the table to drink a cup of coffee.

Maybe I should give Earl a call and see what he thinks about the supper invitation. He will probably think it's pretty strange to be getting an invite now, after living across the street from that Amish family all these months. She blew on her coffee and took a cautious drink. *I bet Belinda only asked out of obligation, or maybe it was a spur of the moment decision.*

Virginia picked up her cell phone and punched in Earl's number. It rang several times before he answered.

"Hey, Earl, it's me. Guess what happened when I went out to get the mail a short time ago?"

"I have no idea, but unless it's something critical, I don't have time to talk. A customer walked in a few minutes ago and I need to speak to him before I lose a potential sale."

Virginia took another drink from her cup; this time without blowing and she burned her tongue. "Ouch!"

"What's wrong, Virginia?"

She grimaced. "Burned my tongue on some hot coffee."

"You shoulda blown on it first."

"I did when I took my first sip, but then I—"

"Gotta go, Virginia. We can talk later, when I get home from work." Earl hung up without saying goodbye.

Virginia pressed her lips together and frowned. "I don't want to wait till you get home, Earl. I wanted to talk now!"

"Now that you're here, and there's food on the table, can I tell you what I called about earlier?" Virginia tapped her husband's shoulder.

"Go right ahead." Earl reached for the bowl of spaghetti and plopped a good-sized mound on his plate. Following that, he sprinkled a hefty amount of Parmesan cheese over the top.

"I saw Belinda King this afternoon, when we were getting our mail."

His eyebrows squished together. "Was that worth bothering me when I was at work?"

"You don't understand. There's more."

Earl grabbed two slices of sourdough bread and slathered them with butter. "Go ahead."

Virginia told him about the supper invitation for one night next week. "Now isn't that something, Earl? I mean, we've been living here all this time, and never once have they invited us for a meal. They didn't even have the decency to include us in one of the suppers following Amy and Jared's wedding."

"Not that again. You shouldn't hold it against them, because you may have misunderstood when Jared said we'd get an invitation."

"I did not!" Virginia's posture stiffened as she scrunched her napkin into a tight ball. "But all that aside, I just don't get why Belinda would want us to come for supper now. Does she really believe we would be willing to go over there and be all neighborly with them?"

"I think it's a great idea. I hope you told her we'd come." Earl dipped a piece of bread in the spaghetti sauce and took a bite.

"You can't be serious." She frowned at him. "After the way those people have treated us, and you think we should go over there and play nicey-nice?"

"Yep."

"What for? You know I'm not comfortable around those Plain folks—we have nothing in common at all." Her lower lip protruded. "I wish Stella could come visit me again."

"Now, where did that comment come from?"

"Don't you remember, Earl, how interested she was in those Amish people? Stella was excited about the prospect of going with us to the wedding across the street. I bet she'd be just as thrilled to come with us on an invite into their home for dinner."

"I don't see how that's gonna happen. Stella can't come racing out here on a moment's notice."

"You never know. Maybe she could. I'll call and let her know of our plans. I will just say to Stella, 'It's too bad you can't be here when we hang out with the Amish and enjoy their home-cooked dinner.'"

"You should drop the silly notion of including your friend, because she was not invited." Earl spun a good-sized amount of spaghetti onto his fork and shoved it into his mouth.

"Like I said before, I have nothing in common with them. Besides, they make me feel uncomfortable."

"It would be rude not to accept their invitation," Earl mumbled around his mouthful of spaghetti.

She shook her finger in his direction. "Didn't your mother teach you that it's not polite to talk with your mouth full?"

"She tried, but I'm not a kid anymore, so I'll do as I please." Earl swiped his napkin across his lips, then picked up his glass of water and took a drink. "So what'd you tell the neighbor lady?"

"I said I'd need to speak with you."

"And now that you have, you can graciously let her know that we'd like to come, and find out what day and time." He bit off a piece of his bread. "Also, you might ask if there's anything we can bring."

Virginia's shoulders curled forward. Her chest felt like it was ready to cave in. The last thing she wanted to do was share a meal in that Amish home. Virginia wished her friend could be there, but Earl had poured cold water all over the topic, so she'd let the matter go. There was no telling what kind of weird thing they might be expected to eat at the Kings' house though. *And, oh my. . . What in the world will there be to talk about?*

With her appetite all but gone, Virginia rubbed her forehead and thought once more, *I wish we had never moved here.*

Monroe had left his store early, planning to stop by Belinda's place to ask her a question. If he could catch her before she started supper, she might agree to go out for another meal with him. He felt that the more time he spent with Belinda, the better his chance would be of winning her over.

I deserve a second chance with her, he told himself as he guided his horse and buggy up the Kings' driveway. *I'll buy her gifts, butter up to her family, and do whatever it takes till she finally agrees to become my fraa.*

When Monroe stepped onto the porch, a delicious aroma wafted out the partially open kitchen window. He couldn't be certain, but it smelled like baked cabbage rolls, one of his favorite meals. Belinda or her daughter must have started fixing supper.

His lips pressed tightly into a grimace. *I should have gotten here sooner.* Then another thought popped into Monroe's head. *If I knock on the door, and Belinda invites me in, I'll mention how good the food she has cooking smells.* Monroe smiled. *Then maybe Belinda will be kind enough to invite me to join her family for the meal.*

With that decided, Monroe rapped on the door. When no one answered, he knocked again, a little louder this time.

Soon the door swung open and Sylvia greeted him. "Hello, Monroe. What can I do for you this evening?"

"Uh nothing, I came to say hello to your mamm."

"She's in the kitchen."

"Okay, guess I can talk to her there."

Sylvia led the way, and after Monroe entered the kitchen, he spotted Belinda in front of the sink, peeling potatoes.

"You have a visitor, Mom," Sylvia announced.

Belinda turned, and when she looked at him, her head jerked back slightly. "Oh, it's you, Monroe. I thought. . ." Her voice trailed off.

He took a few steps toward her and gave a wide smile. "I came by to see if you'd be free to go out for supper with me." Monroe gestured to the potatoes. "But I can see that you've already started fixing your meal. Truth is I could smell the delicious aroma from outside."

Her slightly pink cheeks turned a deep red. "We have company coming for supper soon, so Sylvia and I have been busy trying to get everything ready before their arrival."

He dipped his head slightly. "Oh, I see." Since it sounded like more than one person would be coming, they probably wouldn't want to include one more, so Monroe decided not to try and wangle an invitation to join them. It would seem too pushy and might not set well with

Belinda. He needed to stay on her good side, no matter what.

"I'd best be on my way now, but would there be an evening next week when we could go out to a restaurant again?" he asked.

Belinda glanced at her daughter, and then looked back at Monroe. "Next week is pretty full for me. I'm sorry, Monroe."

"Oh, I see." His gaze flicked upward as he tried to hide the disappointment he felt. Was she looking for an excuse not to go out with him? He turned toward the door. "I'll check back with you in a few weeks. Have a nice evening, ladies."

Monroe barely heard their response as he rushed out the door with his ears ringing. "One step forward and two back," he mumbled. "Something needs to change, because this isn't working out the way I want."

When Monroe headed down the driveway in his rig, another horse and buggy pulled in. He was stunned to see that the driver was none other than Herschel Fisher.

Monroe clenched his teeth. *So Herschel gets an invitation to supper, but I'm left out? What's up with that anyway?*

He snapped the reins and got his horse moving at a good clip. *For ten cents, I'd turn right around and have a talk with that man.*

Chapter 22

As Herschel began his approach to Belinda's house, he felt less nervous than when he'd taken her out to eat. It was either because he'd become more comfortable in her presence or the fact that this evening they wouldn't be in a public place where someone they knew might see them and start a round of gossip. As it was, when Herschel told his folks of his plans, he'd asked them not to mention it to anyone. News traveled fast in Lancaster County, and Herschel didn't want to put Belinda or himself in a position to answer a bunch of curious questions. If and when a stronger relationship developed, he wouldn't care if word got out that an old widower, pretty much set in his ways, and a lovely middle-aged widow lady had begun courting.

Herschel snorted. Since Mattie died, in his wildest dreams, he'd never considered the idea of courting anyone else. But after getting to know Belinda better, a spark had ignited, and the thought of seeing her more often was quite appealing. He hoped she felt the same way about being with him.

After setting the brake, Herschel stepped down from his buggy and tied the horse to the hitching rail. *I wonder what topics of conversation will be discussed this evening or what Belinda has fixed for supper.* He hoped the evening would turn out well and that he wouldn't mess up and say something wrong.

He patted his horse and looked up toward the house with its pretty baskets of hanging flowers. *Come on, Herschel, don't overthink things. All you need to concern yourself about is trying to relax and having a nice time.*

As Herschel moved swiftly across the lawn, Henry rounded the corner with his dog at his side. One look at Herschel and the animal rushed toward him, barking and wagging his tail.

Henry clapped his hands and hollered, "Blackie, you come back here, right now!"

Herschel chuckled when the dog stopped in front of him and pawed at his pant leg. No sign of viciousness here. Blackie clearly demanded some attention.

Herschel bent down and patted the dog's head. "Hey, Blackie. Nice to meet you." He looked up at Henry and smiled, despite the young man's scowl. "Your hund's a nice-looking Lab. Have you taught him to do any tricks?"

"A few." Henry barely made eye contact with Herschel.

"Wanna show me?"

Henry shrugged. "Don't know if he would be willing. Looks like he'd rather be petted right now, but I guess I could try."

Herschel straightened to his full height.

"Okay, Blackie, now do what I say." Henry called the dog and told him to sit. Blackie hesitated at first, but then did as the boy had asked.

"Du bescht en schmaerder buh." Herschel pointed at the dog.

"He's only a smart fellow when he feels like it, or if he thinks I have a treat waiting for him."

Blackie nuzzled Henry's hand. "See what I mean?"

Herschel nodded. "Yep. He's one *schmaert* hund."

"Yeah, but my mutt took off yesterday morning, and I ended up chasing him clear up to old Maude's shanty." Henry frowned. "Had to practically drag him home."

"Who's old Maude?" Herschel asked.

"She's a weird lady who lives in a shack up the road most of the year. Maude vacates the place during the cold winter months, but we don't know where she goes." Henry reached under the brim of his hat and rubbed his forehead. "She's taken some things from our yard and even the greenhouse before. I don't trust her at all."

"Has your mamm called the authorities?"

Henry shook his head. "Naw, she thinks Maude is harmless and has even given her food, not to mention two hinkel."

"Were the pieces of chicken fried or baked?"

"Neither. They were alive when Maude snatched them out of our coop. When we discovered that the old woman had the laying hens,

Mom said she could keep them." Henry shrugged. "Maude probably thinks the chickens will lay enough eggs to provide for her breakfasts, but I'm sure she'll be back here again sometime, looking for something else to steal."

Herschel wasn't sure how to respond. If Belinda had no problem with the old woman taking without asking, there wasn't much he could say about it. She might not appreciate him butting in.

"Something smells mighty good coming from the house." Herschel pointed to the partially open kitchen window from where the aroma wafted toward them.

"Yeah. Mom made cabbage rolls for supper, and I guess we'd better get inside, 'cause I think it must be about ready. First though, I need to put Blackie in his pen. Otherwise, he's likely to wander off again." Henry called his dog and the animal went obediently with him.

Herschel watched as they approached the dog's pen. *Should I go knock on the door or wait for Henry?* He decided on the latter and took a seat in one of the wicker chairs on the front porch.

The cloudless spring evening gave way to the dimming blue sky. It seemed so serene and quiet outside. Herschel looked toward the tilled garden with its deep brown soil and rows of rich green plants. He then surveyed the layout of the property. Everything seemed well thought out.

Herschel pulled a mint candy from his pocket and pulled off the wrapper. *It can't be easy for Belinda and her family to stay up with all this work, plus keep the greenhouse running.*

When Henry returned a few minutes later, he paused by the chair and looked down at Herschel with a quizzical expression. "How come you're sittin' out here? Figured you would have gone inside."

"I could have, but I thought it was best to wait for you. Plus I was admiring how nice your family keeps this place up."

"Oh, I see." Henry grabbed hold of the doorknob. "Let's go in then. I'm *hungerich.*"

As he followed the boy, Herschel heard one of the children asking in Pennsylvania Dutch if they could have milk with their supper. *That does sound good. When I was a boy, I used to drink milk with my suppers.* Herschel had to admit, with that great smell coming from the kitchen, he too was hungry. And he was glad Belinda's son had warmed up to him just a bit.

Belinda greeted Herschel when he and Henry entered the house and suggested they both take a seat in the living room. "Just make yourself comfortable, Herschel," she said. "We'll eat as soon as Dennis and Jared arrive."

"Sure."

Belinda waited until Henry and Herschel headed for the living room before she returned to the kitchen to help her daughters with the final supper preparations.

She pulled the large baking pan from the hot oven. *This is the first time I'm having Herschel over to my house. I hope he's comfortable and will enjoy the meal we've prepared.* Belinda opened the lid to check the contents which looked nicely done, and then she placed the container on top on the stove.

It wasn't long before Jared showed up, and a few minutes later Dennis arrived. While Sylvia rounded up her children, Amy went out to the living room to let the men know they could wash up and join them in the dining room.

Everyone had barely taken their seats around the table and were about to bow their heads for prayer when a knock sounded on the front door.

"Would you like me to see who it is?" Jared directed his question to Belinda.

"Yes, please. We'll wait to pray until you come back."

"Okay."

When Jared reappeared a few minutes later with Monroe at his side, Belinda's eyes widened. Since he'd been here a short time ago, she couldn't figure out why he'd come back.

"Sorry to interrupt your meal, folks, but after I left here earlier, I got to thinking that I must have dropped my *backebuch* in your yard somewhere because it was no longer in my pocket." He shifted his weight from one foot to the other. "So I came on back to look for it, and lo and behold, I discovered the billfold not far from the hitching rail."

Belinda's mind felt a bit fuzzy. *If Monroe came back to look for his wallet and he found it, why'd he feel it was necessary to come up to the house and tell us about it?*

As though he could read her thoughts, Monroe looked right at Belinda and said: "I figured I should come on up to the house to let you know in case someone saw me outside and wondered what I was up to."

"Although it wasn't necessary, danki for letting me know." Belinda tapped her foot under the table. The food was getting cold, and they still hadn't prayed, but she couldn't come right out and ask him to leave.

Monroe sniffed deeply and made a sweeping gesture of the table. "Looks like you're all in for a real treat 'cause those cabbage rolls, and everything else, sure look and smell good."

Belinda's tapping foot went suddenly still. With Monroe standing there with a hungry expression, she could hardly do anything but invite him to join them.

"Umm. . .would you like to join us?" The words almost stuck in her throat.

"Jah, that would be nice, but I don't want to intrude."

"It's fine, really." Without bothering to suggest that he might want to wash up first, Belinda pointed to an empty chair. She just wanted to get on with their meal. "Please, take a seat, Monroe."

A big grin spread across his face as he lowered himself into the chair. Then all heads bowed for silent prayer.

Bless this food and all who sit around my table, Belinda prayed. *And, Lord, please help this evening to go well and pass quickly. Amen.*

After everyone's prayer had been said, the meal began with the passing of bowls and dishes. Monroe took over the conversation almost immediately. Herschel, feeling quite anxious since Monroe had showed up, quickly realized that he'd lost his appetite. He could see by the sappy look Monroe gave Belinda that the overly talkative man most definitely had a keen interest in her.

So now that I'm aware of my competition, I need to figure out what to do about it. Herschel picked up his fork, stabbed one of the cabbage rolls, and put it on his plate. *Would it be best to back off, or should I keep pursuing Belinda and hope that I'm the one she chooses? Of course,* he reasoned, *she may not be interested in either me or Monroe. The invitation I received to join Belinda and her family at this table may only have been made because she's such a nice woman or felt like she owed me the favor because I treated her to supper at a restaurant.*

As the meal came to a close and dessert was served, Monroe became even more obnoxious. Herschel couldn't believe what a braggart the man was, especially when it came to his furniture business.

"Of course," Monroe said with a smug expression, "I've always had a good business head. Fact of the matter—my goal is to own several businesses, which will secure a strong financial future for me and the woman I will marry someday." He looked at Belinda and gave her another sappy grin.

Herschel nearly choked on his piece of shoofly pie. There was no doubt in his mind. Monroe had his sights set on marrying Belinda.

His jaw clenched. *And I guess there isn't much I can do about it. The question is: Does she feel the same way about him?*

As the evening progressed, Belinda's anxiety had advanced to the state of near exhaustion. She couldn't help wondering how the evening would have gone if it had only been Herschel and her family there. *I wish it would've been just him. I'm the one who initiated the invite for Herschel to come over this evening—unlike Monroe, who hadn't been invited at all.*

Belinda went into her room and closed the door. *I felt like Monroe made it impossible for me to say no. I should've gotten up from my seat first thing, led him out to the front door, and sent him on his way.* She felt sure that if Monroe had not been there things would have gone better. Not only had he monopolized all of her time, but poor Herschel had barely gotten a few words in to express his appreciation for the meal. He'd been the first one to leave, and Monroe was the last person out the door. Before he left, he'd mentioned taking Belinda out for supper again. She'd politely said she wouldn't be free anytime soon and told him goodnight.

Now, as Belinda sat on the edge of her bed, she reflected on other things that had gone on this evening. The situation reminded Belinda of her younger days when she was being courted by Monroe and Vernon had come into the picture. She hadn't wanted to hurt Monroe, but her heart lay with Vernon. Fortunately that wasn't the case this time, as she felt no romantic love for Herschel or Monroe. It would take time to get better acquainted with each of them, and Belinda wasn't in any rush to remarry, which meant that she was in control. It didn't make it any easier, though, since both men were obviously interested in her. On top of that, Henry had been even more sullen than usual this evening. No doubt he didn't approve of either man.

Oh my. . . Belinda lay back on the bed. *What am I supposed to do? I don't want to hurt Monroe or Herschel, but I can't allow either of them to think they have a chance at a relationship with me,* she reminded herself. *I can't accept any more supper invitations from either of them, nor will I extend an invitation for them to join us for a meal here. I have to nip this in the bud now, before it gets out of hand.*

Chapter 23

When Belinda stepped into the greenhouse the following morning, she was greeted with a pretty sight. A whole row of impatiens bloomed brightly. It was a cheery display, in spite of the uncertainty hovering over her.

Since only she and her eldest daughter were in the building at the moment, Belinda motioned for Sylvia to step behind the counter with her. While Henry was tending the beehives, she would take this opportunity to talk to Sylvia without anyone listening.

"What is it, Mom?" Sylvia questioned. "Is there something specific you need me to do here today?"

"No, I wanted to talk to you about last night but didn't want to say anything at breakfast, especially since Henry was there and would no doubt want to put in his two cents' worth."

Sylvia placed a hand on Belinda's arm. "What's wrong? You look so serious right now. Has more vandalism been done?"

Belinda shook her head as she took a seat on the wooden stool. "It's about Monroe and Herschel and their behavior last night. I wish I hadn't invited either of them to join us for supper." She released a heavy sigh. "It was a big mistake."

Sylvia's dark brows lifted. "Both men are obviously smitten with you, although they each show it in different ways." She emitted a giggle behind her hand.

"It's not funny." Belinda groaned. "I couldn't believe their expressions every time I spoke to one of them. You'd think I was some prize to be won."

Sylvia laughed a little louder this time. "You'll have to admit, it is a little funny. I mean, when was the last time you had two men vying for your attention?"

"When I was a young woman being courted by Monroe, and then your daed came along and swept me right off my feet." Belinda gave a quick shake of her head as her face heated. "I was flattered back then and felt quite special, but now at my age, it's embarrassing." She glanced at the door to be sure no one had come in and then looked back at Sylvia. "I need to put a stop to this nonsense before it gets any worse."

"Why would you need to stop it, Mom?" Sylvia questioned. "Why not just enjoy the attention you're getting from Herschel and Monroe. If you spend more time with both of the men, you may come to realize that you care deeply for one of them." She wrinkled her nose. "Although, I can't imagine you falling in love with Monroe. He's too full of *hochmut*, always bragging about himself and his accomplishments."

Belinda's head moved up and down. "He's always been that way, even when we were teenagers. But Monroe does have a certain charm. He's adventurous and says nice things to me." She paused and touched her hot cheeks. "I can't believe I'm admitting this, but I feel youthful when Monroe's around."

"And Herschel? How do you feel when you're with him?"

"Herschel is the quiet type, but he's kind and gentle. I feel relaxed when I'm with him."

"Would you like my advice?"

"Certainly."

"If I were you, with one man making me feel relaxed and the other giving me the feeling of being young again, I'd make an effort to spend time with them both—at different times, of course. That's the only way you'll ever reach a decision about which man is right for you."

"There's one problem with that, Daughter. I don't want a serious relationship with Herschel, Monroe, or any other man. I'm content being a mudder and a *grossmammi*. I don't need a romantic relationship."

"Are you sure about that?"

Belinda gave a decisive nod. "I think it's best if I don't see Monroe or Herschel socially any longer."

Sylvia opened her mouth, as if to say something more, but when the bell tinkled above the greenhouse door, she pointed and mouthed the word, "Monroe."

Belinda turned in that direction. *Oh dear. This is not what I need this morning.*

When Monroe walked toward the counter, Sylvia moved away. "I'm going to put out some of the new potholders I made on display, but I'll be available to assist any customers who may come in needing assistance."

"Sounds good. Danki, Sylvia." Belinda turned her attention to Monroe. "Good morning. May I help you with something?"

"I don't need anything from the greenhouse," he replied. "I came by to say how much I enjoyed being with you and your family last night, and I'd like to return the favor."

Belinda gave a brief shake of her head. "As I told you last night, there's no need for that. Besides, I'm going to be quite busy for the next several weeks." She released a frustrated breath. *This man is so persistent. I don't want to be rude to him, but I'll need to figure out a way to deal with his exuberance.*

"Then tell me what you'd like from one of the restaurants that does take-out orders, and I'll bring a meal to you one evening."

"There's no need for that, Monroe. Sylvia and I don't mind cooking."

"But I must insist. It's the least I can do to repay your kindness."

Belinda's resolve weakened. "All right, Monroe, I accept your offer."

He gave her a wide grin. "How about if I bring a couple of pizzas over to your house tonight? Would six o'clock be a good time?"

"That'll be fine. I will see you then." Belinda gestured to the English couple who'd come into the greenhouse. "If you'll excuse me, I need to see what my customers want."

"Sure, no problem. See you this evening, Belinda." With a spring in his step, Monroe left the building.

I hope I haven't made a mistake. Belinda bit the inside of her cheek. *But as Sylvia mentioned, I really haven't given Monroe or Herschel a fair chance. I suppose it's possible that after some time, I might develop feelings for one of them.*

Shaking her troubling thoughts aside, Belinda stepped out from behind the counter and went up to her customers. "Are you looking for anything in particular?"

"We saw your sign along the road and thought we'd pop in for a look around."

"That's good. If you have any questions, don't hesitate to let me know."

The woman appeared to be a tourist, carrying a camera in one hand, while the man munched on a soft pretzel. Belinda saw the wedding bands on their fingers and guessed they were married. It wasn't uncommon for the curious English to visit her greenhouse, and they were usually full of questions. She and Vernon had plenty of years dealing with English folks who came in to look around or snap photos without asking.

Belinda returned to her place behind the counter and watched the couple chatting away as they looked at the plants. She wondered what they might be talking about as she got out a rag and cleaned off some soil from the counter. The two of them made their way over to the gifts, looking at Sylvia's homemade pot holders and some other things. Soon they brought up a few items, setting them near the register.

"I have a question," the woman said.

Belinda could only guess what that might be as she rang up each item. "What is it you'd like to know?"

"Are there other Amish businesses in this area?" She reached into her purse and took out a wallet. "My husband thought I should ask you since we are from out of town."

Belinda pointed north. "There's a shoe shop down this road about a mile. Beyond that is an Amish-owned furniture store, but they do sell other things there as well."

"Good to know. My husband and I will have to go by there and check them out." She handed Belinda the money to pay for her purchases.

"My wife will no doubt want to return to this area sometime in the future. She's fascinated by the Amish culture and has a good many questions," the man interjected.

His wife blushed as Belinda bagged up the items she'd purchased. "I can't help it. Your Plain ways are intriguing to me. I'm especially fascinated with your mode of transportation and how you get around with a horse and buggy."

"It's part of our heritage," Belinda responded.

"It is certainly an interesting way of life."

The couple stepped away from the counter, but the wife turned back around. "Thank you for telling me about other Amish businesses that are nearby. And by the way, you have a nice greenhouse here." She looked at her husband. "If I didn't have to put my things into a suitcase for our flight home, I'd be tempted to pick out some plants here today."

Belinda watched as the man and his wife left the building. *Sylvia will be happy when she finds out that some of her pot holders sold. No doubt, she'll get busy making more.*

Virginia put on a heavy sweater, picked up her cane, and went out the front door. She dreaded going across the road to speak with Belinda King, and even more so this morning, since her bum leg was acting up.

"I don't see why Earl insisted that we accept Belinda's supper invitation," Virginia muttered as she stood on her side of the street, waiting for a horse and buggy to pass. The thought of spending an evening with the King clan caused a tingling sensation in her chest. It would be a miracle if she made it through the ordeal.

Virginia looked both ways before crossing the road. As she made her way slowly up the driveway, a car passed her, coming down from the direction of the greenhouse.

She clenched her teeth. *I hope there aren't a bunch of customers milling around the building right now. I just want to say a few words to Belinda and get out of there as quickly as possible.*

When Virginia entered the building a few minutes later, she spotted Belinda's oldest daughter sitting behind the front counter but saw no sign of Belinda.

"Is your mother here?" Virginia asked.

The dark-haired woman, whose name Virginia did not recall, shook her head. "Not at the moment. She went up to our house to get something. Is there anything I can help you with, Virginia?"

"Umm. . . I came over to speak with your mother."

"You can either wait here for her or go on up to the house."

"Think I'll wait outside on the bench I saw in the area where you sell birdbaths and other yard decorations." Virginia shuffled out the door and made her way over to the bench. She'd only been sitting a few minutes when the old woman, Maude, came along and stopped in front of the bench Virginia sat upon. "Whatcha doin'?" She pointed a bony finger at Virginia.

"I'm waiting to speak to Mrs. King." *Not that it's any of your business.*

"She's probably in there." Maude gestured to the greenhouse.

"Not at the moment, but she should be back soon."

Maude folded her arms and took a seat next to Virginia. "Guess I'll wait here too."

How nice. The last thing I need is some nosey old lady sitting beside me. Virginia shifted to the far side of the bench. *If Belinda doesn't show up soon I'll go back inside the greenhouse and wait for her there. I'd go up to the house like her daughter suggested, but the unkempt woman next to me would probably follow.*

"Where ya from?" Maude asked.

"My husband and I live across the street."

"No, I meant where'd ya live before you moved here?"

"Chicago." Virginia's lips pressed together. *I wish she'd stop asking me questions.*

Maude reached into her coat pocket and pulled out a partial roll of toilet paper. She then proceeded to pull off a few pieces and blew her nose.

After watching the old woman toss the pieces on the ground, Virginia grimaced. *Surely there has to be a trash can around. If not, then Maude should have put the pieces she used to blow her nose in another pocket to dispose of when she got home. If that old shack she lives in could even be called a home.*

"You come here often?" The old woman's question pulled Virginia out of her musings.

"Sometimes."

"I come here a lot. I like to get things from the woman who runs this place." Maude looked at Virginia with furrowed brows. "I think she feels sorry for me, but I don't need no one's pity. I've been on my own ever since. . ." Maude stopped talking when Belinda approached.

"Good morning, ladies." Belinda gave them a pleasant smile. "I'm surprised to see you sitting outside on this chilly spring day."

"I've been waiting to talk to you." Virginia stood up.

"Certainly. Should we go inside, or would you rather have our conversation out here?"

"I'd prefer to speak to you in private." Virginia was not about to talk to Belinda in front of Maude. The old woman didn't need to hear anything they said.

"Okay, I can take a hint. You can have my seat here." Maude got up and ambled into the greenhouse.

Once Belinda was seated on the bench, Virginia got right to the point. She had no plans of sticking around here any longer than necessary.

"I came to tell you that my husband said we will be able to come for supper whatever evening is convenient for you."

"Would Friday at six o'clock be okay?"

"Yes, and is there anything I can bring?"

Belinda shook her head. "Just a good appetite. There will be plenty of food."

"Okay, we'll see you at six then." Virginia stood, and as she headed out of the parking lot, a busload of tourists pulled in. *I sure don't understand what the big attraction is for these English people. I wonder what any of them would say if they knew Earl and I will be eating supper this Friday with the Amish family who run the greenhouse.* Her chin jutted out. *Makes no sense to me, but I bet they'd be jealous.*

"Each to his own, I guess," Virginia mumbled as she made her way across the street. *All those crazy tourists may be fascinated with the Amish people, but not me. I just want to live a peaceful life without all the bad odors their horses put out, not to mention the disturbing noise.*

Chapter 24

Gordonville

Herschel sat in his office at the bulk-food store, eating a sandwich and thinking about how Monroe had showed up at Belinda's last evening, right when they were getting ready to eat.

That man is so full of hochmut, Herschel fumed. *I hope Belinda isn't taken in by him. Even if she isn't interested in me, she deserves better than a braggart like Monroe.*

He shifted his arm to the right and knocked a stack of papers off the desk. "If this is how my afternoon is starting, then I'm in for a tough time." Herschel groaned as he bent over to pick up the mess he'd made. *Monroe may have more money than me, but that doesn't mean he's a happier man. Some Bible verses talk about a person's riches and pride getting the best of them.*

Herschel's half-eaten roast beef sandwich beckoned him to eat. As he began to chew, his mind conjured up questions. *Do I have any chance to win Belinda from Monroe? Can I let myself envision us together as Mr. and Mrs. Herschel Fisher?*

It would be a challenge to go up against Monroe. Not quite like David and Goliath, because from what Herschel had learned, this fellow had been turned down by Belinda before, and she'd married the other guy. But now that Monroe had money and made it apparent to anyone who would listen, maybe Belinda would consider him the right man to make her happy.

Herschel couldn't forget how thick Monroe poured it on while discussing his accomplishments during supper. All the guy did was dominate each topic, and it seemed like he wanted to be the first to respond to every comment.

Herschel nearly choked on his last bite of food, thinking about the pride Monroe emitted. *How does Belinda put up with him? I can't imagine her liking that guy's personality. But if she does, I'm in trouble.*

Herschel felt like giving up, but as he mulled things over, he reached a decision. He would wait a few weeks and then invite Belinda out for supper again. If she turned him down without a valid excuse, Herschel would take it as a sign that she wasn't interested in him and bow out graciously. But if Belinda said yes and they had another pleasant evening together, Herschel would continue to pursue a relationship with her.

Strasburg

When Sylvia came into the house to take her turn at fixing something to eat for her lunch, she found Amy washing dishes.

"Have you and the kinner eaten already?" Sylvia asked.

"Jah, and they're both playing quietly in the living room right now." Amy gestured to the refrigerator. "Would you like me to fix you a ham and cheese sandwich?"

"No, that's okay. I can fend for myself. Besides, you probably need to take a break about now."

"I'm fine, really."

Sylvia opened the refrigerator and took out what she needed. "When I was pregnant with my little ones, I tired easily—more so with Rachel, since Allen was a toddler and always into things. Ever since my son learned to walk, he's kept me busy."

Amy chuckled. "He's a livewire, all right. Always full of energy and eager to investigate things."

"Jah, but he's never gone out of the yard with a stranger, the way Rachel did last year." Sylvia set her sandwich makings on the table. "She sure gave us a scare, and it was even more frightening when Dennis and I found her inside Maude's rundown shack."

"That woman had some nerve taking your daughter out of the yard. If it had been my daughter, I would have reported the incident to the sheriff." Amy tapped the side of her head. "I believe that old woman might be a bit touched."

"She is a strange one all right."

"Our mamm's always been good to Maude though."

Sylvia nodded. "Speaking of Mom, she and I talked privately this morning, before any customers showed up at the greenhouse."

"About the business?"

"No, it concerned Herschel and Monroe."

Amy dried her hands and took a seat at the table. "Sounds interesting. Would you mind filling me in on what was said?"

"Not at all." Sylvia sat in the chair opposite her sister, and as she prepared her sandwich, she told Amy everything their mother had said.

Amy's brows went up. "And so it begins."

"What begins?"

"The race between the two men who are smitten with our mamm, to see who will win the prize." Amy snickered. "Never thought I'd see the day."

"Me neither."

"Who do you think will win Mom's hand?"

"Maybe neither. Mom says she's not interested in getting remarried, but she also said she would be open to seeing both men, so maybe she'll change her mind."

"Hmm. . ." Amy tapped her fingers on the table's surface.

Sylvia leaned forward. "I know it's wrong of me to dislike someone, but I'm hoping Mom doesn't choose Monroe. In any event, it's our mother's decision." She glanced at Amy, who seemed to be in deep thought. "What are you thinking?"

"Oh nothing, just wondering how we might be able to give Herschel a little edge."

Sylvia took a small intake of breath. "I think it would be best if you didn't meddle. Our mamm's old enough to make her own decisions."

"True, but there's a fifty-fifty chance she might choose Monroe, and those odds could turn in the man's favor because of his strong will to win our Mom. In my opinion, that would be a big mistake."

"Maybe so, but it's still Mom's choice." Sylvia covered two slices of bread with mayonnaise and added a piece of ham. "Speaking of Monroe, he's bringing pizza over here tonight and joining us for supper again."

"Another meal with Monroe carrying on about himself? Can you imagine if he were to become our stepfather?"

"No, I can't." Amy's brows furrowed. "How did this invitation come about?"

"He came by the greenhouse this morning and made the offer. Mom told me about it before I came up to the house." Sylvia added some cheese, lettuce, and a pickle slice to finish off the sandwich. "Why don't you and Jared join us?"

"As much as we enjoy eating pizza, we can't come because we've already accepted a supper invitation for this evening from Jared's parents." Amy gave an unladylike snicker. "Guess you'll get to enjoy Monroe's company without us."

"I'll admit he's not my favorite person, and we both know he's not Henry's either. I really hope if Mom chooses one of the men, that it ends up to be Herschel."

"He has my vote too," Amy agreed. "I'm seeing already that his and Mom's personalities blend better."

Henry sat at the dining-room table, staring at the piece of pepperoni pizza on his plate. Normally he would have gobbled it down, but this evening his stomach churned so badly he didn't think he could take one bite. Henry wished he could excuse himself and head to his room or go out to the loft. Instead, he was stuck here, like Sylvia and the kids, being forced to sit through the meal. Henry still hadn't come up with anything that would pin the vandalism on Monroe, even though he was convinced this man had to be the one behind the damage.

Henry filled his glass with root beer and took a long drink. Setting the glass aside, he glanced out the window facing the front yard. *Maybe someday he'll be told by someone that he needs to stop being so into himself. Why did Mom let Monroe bring pizza over here for supper?* He continued to fume. *Doesn't she care how much I don't like him? Truth be told, unless Sylvia has changed her mind, she doesn't care for Monroe either. I can't figure out why Mom is so kind to him. She's gotta see that he's not as nice as he pretends to be.*

"Business was booming at my furniture store today. The customers commented on what finely crafted furniture I carry."

Monroe's loud voice drew Henry's thoughts aside. He picked up his glass of root beer and took a drink. *At least it was Mom who furnished the cold drink, as well as a tossed green salad, so guess I can eat that.* Henry sat stiffly in his chair. *I won't give that man the satisfaction of knowing pepperoni pizza is my favorite. I sure hope he doesn't stay long tonight.*

When the meal was over, Monroe jumped up and began clearing the table. "I'll put the paper plates and cups in the garbage." He smiled at Belinda. "Since you won't have any dishes to wash, maybe we can go outside and sit awhile. It's the perfect night for stargazing."

"I suppose we could." Belinda looked at Sylvia. "Would you and the kinner like to join us?"

"I need to give them both a bath, and then it'll be time for bed, so why don't you go outside without us?" Sylvia responded.

Belinda had a feeling her son would decline the invite, but she decided to ask him anyway. "How about you, Son? You could bring your binoculars out and—"

"Yeah, that's a good idea. I might see an owl or even a *schpeckmaus*."

Belinda was surprised at her son's positive response, but at the same time she shuddered. "I hope we don't see any bats. I remember once when I was a girl, a bat got in our house and my daed had a terrible time trying to catch it. The whole house was awakened by the time he finally shooed the critter out the door."

Monroe snickered. "The only encounter I've had with a schpeck-maus was during a young people's singing when I visited my cousin Timothy's family up in Perry County one summer." His gaze went to Belinda. "Don't think I ever told you about it, but stop me if you've heard this story."

Belinda listened with interest as Monroe gave a vivid account of a bat swooping into the barn where the singing had been held. She couldn't help but laugh when he ducked his head way down and squealed as he emphasized how some of the young women had reacted to the bat. Sylvia laughed too, which caused Allen and Rachel to laugh. But Henry just sat with a stony expression.

"Did the bat fly out of the barn of its own accord?" Sylvia asked.

He shook his head. "My cousin and a couple other real tall fellows chased after the critter, swatting at it with their straw hats. Then one of 'em knocked the bat to the floor."

"Was it dead?" Belinda questioned.

"Nope, just stunned. After that, using two hats, Timothy scooped up the bat and took him outside."

"What were you doing all that time?" Henry spoke up.

"I was sitting there holding my sides from laughing so hard."

"Figures."

Henry's words were spoken softly, but it didn't keep Belinda from hearing what he said. No doubt Monroe did too. Her son's rude behavior whenever Monroe came around did not set well with her. She would need to speak with Henry about it later.

Monroe turned toward the kitchen. "Guess I'd better get the paper dishes put in the trash so we can head outdoors."

Belinda picked up the silverware and followed.

"Mom's not happy with you. Couldn't you tell by her expression?" Sylvia whispered to Henry.

He folded his arms and frowned. "I'm not happy with her either. She shouldn't have let Monroe bring pizza tonight. He's only after one thing, and I—"

Sylvia put a finger against her lips. "Let's take the kinner into the living room. You can read to Allen while I give Rachel her bath."

"Okay, sure. I have nothin' else to do, and it'll be better than sitting outside looking at the stars and listening to Monroe acting all nicey-nice with Mom." Henry pushed his chair away from the table and trudged into the adjoining room.

"Are you sure?" Sylvia asked. "I thought you were going to take your binoculars out like Mom suggested at supper."

"I changed my mind. Decided to stay in the house to help you, and I'm fine with that."

Once his niece and nephew had been bathed and put to bed, Henry planned to spend the rest of the evening alone in his room.

Monroe sat next to Belinda on the porch swing, tempted to reach for her hand. He remembered their courting days, and how the two of them had sat on her parents' porch with no interruptions. His heart felt full this evening, but he wished he felt free to talk about planning a future with her. The only thing that stood in his way was Herschel. *I'm not going to let him steal my girl the way Vernon did. I'll do whatever it takes to make her mine.*

They visited quietly as the swing moved gently back and forth. Monroe was tempted to lean over and give her a kiss. Instead, he kept his composure and folded his hands in front of him.

A cool breeze came up and Belinda shivered. "Are you cold?" Monroe asked. "We can go back inside if you want."

"I am a bit chilly, but I'm in no hurry to quit looking at the twinkling stars and bright moon." Belinda rose from the swing. "Think I'll go in the house and fetch a jacket to wear over my sweater. Can I get you something to drape over your shoulders?"

"No thanks. I'm fine."

Monroe watched as Belinda went back into the house. She was still a fine looking woman. He pulled his shoulders straight back and looked up at the sky. *I will not give up until she agrees to marry me.*

Chapter 25

Belinda glanced at the clock. In thirty minutes, the greenhouse would close for the day and she could go up to the house. Sylvia had already gone up to help Amy start supper. Virginia and Earl would be joining them for the meal and would be there at six o'clock. Since Belinda had invited Amy and Jared as well as Dennis to join them, there would be eight adults and Sylvia's two children. It would give them all a chance to get to know their neighbors better.

Belinda still felt bad that she'd procrastinated in extending an invitation to the Martins, but it was better to do it now than not at all. She wasn't looking for the neighbors to reciprocate—she simply wanted to do the right thing.

Belinda gazed at the row of indoor plants she had for sale. African violets seemed to be everyone's favorite, but other flowers such as orchids and shamrock plants sold well too.

The local landscaper had come by earlier today and placed another order. At the rate things were going, Belinda might be able to hire someone to either add on to the greenhouse soon or perhaps put up another building. The only problem was more room for items to sell meant more work to be done. Once Sylvia and Dennis got married in early August, Belinda and Henry would be on their own. When Amy's baby was born, she'd be a stay-at-home mother. Unless Sylvia found a sitter for the children or brought them to the greenhouse with her, she wouldn't be helping anymore either.

If anything, I should be downsizing, not thinking of adding on. Belinda sighed deeply. *Maybe I should sell out and move to Clymer to live with Ezekiel and Michelle. Another option would be to ask Ezekiel to move back here to help me run the greenhouse.*

The idea of asking Ezekiel to move from a place where he'd established a new business and seemed content held no appeal for Belinda. Just thinking about it made her stomach clench. *No, I will not ask my son to make that sacrifice. If Henry and I can't handle it on our own, I'll see about hiring someone outside the family to help.*

Belinda heard a horse and buggy pull into the parking area and looked toward the door. *Just what I don't need—a last-minute customer.*

She waited behind the counter, and was surprised when Herschel entered the store.

"Hello, Belinda. How are you doing?" That expected little shy smile formed on his lips as he approached her.

"I'm doing fine. How are you?"

"Doin' all right. I came by, hoping you were still open. I want to get a nice plant or something else for my folk's yard, because today is their sixtieth wedding anniversary."

"That's wonderful. Please relate to them my hearty congratulations."

"I certainly will. I'm taking them out to supper at Shady Maple this evening to celebrate the occasion."

Belinda smiled, remembering back to last April, when her children had surprised her with a birthday supper at Shady Maple in East Earl. She'd been even more surprised when Ezekiel and his family showed up unexpectedly.

"Do you have an idea what you would like to get your parents, or should I offer some suggestions?"

"I don't have a clue what they might like," Herschel admitted, "so I'm open to any ideas."

"Is there a particular flower they favor?"

He shrugged his shoulders.

"Do they like solar lights for the yard?"

Herschel bobbed his head. "As a matter of fact, they do."

"Then how about a pretty metal flower that lights up for your mamm? I also have some metal chickens and ducks your daed may like."

"Those are both good options. Jah, I'd like to take a look at them."

Belinda went out the door with Herschel and walked over to where all the solar lights were displayed. "What do you think of those?" She pointed at the flower and then to one of the chickens.

Herschel bent down to check the prices and announced that he'd take a purple flower for his mother and a large rooster for his father.

Belinda led the way back inside the greenhouse. After Herschel paid for the items, she wrapped each one carefully in bubble wrap and placed them in a cardboard box. Belinda didn't voice her thoughts, but she wished she could be there to see Herschel's parents' reaction to the gifts he'd gotten for them. She'd met his mother, Vera, a few times when she'd come into the greenhouse but had not made his father's acquaintance.

Herschel picked up the box and opened his mouth, like he was about to say something more to Belinda, when Monroe stepped into the greenhouse. It took Belinda by surprise because she hadn't heard his horse and buggy come in. Perhaps he'd pulled his rig in while she and Herschel were outside on the other side of the building, looking at solar lights.

Herschel glanced at Monroe, nodded, and then mumbled to Belinda: "I'd better go." Before she could form a response, he was out the door.

Belinda felt a keen sense of disappointment. She'd hoped to talk with Herschel awhile longer.

Turning her attention to Monroe, Belinda wondered what he was doing here at this late hour. Surely he had to know she would be closing the greenhouse momentarily.

"I'm about to close the greenhouse for the day, but if there is something you need, I can wait a few minutes." Belinda smiled, despite her irritation. *It was nice seeing Herschel and it's too bad our chat got interrupted. Monroe always seems to know when Herschel is here. How can I get better acquainted with Herschel if Monroe keeps dropping in whenever Herschel's here?*

"I realize it's a last-minute invitation again, but I stopped by to see if you might be free to go out for supper with me tonight." He put both hands on his side of the counter and leaned a little closer to her. "Or I could head over to the pizza place and bring supper to you. No doubt after working all day, you're not feeling up to cooking."

"Actually, we have company coming this evening, so I won't be able to see you tonight, Monroe. And as I've stated previously, I would appreciate some advance notice if you want to include me in your plans."

"Sorry. It was a spur-of-the-moment decision." Monroe turned toward the windows facing the parking lot. "It's that Herschel fellow, isn't it? He's the one you invited for supper." A visible flush erupted on Monroe's cheeks. "Isn't that why he's still out there talking to your son?"

Belinda glanced in the direction Monroe pointed. Sure enough, Henry stood with Herschel, next to his horse and buggy. She wondered what they might be talking about.

I guess it would be good of me to clear things up, so he'll settle down. "Herschel is not coming to our home for supper. If you must know, we invited our neighbors across the street to join us for a meal."

"Oh, I see." Monroe's eyes brightened a bit. "It's good to be neighborly once in a while, jah?"

Belinda bobbed her head.

"Umm. . . Is it the neighbor with the bright red hair?"

"Yes it is. Why do you ask?"

"When I came by to check on your place when you all were gone to New York, I caught that gal outside on her porch with a pair of binoculars. I couldn't help feeling that I was being watched."

Belinda flapped her hand. "Oh yes, I believe she must have been bird-watching. It seems harmless to me."

"Well, anyway, it's nice of you to be a good neighbor." He straightened his hat.

"Did you come by for anything else?" she asked. "Because if not, I need to close things up and head to the house. I want to get cleaned up and help my daughters start supper."

"Sure. I'll let you get to it then. Maybe in another week or so, you and I can get together. I'd like to take you somewhere special."

"I'll have to wait and see how it goes."

"Okay."

Belinda felt relieved when Monroe said goodbye and went out the door. She wanted to give him a chance, but she'd feel much better about seeing him if he wasn't so overbearing.

"What's taking you so long, Virginia? It's almost six o'clock." Earl stepped into the bedroom and narrowed his eyes as he pointed at her.

"Are you stalling?"

She shook her head, although to tell the truth, Virginia was in no hurry to walk across the street and share a meal in an Amish home.

She stared at her reflection in the full-length mirror attached to the front of their closet door. "I want to make sure I look presentable." Virginia reached down and rolled the lint brush she held across the front of her dark green slacks. "Can you check the back, to make sure none of Goldie's hairs are sticking to me?" She handed Earl the brush.

He stepped behind Virginia, made a few swipes, and gave it back to her. "Okay, let's go."

"Just a minute; I need to put my earrings in."

Earl groaned. "Are you kidding me? We're not goin' out to eat at a fancy restaurant. Those people across the road are Plain folks. In case you haven't noticed, they all dress in simple clothes, and none of the women I've seen wear jewelry."

"I don't care. I am not Amish, and I don't feel fully dressed unless my earrings are in." Virginia walked over to her dresser, opened the jewelry box, and took out a pair of white earrings with blue polka-dots. Once they were in place, she slipped on a sweater and picked up her cane. "All right, Earl, I'm ready to go."

"Someone just knocked on the front door, Mom. Would you like me to answer it?" Amy asked.

"Yes, please. I'm sure it must be our neighbors, since Dennis and Jared are already here." Belinda set the bowl of shredded lettuce on the kitchen table between a bowl of cut-up tomatoes and some chopped onions. "You can escort Mr. and Mrs. Martin to the living room and let them know that I'll be out there soon."

"Okay." Amy hurried from the room.

Belinda looked at Sylvia, who'd been busy chopping olives. "I'll go out and greet our guests and explain that we'll be eating in the dining room but serving from the kitchen."

"No problem, Mom. I should have the rest of the things set out in the next few minutes." Sylvia touched Belinda's shoulder. "You look kind of stressed. Take a few deep breaths and try to relax."

"You're right. I do need to calm myself a bit before greeting our guests."

"Are you nervous about having Virginia and Earl here for supper?"

"A little. It's the first time they've been in our home, and they may feel uncomfortable with our simple surroundings compared to their modern furnishings."

"It'll be fine, Mom. You'll see." Sylvia's confident tone did little to relieve Belinda's nervousness. The few encounters she'd had with Virginia had caused Belinda to believe her English neighbor didn't care much for her. Hopefully the evening would go better than she expected.

Virginia sat stiffly on the couch beside Earl, wondering if she'd lost her mind agreeing to come here and eat supper with these Plain people with whom she had nothing in common. Belinda had entered the room a few minutes ago and introduced Virginia and Earl to each of her family members. "It's too bad our son Ezekiel and his wife and two small children couldn't be here as well," she said.

"I didn't realize you had other family living in the area," Virginia commented.

"Ezekiel moved to Clymer, New York, a few years ago, not long after he and his wife got married."

"My brother's wife used to be English," Henry spoke up. "But she decided to give up her worldly ways and join the Amish church."

Virginia rubbed the bridge of her nose. *Who in their right mind would want to leave all their modern conveniences and stylish clothes in order to live the Plain life?* She glanced around, gazing at each of the Amish people gathered in this simply decorated room, devoid of a television or electric lights. *No way could I ever live like this, especially in the summertime with no air-conditioning.*

"It must have been a difficult transition for your son's wife to become Amish," Earl said.

"It was," Belinda responded, "but my daughter-in-law seems to have adjusted quite well."

What's this conversation have to do with anything? Virginia reached up and fingered the necklace matching the earrings she wore. *We came here to eat supper, not discuss Belinda's family members, who I care nothing about. I'd just like to get this evening over with so we can go home and maybe watch an hour or so of TV before it's time for bed.*

"New York, huh?" The question came from Earl. "That must mean you don't see your son too often."

"Not as much as we'd like, but we try to get together as often as we can." Belinda gestured to the adjoining dining room. "We'll be eating in there, because our table is quite large, but we will put the food on our plates from the items set out on the kitchen table. So Virginia and Earl, if you'll come with me, you can dish up first and the rest of my family will follow. Then once we are all seated around the table, we can pray."

Pray? Virginia glanced at Earl and struggled to keep from rolling her eyes. She hadn't uttered a prayer since her mother made her attend Bible school one summer when she was a girl. Virginia and Earl had never really talked about it, but she felt fairly sure he'd never been a praying man either. If he had, he'd chosen to kept it private.

I hope they don't call on me or Earl to recite a prayer, because I have no idea what either of us would say.

When they entered the kitchen, Virginia was surprised to see a stove and refrigerator, not that much different than hers. Other than the absence of a dishwasher or microwave, Belinda's kitchen didn't look too terribly plain. A calendar with a colorful sunset picture hung on one wall, and a pretty vase with pink flowers in it sat on the roll-top desk across the room.

When Belinda directed their attention to the items on the table, Virginia's brows squished together.

"Are you folks familiar with haystack?" Belinda questioned.

Virginia looked at Earl, and when he shrugged his shoulders, she shook her head. "Never heard of it before."

Belinda explained that they should choose from whichever food items they wanted and layer them on until their plate was full, making it resemble a haystack.

"I'm guessing it must be similar to a taco salad." Virginia looked at Belinda. "Is that right?"

"Yes, only some of the ingredients we're offering tonight are not included in any taco salad I've ever eaten."

"Well, it sounds good to me." Earl rubbed his hands together with an eager expression. "Should we start filling our plates?"

"Please do. Once you have everything you want, go ahead to the dining room and take a seat. The rest of us will join you shortly."

Virginia went first, starting with some crushed corn chips, forming the bottom layer of her haystack. Following that, she added lettuce, tomato, a few onions, several sliced black olives, and some of the ground beef mixture. On top of that she poured some melted cheese, added a dollop of sour cream, and topped it off with a spoonful of picante sauce. Carrying her plate, she hobbled into the dining room without the aid of her cane, which she'd left propped inside the entryway near the front door.

She took a seat on one side of the table and picked up the glass of water sitting there to take a drink. *I'll be glad when this evening is over and Earl and I can go back to the comfort of our home.*

Chapter 26

The next few weeks went by in a blur, with many more customers coming to the greenhouse in preparation of planting their gardens. Despite the fact that the big garden center in town absorbed a good many customers, it hadn't seemed to have hurt Belinda's family business. Now that it was April and more tourists were arriving, her greenhouse attracted people from far and wide. She'd had a customer the other day visiting from Canada. The gentleman stated how intrigued he was with the Amish and said he'd been to a couple of communities close to where he lived.

An older couple had come in yesterday from Texas. They'd driven up for a book signing to meet their favorite author who wrote about the Amish and also to see the Plain people. The man seemed as interested in what was being said as the woman. They'd asked Belinda about the Pennsylvania Dutch language, and she'd answered their questions. But as the greenhouse continued to fill with more customers, she'd had to excuse herself and tend to others who needed assistance.

So far today they'd been exceptionally busy, but Belinda had no problem with that. It kept her mind off the fact that today was her birthday, and how two years ago, her husband, son, and son-in-law had been killed. It was hard to think of celebrating anything when painful memories surfaced. She'd hoped her birthday might go unnoticed, but it was not to be. Sylvia had fixed Belinda a special ham-and-egg omelet this morning. Then when Amy arrived to watch the children, she'd informed Belinda that she and the rest of the family would be going to her house for supper that evening.

A lump formed in the back of Belinda's throat. While she looked forward to spending time with her loved ones, she wasn't in the mood to celebrate. The card she'd received in the mail this morning from Ezekiel and Michelle wished her a happy birthday and said they hoped she would have a good day. Belinda missed them so much, and the distance between them didn't help.

It would be better if they could be with us this evening, she thought. *But for my family's sake, I must put a smile on my face and try to have a pleasant time.*

Belinda glanced at the clock and heaved a sigh. Several people wandered up and down the aisles, and it would be another two hours before quitting time. She wished she could go up to the house, stretch out on her bed, and take a nap. But she had to keep pushing until the last customer left the greenhouse.

An English lady came up to the cash register with an outdoor plant and several pot holders that Sylvia had made. After the woman paid for her purchases and left, Belinda got up from the stool where she'd been sitting behind the counter. She'd noticed the give-away containers for the customers to use for their plants were running short.

Belinda headed to the area where the surplus was stored, but on the way back, something caught her eye. Henry was watering some plants while visiting with an Amish girl about his age. Belinda had seen the young lady and her family last week at church. She'd met the girl's mother and found out they were visiting from outside the area.

Belinda stepped up next to Henry and smiled at the girl. "I didn't see you come in, but it's nice to see you have found our place."

"Jah, I took a walk after breakfast and spotted this place. The hanging baskets on display out front look beautiful."

"Thank you." Belinda looked at her son. "I should get back up to the counter and take the supplies I came here for. When you're done watering, I'd like you to bring in more bags of potting soil."

He nodded. "I'll take care of it, Mom, as soon as I'm done talkin' to Anna."

It did Belinda's heart good to see Henry socializing with someone his age. He spent long hours working in the greenhouse and doing chores around the place.

She returned to the counter and added the containers to what was left. An English woman stood near the register, ready to pay for her things. "I'm glad I came here today. You've got some cute birdhouses. I'm getting one for my sister's birthday next week. The second one I will keep for myself."

The word *birthday* was another reminder to Belinda that she would be getting together with her family this evening. She rang up the items, and when the lady left the greenhouse, Belinda walked down the aisle where she'd last seen her son. He seemed to be taking his time getting done with the plants, and there was only one bag of potting soil left. *I wonder if he's still talking to that girl.*

She walked over to the area where Sylvia stood putting more pot holders on the gift items shelf. "Your homemade things have been selling well."

"Henry's sold a few of his painted horseshoes too," Sylvia reported.

"Business has been booming all right. I'm sure it'll be even busier throughout the summer months."

"Yes, and I've been thinking about that. In fact, Dennis and I have decided to change our wedding date from August to October, when things have slowed down here a bit." Sylvia put a few more pot holders in place. "There won't be as many customers in the fall, so you and Henry won't be quite as busy and can hopefully handle things okay without me by then."

Belinda swallowed hard. The thickening in her throat had returned. As much as she dreaded the day Sylvia would no longer be working here, she did not wish to stand in the way of her daughter's happiness by making her wait two extra months to get married.

"I do not want you and Dennis to change your wedding date because of me."

"It'll only be a few months later than planned, Mom. And it'll give Dennis more time to make some changes to my house before the kinner and I move in with him after the wedding."

Belinda's eyes widened as she touched the base of her throat. "You're going to move back to your old house?"

"Jah."

"But I thought you weren't comfortable with living there since it had once been yours and Toby's home and it holds so many memories."

"That's true, but with all the changes Dennis and I have in mind, it'll be like a new house. Plus, there will be more bedrooms for guests and children, should the Lord bless us with babies."

Belinda gave a closed-lip smile. Her daughter's announcement came as a surprise, and she hardly knew what to say. For many months after Toby's death, Sylvia could not even go to her house without falling apart. When she forced herself to go there, someone in the family always went along to offer their help and emotional support.

"So you're okay with us waiting till the first Thursday in October?"

Belinda slipped her arm around Sylvia's waist and gave her a hug. "Whatever decisions you make, regarding your wedding date or where you'll live after you and Dennis are married, are between you and him."

Sylvia smiled. "Danki, Mom. I was certain you'd understand and accept our reasons for waiting."

"A final note: if you need help painting any rooms or cleaning down the walls, please let me know."

"I will."

When Belinda heard someone come into the greenhouse, she made her way back to the counter. She was surprised to see Monroe walking toward her with a huge green gift bag and a bouquet of roses. "*Hallich gebottsdaag*, Belinda."

Her cheeks warmed as he handed her the flowers and placed the gift on the counter. "Danki, Monroe, but you didn't have to do that. I wasn't expecting anything from you."

He shook his head. "There was no way I could let your birthday go by and not give you a gift."

Belinda sniffed the roses. "They smell delightful."

He gestured to the other bag. "Go ahead and look in there."

Belinda placed the roses on the counter, reached inside the pretty bag, and withdrew two large battery-operated candles—the kind that looked like the flames were real. She'd seen them for sale in some of the stores in town and knew they were more expensive than the average candle with batteries.

"They're very nice, Monroe. Danki for thinking of me with these lovely gifts."

With his chin held high, and both thumbs positioned under the front of his suspenders, he gave her a wide smile. "You are most welcome. And now I have a question to ask."

"Oh?"

"May I help you celebrate by taking you out for supper?"

Belinda blinked. *Why does he keep asking me out for supper at the last minute? I thought I'd made it clear that I would prefer some advance notice.*

She looked at him and said: "It's kind of you to offer, but my family and I have already made plans for this evening."

His shoulders sagged. "Guess I messed up again by not asking sooner. Sorry about that."

"Maybe we can do it one night next week. How about Friday? Would that work for you?"

He reached out and touched her arm. "Jah, that'd be great. I can finally take you someplace special where they serve really good food."

Belinda couldn't imagine where it might be. Most of the restaurants in their area served simple fare—nothing fancy. Well, she'd only have to wait a week to find out where the location of the special place was.

When Belinda and her family arrived at Amy and Jared's that evening, she noticed two carriages parked in the yard. She was quite sure one belonged to Dennis, which was no surprise, since she'd assumed he would be included in their plans for tonight. The other buggy, she wasn't sure about. Had Amy invited someone else to this gathering?

Belinda stepped down from the carriage, and while Henry took care of putting the horse in the barn, Sylvia handed Rachel to her.

Belinda began walking toward the house with her granddaughter, until Sylvia called out: "Would you mind waiting for me and Allen? That way we can all go in together."

"Okay." Belinda thought her daughter's request was a little odd, but she came back to the buggy and waited for Sylvia to help Allen down. It was also a bit strange that Sylvia hadn't brought anything to contribute to their supper. It wasn't like her to allow Amy to provide everything for a meal—even one that took place in Amy and Jared's home.

"Let's take a walk out to the barn before we go up to the house," Sylvia suggested. "Amy mentioned that one of their barn cats had a batch of kittens last week. It'll be fun for the kinner to see them."

"Maybe we should wait and do that later," Belinda suggested. "Amy may have supper ready, and I'm sure she would appreciate it if we ate the food while it's warm."

"I believe she's making *hoischtock*, so there's really nothing involved that needs to be kept warm."

The mention of haystack caused Belinda to think of the evening they'd had their neighbors over for supper. Earl had eaten the meal heartily, and even complimented Belinda and Sylvia. Virginia hadn't said whether she enjoyed it or not. In fact, she hadn't contributed much to the conversation that evening and kept checking her watch. Belinda figured Virginia may have felt uncomfortable in a home lacking modern conveniences. Although she hadn't admitted it to anyone, Belinda had felt relieved when the Martins returned to their own home. It wasn't that she was prejudiced against English folks. She just didn't feel comfortable around Virginia, because she had very little in common with her neighbor. *Even so,* Belinda told herself, *I will try to be a good neighbor to Virginia and her husband.*

"Allen, wouldn't you like to see the new kittens in the barn?" Sylvia's question had been spoken in Pennsylvania Dutch, and it halted Belinda's musings.

The boy bobbed his head and took off running in that direction.

Sylvia looked at Belinda. "Looks like we have no choice but to go after him."

When Sylvia began walking quickly toward the barn, Belinda felt obliged to follow—especially since Rachel had begun shouting that she wanted her mamm.

Sylvia had a head start, and by the time Belinda got there with Rachel, both Sylvia and Allen had entered the barn and shut the door. It made sense that they would close it to keep so many flies from getting inside, because even in April the pesky insects could be a problem for the horses.

When Belinda entered the building, with the exception of horse whinnies, everything was quiet. Belinda glanced around the dimly lit barn but saw no sign of Sylvia, Allen, or Henry.

Holding tightly to Rachel's hand, she made her way toward the sound of the horses, where she assumed her daughter, son, and grandson had gone.

As Belinda approached the first stall, a chorus of voices shouted, "Surprise! Happy Birthday!"

Astonished, Belinda teared up when Ezekiel stepped out of the shadows and gave her a big hug. She looked around and saw Michelle smiling while she held on to little Vernon. Their daughter, Angela Mary, wearing a big grin, stood beside her mother. The rest of Belinda's family stood there too, along with Herschel.

"Did we surprise you?" Ezekiel asked. "Did we get ya good?"

"Oh jah, you fooled me again, just like last year when you showed up at Shady Maple." Happy tears welled in Belinda's eyes. She looked at both of her daughters. "Did you two plan this?"

Sylvia and Amy nodded. "It wasn't easy to keep you from finding out, but things fell together quite well, and we're glad you were surprised." Amy slipped an arm around Belinda's waist, and Sylvia did the same.

"Danki for making me feel so special." It was difficult for Belinda to convey her emotions without breaking down. The only thing that would have made this gathering more special would be if their departed loved ones could be there too.

"I hope you don't mind my being here, since I'm not part of your family," Herschel spoke up. "Amy and Jared invited me, and I sure didn't want to say no."

"It's perfectly fine, Herschel. I'm glad you're here." Belinda went around to each family member and gave them a hug. She could hardly believe they were all here. This was the first time she had seen Ezekiel, Michelle, and the children since she and the rest of their family had gone to Clymer for Christmas. This birthday had turned out to be joyful after all.

Chapter 27

"Should we take a look at the *busslin* before we go in the house?" Jared asked Belinda.

"Of course. That is the reason I was told we were coming out to the barn." She gave a small laugh.

"Okay everyone, follow me." Jared led the way to a wooden box near the back of the barn. Within the crate, a silver-gray mama cat lay next to her kittens. The children squealed with obvious delight, while the adults looked on.

It pleased Belinda to see her family so happy. Even Herschel wore a grin when each child was given the chance to pet one of the six kittens. Mama cat didn't seem to mind, as she lay in the box with her eyes closed. No doubt she was in need of a nap.

As she watched her young grandchildren interact with the squirming, meowing kittens, Belinda recognized again how much joy they brought to her heart.

She closed her eyes and lifted a silent prayer: *Heavenly Father, thank You for the privilege of being a part of my grandchildren's lives. Please bless and protect each member of our family and keep us from wandering off the narrow path. Help me, as well as the other adults in our family, to be a Christian example to the younger ones in all we say and do. Bless and protect Herschel too. He's such a kind man, with a servant's heart. Please be with us all in the coming days as You guide and direct each of our lives. Amen.*

When everyone headed into the house a short time later, Herschel held back and brought up the rear. The look of joy he had seen on Belinda's face when she'd entered the barn and discovered the surprise her children had planned for her caused Herschel to be filled with happiness too. Oh, what he wouldn't give to be part of a family like this.

If I were married to Belinda. . . But it's too soon in our relationship to be speaking of that to her. I wouldn't want to say anything that might scare her off. Besides, I have no idea how she feels about me. He pulled his fingers through the back of his hair. *Sure wish I could ask, but it would be too bold, and Belinda might think I was trying to push her into a relationship she isn't ready for or may not even want.*

In addition to his desire to respect Belinda's feelings, Herschel was concerned about his rival. A man like Monroe, with good looks, charm, and plenty of money, might succeed in winning Belinda's heart.

As Herschel drew closer to the house, he paused and looked around the yard. Despite Amy dealing with pregnancy and babysitting Sylvia's children sometimes six days a week, the young woman managed to find the time to keep her lovely flowerbeds from being overrun by weeds. *She must get up early in the mornings to do it, or maybe Jared helps out. I was smart to rent this house to them,* Herschel thought as he stepped onto the porch. *It's clear that they've been maintaining it well.*

When Herschel entered the house, he hung his straw hat on the coat rack in the entryway. Jared, Henry, and Ezekiel's hats were there too.

Amy asked everyone to wash up and meet in the dining room, where she'd placed the ingredients for haystack on an extended side table positioned on one side of the room.

A short time later, everyone gathered around, with the adults at the longer dining-room table and the children at a smaller folding table. Belinda's two youngest grandchildren were seated in high chairs.

When Jared announced it was time for prayer, Herschel bowed his head, along with the others. *Dear Lord,* he prayed, *please bless this food and the hands that prepared it. Bless those who are gathered in this room. And most of all, give Belinda a special blessing, for she is certainly a woman who follows after You.*

The evening went by too quickly, and Belinda enjoyed every moment of her birthday celebration. Today had turned out better than she could have imagined. Still full from supper, she could barely eat the piece of birthday cake Sylvia had cut and put on her plate.

Belinda mentioned the work Amy had done to make the evening happen, but her daughter brushed the compliment aside. "I can't take all the credit. Sylvia came over yesterday evening when you thought she went to visit Lenore Smucker. She helped me clean the house, baked your birthday cake, and prepped most of the ingredients for our haystack meal. She's also the one who got in touch with Ezekiel about hiring a driver to bring them here so they could be part of the celebration."

Belinda gave Amy a hug. "I appreciate everything you both did to make tonight possible."

"Are ya ready to open your birthday presents, Grandma?" Angela Mary tugged on the sleeve of Belinda's dress.

Belinda tweaked the young girl's nose. "I most certainly am."

"Why don't you open ours first?" Ezekiel handed Belinda a box wrapped in pink paper. "Sure hope you'll like what we got for you."

Belinda pulled the paper off and opened the lid. A pretty teapot with red roses on it was cushioned in tissue paper. Also in the box was a tin filled with mint-flavored teabags—Belinda's favorite kind. She smiled. "Danki, Ezekiel, Michelle, and grandchildren."

"We chose that teapot because we know how much you like roses," Michelle responded.

"Yes, I certainly do."

Next came a gift from Amy and Jared. Belinda was pleased to discover a plastic tote filled with material in various colors. "Danki. These pieces of cloth will come in handy the next time I need to make a new dress or apron."

"Here's a gift from me, Dennis, and Henry." Sylvia handed Belinda a box covered with bird-designed wrapping paper. "There's a picture inside too that Rachel colored with the help of her big brother." Sylvia placed her hand on top of Allen's head.

When Belinda opened the box, the children's drawing was on top, so she pulled it out first. "Well, isn't this nice? It's a picture of a robin, right?" She reached out and touched Rachel's arm, and then Allen's.

"Amschel!" Rachel declared.

Allen bobbed his head and spoke in Pennsylvania Dutch. "It's a robin all right."

Everyone laughed.

"Did you see what else is in the box?" Dennis questioned.

Belinda reached inside and withdrew a pair of binoculars. With a slight tilt of her head, she looked at her eldest daughter.

"You enjoy feeding the birds that come into your yard, so we thought you might like to take up bird-watching," Sylvia explained.

"That's right, Mom," Henry interjected. "Just think how much fun it'll be when we go on picnics this spring and throughout the summer. "You, Dennis, Sylvia, and I all have field glasses to look through now, so you can officially become a bird-watcher."

Belinda had never considered taking up bird-watching, but thought it might be kind of fun, and she didn't want to disappoint the three people who had chipped in on this gift. "Danki," she said with enthusiasm as she held the binoculars up for everyone to see. "I'll be eager to try them out."

"Here's my present." Herschel handed Belinda a small gift bag. "It's not much compared to the rest of your gifts, but I hope you'll like it."

Belinda reached inside and withdrew an alarm clock.

"It plays a hymn, instead of waking you with an irritating beep, beep." Herschel gave her one of his shy grins. "I have one, and waking up to Christian music helps to put me in a good mood before I get out of bed."

"Thank you, Herschel." Belinda smiled at him. "What a thoughtful gift. I'm sure I'll enjoy waking up to the inspirational music too."

"Hey, Mom, sorry for the change of subject," Ezekiel interjected, "but is it okay if we go home with you tonight and then spend a couple of days?"

"Of course." Belinda's cheeks grew warm with pleasure. "You're welcome to stay as long as you like."

Angela Mary hopped up and down. "We're goin' to Grandma's house to spend the night!"

Belinda scooped the little girl onto her lap. "And tomorrow you can visit me in the greenhouse."

"It's not just our daughter you'll be visiting, Mom," Ezekiel said. "I'm planning to help Sylvia and Henry so you can take the day off to enjoy all four of your *kinskinner*."

Belinda released a gratifying sigh. "That would be wunderbaar, Son."

"How are things going for you these days?" Ezekiel asked as he and Henry fed the livestock in the barn the following morning.

"Not that great."

"How come?"

Henry kicked a clump of straw beneath his feet and closed the bag of oats they'd just given the horses. He wished he could share his frustrations over the vandalism that had gone on since their loved ones died, but Mom would be upset if he said anything. He'd also like to mention his decision to try and figure out who was behind the terrible things that had been done, but that was also out of the question.

"What's bugging you, Henry?" Ezekiel put both hands on his hips. "Come on. . .out with it now."

"Umm. . . Well, one of the things bothering me right now is that our mamm has two suitors."

"I assume you're referring to Herschel and Monroe?"

"Jah." Henry removed his hat and swatted at an irritating fly that began buzzing around his head. "If something isn't done soon, one of those men is likely to talk her into marrying him."

"Would that be such a bad thing, Henry?"

"Jah."

"How come?"

"Because Mom's still in love with Dad, and she don't need another husband."

"Maybe she wants one. Did you ever think of that?"

Henry shook his head vigorously. "I don't see why."

Ezekiel put his hand on Henry's shoulder. "Our mother might want the companionship that goes with marriage. She may also develop strong feelings for one of the men. If she does choose to remarry, we should be happy for her."

Henry's shoulders slumped as he dropped his gaze to the floor. "Don't think I can. The thought of her gettin' married again makes me feel *grank*."

"That's *lecherich*. You should not feel sick if our mamm falls in love and chooses to get married again."

Henry looked up at his brother and frowned. "It's not ridiculous.

I have a right to feel this way, and nothin' you say is gonna change my mind. Anyway, there's been enough changes around here for me to last a lifetime."

Henry left the horse's stall, poured some food into the cats' dish, and stormed out of the barn. *Sure hope Ezekiel doesn't say anything more about this while we're working in the greenhouse today. I can't believe he thinks it's okay for Mom to be courted by another man—let alone two! Doesn't he care how this affects me?*

Belinda smiled as she stood behind Angela Mary and Allen, watching as they drew pictures and colored them in. Michelle was in the living room with Rachel and Vernon, keeping them occupied with some age-appropriate toys. Amy had stayed home today, since Michelle had mentioned at the party last night that she'd be happy to keep an eye on Sylvia's children. Belinda could have watched them, but with Michelle here, it gave her the opportunity to bake some cookies for everyone to enjoy. She also relished this chance to be with all of her grandchildren.

"Your pictures look nice." Belinda put one hand on each of the children's shoulders.

"Danki," Allen and Angela Mary said in unison.

"How would both of you like to walk down the driveway with me so I can get the mail?" Belinda asked.

"Okay." Again, the children spoke at the same time.

Belinda bit back a chuckle. She didn't want Angela Mary or Allen to think she was laughing at them. "When we come back to the house, who wants to help me bake some oatmeal cookies with raisins?"

"I do! I do!" The children clapped their hands.

"All right then, let's head out the front door."

Virginia looked both ways before heading across the road to get her mail. She'd no more than stepped up to her mailbox when Belinda showed up with two young children—a girl and a boy. The boy she recognized, because she'd seen him playing outside several times and had met him personally the evening she and Earl had eaten supper at

Belinda's. She didn't think she'd seen the girl before, but she was a cute little thing with rosy cheeks and braided reddish-brown hair.

"Hello, Virginia." Belinda smiled. "How are you this fine spring morning?"

"Doin' okay. How about you?"

"Very well. I'm privileged to have my son Ezekiel and his family visiting with us for a few days. Today my eldest son is taking my place in the greenhouse so I can spend more time with my grandchildren."

"How nice." Virginia reached down and rubbed her throbbing leg. She'd left her cane in the house and wished she had it right now. Not that it took away the pain she often felt in her bum leg, but it did offer some support when she walked.

"You've met Sylvia's son, Allen, already, and this is Ezekiel's daughter." Belinda gestured to the girl. "Her name is Angela Mary."

"Pretty name." Virginia opened her mailbox and took out the contents. *She's a cute girl. It's a shame these kids will have to grow up in such a sheltered environment. I wonder when they get older if they might decide not to join the Amish church, like some of those Amish young people I saw on that reality TV show some time ago.*

"When we get back to the house, we're going to bake cookies. You're welcome to come over in a few hours and have some," Belinda said. "Or I could bring them over to your house."

"Thanks anyway, but I'm trying to watch my weight these days." Virginia gave her stomach a few pats.

"Okay, but if you change your mind, let me know. Perhaps your husband would like some cookies."

"Earl's on a diet too." *Or at least he should be.* "Well, have a nice day." Virginia turned and limped to the other side of the road.

When she entered her house and took a seat on the couch to go through the mail, Virginia thought about her own childhood and what a rebellious teenager she had been. She'd grown up as an only child in a dysfunctional home and gotten married to the first man who asked, so she could get away from her parents. But getting married hadn't changed much of anything in Virginia's life. Her first husband had been physically and mentally abusive, and she'd been relieved when he died. Until Virginia met Earl, she'd never felt truly loved. Even with her husband's quirks and sometimes stubborn ways, she felt certain that he loved her.

"Although my marriage to Earl is better than the first one," Virginia mumbled, "I'd give almost anything to have even one grandchild right now. At least then I'd have someone besides Goldie to dote over."

Tears escaped Virginia's eyes, splattering onto the envelope she held in her hand. *Guess I need to quit feeling sorry for myself and find something sensible to do. Maybe I'll give my friend Stella a call and see how things are going in Chicago. That would be better than sitting around here giving in to unwanted tears that won't change a thing.*

Chapter 28

Belinda stood on the back porch, looking at the birds in their yard through her new binoculars. She spotted a baby robin and watched it for a while. The homely little bird couldn't fly well yet, but it wouldn't be long before it would be soaring from tree to tree in her yard.

Belinda reflected on the wonderful birthday she'd had with her whole family there to celebrate. She looked forward to Ezekiel, Michelle, and the children coming back for Sylvia and Dennis's wedding in October.

Before going home, Ezekiel had mentioned that if they could get away, he and his family might come sooner—maybe when Amy and Jared's baby was born. Otherwise, they would come a few days before the wedding so they could help with the preparations.

Shifting gears again, Belinda focused the lenses of her field glasses on something else in the yard, and her mouth opened slightly. So many goldfinches flew toward the new feeders Henry had put up recently, it looked like a bunch of leaves falling from the trees. She watched in awe for several seconds before going back into the house to help with breakfast. Today was likely to be busy in the greenhouse again, and this evening was her promised date with Monroe. She was eager to see where the special place was that he said he'd be taking her for supper.

Belinda was almost to the door when a vehicle pulled in. She turned and watched as Amy got out of her driver's car and began walking toward the house.

"I hope I'm not late," Amy said after she joined Belinda on the porch. "I got up a little later than planned and it set me back a bit."

"Not a problem." Belinda gave her daughter a hug. "We haven't had breakfast yet."

"Oh good. Guess I wasn't as late as I thought."

"You're welcome to join us at the table. Sylvia's fixing pannekuche at Allen's request."

"That little man does enjoy pancakes." Amy grinned. "Jared and I only had toast and tea this morning. His driver picked him up early to bid on a job in Lancaster, so there wasn't time to fix a big breakfast."

"Then you definitely need some pancakes." Belinda opened the door for Amy, allowing her to go in first, and then she stepped in behind her. Oh, how she would miss seeing her daughter every day once the baby came, but she understood the importance of Amy staying home to be a full-time mother.

When Henry entered the phone shack and shut the door, he drew in a couple of deep breaths to steady his nerves. Mom had asked him to go out and check for messages, but he'd gotten waylaid until now. On the walk down the driveway earlier, he'd discovered a whole bunch of nails had been scattered about. Henry felt certain they had not been there the evening before when he and Blackie played fetch. Someone had obviously come onto their property during the night and dumped out the nails.

Since the greenhouse would be open for business in less than an hour, Henry had gone to their storage shed for a cardboard box to put the nails in. It had taken him awhile to gather all the nails. He probably should have gone up to the house and asked Mom or Sylvia to come out and help, but he'd done it himself. This gave Henry an opportunity to check for clues. But the only thing he'd found were some shoe prints, which could have been anyone's, since some local people came to the greenhouse on foot.

Wish I knew who threw all these nails out. Henry rubbed his damp forehead and set the cardboard box on the counter inside the phone shed. *No doubt it was the same person who did all the other destructive things.*

Henry eyed the blinking light on the answering machine, indicating that some messages had come in.

His finger came down on the button and he listened to the first message. It was from Ezekiel, calling to see how they were all doing.

Henry paused the answering machine. *I wonder what my bruder would have to say if I told him our mamm's going out to some fancy place with Monroe this evening. Maybe Ezekiel wouldn't care. He might think it's fine and dandy that Mom's acting like a teenage girl with two fellows hanging around all the time, trying to impress her.*

Henry stared at the box of nails. *Bet he'd really be upset if I told him about these. Sure don't like keeping secrets from my brother.*

Henry wrote Ezekiel's message on the tablet but froze when he heard the next one: "When are you going to listen? I told you to get out. You have until the end of the year, and there will not be too many more warnings."

The voice sounded muffled, but Henry understood every word. He listened again and wrote the message down exactly as he'd heard it. Without waiting to hear any other messages, he grabbed the tablet and the box of nails and flung the shed door open. He needed to share this with Mom right away. Maybe now she'd wake up and call the sheriff.

Belinda had entered the greenhouse and was about to put the OPEN sign in place when Henry rushed in. One look at his sweaty, flushed skin and wide eyes and she knew something was wrong.

"What is it, Son? You look like you've encountered a *schpuck*."

"Not a ghost, Mom, but more *druwwel*."

Belinda's throat constricted. "What kind of trouble?"

Henry showed her the box. "I found all these *neggel* in the driveway and had to take the time to pick them all up. Sure wouldn't want some car to drive over the nails and end up with a flat tire."

She blinked several times. "I wonder how they got there."

"I'm pretty sure the person who left this message on our answering machine threw the nails all over our driveway sometime during the night." Henry handed the notepad to Belinda.

She barely took notice of the message from Ezekiel. It was the second message that caught her attention. "Was the voice muffled, or could you hear the person who spoke clearly?"

"It was muffled, but I understood every word they said." With the back of his hand, Henry wiped the sweat off his forehead. "Whoever's been doing all these things wants us gone. They expect us to get out by the end of the year."

The back of Belinda's neck prickled. "I can read, Son. You don't have to repeat what's written on the tablet."

"Sorry, I was just trying to make sure you got the point." Henry pointed to the nails. "Are you ready to call the sheriff now?"

She shook her head as determination welled in her chest. "We will not be run off our property because someone, for some reason, dislikes us. Involving the sheriff would make all of this public knowledge, because I'm sure the word would get out." She made little circles on her forehead, hoping to ward off a headache. "The thing we have to do is hold steady and not give in to this person's demands. We must be steadfast in our prayers and trust God to protect us and our property." She stepped closer to Henry and put one hand on his shoulder. "Let's keep this latest event to ourselves, okay? I don't want to upset your sisters."

Henry sighed. "I won't say anything to Amy or Sylvia, but I will keep a closer watch on things, even if it means sleeping outside at night until the weather turns cold."

Belinda shook her head. "There's no need for that, but we could let Blackie sleep in your room, since it faces the front of the house. If anyone enters our yard, the dog's bound to alert us with his super-loud barks."

"Okay, if that's what you wanna do, but I'm still gonna keep my eyes and ears open anytime I'm awake."

"Good idea, and I shall do the same."

Belinda turned the OPEN sign over and took a seat behind the counter after she instructed Henry to take the box of nails outside to the shed. She sat looking at the tablet he had brought in from the phone shed until Sylvia came in. Belinda quickly tore off the page with the messages, folded it, and put it under the front band of her apron.

"Looks like there are no customers yet," Sylvia commented.

"Right, but I'm sure we'll have people here soon."

Sylvia stepped up to the counter. "Did Henry come back from the phone shed? Dennis was supposed to call with a message about what time he'd be by to pick me and the kinner up so he can show us the colt that was born two days ago."

"Henry did come back," Belinda responded. "But he made no mention of a message from Dennis."

"Maybe I'll go see. He may have called and left a message after Henry came out of the phone shed."

"If you'll take my place behind the counter, I'll go check for you. I need to make a few phone calls anyway." The last thing Belinda wanted was for her daughter to hear the threatening message.

"Sure, no problem." Sylvia came around and seated herself on the stool as soon as Belinda stood up. "Where's Henry?" she asked. "I figured he'd be in here by now."

"He was, but he went out to the storage shed to put something away for me. He should be back soon I expect."

"Okay." Sylvia picked up the tablet Belinda had left on the counter. "Isn't this the one we keep in the phone shed to write messages on?"

"You're right, it is. Henry brought it in when he told me that Ezekiel had called to see how we're all doing. I'll call him back while I'm in the phone shed." Belinda took the notepad and started for the door, glad she'd torn off the page with the messages on it. She'd barely opened the door when Maude stepped in.

"Ya got anything set out in here to eat?" The old woman pressed a gnarly hand against her stomach. "There ain't much at my place for breakfast 'cause those fat hens you gave me haven't laid any eggs for a couple of days."

Belinda felt compassion for Maude. She couldn't imagine what it must be like for her to live all alone and in such poor conditions. It was a wonder she could even survive.

"I don't have anything here at the moment, but if you'll wait in the greenhouse a few minutes, I'll bring you something from the house."

"I can stay here." Maude lifted both hands and let them fall to her sides. "There ain't no other place I need to go anyways, so I'll just wander around here till you come back with some food."

Belinda glanced at Sylvia. She had a pretty good guess of what her daughter was thinking by the way her gaze flicked upward.

When Maude wandered down one of the aisles, Belinda returned to the counter and whispered to Sylvia, "I'll be back soon with something for Maude, and then I'll check the answering machine in the phone shed."

After Belinda gave Maude a box filled with a dozen cookies, several apples, a loaf of bread, a package of cheese, and a jar of honey, she hurried down the driveway to the phone shed. She would listen to all the messages, including the threatening one Henry had told her about, and then she'd make a few calls. One would be to Ezekiel, letting him know they were all fine, and the other would be to Monroe. After beginning her day with such stress, there was no way she could go out to supper with him this evening. Undoubtedly she would be thinking about the threat off and on all day, and by this evening she would not only feel tired but also wouldn't be good company. The best thing to do was cancel right away and make plans to see Monroe some other time.

Belinda clicked the button to retrieve messages. The first one was from Ezekiel, just as Henry had said. Next, came the muffled threatening call, which sent a chill up Belinda's spine. She deleted that message before moving on. A potential customer called, asking if they had any birdbaths for sale. The last message was from Dennis, telling Sylvia that he would be there around five thirty that evening. He said he'd take Sylvia and the children out for supper first and then head over to his place to see the colt.

Belinda wrote Dennis's message on the tablet for Sylvia and called Ezekiel. She left a message saying everyone was fine and she hoped that he and his family were doing well too. After that, she called the lady who'd asked about buying a birdbath, and finally she punched in Monroe's number. She hoped he wouldn't answer and that she could simply leave a message, but as luck would have it, Monroe picked up and said, "Hello."

"Good morning, Monroe. It's Belinda."

"It's good to hear your voice. What a nice way to begin my day." He spoke in a bubbly tone.

Belinda fanned her face with the tablet. *When he hears what I have to say, his mood will probably change.*

"I called to let you know that I'm not feeling up to going anywhere tonight, so we'll have to postpone having supper out." She sat quietly, waiting for his response.

"Are you grank?"

"No, I'm not sick. Things have been quite hectic around here this morning and I've developed a *koppweh*." It wasn't a lie. She truly did have a headache.

"Sorry to hear that, but it might be better by this evening. Maybe relaxing and enjoying a tasty meal at a nice restaurant is what you need."

Belinda clenched and unclenched her fingers. This was not going well. It would have been easier if she could have left Monroe a message. "When I get a bad headache, it rarely gets better until I've gone to bed."

"Why don't you go up to the house right now and take a nap? Then by the time I get there with my driver to pick you up. . ."

"Sorry, Monroe, but I need to cancel."

Several seconds went by before he spoke again. "Is something wrong? Have I done anything to upset you? Is that why you don't want to go out with me?"

Belinda pressed her lips together in a grimace. *Why does he have to be so persistent? And now he's caused me to feel guilty. Would it be better if I forced myself to go out for supper with him, or should I stick with what I first said?*

"Have I done something to upset you?" Monroe asked again.

"I am not upset. I'm just not feeling my best, and I would not be good company tonight."

"I understand if you're not feeling up to it. I only hope that when we make plans again you won't need to cancel."

"I hope not too, Monroe, and I appreciate your understanding." Belinda closed her eyes briefly.

"Goodbye for now. I'll talk to you soon."

When Belinda hung up, she sagged against the chair. Perhaps the next time Monroe contacted her, she'd feel better about things.

Chapter 29

Throughout the rest of April and the first half of May, Blackie slept upstairs in Henry's room. Not once had he awakened Henry with barking, nor had any more vandalism been done. Mom saw it as a good sign, but Henry figured it was just a calm before the storm. If his mother didn't put her place up for sale and move somewhere else, there was no telling what might happen.

"I've gotta figure out who's responsible for the vandalism, threatening phone calls, and notes," Henry muttered as he put on his protective gear in preparation of checking on the bees and the prospect of gathering more honey. He'd talked to his mother about all this two days ago, and she'd said that if she knew for certain who'd done all the mean things to them, she would either notify the sheriff or try to convince the guilty party not to do any more harm to her property.

Yeah, right. Henry kicked a small stone and sent it flying into the field that bordered their yard. *I don't think anything Mom could say would put a stop to the attacks. Whoever this person is, they need to be fined and put in jail.*

When Belinda left the register and started down aisle 1, she tripped on the end of the hose, nearly losing her balance. "Whew, that was close! I need to do a better job of putting that away so that no one gets hurt." She yawned and recoiled the green tubing out of the walkway.

Belinda figured the reason for her fatigue was because she had lain awake last night thinking about this evening's supper date with Monroe. She wondered how it would go, trying to keep things on a strictly friendship basis.

Before she'd turned in last night, Belinda had set the musical alarm clock she'd received from Herschel. She thought of him often and his sweet personality. *I had a nice time when we were together for my surprise party. Herschel is so easy to get along with. Even though he's older than Monroe, he keeps himself in good shape, and I've noticed he likes to eat healthy too.*

Belinda smiled while cleaning the dirt left from putting the hose away as she thought once more about the clock Herschel had given her. *I think his gift is perfect, and it's nice to be woken up in the morning by its cheerful songs.*

Since there were no customers at the moment, Belinda walked to the back of the greenhouse where Sylvia had been putting some new plants in place.

"How are things going?" Belinda asked.

"Good. I'm just about done. How are things up front?"

"There are no customers right now, but I'm sure there will be more before the day is out."

"Are you looking forward to your supper date with Monroe this evening?" Sylvia asked.

"It will be nice to eat out, and I really couldn't put off Monroe any longer. He's waited several weeks to take me out, but we've had to put our plans on hold because things have been so hectic around here." Belinda made a sweeping gesture with her hand.

"It's true, Mom, and we're just as busy as we were three weeks ago."

"I know." Belinda yawned. "And I'm as tired as ever. But with Monroe's continued insistence, I felt I had no choice but to go out with him tonight."

"Can I give you some advice?" Sylvia looked directly at Belinda.

"Jah, of course."

"I sense that you're not in love with Monroe."

"That's true."

"So why go out with him at all?"

Belinda dropped her gaze. "I do consider him to be a friend, and friendship should always come first, but falling in love takes time."

"Good point. With me and Toby it wasn't love at first sight. But the more time we spent together, the more we both realized how much we cared for each other. It was the same way for Dennis and me," Sylvia added.

Belinda's shoulders loosened slightly as her tension ebbed. "Guess I need to stop worrying about this and just wait and see how things go." She reached over to pluck a dead bloom off one of the African violets. "What's the latest with the remodeling project on your old house? Has Dennis hired a contractor to do the work, or is he trying to do most of it himself?"

"He's doing the things he feels capable of, but he's had several horses to train of late and doesn't have time for much else."

"Has he considered having a work frolic to help with the remodel?"

"I'm not sure. He hasn't said."

"Probably many people from our community would be willing to help out."

"When Dennis comes over to join me, Henry, and the kinner for supper tonight, I'll mention the idea of a work frolic." Sylvia pointed to the row of plants ahead of them that still needed pruning. "Right now though, I'd better get back to work."

"Same here," Belinda agreed. "I hear a vehicle pulling in, which means another customer to wait on."

"So you and your woman-friend will be going to a fancy restaurant in Lancaster, huh?" Monroe's driver, Bill, glanced over at him and grinned. "Must be a pretty special woman, huh?"

Monroe bobbed his head. "I've been in love with Belinda since I was a teenager."

"But she married someone else, right?"

"Yeah, Vernon King." Monroe's fingers clenched around the brim of his hat, which he'd taken off when he got in Bill's car and placed on his lap. "Belinda's a widow now, and I've been courting her for a while."

"I'm guessing your plan is to marry the woman?"

"Yes."

"Gonna ask her tonight?"

"Nope. It's too soon for that. I'm just layin' the groundwork is all."

Bill chuckled. "I heard someone say once that they didn't think Amish men were romantic, but you're proving them wrong."

"I hope so." Monroe puffed his chest out as he mentally encouraged himself to succeed. He was aware that there were other romantic Amish men, but he didn't believe Herschel Fisher was one of them. During the times Monroe had spent in Herschel's presence, he'd perceived that the quiet man was rather boring. Monroe felt pretty smug about that. He'd convinced himself that after tonight, he would have a definite edge over Belinda's other suitor.

Monroe stared out the window at the passing scenery and smiled. *When Belinda sees how romantic I can be, she is bound to realize that the two of us are meant to be together.*

"I wonder where our mamm and Monroe ended up going for supper this evening." Sylvia passed the steaming bowl of spaghetti over to Henry.

His features tightened as he forked some noodles onto his plate. "I'm not in the mood to talk about Monroe, and I have no idea where they went. Mom's never made any mention of where he planned to take her."

"I don't think she knew. According to her, Monroe was planning to keep it a secret until they arrived at their destination." Sylvia sprinkled some Parmesan cheese over her spaghetti and then wiped a glob of red sauce off Rachel's face. "The only thing I know for sure is that Monroe said it was someplace special."

Henry looked over at Dennis and rolled his eyes. "That Monroe fellow is not the man for our mudder."

Sylvia slid the bowl of spaghetti sauce between them and ladled some onto hers and Rachel's pasta. "I know you aren't a fan of his, and I'm not sure about him either."

Henry remained quiet as he went next and spooned a fair amount onto his plate, and then passed it on to Sylvia's boyfriend.

Dennis glanced at Sylvia then back at Henry. "Not to change the subject or anything, but there's something I wanted to share with both of you."

"What's that?" Henry's tone sounded less than enthusiastic.

"I called the birding hotline this morning and listened to several reports on some local sightings of the ruby-crowned kinglet."

"I'm not familiar with the name. What kind of bird is it?" Sylvia questioned.

"It's a small, teardrop, greenish-gray bird with two white wing bars and a hidden ruby crown."

"Think I read about that species in one of the birding magazines." Henry's eyes brightened as he sat a little straighter. "Isn't it the second smallest bird in the state of Pennsylvania?"

"That's right." Dennis winked at Sylvia. He'd definitely succeeded in catching Henry's attention and altering his mood.

"The ruby-crowned kinglet is usually seen during migration in the spring and fall. You should look for it flitting around thick shrubs that are low to the ground."

"Where does the name *kinglet* come from?" Sylvia asked after she'd given Allen another piece of sourdough bread.

"It's from the Anglo-Saxon word *cyning* or 'king,' which refers to the male's ruby red crown," Dennis explained. "And the *let* part of the word means 'small.'"

"That's quite interesting."

They discussed some other birds Dennis said he had heard about while listening to the birding hotline, and then the topic changed to the prospect of a work frolic to help with the additions being made on Sylvia's old house.

"Things always get done quickly whenever there's a work frolic." Sylvia smiled at Dennis. "You sure can't be expected to remodel our house alone."

He grinned back at her. "I will if I have to, but I think a frolic might be a good way to go."

"I'm sure Jared, as well as Lenore's husband, will be there to help, and I wouldn't be surprised if Herschel and Monroe show up too." She laughed. "If for no other reason than to make an impression on Mom."

"Do you think there's a possibility your mamm could end up marrying one of those fellows?" Dennis helped himself to some bread.

"I don't know. . .anything's feasible. I'm pretty sure both men are hoping Mom will choose soon."

"I'm done eating, and I've heard enough of this conversation." Henry picked up his empty plate and stomped off to the kitchen.

Dennis looked over at Sylvia with raised brows. "I wonder what's wrong with your bruder. Normally he likes to sit and talk whenever I'm here."

"He's upset because Mom has two suitors. The idea that she might end up marrying anyone doesn't set well with Henry."

"No one can ever take his daed's place," Dennis said. "I understand that quite well. Thankfully, my mamm has never shown any interest in a prospective husband since my dad died. But if she had, I'd probably have a hard time with it too."

Sylvia heaved a big sigh. "I'm not thrilled with the idea of my mother getting remarried either, but if I had to choose which man she would marry, it would not be Monroe."

Lancaster, Pennsylvania

The minute Belinda entered the Greenfield Restaurant with Monroe she knew why he'd referred to it as special. The main dining room, which she assumed was where they'd be seated, offered a cozy fireplace, and that suited Belinda just fine, since it had become a bit chilly this evening. However, as their hostess walked with Belinda and Monroe, she did not escort them to a table in the dining room. Instead, she led them downstairs to a table near the wine cellar. "I'll give you two a chance to look over the menu and then your waitress will be here shortly to take your orders."

"Thank you." Monroe pulled out a chair for Belinda and waited until she was seated before seating himself across from her.

Such a gentleman, Belinda thought. *He does know how to court a woman.*

"This is the perfect spot for a special occasion." Monroe smiled at Belinda in such a tender fashion that she felt like a young woman on her first date. "That's why I requested it when I made the dinner reservations," he added.

She tipped her head slightly. "What are we celebrating, Monroe? I didn't realize this was a special occasion."

"Anytime is special when we're together. You make my heart sing, Belinda. When I'm with you, I feel like I did when I was a young man and first fell in love with you." He leaned closer. "Don't you feel it too?"

A warm flush spread across Belinda's cheeks, and her fingers trembled as she fumbled with her menu. *How do I respond to that? I can't tell Monroe what he wants to hear. Why has he put me in this awkward position and with no place to hide or escape?*

For a diversion and change of topic, she glanced at her menu. "Some of the entrées are a bit expensive."

"Not a problem. Money is no object, so go ahead and choose whatever you want. And if you'd like an appetizer before the main meal, that's fine and dandy too."

"Maybe I'll just have a *zelaat*." She pointed to the menu. "The Farmer's Market Salad sounds pretty good."

Monroe shook his head. "No way! You can have a salad anytime. Why don't you order a steak, the grilled pork chop, or one of the seafood items?" He pointed to himself. "Think I might try the South African rock lobster tail."

Belinda scrutinized the listed items some more, until a waitress came to take their order. At that point, Belinda figured she'd better choose something, so she pointed to the grilled petite filet mignon and said, "I'll try this."

The young woman nodded. "How would you like it cooked?"

"Medium-well, please."

"It comes with a fresh tossed salad. Would you like to add some steamed broccoli or fingerling potatoes?"

Belinda shook her head. "No, thank you. Steak and salad will be plenty for me."

The waitress turned to Monroe. "What would you like to order, sir?"

"I'm in the mood for lobster tail."

"That's a good choice. Would you like one or two?"

Monroe chuckled. "If one's good, then two's bound to be better."

Belinda looked at the menu again and noticed that the price for two lobster tails was sixty-eight dollars. In all the times she'd gone out to eat, Belinda had never spent that much on a single meal. Apparently money was no object for Monroe. Either that or he was simply trying to make an impression on her. And for the moment at least, he truly had.

Just relax and enjoy the evening, Belinda told herself. *It's not every day you get to eat at such a fancy place.* Belinda had to admit, she did feel kind of special this evening.

Chapter 30

Strasburg

By the middle of July, life was busier than ever for Belinda—working in the greenhouse, tending the garden, doing household chores, and socializing. She'd continued to see Herschel and Monroe as regularly as possible during what little free time she had. Her friendship with the men had deepened, but so far, Belinda's feelings had not turned to love.

And maybe they never will, Belinda thought as she guided her horse and buggy in the direction of her dear friend Mary Ruth Lapp's home. The older woman had come home from the hospital a few days before, after a right knee replacement. It was definitely time to drop by and see how Mary Ruth was doing.

Belinda glanced over at Sylvia, sitting on the front seat beside her with Rachel in her lap. Allen sat in the seat behind them, remaining quiet, which was unusual for a boy who often talked nonstop. It was a good thing his sister wasn't sitting next to him, because he'd probably be teasing her all the way to Mary Ruth's house.

"The wind's picked up, and the clouds have darkened," Sylvia spoke up. "I wonder if a summer storm might be coming."

"Could be. It's been dry here of late, so the crops and gardens could use a good dousing of *rege*."

"True. I only hope if it does bring rain that it won't go on for too many days. There's laundry to be done, and I'd prefer to hang things outdoors instead of in the basement."

"Same here, but unfortunately, we don't always get what we want."

Sylvia reached over and placed her hand on Belinda's arm. "I know, Mom. I know."

They rode in silence until the driveway leading to Mary Ruth's home came into view. "Come on, girl," Belinda coaxed, "This is where we make our turn." With the skill from many years of managing a horse and buggy, she guided her mare up the driveway to the hitching rail.

Sylvia placed Rachel on the seat beside Belinda, stepped down, and secured the horse to the rail.

A short time later, they walked with the children up to the house. "I hope you got my message about us coming by this evening," Belinda said when Mary Ruth's granddaughter Lenore greeted them at the door.

"I did, and my grandma has been looking forward to seeing you ever since I told her you'd be coming." Lenore let them in, and after Belinda handed her a container of brownies, she led the way to the living room, where Mary Ruth reclined on the couch with her leg propped on a pillow.

A wide smile graced the older woman's face as she beckoned them to come closer. "It's ever so nice to see you both. Danki for coming over."

Belinda reached down and took her friend's hand. "How are you feeling? Is there much *schmatze*?" She gestured to Mary Ruth's leg.

"To be honest, recovery from the surgery is not without pain, but thanks to the medicine I was given, I'm managing okay." Mary Ruth motioned to the two closest chairs. "Please take a seat so we can visit awhile."

"While you're doing that, I'll go to the kitchen and fix us all a cup of tea." Lenore smiled. "We can enjoy some of the brownies Belinda and Sylvia brought." She looked down at Allen and Rachel, hiding shyly behind their mother. "My kinner are at the kitchen table, coloring pictures. Why don't you two come along and join them?" As usual, Pennsylvania Dutch was spoken to the children.

Allen followed Lenore right away, but Rachel hung back.

"Guess I'd better walk out there with her," Sylvia said. "I'll come back with Lenore when the refreshments are ready. By then, my daughter will be happily coloring with the other children, and probably enjoying a brownie too."

After Sylvia left the room, Belinda pulled a straight-back chair close to the couch. "How long will you be convalescing, Mary Ruth?"

"I'm able to get up and move around with that." Mary Ruth pointed to the walker parked within her reach. "I'll start physical therapy soon, but it'll be several weeks before I'm pronounced to be good as new." The wrinkles in her forehead deepened. "If my dear husband was still alive, he'd probably keep me under his watchful eye, afraid I'd try to do too much too soon."

"I bet he would."

"So tell me, what's new with you?" Mary Ruth placed her hand on Belinda's knee.

"I've been working in the greenhouse, helping with household chores, and trying to keep up with the weeds in our vegetable garden. Sylvia's a big help, but since she began working in the greenhouse, she's just as busy as I am."

"Sounds like you have your hands full." Mary Ruth's voice lowered. "I hear tell you have two eager suitors hanging out at your house a lot these days. Has one of them stolen your heart or are you still trying to decide?"

It's funny how much she knows when we haven't spoken to each other for a spell. I'd say the grapevine in this community is healthy and strong. Belinda moistened her lips with the tip of her tongue and swallowed a couple of times. She'd rather not talk about this, but knowing Mary Ruth, she wouldn't stop questioning until she had some answers. "They're both quite different, but each has some good qualities that I admire."

"Enough to marry one of them if they should ask?" Mary Ruth tipped her head.

I think my friend here would make Monroe a good companion. They both seem to possess the strong desire to make me feel pressured. Belinda shuffled her feet against the hardwood floor while rubbing the back of her warm neck. It was embarrassing to be put on the spot, but it was just like Mary Ruth to ask lots of questions and say whatever was on her mind.

"If you'd rather not talk about it, I understand." Mary Ruth reached up and plumped the pillow behind her head. "It's really none of my business."

Belinda leaned closer and whispered, "When I'm with Monroe I feel like a young woman enjoying her boyfriend's attention."

"And Herschel? How do you feel when you're with him?"

Belinda lowered her hand and gave her dress sleeve a little tug. "He makes me feel calm and relaxed."

Mary Ruth's brows moved up and down as a playful smile spread across her face. "Well, there you have it—all you need to do is decide whether you want to spend the rest of your life enjoying your husband's attention or feeling calm and relaxed."

Belinda lowered her hand. *If it were only that simple. And who said anything about a husband?*

Henry wandered around the yard with Blackie at his side. It was kind of nice having Mom, Sylvia, and the kinner gone for a few hours. It gave him time for some things he wanted to do without having to worry about someone asking him to do something he'd rather not do. That seemed to have become his way of life since his dad and brother died.

"Work. . .work. . .work. . ." Henry muttered as he picked up a stick and tossed it for Blackie.

The dog took off on a run and came back soon with the piece of wood in his mouth. He promptly dropped it on the ground and, with tail wagging, looked up at Henry as if to say, "Throw it again."

"Enough already! We've done it too many times. Go lie down now, so I can sit and think awhile." Ignoring the stick, Henry pointed to the porch and headed that way himself. His faithful dog followed.

Blackie flopped onto the porch with a grunt, and Henry went inside to get them both some water. When he returned, he placed a plastic bowl, brimming full of water, beside the dog and took a seat on the porch swing with the glass he'd filled with ice and cold water.

Henry took a drink and grinned when Blackie began lapping thirstily from the bowl. It had been a hot, humid day, and now the wind had begun to blow, while the sky darkened with ominous-looking clouds. Off in the distance Henry heard the rumble of thunder. He watched the sky in anticipation of a bright flash appearing. Not long after, it happened.

"Oh, wow. . .that was a good one!" Henry heard Blackie's whimper. Soon a loud boom echoed across the landscape. The wind picked up, and the trees swayed even more. Henry felt the temperature drop and smelled the essence of rain in the air. He watched another flash, and not long after, the crack of thunder boomed.

Blackie got up and came over to Henry. "Aw, it's okay, boy. I'll take care of you." He combed his hand down the dog's back a few times and patted him.

Henry took another drink and set his glass on the small table next to the swing. *Oh boy, I bet we're in for a summer storm, and from the looks of that sky, it could be a bad one. Sure hope it doesn't hit hard—at least not till Mom, Sylvia, and the kinner get home.*

Belinda clung tightly to her horse's reins as a torrential rain poured from the sky, making it difficult to see out the buggy's front window, even with Sylvia working the hand-operated window wipers.

The poor horse looked soaked to the bone as it pulled them home. Belinda felt bad for the animal. It seemed as though they were right in the middle of this terrible storm.

A gust of harsh wind rocked the buggy as a clap of thunder boomed. Rachel and Allen both screamed.

"Maybe we should pull over and wait the storm out." Sylvia's voiced trembled. "The children are frightened, and the rain's coming down harder. The wind's grown stronger too. If we keep going, your buggy might topple over."

Speaking in short, strong sentences, Belinda said, "We're not far from home. We need to press on. If the weather gets worse, we'll be safer there."

Sylvia turned in her seat and spoke in a reassuring tone. "It's okay, little ones. Soon we'll be back at Grandma's."

As they continued on, although the sky had darkened, Belinda saw some trees on her side of the road that had been uprooted. If they didn't get home soon, there was a good chance her carriage could be upended.

Dear Lord, she prayed, *Please help both me and my horse to stay calm, and protect us from harm. Also please be with others who are out on the road this night too.*

As Belinda's prayer ended, a sheet of lightning lit up the sky, enabling her to see several feet ahead. To Belinda's surprise, she saw someone bent over and appearing to be struggling against the wind. Upon closer look, it became clear that the person was Maude.

Belinda leaned closer to Sylvia. "We need to stop and give her a ride. On foot, it'll be a miracle if she makes it back to her shanty in one piece."

"It's certainly the right thing to do," Sylvia responded, "but listen to my kinner and their terrified whimpers. They might be as afraid of Maude as they are the storm."

"Rachel wasn't scared when Maude took her to the shanty last year. I'm sure they'll be fine." With no further discussion, Belinda guided the horse and buggy to the side of the road. Although opening the door of the driver's side meant she'd be drenched within seconds, Belinda did it anyway. "Maude, it's Belinda King!" she shouted against the howling wind. "We've stopped to give you a ride to your home."

Maude didn't have to be asked a second time. Sylvia got out of the carriage and climbed in back with the children. Then Belinda instructed Maude to take the seat up front beside her.

"What are you doing out on a night like this?" Belinda asked once she got the horse moving again.

Maude looked over at her. "I could ask you the same thing."

She smiled. "Good point, but why don't you explain first?"

Maude shifted on the seat. "I went for a walk. Didn't realize bad weather was comin'."

When Maude spoke, Belinda had to hold her breath, for the pungent odor of garlic permeated the buggy. It was so bad Belinda figured the obnoxious smell was not only coming from Maude's breath but also leaching out of her body. No doubt this near-homeless woman had eaten a lot of garlic, either for the sake of her health or to ward off insects.

I wonder if Maude's been taking garlic from my garden. Belinda had noticed that it seemed to be disappearing rather quickly, but she figured Sylvia might have picked more than normal to use in upcoming suppers.

"So how 'bout you folks? What are you doin' out on a night like this?" Maude bumped Belinda's arm with her elbow.

"We were visiting some friends, but the weather didn't turn bad until we began our journey home."

The elderly woman made a clicking noise with her tongue. "I see."

Rain continued to pelt Belinda's buggy as stronger winds made it more difficult to stay on the road. When Belinda's mailbox, near the beginning of her driveway, came into view she directed her horse to go right.

"You turned too soon." Maude leaned closer to Belinda. "My little cabin is farther up the road."

"I'm aware of that, Maude, but the weather has turned so frightful, I don't think we should chance going any farther."

"Okay, well then, I'll get out and walk the rest of the way." Maude coughed a couple of times, making the odor of garlic permeate the carriage even more.

Belinda reached over to touch the woman's arm. "If the storm gets worse, you may not make it to your place. I would like you to come to my house and sleep in the guest room tonight."

Even with the wind howling, Belinda heard Sylvia's intake of breath from the back of the buggy. However, Belinda held firm in her decision. *Surely my daughter must realize the importance of helping out a neighbor, or anyone else, during a time such as this.*

Chapter 31

Henry had settled into a chair in the living room with the latest birding magazine, when Sylvia and her children entered the room with wide eyes and flushed faces.

Sylvia stopped in front of his chair. "How can you sit here so calmly when there's such a wicked storm outside? Haven't you seen the damage it's doing?"

"Where's Mom?" Henry asked without answering his sister's questions.

"She's outside trying to get the horse unhitched and put in the barn. Maude's with her."

His brows shot up. "Maude? What's she doin' here?"

"She was walking and got caught in the storm, so we picked her up and Mom decided to bring her here to spend the night."

Henry's mouth dropped open. "Why would she do something like that?"

"She feels sorry for Maude and wants to do right by the poor woman," Sylvia whispered. "Now would you please go out there and help her so they can get inside where it's warm and dry? While you're doing that, I need to get my little ones put to bed."

"Okay." Henry set down his magazine and stood. He didn't mind helping to put the horse away, but the thought of Maude spending the night in their home didn't sit well with him. His finger's clenched. *Just a few hours in this house and that old woman might steal anything she can get her hands on.*

Henry wished he could stay up all night to keep an eye on things, but his mother would never go for that. *Think I may sneak downstairs with Blackie and sleep on the couch after Mom, Sylvia, and Maude go to bed. That way, if the old woman comes out of the guest room and tries anything funny, the dog will let me know, and I can hopefully catch her in the act.*

The following morning, when Belinda woke up, the first thing she did was go to her bedroom window and look out. The sky was overcast, but at least it wasn't raining. The harsh winds had subsided too. However, the sight that greeted Belinda was disturbing. Two of the smaller trees in their yard had been uprooted. It made her feel sad, because those were the ones Vernon had planted the same year he'd died.

As she continued to scan the property it became apparent that broken branches lay scattered across the yard and one section of their fence had been knocked down. It would take some doing to get it all cleaned up, and it certainly wouldn't happen today.

Belinda stepped away from the window. *I can only imagine the state of other properties around our area. I pray no one was injured due to the storm that went through here last night.*

She hurried to get dressed so she could check and see if any damage had been done to the house.

When Belinda passed through the living room, she was surprised to see Henry sleeping on the couch, with Blackie lying on the floor nearby.

"Wake up, Henry." She shook his arm.

Henry rolled over and opened his eyes. "Morning, Mom."

Her brows furrowed. "Why are you and your hund sleeping down here?"

Henry sat up and yawned as he averted his gaze. "I...um...thought it would be good if I slept on the couch."

"How come?"

He pointed in the direction of the guest room down the hall.

She glanced that way then looked back at him. "What are you talking about?"

"I wanted to make sure our overnight guest didn't help herself to anything during the night." Henry spoke in a near whisper. "Don't think she came out of her room while I was sleeping though, 'cause I'm sure I woulda heard her."

Belinda's jaw tightened as she folded her arms. "Why must you be so suspicious?"

"Because Maude's given us plenty of reasons not to trust her."

"We'll talk more about this later. Right now, while I start breakfast, I'd like you to get dressed and go outside. Last night's storm left our yard in a terrible mess, and a good deal of the debris is blocking the parking lot of the greenhouse." Belinda bit down on her bottom lip. "If the building is still standing, that is."

Henry got up, grabbed his binoculars, and hurried over to the living-room window. "Wow, Mom, you're right, the yard is a mess, but from here, I can't tell much about the greenhouse except that it's still there."

She sighed softly. "That's a relief. Even so, I'd like you to walk down there and check on things. For today, at least, we'll need to keep the CLOSED sign on the greenhouse door. There is too much work to be done in the yard today, and I don't want anyone to get hurt with all the mess scattered around. Also, please take a look at all sides of our house," Belinda added.

"Okay, I will let Blackie out right now, and then I'll get dressed."

"At least the damage from the bad weather we had last night isn't due to another senseless attack," Belinda stated. "There have been no more incidents for quite a while, so I think maybe whoever did those things may have given up or realized what they were doing was wrong."

Henry shook his head. "I'm not sure about that. I think the person behind the attacks is waiting to see if we'll take his or her threats seriously and put our place up for sale."

Belinda's thoughts raced as she remembered the last threatening message they'd received. She hoped and prayed the person behind the message had changed his or her mind, because she had no plans to sell her home or the greenhouse she and Vernon had worked so hard to establish.

Henry tapped Belinda's shoulder. "Mom, did you hear what I said?"

"Jah, I did, but I don't want to talk about this right now." She glanced toward the guestroom door, noticing that it was partially open. "While you're outside, I'll get breakfast started and check on Maude. She'll no doubt be hungry and ready to eat."

Henry opened his mouth as if he wanted to say something more, but instead he called his dog and let him outside.

Belinda shook her head. *That boy of mine; I can't believe he slept down here to keep an eye on Maude.*

She moved across the hall to the guestroom and rapped on the door. When there was no response, Belinda pushed the door open a little farther and peaked in. The bed had been made, and the nightgown Belinda had given the old woman to wear last night lay at the foot of the bed, but there was no sign of Maude.

"Well, for goodness' sake." Belinda hurried down the hall to the bathroom to see if Maude may have gone there, but that door was open and no one was inside.

Belinda checked the kitchen next, but Maude wasn't there either. When she spotted a note on the table, she slipped on her reading glasses and read it aloud: "Thanks for the soft bed to sleep in. I helped myself to four cookies and an apple before I left. —Maude."

Belinda felt a tight sensation in her throat. *I wish there was something more I could do to help that poor woman. I can't imagine what it must be like to live in that old shack with barely any furnishings and no family around. There must be something our Amish community can do to help her out.*

Belinda tapped her chin. *The next time I see Maude, I'll ask her some questions. Surely she must have some family somewhere who would be willing to take her in. If not, then I'll speak to some of our church members and see who might be willing to do something to help out.*

"Would you look at that mess!" Virginia pointed out the kitchen window at their backyard. "That horrible storm we had last night left our yard in shambles."

Earl set his coffee cup down and joined her at the window. "We did lose a lot of tree branches, but at least my garage roof is still intact." He turned to face Virginia. "I'll pick up the larger branches when I get home from work this evening. In the meantime, maybe you can gather the smaller ones."

Virginia's fists tightened and her fingers curled into the palms of her hands. "I'd planned to do some shopping today, and there's also a batch of laundry that needs to be done. I'm tellin' you, Earl, if we still lived in Chicago, my life would be much easier and I wouldn't be expected to pick up tree branches today. It's like I'm a pioneer woman having to gather wood up to start a fire."

He rolled his eyes at her. "For heaven's sakes, woman, we had storms in Chicago."

"Yeah, but we didn't have a yard full of trees. Besides, I see myself as more of a city gal who's used to not doing unnecessary work."

Earl picked up his cup, took a drink, and then placed it in the sink. "I'm glad you've figured out that you're a city girl, Red, and that's all right by me. But it would still be helpful if you moved your caboose and got busy with those branches. I've gotta head out now. I'll see you when I get home." He grabbed his cooler and went out the back door.

Virginia flopped into a chair at the table, looked down at her cat who curled up near her feet, and groaned. "I think Earl's irritated, Goldie. I didn't even get a goodbye kiss. I long for the good ole days when picking up wood meant I'd be going to the store to buy a few Pres-to-Logs for the fireplace." She reached down and stroked the cat's fur. "But on a positive side, my bum leg has eased up some in the last day or two. Of course that'll probably change after I'm done working in the yard."

Virginia remained at the table until she'd finished her coffee, then ambled into the living room and picked up her binoculars. *I may as well look out front and see how things held up in the neighbors' yard across the road.*

Holding the field glasses up to her face, she was stunned to see that two trees in the Kings' yard had been uprooted. There were also plenty of limbs lying around.

Guess we were the lucky ones with only tree branches down. It's strange how a storm that hits the same area can do different kinds of damage from one individual's property to another's.

Continuing to observe through the binoculars, Virginia was even more surprised when she spotted a woman on the lower roof of the house that extended out under part of the second floor. She couldn't be sure if it was Belinda or her daughter, Sylvia, but whoever it was, they were sweeping off debris, no doubt left from the storm.

"What a foolish thing to do," she mumbled. "You couldn't pay me enough to go up there. It's bad enough Earl expects me to clean up some of the fallen debris in the yard." Virginia's brows knitted together. "Sure hope I don't have to witness that woman taking a tumble. Even if she survived the fall, she'd no doubt be seriously injured."

Herschel's eyes widened when he guided his horse and buggy into Belinda's yard and saw so many downed tree limbs, branches, and even a couple of uprooted trees. Apparently this part of Lancaster County had been hit pretty hard by last night's storm.

Herschel brought the horse up to the hitching rail, got out and secured the animal. When he turned toward the house, he pressed a fist to his mouth. *Oh my. . .what on earth is Belinda doing on that flat roof? Just one slip and she could be on the ground.*

Herschel saw Henry in the yard, picking up branches and loading them into a wheelbarrow. He hurried over to him and pointed to the roof where Belinda stood. "What's your mamm doing up there?"

Henry glanced in that direction and shrugged. "She's sweepin' the roof to get rid of everything the wind blew on it."

"Well, she needs to come down. It's not a safe place for her to be." The concern Herschel felt for Belinda was almost overwhelming. He hadn't experienced this feeling of protectiveness since Mattie died. "Is it okay if I go up?"

"On the roof?"

"Jah."

The teenage boy shrugged his shoulders. "Suit yourself, but I don't know what you're so worried about. My mamm's been on that flat roof before and she's never had a problem."

"What room is she near, and how do I get there?" Herschel didn't care what Henry said. With every second that passed, his concern for Belinda grew. His heart beat twice as fast as normal, while looking up at her and thinking about what might happen.

"Once you enter the house, go partway down the hall and then up the stairs to the second level. The room Mom is working from will be the first door to your left." Henry went back to picking up branches.

Herschel hurried up the front porch steps and knocked on the door.

A few seconds later, Sylvia answered. "Hello, Herschel. How are you this morning?"

"I'm fine, but I saw your mudder up on the flat roof, and I'm worried about her. Henry said I could go on up."

"Of course, but—"

Herschel didn't wait for Sylvia to finish her sentence. He hurried down the hall and raced up the stairs. When he reached the second floor and found the door Henry had mentioned, he jerked it open, nearly colliding with Belinda.

"Oh my! You scared me, Herschel. I didn't know you were here, much less in this room."

"I saw you on the roof and was worried you might fall."

Belinda gestured to the partially open window. "I went out there to sweep off the debris from last night's storm."

"So you crawled out through a *fenschder*?"

She bobbed her head. "It's not the first time I've crawled out that window, so there's no need to look so serious."

"I—I can't help it. I'd feel terrible if you fell and got hurt or. . ." Herschel's voice trailed off and he blinked several times, hoping to control his swirling emotions. He'd never admitted it to himself until now, but he had fallen in love with this sweet woman and was on the verge of telling her so. The question was, how would she respond?

Chapter 32

Plink! Plink! Something wet landed on Herschel's arm. "What in the world?" He looked up just as another drop of water came—this one targeting his nose.

Herschel stepped aside and Belinda did the same. "Oh dear, it looks like there may be a leak in my roof. I bet it's from all the rain we had last night."

"Yes, and we had a lot of wind too. Maybe your shingles took a beating from it, like some of the other houses I spotted on the way over here this morning." Herschel went to the window and looked out. "Jah, and it's raining lightly right now." So much for declaring his love for Belinda. The matter of her roof in need of repair took precedence over anything else at the moment.

"If you have an extension ladder I can go up there and take a look," he offered.

Belinda shook her head. "My son-in-law's a roofer by trade, so I'll ask him to come over and look at it as soon as he's able."

"Are you sure? I don't mind going up there to check things out. I could patch any holes temporarily."

Before Belinda could respond to Herschel's question, her daughter hollered up the stairs: "Amy left a message on our voice mail, Mom! There's a fallen tree blocking the road between their place and here, so unless it gets cleared soon, she won't be able to make it over today to watch the kinner."

Belinda cupped her hands around her mouth. "I'll be right down!" She turned to face Herschel again. "I'd better go downstairs and talk to my daughter."

"Of course." Herschel followed Belinda down the stairs. When they reached the bottom step, he placed his hand on her arm. "It may be awhile before the road gets cleared, which means Jared might not be able to take a look at your roof today, or even tomorrow. So if you don't mind, I'd really like to go up there and see what I can do to stop the water from coming in."

"Very well, but only if you allow Henry to hold the ladder for you."

Herschel smiled. "I have no problem with that."

After Herschel went outside, Belinda sought Sylvia out. She found her at the kitchen sink, washing a batch of canning jars.

"Did you respond to Amy's message about not being able to come over?" Belinda asked.

"Jah. I said it was fine because we're not opening the greenhouse today."

"That's good, but I'm going out to the phone shed again to leave an important message for Jared."

"Oh?" Sylvia turned to face Belinda. "Is something wrong?"

"Apparently there's a leak in our roof. When I was talking to Herschel upstairs, we discovered water dripping through the ceiling."

"Do you think it will require putting on a whole new roof?"

Belinda shrugged. "I don't know. Herschel went out to ask Henry to get the tall ladder, and then he plans to go up on the roof to check things out."

Sylvia's brows lowered. "Henry?"

"No, Herschel. Your bruder will hold the ladder."

"That's fine, but it might be better if we waited until Jared can come over. Herschel's not a young man anymore. He might lose his footing and fall off the roof."

Belinda pinched the skin near the base of her throat. "I hope not. I would feel terrible if something bad happened to him."

"That's interesting, because Herschel was concerned about you being on the lower flat roof. He couldn't wait to get upstairs and see if you were okay." Belinda detected a gleam in her daughter's eyes as she leaned closer to her. "I think that nice man is in love with you, and I have a hunch the feeling is mutual."

"Now, don't be silly." Belinda's chin dipped down as she tucked her arms against her sides, unable to look her daughter in the eye. She couldn't deny that strong feelings for Herschel had begun to surface, but she wasn't willing to admit it to Sylvia or anyone yet. Truth was, Belinda could barely admit it to herself.

Her thoughts went to Monroe and how she felt whenever he was around. At times she enjoyed herself, but her feelings for him had not developed into anything close to love at this point. *I doubt they ever will,* she told herself. *In all fairness, I should let Monroe know that there's no hope of us having a future together, before he becomes too serious and proposes marriage. I'm not quite sure how to bring up the subject or form the right words.*

Belinda removed a wicker basket from the storage room and placed it on the kitchen counter.

"What are you going to do with that, Mom?" Sylvia questioned. "It's still drizzling outside, so this isn't picnic weather."

"Since Maude left before any of us got up this morning and didn't have breakfast with us, I want to take her something to eat."

"I'm sure she must have some food in her shanty."

"That could be, but it's probably not enough." Belinda placed a loaf of bread in the basket, along with a jar of honey, and some home-canned fruits and jellies.

"Do you think that poor woman has some sort of mental problems?" Sylvia asked.

"Perhaps, which is all the more reason she needs some help."

"Henry thinks she could be the person who has done the vandalism around your property."

"I know." Belinda rubbed at an itch on her arm. "Do you realize your bruder has made a list of suspects, but without any proof?"

"I'm well aware." Sylvia gave a small laugh. "But at least Henry playing detective keeps him occupied and out of trouble. And maybe he will discover who's been responsible for all the upsetting things that have happened."

"That would be nice, but right now we have other things to worry about." Belinda moved toward the back door. "The rain seems to have let up, so I'm going outside to leave a message for Jared, and then I'll see how Herschel and Henry are doing. Afterward, I may pick up a few of those branches that are scattered all over our yard before I head to Maude's."

"I know it's a mess out there because the children walked with me earlier to the phone shed. We had to make our own pathway to it, and the little ones were sure intrigued with the branches and the fallen trees." She continued to fill the basin with warm water. "I'd like to help you but I can't leave Allen and Rachel alone in the house." Sylvia grimaced. "No telling what kind of mischief they'd get into while I was outdoors. And I certainly can't allow them in the yard by themselves until everything's been cleaned up." Sylvia set the last jar in the sink and added more soap and water. "I also need to get started preparing the tomatoes we want to can."

Belinda flapped her hand. "Not a problem. If you decide you want to come outside later on, we can switch places."

"True, but you probably won't want to come inside until Herschel is gone." Sylvia gave Belinda a little smirk, and then plunged her hands into the water to begin her task.

Belinda ignored her daughter's last comment and went out the back door. She had no more than stepped onto the porch when she spotted Monroe's horse and buggy coming up the driveway. *Oh boy. . .both men are here at the same time. I wonder how this will play out.*

As Monroe pulled his rig into Belinda's yard, he noticed another horse and buggy at the hitching rail. He wondered if it belonged to a family member or if Belinda had company. Her yard was sure a mess. Last night's storm had done a number on the trees in Belinda's yard. No doubt she would need help cleaning it up, and he planned to volunteer his services.

Once Monroe stepped down from the buggy and secured his horse, he looked toward the house and noticed Belinda on her front porch. She wasn't the only person he saw, however. Her son, Henry, held a ladder against one end of the house.

Monroe's gaze traveled up to the roof. There stood Herschel, looking as though he was about to descend the ladder.

Monroe's lips pressed together. *Oh great. What's he doing here? Probably came over to see if Belinda needed anything. If I had gotten here sooner, I'd be the one fixing her roof instead of Herschel. I wonder if he's capable and can do a good job.*

Monroe approached the house and stepped onto the porch. "Morning, Belinda. I came by to see how you are doing after last night's unexpected storm." He turned slightly and gestured to the yard. "It looks like your place got hit pretty hard."

"It did, and now we have quite the mess to clean up. I'll need to find a good place to pile all this debris until we can dispose of it."

"That shouldn't be too hard since you've got plenty of property to keep it out of the way until then." He smiled. "I'm available for part of the day, so just tell me what you'd like done first and I'll get started."

"Well, umm..." A pink flush appeared on Belinda's face and neck as she looked over at Herschel, who'd just stepped off the ladder.

Before either of them could say anything more, Herschel walked past Monroe and stood in front of Belinda. "I found the problem. Several shingles were blown off, so that's why water's been getting in."

"I figured as much. I'll head out to the phone shed and leave a message for Jared."

"Would you like me to see what's in your toolshed and take care of patching it for now?" Herschel asked.

"I suppose it would be good to get something in place, because Jared might not be able to come over anytime today."

"No problem." Herschel looked over at Henry who had joined them on the porch. "Would you mind coming with me to the shed to get the supplies we need?"

Henry glanced briefly at Monroe, then back at Herschel. "Sure, I can do that, and I'll go up on the roof to help you too." The boy pointed to the barn on the other side of the yard. "I sit up in the hayloft sometimes and look out the front opening to watch for birds and other things, so I ain't scared, 'cause I'm used to being up high."

"All right, if your mamm has no objections, neither do I." Herschel gave Henry's shoulder a few taps.

Oh brother, this fella is too much. Monroe almost gagged. It seemed obvious that Herschel was trying to win over Belinda's son. He probably thought if he succeeded with that, he'd win Belinda's hand in marriage. *Well, I've got news for him. I'm the better man for Belinda. Besides, we have a history, and the fact is, she would've picked me to be her husband if Vernon hadn't come along and snatched her away.*

Monroe's fingers twitched as he held them behind his back. *Well, Herschel can try all he wants, but he will never succeed. I'm not about to let him steal my girl.*

Herschel looked down from the roof and frowned. Monroe pushed a wheelbarrow full of branches he'd picked up in the yard, and Belinda appeared to be helping him. "I'm glad I came by to check on you, and see how things are here," Herschel heard the man say. Monroe stopped briefly to pick up more branches. "You definitely need some help, and I'm the right man."

"That man," Herschel mumbled behind clenched teeth. Using the back of his hand, Herschel wiped sweat from his forehead.

"You talkin' about Monroe, by any chance?"

Herschel looked at Henry and nodded. "He seems to know everything and is always bragging. When we came out of the toolshed I heard him telling your mamm that even at the age of fifty-three, he could work twice as hard as any man half his age."

Henry's nose wrinkled. "Monroe says all that stuff, hopin' Mom will be impressed. He thinks that because he used to court her before she married my daed, it gives him an edge with her now." Henry handed Herschel another roofing nail. "Don't know what I'm gonna do if he talks her into marrying him. The last thing I want is a stepfather—especially a man like Monroe."

What about me? Herschel was tempted to ask. *Would you be okay if your mother and I got married?* Herschel's good sense kept him from asking that question. He wasn't about to let on to Belinda's son that he would like to marry his mother—especially since he hadn't asked Belinda yet.

As Herschel began patching the roof, he heard Monroe down below, bragging about his new open buggy. *Here we go again.*

When he looked down another time, and saw Monroe move closer to Belinda, Herschel's stomach tightened. *If I don't get my courage up soon and declare my feelings for Belinda, she'll be married to Monroe before I ever have a chance to ask for her hand in marriage.* He set a nail in place and lifted the hammer. *I need to act fast.*

Chapter 33

Monroe tossed a few more branches into the wheelbarrow, then reached into his trousers pocket and pulled out his timepiece. "Sorry, Belinda, but I need to go. I have a meeting soon with a Realtor about a home I may be interested in purchasing."

"No problem. I appreciate the help you've done here this morning. Before you go, though, let me run into the house and get a container of applesauce-raisin cookies for you."

A pleasing smile crossed his face. "Danki, Belinda. That's kind of you." He glanced across the yard, where Herschel was busy cutting limbs off one of the uprooted trees. "I figured Herschel would be gone by now. Doesn't he have a store to run in Gordonville?"

Belinda blinked. "Well, jah, but he also has employees who can run the store while he's away. Isn't that how it is with you?"

With a tight expression, Monroe gave a brief nod. "I'll wait over by my horse and buggy for you to bring me the cookies," he added, then left before Belinda could comment. The reality hit her that Monroe was jealous of Herschel. She felt sure it had nothing to do with his business dealings either.

Belinda went into the house and filled a disposable plastic container with cookies, then hurried outside and handed it to Monroe. "Thanks again for coming over to help out."

"It was my pleasure." His lips formed into another wide smile. "I would do most anything for you."

She swallowed hard. *I hope he doesn't say anything more. I'm not ready to tell him how I feel today.*

Belinda felt relief when Monroe said goodbye, untied his horse, and got into his carriage. She waved and watched until he was out of sight, then walked over to the section of yard where Herschel and Henry worked. "I have an errand I need to run," she said, looking at Herschel. "When I get back, I'll help Sylvia start lunch preparations, and I'd be pleased if you would join us for the meal."

Herschel brushed the cuff of his shirtsleeve across his damp forehead. "Between what I did on the roof, and now down here, I've worked up quite an appetite, so I won't turn away your invitation for lunch. Danki, Belinda."

"It's me who should be thanking you." She gestured to the tree he'd been cutting. "There's no way Henry and I could have accomplished this much by ourselves today, and we truly appreciate all your help." She looked at Henry. "Right, Son?"

Henry gave a weak smile as he bobbed his head. "Uh-huh, right."

"I'll let you two get back to work now. I shouldn't be gone long—just walking over to Maude's place."

Henry's forehead wrinkled. "What are you going there for?"

"I have a food basket for her."

Henry's mouth slackened before his gaze turned skyward. "You must be kidding, Mom."

The heat and humidity of the day accentuated the warmth she felt on her cheeks. "I most certainly am not."

"As many times as that woman has stolen from us, and you wanna give her some food? I still don't understand why you let her sleep here last night."

"The Bible says in Mark 12:31, that we should love our neighbors as ourselves." Belinda paused before continuing. "And in Luke 6:35 we are reminded to love even our enemies, and lend, hoping for nothing."

"But Maude ain't borrowin', Mom. She's taking and you're giving to her. That strange old woman's done nothing but cause us trouble."

"I don't believe you quite understand the concept of the scriptures your mamm speaks of," Herschel interjected. "God wants us to love others and do good to people, whether they have done good to us or not."

Henry's facial features tightened. Mumbling under his breath, he moved away and began picking up more limbs that had been scattered on the other side of the yard.

"I don't think your son appreciated my words on the matter,"

Herschel said to Belinda, "Guess maybe I spoke when I should have kept silent."

She shook her head. "What you said was the truth, based on God's Holy Word, and Henry needs to take those words to heart."

"Hopefully, someday he will." Herschel placed his hand on her shoulder. "In the meantime, Belinda, I'll be praying for your son and you as well—that God will give you words of wisdom and guidance as you continue to set a good example to each of your family members."

"Danki." Belinda's body felt weighed down. Being a single parent was a huge responsibility. There were many days when she didn't feel up to the task. If only she had a husband to share in the responsibilities and offer wise counsel the way Herschel just did. He truly was a good friend. She looked into the depths of his blue eyes and saw sincerity. Was it any wonder she'd fallen in love with him? If only she knew how he felt about her.

Belinda was halfway to Maude's when she saw a horse and buggy going down the road in the opposite direction. She blinked several times, barely able to believe her eyes. A full grown sheep sat in the front seat next to the Amish man who drove the rig. What a humorous sight to behold. Belinda remembered hearing that one of her English neighbors had planned to buy a new ewe. She figured this sheep might be on the way to its new owners, but having it ride in the front of the Amish man's buggy was a strange way to make a delivery.

"Each to his own, I guess." She chuckled. It was good to witness something humorous once in a while. Life often became too serious, and sometimes it was difficult to find anything to laugh or even smile about.

Belinda felt grateful for the two grandchildren who had lived with her since their daddy was killed. Rachel and Allen did cute or funny things almost every day. Other things in life brought joy to her too, such as the martins who had taken up residence in the martin boxes her husband had built before his untimely death.

Another thing that always brought a smile to Belinda's lips was watching the hummingbirds busy at the feeders she'd hung on shepherd's hooks near the front porch. Sometimes as many as five or six hummers tried to feed at the same time, which often meant some of the little birds tried to fight each other off. Belinda would miss their frenzied activity when it came time for the hummingbirds to leave, just like she would miss Sylvia and her children when they moved in with Dennis after the wedding in October.

But life moves on and we always have changes to deal with, Belinda told herself. *I'll need to keep my focus on keeping the greenhouse running, even if it means hiring someone outside the family to help out.* She stopped walking as another thought popped into her head. *What if I got married again? Would it mean giving up the greenhouse?*

As Belinda approached Maude's rundown shack, she wondered once more where the elderly woman went during the harsher winter months. She'd checked the cabin a few times last winter and found it empty, so Maude must have gone someplace until she returned in the early spring. The chickens were gone too. She'd either cooked and eaten them, or taken the hens with her—which seemed unlikely. *Maybe I'll ask her about that when I drop off the basket of food.*

A short time later, the shanty came into view and Belinda saw Maude sitting outside on a rickety-looking wooden chair. In her lap lay a beautiful cat with golden-colored hair.

"Hello, Maude. I brought you a few items of food you might enjoy." Belinda held out the basket. "I would have given them to you after breakfast this morning, but you left my house before I got up."

"I woke up early and didn't want to disturb ya." Maude put the feline on the ground and stood. "I'll take the food inside and put it away. Then you can have your basket back." She motioned to the cat. "Would you mind watching her for me so she don't run off?"

"I didn't realize you had a cat." Belinda bent down, and when she picked the animal up, it let out a loud, *Meow!*

"Didn't have it till this morning. The critter was here when I came back from your place. I think it must be a stray."

"That's possible." Belinda knelt down and stroked the cat's silky head. She wasn't much of a cat person, but this one seemed quite tame and lovable.

"Have a seat." Maude motioned to the chair she'd been sitting in. "I'll be back soon." She quickly disappeared into her sad-looking dwelling.

When Belinda sat down, the cat began to purr. All the cats she had were either outside or in the barn. Although it might be nice to have a cat inside for companionship, it would also mean having to stay on top of all the cat hair that would most likely get on the furniture.

Belinda stopped petting the cat when Maude came back out and set the basket on the ground by her feet.

She got up and offered Maude the chair and then handed her the cat. "I need to get home, but before I go, there's something I've been meaning to ask you."

The older woman sat down and placed the feline over her shoulder, like a baby. "What do ya wanna know?"

"I've noticed that you're not here during most of the winter and wondered where you spend the colder months."

"I stay with my late sister's daughter, Bonita. She lives in South Carolina." Maude stroked the length of the cat's body, which brought about more purring.

"I'm glad to hear you have someplace warmer to go. Our winters here can get pretty cold."

"Yep." Maude placed the cat back in her lap, and it began licking its paws.

The beautiful katz might be just what this poor woman needs, Belinda mused. *Of course, what will she do with it during the winter months when she's gone? Will Maude take the cat with her? Surely she wouldn't leave it here to fend for itself. Speaking of which. . .I still haven't asked about those hinkel.*

"I have another question." Belinda looked directly at Maude. "What happened to the hens you had in your possession?"

Maude blinked several times. "Well, I put 'em back in your coop, and got 'em out again when I returned from South Carolina."

Belinda's mouth nearly fell open. "Oh, I–I see." *How odd that Henry never said anything about the return of those chickens, or the fact that they were missing from the coop again. He must be too focused on playing detective these days.*

Belinda bent down to pick up the basket. "I'm glad there wasn't much damage done to your yard from last night's storm. It sure caused a mess in our yard."

"Yeah, I saw that this morning." Maude motioned to her shanty.

"Figured when I arrived here I'd discover that not much of my place was left. But for some odd reason, the only damage I saw was a few places on the roof that were leaking."

"We had a leak in our roof too." Belinda put two fingers under her nose, to hold back a sneeze. When the feeling passed, she asked another question. "Would you be okay if some men from my Amish community came over and put a new roof on your cabin?"

Maude shook her head. "I don't have enough money to pay 'em."

"No, no. Their work would be free." Belinda clamped her mouth shut. *I shouldn't have said anything until I talked with Jared. He might be too busy to replace or even repair Maude's roof and may not appreciate me volunteering him to do it without pay. I should have thought things through before I spoke.*

Maude looked up at Belinda with her chin dipping slightly. "I'd be much obliged."

"All right, I will talk to my son-in-law who's a roofer, and either he or I will get back to you about it."

"Thanks." Maude picked up the cat and nuzzled it with her nose. "It's nice to know that some folks care about someone besides themselves."

Belinda reflected on the scripture verses she had shared with Henry awhile ago. This was an opportunity for some members in her church to do something good for someone in need.

With a sense of urgency, Virginia called Goldie's name over and over as she went from room to room. Shortly after Earl left for work this morning, she'd discovered the cat was missing. Goldie had disappeared one other time, and Virginia had been relieved to find her still in the house. This time, however, she'd looked high and low but had seen no sign of Goldie.

Virginia always kept the cat indoors, so if Goldie had gotten out, she probably ran off and wouldn't know how to find her way home. The idea of her furry companion being out on her own caused Virginia's chin to tremble. "Oh Goldie, what will I do if I can't find you?"

She stepped outside, checking both the back and front yards, while calling numerous times for the cat.

Virginia was about to look in the front yard again, when she spotted Belinda walking up the road. "Have you seen a gold-colored cat anywhere?" she hollered.

"As a matter of fact, I have." Belinda crossed the street and stepped into Virginia's yard. "I stopped by to see Maude, who lives in that old shack down the road, and she was holding a cat with gold-colored hair when I got there. She said it showed up at her place this morning."

"Oh, what a relief. It must be my Goldie. I'll get in my car and head over there right now." Virginia hurried to the garage without saying goodbye to Belinda.

A short time later, she pulled up to Maude's rundown shack. There was no sign of the old woman, or Goldie, so Virginia got out of the car, walked across the brown patches of grass, and knocked on the rickety front door. She'd only seen the cabin from the road before, and seeing it up close, she was appalled at the condition it was in. She could only imagine what the inside must look like.

I bet the old woman who lives here is a squatter, using the shanty without permission of the owner. Virginia pursed her lips as she waited outside the door. *How could anyone live in this place? I bet there's no indoor plumbing or electricity.*

Virginia's thoughts were stalled when the squeaky door swung open. There stood Maude with Goldie in her arms.

"Who are you, and what do ya want? If you're selling something, I ain't interested." Maude's gruff-sounding question caught Virginia off guard.

"I came here looking for my cat." Virginia pointed at Goldie. "That's her. She escaped from my house sometime this morning—probably when my husband left for work."

"Can ya prove she's yours?" Maude stroked the top of Goldie's head.

Virginia's muscles tightened. She was tempted to snatch her cat right out of the old woman's hands. "Can you prove she's yours?"

Maude looked down at Goldie, then back at Virginia. "Well, she's been with me since early this morning, so that oughta prove something."

Virginia poked her tongue against the side of her cheek as she released a long breath. Things were not going as well as she'd hoped. "I don't know why Goldie ended up on your doorstep, but I assure you, she is my cat. I've had her for several months, and if you'll put her on the ground right now, I'll prove that she belongs to me."

Maude hesitated a few seconds but finally did as Virginia asked.

Virginia took a few steps back, held out her arms, and called, "Come here, Goldie. Come to me, sweet kitty."

The cat let out two loud meows and pranced over to Virginia.

Without another word, Virginia scooped Goldie up, limped over to her car, and climbed in, placing the cat on the seat beside her.

Maude began walking toward the vehicle, but Virginia put her key in the ignition and backed out of the dirt driveway before the old woman could make it halfway across the unkempt yard.

"Don't you ever run off like that again." Virginia reached down and stroked Goldie's head. The contented cat curled up in Virginia's lap, and she felt the vibration of the feline's purring. She was ever so happy to have her furry friend back.

Chapter 34

As Amy made her way to the phone shed, she paused in the front yard to take in the damage left from last night's storm. No trees had been uprooted, but many branches lay scattered across the lawn. Jared had already cleared out the ones in their driveway and was out back, picking up more debris.

Amy had wanted to help her husband clean the yard, but he'd insisted that he could do it himself and said he didn't want her doing any strenuous work. Although Amy had assured him she wouldn't pick up anything too heavy or overdo it, Jared remained insistent.

Even though some people might believe Jared was too protective, Amy respected his decision, knowing he had her best interest at heart as well as that of their unborn child.

Amy entered the phone shed with a small pillow, and placed it on the chair before taking a seat. At Sylvia's suggestion, Amy had decided to sit on a soft pillow so she'd be more comfortable on the hard stool.

After Amy sat down, she placed both hands on her belly and gave it a massage, while thinking about the baby she carried and how exciting motherhood would be. Although her nieces and nephews were special, Amy looked forward to having her own precious child to love and care for.

She glanced out the open door and watched a robin outside of the shed as it hunted for a worm. The red-breasted bird hopped along until it grabbed hold of a worm and flew off. Amy continued to watch other robins in the grass and finally clicked on the answering machine. *I hope Mom and everyone in my family are doing well after the storm we had last night.*

Hearing her mother's voice, Amy leaned closer to make sure she would hear everything correctly. She felt relieved when she heard that the rest of the family was okay. It was too bad about the uprooted trees and leaky roof though. As soon as she listened to the rest of the messages, Amy would tell Jared that Mom had asked if he would come over at his convenience to check on the roof. Mom had also mentioned that Herschel had patched one section where water had gotten in due to last night's heavy rains.

The fact that Herschel had gone over to help was a confirmation to Amy that he cared about Mom's welfare as well as the rest of the family's.

Amy tapped her chin with the end of the pen she'd used to write down her mother's message. *I wouldn't be surprised if not too far in the distant future Herschel declares his love for my mamm.*

"How'd things go when you went over to Maude's?" Sylvia asked as she and her mother prepared sandwiches for lunch.

"Fine. She took the food inside, and when she came back out we talked for a bit." Mom opened four cans of tuna fish and emptied them into a bowl. "I learned that Maude spends her winters in South Carolina with a relative, but I didn't think to ask a few other questions I've been wondering about."

"Like what?" Sylvia took a jar of sweet pickles from the refrigerator and cut several into small pieces, which she would add to the tuna Mom had begun mixing with mayonnaise.

"I wanted to ask if she's ever been married, and more importantly, how she came to acquire the rundown shack she's been living in, but it slipped my mind. Guess with everything that's gone on here today, I'm feeling kind of befuddled."

"Those questions would be worth knowing. I'm surprised none of us have thought to ask her about it before."

"I get busy in the greenhouse, but the next time she drops by, I'll try to remember to question her more." Sylvia's mother added some diced onion to the tuna mixture. "That old shack needs some repairs, so I'm going to talk to Jared and some of the other men in our district about fixing the place up to make it more livable."

"What if you find out she doesn't own the rundown cabin?"

"Then we'll ask who the owners are and find out if it would be all right if our men make some repairs on the building." Mom sighed. "I should have tried to get the poor woman some help long ago, but I suppose it's better late than never."

Sylvia added the pickles she'd cut up to the bowl of tuna fish. "You're always doing kind things for others. Inviting Herschel to join us for lunch today is just one example."

"It was the least I could do to thank him for coming all the way over here to check on us and help out this morning." Mom kept her gaze on the tuna salad, while speaking in a quieter tone than normal.

"Did Herschel say how things were at his parents'?" Sylvia asked.

"No, and I didn't think to ask." Mom thumped her head. "I don't know what's wrong with my memory today. I hope it's not a sign of old age creeping in."

"You're just a bit rattled because of all the cleanup due to the storm on top of everything else that's been happening around here."

"Jah, I suppose."

Sylvia felt certain that her mother's problem today was feeling giddy with Herschel around. She was sure showing gratitude wasn't the only reason Mom had invited him for lunch. Mom's relaxed posture and smiling face whenever Herschel came around was enough for Sylvia to believe something special had developed between the two of them. Truth was, Sylvia figured Mom might have fallen in love with the nice man, and she was almost certain the feeling was shared.

At least it wasn't Monroe who won my mamm's heart. Sylvia's lips twitched. *I've never seen Mom respond to him the way she does to Herschel. I'm sorry, Mr. Esh, but I think you've lost out on your quest to gain my mother's favor.*

Belinda heard a familiar *clip-clop. . .clip-clop* and looked out the kitchen window. She was pleased to see Jared's horse and buggy come into the yard, and glad that Herschel and Henry had gotten the driveway cleared.

Belinda watched as Jared brought the horse up to the hitching rail and was happy to see Amy step down from his buggy as well.

She turned to face Sylvia. "Jared and Amy are here. I'm going out to greet them and see if they'd like to join us for lunch."

Sylvia smiled. "That'd be nice. I'll set out some other sandwich fixings, in case anyone prefers something other than tuna."

"Okay, we'll be in soon." Belinda wiped her hands, and hurried out the door, where she met Jared and Amy on the lawn.

"We got your message," Jared said. "The road between our place and yours has been cleared, so I'm here to do a check on your roof." He grinned at his wife. "As you might expect, Amy wanted to come along."

"Danki, I'm glad you're both here." Belinda gave them each a hug. "We're getting ready to serve lunch, and if you haven't eaten already, we'd like you to join us for the meal."

"Sounds good to me." Amy looked at Jared. "Is that okay with you?"

"Of course. After we eat, I'll climb up on the roof and take a look."

"I'll let Herschel and Henry know that it's time to wash up, and then we can all gather around the dining-room table."

"I can tell them," Jared offered. "It'll give me a few minutes to talk to Herschel about the condition of the roof and what all he found." He gave Amy's arm a squeeze and started across the yard.

Belinda turned to her daughter. "Did the storm do much damage to your yard?"

Amy shook her head. "A few tree branches came down, but nothing major. I'm sure Jared will be getting lots of calls from people in the area who had roof damage though."

Belinda looped her hand through the crook of Amy's arm. "Speaking of damage, I went to see Maude earlier today, and that old cabin she lives in could sure use some repairs. Some of it probably came because of the heavy winds and rain we had, but the building has been neglected for a long time and needs sprucing up. I'd like to ask Jared and some other men in our church district to have a work frolic over at her place sometime in the near future."

Amy bobbed her head. "Good idea, Mom. We need to help others in our area, and not just our Amish community."

While Herschel ate his tuna sandwich, all he could think about was the joy he felt sitting here at Belinda's table. With the exception of Henry, Herschel felt fully welcomed by her family members. Since he and his late wife had never had children, Herschel hadn't experienced the joy of raising a family. And since he hadn't known about his daughter, Sara, until she was an adult, he hadn't fully understood what fatherhood was about. Sara had a baby now, which made Herschel a grandfather, but he didn't get to Lancaster to see Sara, Brad, and the baby very often. They came by to see him whenever they could, but Brad's job as a minister kept him pretty busy.

Herschel looked across the table at Belinda and smiled. *If I married her, I'd have a ready-made family as well as a loving wife. If only I could work up the nerve to express the way I feel about Belinda.*

Herschel's biggest concern was not in finding the words to convey his love, but how he would deal with it if she didn't return his feelings. His chest tightened as he shuffled his feet underneath the table. The thought of her rejection lay heavy on his mind. After Mattie died, Herschel had been sure he could never fall in love again, and now that he had, he felt fearful and more than a bit overwhelmed. He'd spoken to his mother about it the other day, and she'd encouraged him to tell Belinda how he felt about her. He just needed to find the courage.

"Danki for the meal, ladies, but now it's time for me to go up on the roof to check things out."

Jared's statement brought Herschel out of his musings. "Would you like me to tag along? I can show you the spot that I patched."

"That would be helpful."

Herschel slid back his chair. "The sandwiches hit the spot." He looked right at Belinda, forcing himself not to lose eye contact with her. Sometimes in her presence, Herschel felt like a shy, tongue-tied schoolboy with a crush on a pretty girl.

"When I come off the roof, would you mind if I take a closer look at your garden?" Herschel shifted from one foot to the other as he continued to look at Belinda. "I glanced at it earlier, when I picked up some debris nearby, and was surprised at how well everything looked in spite of last night's storm."

"I don't mind at all." Belinda smiled. "Let me know when you're ready, and I'll join you in the garden."

"Will do." Herschel hesitated a moment, wondering if he should say something more, but decided he'd said enough and followed Jared out the door.

While Sylvia took her children down the hall to wash up after the meal, Belinda and Amy cleared the table.

When they entered the kitchen, Amy placed her stack of dishes in the sink and turned to face Belinda. "Is there something happening between you and Herschel? I'd sure like to know."

Belinda placed both hands against her warm cheeks. "What made you ask such a question?"

Amy held up one finger. "Let's see now. Herschel gets a bird dog expression whenever he looks in your direction." A second finger came up. "And you, Mom, blush, like you're doing now, when you're talking to, or even looking, in his direction."

"It could just be the heat. It's quite warm in the house today, you know."

Amy shook her head. "Today was not the first time I've seen blotches of pink on your cheeks when Herschel's been present."

Belinda dropped her gaze for a few seconds before looking up. "If you must know, I have come to care for Herschel."

"I am glad to hear it." Amy moved closer to Belinda. "Have you told him how you feel?"

"Of course not. That would be too bold. Besides, if I were to admit it, and he doesn't feel the same way about me, it would be quite embarrassing for me as well as Herschel. It might even be the end of our friendship."

"Are you willing to take the risk?"

"No, I'm not. If Herschel and I are meant to have a serious relationship, then he has to make the first move."

"I guess that would be more proper." Amy grinned. "Maybe I'll ask Jared to speak to Herschel. He might need a little nudge."

Belinda held up her hand. "Please don't involve Jared. This is between me and Herschel, and I'm sure he wouldn't appreciate your husband or anyone else trying to get us together."

"Okay, Mom. I just want you to be happy, and I'm sure you wouldn't be with a man like Monroe."

"I have come to the same conclusion. I've tried to give Monroe a chance by spending time with him and even accepting his gifts, but I know in my heart that I will never feel anything more for him than a casual friendship."

Amy wrinkled her nose. "Sometimes Mr. Esh can be so irritating. I doubt that any *weibsmensch* could fall in love with him."

"You never know. . . He does have some good qualities, and the right woman might see things about him that would appeal to her." Belinda filled the sink with warm water and added liquid detergent. "And if things don't work out between me and Herschel, I shall keep my focus on running the greenhouse and being a loving, helpful mother and grandmother until God chooses to take me home."

Amy gave Belinda a hug. "I hope you'll be around for a good long time."

"Me too, my precious daughter." The back of Belinda's throat thickened. *Me too.*

Chapter 35

Virginia sat on the front porch with a cup of coffee. She'd raked up the last of the fallen leaves and picked up a bunch of smaller branches, all the while grumbling about it. Earl would take care of the large limbs that had come down during last night's storm when he got home.

"My life stinks," Virginia muttered. "Nothing's been right since Earl and I moved to Lancaster County. Why couldn't he have been happy to remain in Chicago?"

She looked across the street and saw two men on the roof of Belinda's house. *I bet they had some damage. I wonder if our roof is okay. Maybe Earl oughta climb up there and check.*

She set the cup down on the small table beside her chair and folded her arms. *We'll probably have to call that Amish roofer, Jared, and end up using the money we've been saving for a vacation to fix the stupid roof.*

Virginia glanced at the sign near the front of the Kings' driveway. A large piece of tape with black lettering had been placed over the greenhouse sign, letting people know that the business was closed for the day. No doubt it was due to the storm and the mess it had created in most people's yards.

When she saw Maude walking up the road, her jaw clenched. *I still can't believe that silly old woman treated my Goldie like she belonged to her. I think she would have kept my cat for herself if I hadn't shown up.*

Virginia limped inside to the kitchen, where she poured herself another cup of coffee, adding extra vanilla creamer to it, and placed it on the table. She smiled when Goldie rubbed against her leg. "Hi, pretty kitty." Virginia reached down and scooped up the cat. "Are you hungry? Well don't worry, because I'll put some food in your bowl in a little bit." Goldie rubbed against Virginia's chin and purred like a motor boat. "You're one of the few good things that has happened to me since Earl and I moved here."

Virginia thought about how the Kings had all that help over at their place. *You'd think they would have asked us if we could use some help. Maybe they figure Earl is a capable man who can get things done around here.*

She drank her coffee and went outside again to take another look at the house. Tipping her head back, Virginia noticed some branches hanging from the roof. *I think it's possible for me to get a few of them down. I just need something long enough so I can reach them.*

Virginia went into the garage to see what was there that she might be able to use. She dug through the section where Earl kept all the lawn tools and frowned. *My husband sure isn't organized. How does he manage to find anything in this mess?*

Virginia located a metal rake. The handle looked long enough, so she went back to the yard and tried to reach one of the dangling branches. With a little determination, Virginia managed to hook it and pulled the branch down. "Now how 'bout that?" She looked up and saw another one hanging farther down from her. "I'll get that one too." As she stepped forward, Goldie zipped in front of her and ran across the yard.

Virginia looked toward the door that hung open. "Oh boy, look what I've done. I can't believe I forgot to shut the door."

She laid the rake on the ground and headed for her cat. "Here kitty, kitty. Come on, Goldie. It's time to go back inside." Virginia felt relieved when the cat stopped running and came over to her. She went to grab Goldie and noticed that her slacks had gotten grease on them from something in the garage she must have rubbed against. *Guess this is what I get for trying to be helpful. Sure hope these pants aren't ruined.*

"Jared and Herschel are off the roof now." Amy pointed out the kitchen window. "Should we go see what they found out?"

"Jah, let's do." Since the dishes had been done, Belinda drained the sink and dried her hands. She stepped into the living room to let Sylvia know that she and Amy were going outside, and then the two of them went out the back door.

"Herschel did a good job patching your roof, and I didn't see any other serious issues." Jared looked at Belinda. "I don't think we'll have to do any more work on it right now."

Belinda smiled. "That's a relief, but I do have something else for you to consider."

"What's that?"

She explained about the condition of Maude's shanty. "When you have time, could you take a look at it and let me know if you, and maybe some of your crew, would be willing to make the place more livable?"

"I can do that, and I'm sure others in our community will make themselves available when we let it be known that there's going to be a need for workers."

"I'd be happy to assist with the project," Herschel put in. "I've given my store manager more responsibility at the bulk-food store lately, so I have some free time to do other things."

"We'll take all the help we can get." Jared turned to face Amy. "I need to stop at a few other places before going home. Do you want to ride along, or would you rather wait here and have me pick up in a few hours?"

Amy yawned. "I'm feeling kind of tired, so maybe I'll stay here and rest."

"Good idea." He gave Amy's shoulder a few pats and headed toward his horse and buggy. "Danki for lunch, Belinda," Jared called over his shoulder.

"You're welcome." Belinda looked at Herschel. "Do you still want to take a look at my garden?"

He bobbed his head. "You bet."

Before heading into the house, Amy looked at Belinda with a smirk, and Belinda could guess what her daughter was thinking. *She's probably hoping I'll tell Herschel how much I've come to care for him. I can't believe she would even suggest such a thing. It wouldn't be right.*

The day had turned hot and humid, and Herschel undid the top button of his shirt as he walked beside Belinda along the outer edge of her garden. "All of your vegetable plants look healthy," he commented. "You must be quite the gardener, because you sure have a knack for it."

"I don't know about that, but my interest in growing vegetables and flowers began when I was a girl, helping my grandma plant things in her yard."

"I've always wanted a big garden with lots of fresh veggies." Herschel's shoulders lifted then lowered. "But then, who would I be growing it for, when it's just me and my hund livin' in my house?"

"I'd be happy to share some of our produce," Belinda offered. "In fact, we can pick some now for you to take home."

"That'd be nice, but can we talk awhile first?"

"Certainly. Let's have a seat over there." Belinda motioned to the picnic table.

Herschel ambled over and took a seat on the closest bench. His nervousness increased when Belinda seated herself next to him. Did he have the courage to say what was on his mind?

"Was there something specific you wanted to talk to me about?" Belinda asked. She sat so close that Herschel felt her soft breath on his face, making it all the harder to think of the exact words he wanted to say. "Jah, I. . .umm. . ."

"Is something wrong?" Belinda's brows drew together. "You seem a bit *naerfich* right now."

Herschel's knuckles whitened as he pulled all eight fingers into his palms. *Of course I'm nervous. Who wouldn't be when they're about to blurt something out that could ruin a perfectly good relationship?*

Belinda sat quietly, and then unexpectedly she laid a hand on his arm. "What was it you wanted to tell me?"

Herschel's muscles twitched at her gentle touch. "I hope you won't think I'm being too forward or hold it against me if you don't like what I say."

She touched the base of her throat and gave a slight shake of her head. "I can't imagine what you could say to me that I might not approve of." Belinda looked at him with sincerity and spoke in a kind, gentle tone, which helped relieve some of his anxiety.

"The thing is. . ." Herschel paused and swallowed a couple of times. "I enjoy your company very much."

"I like being with you too."

Enough to marry me? Herschel almost bonked himself on the head. *Don't be stupid. I can't blurt that out—at least not till I find out how Belinda feels about me.*

Herschel pulled in a quick breath and started again. "The truth is, I've fallen in love with you." There, it was out. Now all he had to do was wait for her response.

Belinda stared at him with her mouth partially open.

I wish she would say something, even if it's not what I want to hear. Anything would be better than her silence.

A few seconds passed, which seemed like hours, and then Belinda finally spoke. "I'm pleased to hear you say that, Herschel, because I love you too."

A sense of relief flooded his soul as he clasped her hand. "I'm so relieved. I didn't think I stood a chance against Monroe. He has a lot more to offer you than I do."

Belinda shook her head. "Monroe's a friend, nothing more."

"I bet he doesn't see it that way. It's obvious to me that Monroe is determined to have you as his own, and I doubt he'll be willing to give up on his quest."

"I chose Vernon over Monroe when we were courting many years ago, and now I choose you."

A new sense of joy and hope sprang into Herschel's chest, such as he'd not felt in a long time. "After a proper time of courting for us, would you consider becoming my fraa?"

"I would be honored."

Herschel wanted so much to take Belinda into his arms and give her a kiss, but someone might be watching from the house. Instead, he gave her fingers a gentle squeeze and said, "You've made me the happiest man in Lancaster County."

A short time later, after Belinda told Herschel goodbye and sent him on his way with a sack full of freshly picked produce, she headed into the house, feeling as though she was floating on a cloud. It didn't seem possible that Herschel had declared his love for her or that he'd proposed marriage. Even more surreal was the fact that she'd admitted her love for him and said yes to his proposal. In her wildest dreams Belinda had never imagined she could love any man but Vernon or that it would happen so quickly.

It's been over two years since I became a widow, she reminded herself. *So that part didn't occur quickly. The fact that I've fallen in love with Herschel in such a short time is what amazes me.*

While it was true that Belinda had been acquainted with Herschel Fisher a good many years, she hadn't really gotten to know him until the last year or so. It amazed her that in the few short months Herschel had been coming around more often, she'd allowed herself to be drawn to him, like a moth attracted to light. Herschel was a good man—patient, helpful, and easy to be with. He'd never pressured her or tried to make an impression, the way Monroe always did. Herschel had won Belinda's heart just by being himself.

It wouldn't be easy, but she would have to let Monroe know that she and Herschel were planning to get married. He'd likely do everything he could to try and change her mind, just as he had when she'd picked Vernon over him. But Belinda would hold fast to her decision, because deep down in her heart, she knew Herschel was the man God had chosen for her.

She opened the front door. *And now I must tell my family.*

When Belinda entered the living room, she found Amy sprawled out on the couch, but she wasn't asleep. Sylvia sat in the rocker, with a stack of pot holders in her lap, while Allen and Rachel played on the floor nearby.

"Where's Henry?" Belinda asked. "I have something to tell all of you, and then I'll be going to the phone shed to call Ezekiel."

"What's wrong, Mom? Has something bad happened?" Amy sat up, and with wide eyes, she turned to face Belinda.

"I think Henry's in the barn," Sylvia said. "Should I go get him?"

"Please do."

Sylvia set the pot holders aside and went out. She returned several minutes later with Henry.

"What's up, Mom? Sylvia said you wanted to talk to us."

"Yes, I do." Belinda sat down and pointed to an empty chair. "Please take a seat."

Henry flopped onto the couch instead. "What's this about?"

There was no easy way to say this, so she just blurted it out. "Herschel has asked me to marry him, and I said yes." Belinda folded her arms and waited for their response.

It didn't take long, and Amy was the first to say something. "That's wonderful news. Congratulations, Mom!"

"Danki." Belinda looked at Sylvia.

"I think you chose well, and I'm happy for you." Sylvia smiled. "When's the big day? Will it take place before my wedding to Dennis or a few months later?"

"We haven't had a chance to talk about that yet." Belinda turned to face Henry. "What about you, Son? How do you feel about Herschel and me getting married?"

He pressed his knees together and shook his head. "I ain't one bit happy, and I hope you change your mind 'cause I'll never accept Herschel or any other man as my stepfather."

Before Belinda could respond to her son's outburst, he jumped up and raced from the room. She cringed upon hearing heavy footsteps clomp up the stairs and pressed a fist to her lips when his bedroom door slammed.

"Don't let Henry's attitude get to you," Amy said. "He'll come around when he realizes what a wonderful man Herschel is and how much you love each other." The joy on her face was evident when she got off the couch and came over to give Belinda a hug. Sylvia quickly followed suit.

Tears welled in Belinda's eyes. While it did her heart good to witness her daughters' acceptance of Herschel, she couldn't help but be concerned about her son's reaction. She hoped Henry would change his mind but wasn't sure what to do if he didn't.

I'll need to pray about it, Belinda reminded herself. *Pray and ask God to soften my son's heart so he will see for himself what a kind, loving man Herschel truly is.*

Chapter 36

With summer came lightning bugs and sweet corn, and by August, Lancaster County had plenty of both. Belinda enjoyed eating fresh corn on the cob with plenty of melted butter, salt, and pepper. She also liked spending her evenings sitting outside with her grandchildren watching the fireflies rise up from the grass.

Except for Henry's sour-grapes attitude toward her engagement to Herschel, things were going along well in Belinda's life. It bothered her that Henry wouldn't let Herschel into his life, but she continued to hold out hope that after more time her son's attitude would change.

Surely Henry can see Herschel's attributes, Belinda thought as she went down one of the aisles in the greenhouse, giving each of the potted plants some liquid food to help them grow and remain healthy.

Her thoughts went to Monroe. He'd been out of town on business for the past week, so she hadn't had a chance to tell him about her engagement to Herschel. Belinda dreaded the encounter when it came but knew she couldn't avoid it. She hoped she could say it in a way that wouldn't hurt Monroe's feelings. He had, after all, been kind to her in many ways, but he also had qualities and mannerisms that got on her nerves. Belinda couldn't pretend to be in love with Monroe or keep seeing him socially now that she'd given her heart and a promise of marriage to Herschel.

Pushing her concerns to the back of her mind, Belinda finished her plant-feeding project and went up front to take Sylvia's place at the counter so she could go to the house and eat lunch with her children.

"All done with your chore?" Sylvia asked as she picked up her drink container.

"Jah, and I'm here now to take over for you."

"Okay, but before I go up to the house, can I talk to you about something?"

"Of course."

"While you were checking phone messages this morning, after Amy came to watch the kinner, she mentioned that Jared's concerned about working on the shanty Maude lives in."

Belinda's brows lowered. "Really? He hasn't said anything about it to me, other than that he would put the word out and get things lined up for the repairs. Do you know what he's worried about?"

"Jah. He can't proceed with any repairs to the building without the owner's permission." Sylvia shrugged. "As far as I know, Maude has never mentioned to any of us about who owns the cabin. I've just always thought the place had been abandoned and she decided to take refuge there during the warmer months."

"You're right. We don't know who owns it. I'd planned to ask, but things have been so busy here in the greenhouse lately, it's been hard to focus on too many things at once. Also with Herschel coming by every evening since he asked me to marry him, talking to Maude slipped my mind yet again."

"Dennis and I could go over and talk to her," Sylvia offered. "She responded fairly well to him the last time we were there when we found out she had Rachel with her."

"If Dennis is willing, I'd be most grateful." Belinda smiled. "I can't believe how many exciting things will be happening for us in the next few months. The birth of Amy and Jared's baby is only a month away, and then yours and Dennis's wedding will take place in October."

"Two months after that, you and Herschel will get married." Sylvia clasped Belinda's hand. "I'm so pleased for you, Mom. Having both lost your mates, you and Herschel deserve to find happiness in love and marriage again. And I believe you are well suited."

"I'm happy to hear that, but do you think I'm rushing into things, getting married so soon?"

Sylvia shook her head. "Herschel's declared his love for you, and you have admitted that you love him, so what's the point in waiting to begin your new life together as husband and wife?"

"But you postponed your original wedding plans in order to help me here during the busiest season." Belinda paused to moisten her parched lips. "Maybe I'm being *eegesinnisch*, and perhaps a bit *narrisch*, trying to plan a wedding by December."

"You're not selfish or foolish, Mom. You deserve to be happy with the man you love. If Dad could look down from heaven, I am sure he'd approve of your choice for a second husband."

"You really think so?"

"*Jah*, I do. And don't forget—Ezekiel and Michelle are happy for you too. They made that clear when you called to give them your news."

Belinda's voice cracked as tears dribbled down her cheeks. "*Danki*, Daughter, for your words of affirmation and encouragement."

"You're welcome." Sylvia rose from the wooden stool behind the counter. "I'll head up to the house now, but before I go, I'll give Dennis a call and find out when he might be free to go with me to see Maude." Sylvia started for the door, but stopped walking when a horse and buggy came into the parking lot. "It's Monroe, Mom. Would you like me to stay here while you talk to him? I'm sure it won't be easy to tell him your news."

"No, that's okay. Telling him that I've accepted Herschel's marriage proposal is something I need to do alone. And as long as no customers come in who might overhear us, it's time for me to face Monroe and tell him the truth."

Monroe walked with a spring to his step as he made his way to Belinda's greenhouse. He could hardly wait to share his good news and hoped she'd be as excited about it as he was.

Upon entering the building, he was pleased to see her sitting behind the front counter. Since there were no cars or other horse and buggies parked in the lot, he assumed she didn't have any customers at the moment, which was good. *I'll have my bride-to-be all to myself,* he thought with confidence. *And none of her children appear to be around, especially that unfriendly son of hers. If I become Henry's stepfather I'll have my hands full. But I'm not worried. I'm sure things will work out in time.*

Unable to keep from smiling, he stepped right up to the counter and said hello. Then with feet pointed forward and shoulders straight back, Monroe announced: "I have some good news that could affect both of us."

Belinda squinted as she pushed her reading glasses up to the bridge of her nose. "Really? What kind of good news?"

"While I was gone this past week, I made a lucrative business transaction in the outskirts of an Amish community near Harrisburg."

"I see."

"Aren't you interested in what it was?" Monroe shuffled his feet. *Something seems off, but maybe it's my imagination playing tricks on me.*

"Certainly, if you wish to tell me."

Monroe leaned slightly forward, resting his hands on the counter. "I bought another furniture store, and the business is thriving, so I'll soon be making even more money than I am now." He grinned at her. "I'm becoming a real entrepreneur." *Herschel doesn't have a chance. Belinda must see that I'm the perfect man and only true love for her.*

"Well, I guess you are."

Belinda's placid expression had Monroe worried. Wasn't she excited for him? "Would you like to hear more?" he asked.

She nodded slowly. At least she hadn't said no.

"I've been looking for houses in the Strasburg area, and I think I've found the perfect one for us."

Belinda's eyes widened. "Us?"

He pointed to her and then himself. "You and me, for after we're married."

"Oh. . .uh, Monroe. . .where did you get the idea that you and I were going to get married?"

"I just assumed, since we've been courting for a while. . ."

She held up her hand. "We've gone to supper a few times, and you've come here fairly often, but we haven't been officially courting."

"Really, well, I thought we were." Monroe turned his palms upward. "But okay, whatever. The point is, I've spent a good many months trying to prove my love for you, and I figure it's about time for us to get married."

Belinda glanced around, as though looking for someone, and then her facial muscles went slack.

What's going on here? His gaze rested on Belinda. *I've done everything right. Has something changed between us while I've been away?* "Say something, please."

The silence deafened Monroe's senses as he waited for her response. This was supposed to be a most happy moment, but things weren't going the way he'd hoped. He looked around, making sure they were still alone and hoping they could continue their private conversation.

"I am sorry, Monroe, but I cannot marry you."

Monroe stood frozen, unable to digest this information. *Belinda's rejection brings me right back to the day she turned me down for Vernon. It hurt then, and it is just as painful now.*

"How come? Haven't I proven my devotion to you? Don't you realize that I can provide well for you?" He made an arc with his arms, as he turned in several directions, and then back to face her. "You'll be faced with running this place with only the help of your teenage son after Sylvia is married. Think about it, Belinda. If you marry me, you won't have to do that anymore. We'll be co-owners of this business and we can hire someone else to run it." Monroe leaned in closer. "I love you, Belinda. I always have, and if you'll think it through, you'll realize that we were meant to be together."

Belinda covered her mouth with her hand as she slowly shook her head.

He reached over and pulled her hand away. "Please don't say no. It's okay if you don't love me as much as I love you. In time, after we've been married awhile, you could develop stronger feelings for me. I'm sure if you think about it, you'll come to realize that I'm the best man for you."

Belinda pulled her hand back. "I can't marry you, Monroe, because I'm in love with Herschel, and I've promised to marry him in December."

"What?" Monroe felt like his eyes were about to bulge right out of their sockets. "You can't be serious, Belinda. This must be a joke!"

"I am telling you the truth. Herschel proposed to me a week ago, and I said yes."

"A week ago?"

"Yes, it was the same day he came here to help clear away the debris left from the storm."

"Is that so? Guess it must have taken place after I left then, huh?"

"Yes, Monroe. Herschel and I were sitting in my yard after lunch, and—"

His face heated, and he slapped his hand on the surface of the counter. "That's lecherich! He is not the man for you."

"It's not ridiculous. I love Herschel very much, and he loves me."

Monroe shook his head determinedly. "Not as much as I do. Besides, what does that boring old man even have to offer you?

"Herschel is not boring or old. He's a fine person, with kind, gentle ways."

"Are you implying that I'm not a good person?"

"You have many fine attributes." Belinda's voice softened as she lowered her gaze. "I don't want to hurt your feelings, Monroe." She paused a few seconds before continuing. "I'm not in love with you, and I am sorry if I've said or done anything to make you believe we could be anything other than friends."

Monroe's muscles quivered and his heart pounded in his chest. "You'll be sorry you chose him over me, Belinda. *Jah*, you can count on my words." Monroe whirled around and stomped out the door. All this time he'd worked so hard to win Belinda's heart and hand, and now she'd chosen an older man with a graying beard?

He gritted his teeth. *That woman must be touched in the head.*

Henry stood inside the back door of the greenhouse, wondering if he should have made himself known and said something to Monroe the minute he started pressuring Mom about marrying him.

Henry's toes curled inside his boots. *The nerve of that man expecting my mamm to accept his proposal—such as it was. Monroe's pushy and arrogant, and he's still on my list of suspects.* He wiped the sweat from his brow. *With Monroe's tone when he basically told Mom she'd have regrets if she married Herschel, I have to say that her ex-boyfriend has some serious issues. Since he's so upset, I bet we'll have more problems, because I still think he is the one behind all our troubles.*

Although no vandalism had been done to their place recently, Henry remembered the last threatening phone message they'd received, saying they had until December to put the place up for sale and move. Mom hadn't done it, of course, and Henry couldn't blame her. She and Dad had started the greenhouse together, and there was no way she'd let it go and move off this land.

Henry had given up playing detective for the time being, since there'd been no more attacks, but if anything else should happen again, he'd be more determined than ever to find out who was behind their problem.

Henry's thoughts returned to Monroe. He was glad Mom had stood up to the man, letting him know she didn't love him and couldn't accept his proposal.

Henry bit the inside of his cheek. *I wish Mom would do the same with Herschel. She needs to break things off with him, and I have to think of some way to make it happen, because I can't stand the thought of Herschel moving into our house and trying to replace my dad.*

Henry's face heated as another thought popped into his head. *What if Herschel expects Mom to sell this place and move to Gordonville to live with him? Just where would that leave me?*

More sweat formed on Henry's forehead and dribbled onto his face. *There's no way I'm moving into that man's house. If necessary, I'll leave Strasburg for good. I wonder if Ezekiel and Michelle would take me in. If not, then I'll get a job and strike out on my own, 'cause I won't be any man's stepson.*

Chapter 37

Clymer

"I still can't believe your mamm and Herschel are engaged," Michelle said to Ezekiel as they sat at the supper table with their children.

"I know. I was surprised myself when I listened to Mom's voicemail message, telling us about it."

"Surprised in a good way though, right?"

"Jah. I think Mom made the right choice when she picked Herschel over Monroe. He's a nice fellow, and his personality is better suited to hers."

Michelle smiled. "We will go down for their wedding in December, I hope."

"Definitely. Wouldn't miss it for the world." Ezekiel reached for a piece of bread and spread creamy butter over it. "We'll go to Strasburg in September after Amy's baby is born, and make another trip for Dennis and Sylvia's wedding in October."

Michelle's face broke into a wide smile. "Oh good. That certainly gives us a lot to look forward to."

"It sure does. I'll see about hiring a driver for the first trip as soon as we get word that my sister's had her baby."

Michelle reached over and wiped little Vernon's messy face. "I wonder if she and Jared are hoping for a boy or a girl."

"I'm sure they'll be happy with either one, but Jared might like a son who he can eventually train to join him in the roofing trade."

"And Amy may want a daughter she can teach to cook, sew, tend her garden, and do many other things." She placed her hand on Angela Mary's shoulder and gave it a squeeze. "We are fortunate, Ezekiel, because God gave us one of each."

"It's too hot out here, and the flies are bad," Virginia complained as she and her husband sat at the picnic table in their yard, eating the evening meal. "I'd rather be in the house where it's air-conditioned."

"Aw, don't be such a sissy. It ain't summer unless a person enjoys a meal outside now and then." Earl grabbed another hot dog and slapped it in a bun. "You oughta be happy sitting out here where you can listen to the birds carrying on." He gestured to an area across the yard. "And just feast your eyes on all those pretty white posies over there."

Virginia turned her head to look in the direction he pointed. "Those aren't posies, they're daisies, and boy, do they stink!"

His brows furrowed. "Really? I thought most flowers smelled sweet, like perfume."

"Not those. Their odor is worse than the horse droppings on the road out front." Virginia plugged her nose. "Phew!"

"If they're so bad, why don't you remove 'em from the flowerbed?"

"I pulled them out last year after they'd finished blooming, but some must have reseeded."

"Well the next time you yank out the smelly daisies, let me know and I'll spray some weed killer all over the spot where they'd been growing."

"That might work, but then nothing else will grow there either."

"Guess you'll have to decide what's more important to you—an empty flowerbed or flowers that look pretty but stink." Earl snatched up his hot dog and held it close to his mouth. "Now can we quit talkin' long enough for me to eat this?"

"Sure, Earl, enjoy yourself while I try to eat the potato salad I worked so hard to make today. Just be careful you don't end up eating one of those pesky flies that's been buzzin' our heads ever since we sat down."

He snorted and shrugged his shoulders. "If I do, it'll be a little more protein added to my meal."

Virginia rolled her eyes at him. Earl might think what he'd said was funny, but she thought it was gross—enough to ruin her appetite.

"I'm glad that bad storm we had didn't damage our roof," Earl commented after he finished eating his hot dog. He eyeballed the pan of hot dogs and forked another. "Sure do like this brand of dogs you bought us, but now back to the topic of the roof. I'm relieved that it all stayed intact and we're not stuck with more expenses."

Virginia took a sip of her iced coffee. "Me too. I felt relieved when Jared looked at it and said the roof was fine. That means we won't have to use any of the vacation money we've been saving up."

Earl grabbed a handful of potato chips and dropped them onto his plate. "About that, Virginia—"

"Are you planning a surprise trip for me?"

He shook his head. "How would you feel about foregoing our vacation plans and buying a big-screen TV instead?"

Her jaw clenched. "Oh, so you can waste more time sitting in front of the TV with the volume blaring until it gives me a headache? I don't think so, Earl. I want us to take a trip so we can get out of this boring place for a while."

Earl patted her hand after taking a swig from his sweaty glass of cola, apparently unshaken by her outburst. "We both have our favorite shows on TV, and just think how much more enjoyable it would be to watch them on a bigger screen."

She grimaced and wiped her hand with a napkin. "Can't we go on vacation and get a new TV too? I don't think they're that expensive."

"The really good ones are over a thousand dollars."

He'll never budge from that television set if we get the big expensive one. "That's ridiculous, Earl. We don't need anything that fancy."

"We do if we wanna keep up with the latest technology. You have a smartphone, right?"

"Yeah, but what's that got to do with—"

"The television I have my eye on is a smart TV. We'd be able to go on the internet with it and access YouTube and many other places where you can watch all kinds of movies."

Virginia groaned. "Let's forget the TV and go on a nice vacation to the shore this fall like we've talked about. We can rent a little cottage and stay for a week."

"We can discuss this later. Right now, I'd like to eat the rest of my meal in peace." Earl's shoulders pushed back, and Virginia saw the determined set of his jaw. No doubt he would win out and buy a new television, but if she had anything to say about it, they'd be going to the beach too.

"I'm a little nervous about talking to Maude and wondering how we should bring up the topic of who owns the old cabin," Sylvia said to Dennis as they walked along the shoulder of the road in the direction of Maude's rundown shack. She wondered if the older woman might not be straightforward with them.

Sylvia looked over at him. "Mom has been the one person that Maude seems to like. I sure hope we don't offend her with our questions."

"Would you like me to bring up the topic?"

Her tone perked up. "If you don't mind. I'd probably end up saying the wrong thing, and then she might clam up and refuse to tell us anything."

He agreed. "That might be especially true if she is living there without the permission from the person who owns the place. Maude may not even know who the owner is."

"I hope that's not the case. I don't think we can do any renovations without the proper person's approval."

"We're almost there, so we should know something soon." Dennis pointed up ahead when the shanty came into view. "This place could use more than just some work on the roof. It looks like it's been neglected for a long time and in need of much care."

As they drew closer, Sylvia spotted Maude sitting outside on a tattered-looking wicker chair that looked like it should have been thrown out with the trash. It had definitely seen better days.

"Hello, Maude," Sylvia said as she and Dennis approached the woman.

"Howdy. What are you two doin' over here?"

"We came by to talk about the cabin you live in," Dennis responded.

"Yeah, well, it ain't much, but a least it's a place for me to sleep, eat, and get outa the weather when it rains." Maude gestured to a wooden bench that didn't look much better than the chair she sat upon. "Take a seat."

Sylvia looked at Dennis, wondering if it was strong enough for them both to sit on, but when he sat down, she did the same. The bench didn't give way, so she figured they might be okay.

Dennis cleared his throat. "As Sylvia's mother mentioned to you previously, we would like to spruce the cabin up so it's more livable, but we need to know who the owner is so we can ask their permission."

Maude carved her fingers through the ends of her shoulder-length hair, pulled it away from her face, held it back, and then released it. "The place is mine, fair and square."

"Oh, so you bought it from someone?" The question came from Dennis.

"Nope. It belonged to my grandparents, on my daddy's side." Maude paused and flapped her hand in front of her face. "Whew, it sure is hot this evening. Thought it woulda cooled down some by now."

Sylvia gave Dennis a gentle nudge, hoping he would turn the conversation back to the cabin. He must have gotten her message, for he looked at Maude and said, "Did they leave it to you legally?"

"Yeah, it was in their will. Grandpa died first, and then a year later, Grandma followed, but I didn't come here to stay in this place till a few years ago. I'd been living with a friend at that time and didn't have any need to hurry here and settle down. I suppose I should admit that in my younger days my life took off in a bad direction." Maude paused once more—this time to blow her nose on a hanky she'd pulled from the pocket of her faded trousers. "I ain't got much money, except for the small monthly pension I've received since my husband, Fred, died five years ago." She sniffed and blew her nose again. "I manage to get by, though sometimes it's slim pickings for me."

Sylvia's heart went out to Maude. She couldn't imagine what it must be like to live all alone with so little money in this small, dilapidated shanty. She figured it must be hard for the poor woman to talk about it to people she hardly knew.

"Did your grandparents live in this cabin at one time or were there other buildings on the property?" Dennis asked.

Maude pointed to the shack. "This is where they lived, but I'm sure it looked better at that time than it does now. From what I've been told, they planned to build a bigger home, but that never happened because they ended up movin' to Minnesota when my great-grandpappy died."

"Thank you for sharing the information." Dennis spoke in a kindly tone. "We'll be on our way now, but someone will be over to see you soon about when we can begin fixing some things in and around your cabin."

Maude gave the hint of a smile. "Sounds good."

Sylvia rose from the bench. "If you need anything between now and then, please let us know."

"Okay."

"We'll see you later, Maude. I hope you have a pleasant rest of your evening." Sylvia gave a wave and followed Dennis across the overgrown yard.

"It sure is nice to have some time alone with you and chat," Belinda said as she and Herschel sat together on her front porch swing. He had stopped by shortly after Sylvia and Dennis left to talk to Maude, and they'd been visiting for the last forty-five minutes or so, while Allen and Rachel chased after the fireflies rising up from the grass.

"Monroe dropped by the greenhouse today." Belinda looked over at Herschel to see how he would react.

"I'm guessing he didn't come to buy anything?"

"No, he wanted to talk to me." Belinda fingered the front of her apron. *Should I tell him everything Monroe said or just the basics?* She opted for the latter.

"He asked—no pretty much stated—that he and I should get married and was quite upset when I told him that I'd accepted your marriage proposal."

"I'm not surprised." Herschel reached over and clasped Belinda's hand, giving her fingers a gentle squeeze. "I still can hardly believe you chose me over him."

"It was an easy choice, because you're the man I love." Belinda smiled. "I could never be as happy with Monroe as I am with you."

The blue in Herschel's eyes deepened as his gaze remained fixed on her. He pulled Belinda into his arms and gave her a kiss on the mouth that felt as soft as butterfly wings.

Belinda's pulse raced as she melted into his embrace. Although her love for Herschel was different than what she'd felt for Vernon, it was equally strong. She knew without a shadow of a doubt that he was the man for her.

Their lingering kiss was interrupted when Belinda heard Sylvia call out to her children: "How many *feierveggel* have you caught?" Belinda quickly pulled away from Herschel.

Oh, I hope she and Dennis didn't see us kissing. Belinda felt heat on her cheeks as she rose from the swing and was glad when Herschel followed her into the yard.

"How'd it go at Maude's place? Did you have a chance to talk to her?" Belinda asked.

"Yes we did," Sylvia responded.

"Why don't we all take a seat on the porch and then we can talk about it," Dennis suggested.

As they stepped onto the porch, Sylvia came alongside Belinda and whispered in her ear: "Was that the first time Herschel's kissed you?"

Belinda's face grew hotter as she nodded.

"I'm glad you've found such a nice man. You deserve to be happy, Mom." Sylvia gave Belinda's arm a tender squeeze. "And don't let anything Henry says discourage you."

"I'll try not to," Belinda responded. *But my son's making it quite difficult for me,* she admitted to herself. *I hope he changes his attitude toward Herschel.*

Chapter 38

Things moved along quickly during the remainder of August. Maude's cabin got a makeover, and the remodels to Sylvia's house were almost finished.

On the first day of September, before she opened the greenhouse, Belinda went to the phone shed to check for messages. To her delight there was one from Jared, letting them know that Amy had delivered a baby boy at two o'clock that morning. The home birth with the aid of a midwife went well. Both mother and son were doing fine, and they would welcome company later today when Amy felt more rested. The name they'd chosen for their baby boy was Dewayne Aaron, named after Jared's and Amy's paternal grandfathers.

Tears welled in Belinda's eyes, almost blurring her vision. *Thank You, Lord, for my new grandson's safe delivery.*

She lifted the cover on the notepad, to write down the baby's weight, length, and his name. Seeing that something had already been written on the new page, she wiped the tears from her eyes and slipped on her reading glasses.

"Oh my!" Belinda's body broke out in a cold sweat as she stared at the words: *"Are You Ready to Sell? Your time's running out."*

There had been no vandalism for some time, nor more threatening notes or voice-mail messages. Belinda shivered. *Someone must have come into the phone shed during the night or earlier this morning and written this note. But why? What were they trying to prove?*

Wondering if the person responsible may have also left a message on her answering machine, Belinda clicked the button and listened. The only message besides Jared's was from the man who owned the landscaping business, wanting to place another order.

Belinda sat in the chair, rocking back and forth, as she tried to figure out what to do. *Should I tell anyone in my family about this note or keep quiet?*

Thinking how someone had entered her phone shed and written the threatening message caused another chill to course through Belinda's body. *Guess I ought to at least let Henry and Sylvia know about this so they can help me figure out what, if anything, we should do. Telling Ezekiel is out of the question, because if he knew what has been going on the past two-plus years, he'd not only be upset with me for keeping him in the dark, but would insist on selling his place and moving back here.*

She shifted on the chair. *I don't want to feel this way, but I am wondering if Monroe has something to do with this because I chose Herschel over him.*

Belinda sat quietly for a while, thinking things through and praying for God's guidance. Finally, she picked up the notepad, stepped out of the shed, and headed for the house. Her excitement and joy after hearing Jared's message had been dampened, but at the same time, it was something positive to focus on.

"What took you so long?" Henry asked when his mother returned to the house. "I thought you wanted to go over a few things with me and Sylvia before we head out to the greenhouse this morning." He noticed the notepad in his mother's hand. *Why does Mom have the tablet from the phone shed? Usually we write down the information from the answering machine on it and tear off the page to bring into the house, not the whole pad.*

"Sylvia won't be working with us today after all," Mom answered. "Jared left a message saying Amy had her boppli earlier this morning, so she obviously will not be coming to watch Allen and Rachel today."

"How exciting!" Sylvia gave Mom a wide grin.

"What'd she have?" Henry asked.

"Is the baby healthy? Is Amy doing okay?" More questions from Sylvia.

Mom held up her hand. "Please slow down, you two. I can only answer one question at a time."

"Sorry." Sylvia took a seat at the kitchen table, and Henry did the same. After their mother joined them, she replied to each of their questions.

When finished, she looked over at Henry and said, "We'll close the greenhouse at four o'clock this afternoon so we can have an early supper, and then we'll all go over to Amy and Jared's to see the new *boppli*."

"That sounds good," Sylvia said, "but if I don't work in the greenhouse, you'll be shorthanded."

"Henry and I can manage by ourselves today," Mom replied. "But before Monday, we will need to find someone else to either watch the *kinner* or help in the greenhouse."

"It would take time to train someone to work in the greenhouse, unless they'd had experience working in that capacity," Sylvia responded. "I'll call Lenore and see if she'd be willing to watch Rachel and Allen so I can keep working in the greenhouse. Maybe I can take them over to her place, which would make it easier for Lenore, since she needs to stick close to home to help with chores Mary Ruth is not able to do."

Mom smiled, but Henry noticed that her eyes held no sparkle. He figured she'd be so excited about Amy and Jared's new baby that she wouldn't be able to stop smiling.

Mom put the notebook on the table. "The thrill of hearing the news that I have a new grandson was dampened when I read this note someone had written on the tablet we use in the phone shed for messages."

"Someone?" Henry tipped his head. "You mean one of us?"

"No, this was written by somebody who must have gone into our phone shed during the night or very early this morning." Mom pushed the notepad over to Henry. "Open it to the first newly written page."

Henry did as she asked, and his eyes widened as he stared at the printed message.

"What does it say?" Sylvia asked. "Your *gsicht* is bright red."

"Your face will be red too after you read this." He pushed the tablet over to her.

When Sylvia spoke again, her voice trembled. "Who keeps doing this to us? Just when we think there will be no more vandalism or threats, another one comes." She heaved a sigh. "This is so discouraging."

Henry looked at his mother. "Know what I think we oughta do?"

"What's that? And please don't say I should call the sheriff."

"Instead of letting Blackie sleep inside the house, wouldn't it be better if he stayed outside at night? That way, if an intruder comes onto our property while we're sleeping, my hund's bound to see them and bark out a warning."

"That might be advisable, but I'm beginning to think it may be best if I sell the greenhouse as well as our home."

"You're kidding, right?" Henry couldn't believe his mother would say such a thing. The business had been part of her life for a good many years, and she'd said many times that she would not let it go or be run out of here by somebody who obviously didn't like them.

"Since your daed died, I've held on to the business for sentimental reasons and to provide for my family," Mom said. "But the fact is, once Herschel and I are married, my needs will be provided for, and yours too, Henry. I'm sure my husband will want us to sell this place and move to his home in Gordonville."

"That's too much change for me. My life is here, where I was born." Henry slapped the palm of his hand against the surface of the table. "I don't wanna move to Gordonville, and I don't need Herschel to provide anything for me."

"Calm down, Henry, and please lower your voice." Sylvia pointed to the door leading to the living room across the hall. "It upsets my kinner when people shout, so please try to control your emotions."

His tone lowered. "I'm weary of this family going through the trial we seem to be facing. I just want it to end and things to go back to normal." Henry's mouth clamped shut, and he tapped his fingers along the tabletop. *I wonder who wants us to sell out and move away. I still think it must be Monroe.*

He sat up tall in his chair as once more, his thoughts took him down the list of suspects he'd created. Whether it was Monroe or not, Henry was more desperate than ever to find out who was behind all of this.

Although Virginia had seen the mailman's vehicle go by a few hours ago, she'd waited until after lunch to cross the street and get it. Now, back in her yard, she took a seat on the front porch and shuffled through the letters. One in particular caught her eye because it had the Kings' address in one corner.

Now why would they send anything to me and Earl? Maybe they're planning some sort of get-together and have invited us to attend.

Virginia tore the letter open and nearly dropped the card when she realized it was an invitation to Sylvia and Jared's wedding, which would take place the first Thursday of October. "Now this is a surprise."

Continuing to stare at the invitation, Virginia wondered if she ought to call her friend Stella and tell her the news. She held the card against her chest and pondered the situation. *When Earl gets home, I'll talk to him about this. If he says we can go to the shindig, I'll let Stella know. She was fascinated with the Amish way of life when she was here visiting the last time. I'm sure she would jump at the chance to attend an Amish wedding.*

She placed the invitation in her lap and focused on the house across the road. *For that matter, it might be kinda interesting for me and Earl to see up close what the Plain people's wedding is like.*

Belinda's throat clogged as she gazed at her newest grandson, resting peacefully in his mother's arms.

"He's a beautiful boppli," she whispered. "Welcome to the world, Dewayne Aaron Riehl."

"Such a big name for a little guy. I assume everyone will just call him Dewayne?" Sylvia looked at Jared.

"I guess so, unless Amy prefers to call him Aaron. We haven't really talked about it."

Although Amy looked tired, her smile was radiant as she stroked the top of her son's downy dark head. "Either one is fine with me, but I kind of favor the name Dewayne."

"Have Jared's parents been by to see the boppli yet?" Belinda asked. "I'm sure they're as thrilled as I am about having a new grandson."

"I spoke with my mamm earlier," Jared responded. "Dad developed a pretty bad headache today, so she said they'd come by sometime tomorrow. Oh! I called Ezekiel too, but young Vernon has a cold, so they won't be coming to see the baby right away."

"I can't believe your little guy came almost a week earlier than your due date." Sylvia touched the baby's wee hand. "Both of mine came nearly a week late."

Amy shrugged. "Maybe we miscalculated."

"Well it doesn't matter. He's here and is healthy, which is all that counts." Sylvia turned to face Henry. "You're awfully quiet. What do you have to say about your new nephew?"

"He's sure *bissel*."

"You were that small once too," Belinda said.

"That's right. All *bopplin* are little when they're first born." Jared chuckled and bumped Henry's arm. "You need to know things like this, because someday you'll get married and have some babies."

"Yeah, right," Henry muttered. "I ain't never gettin' married."

"Bet you'll change your mind once the right girl comes along." Amy looked at her brother and grinned. "First comes love and then marriage."

"Yeah, I know. . .and sometime after that I'm stuck pushing a baby carriage."

Everyone laughed, including Rachel and Allen, although Belinda felt sure they didn't know what was so funny.

They visited awhile, and all the adults except Henry took turns holding little Dewayne.

Belinda couldn't help but notice her son's placid expression as he sat cross-legged on the floor by the children. She figured he might be thinking about the note she'd found in the phone shed earlier today. It had been on her mind too, but Belinda refused to let it ruin her day or suck the joy out of being here right now as they welcomed a new member of their family.

She closed her eyes briefly and prayed. *Heavenly Father, please bless Jared, Amy, and their precious little boy. May he grow up with the wisdom and knowledge that the only way to heaven is through Jesus Christ, Your Son.*

Chapter 39

September went by quickly, and Belinda divided her time between the greenhouse, working in her garden, spending time with the family, and helping Sylvia with all the final wedding preparations. Belinda also saw Herschel several times a week, and with each visit, she fell more deeply in love with him.

When Belinda shared with Herschel about the vandalism that had been done in various places on her property, he suggested putting some bright motion-activated solar lights around the yard. Belinda didn't know why she hadn't thought of the idea herself, since she sold several kinds of solar lights in one section of the greenhouse.

I could see the look of concern on his face, and when he spoke to me, his tone was calming to my ears. I'm blessed to have a man I love and who cares for me and my family. And Herschel is determined to get to the bottom of the vandalism, Belinda thought as she made her bed.

She hoped the reason there hadn't been any problems on the property lately was because Blackie had been sleeping outside in his pen and would surely have warned them if anyone came into the yard.

Something else that hadn't been resolved was whether Belinda should hire someone to help in the greenhouse or try to manage things on her own with only Henry's help. She thought it might be doable, since she'd be closing the business for the winter by the end of November and possibly indefinitely. It would depend on where Herschel wanted them to live after they got married. This was a subject they had not yet talked about, but would need to do so soon.

Lenore had agreed to watch Sylvia's children, but in just a few weeks that would no longer be necessary. Once Sylvia and Dennis were married, she would stay at home with the children instead of helping in the greenhouse. Many changes were happening within the family, giving her so much to think about.

Monroe hadn't come around since the day Belinda told him that she and Herschel planned to be married. Belinda had been concerned that he might try to persuade her into choosing him over Herschel. But the more days and weeks that passed, the better Belinda felt. She hoped he had accepted her decision and would move on with his life. Belinda wished she had never agreed to see Monroe socially because it had caused him to believe he had a chance at winning her hand in marriage.

After Belinda got dressed for the day, she opened up the window shades in her room before leaving. *I pray that a good woman will come into Monroe's life. He is deserving of someone, and only You, Lord, can provide a suitable mate for him.*

As Belinda entered the kitchen to prepare breakfast, she glanced out the window by the sink and gasped. A good portion of their vegetable garden had been trampled, leaving only one section untouched. *So much for solar lights and a dog that didn't bark. Of course,* Belinda reasoned, *it may not have been a person who destroyed part of the garden. It could have been some animal tromping on the vegetable patch.*

That idea had no more than flitted through her head when she heard a familiar *m-a-a. . .m-a-a. . .m-a-a. . .*

What is going on outside? Belinda wondered. A few seconds later, three frisky goats pranced across the lawn, heading toward the garden. *Oh no, you don't. You've done enough to our nice garden that we've worked hard to grow.*

Belinda grabbed a broom from the utility porch and raced out the back door. Shouting and shaking the end of the broom at the ill-mannered animals, she hoped they would have enough sense to go back to the yard from which they had apparently escaped.

"What is all the ruckus about?" Sylvia asked, leaving the house and joining Belinda in the yard.

Before Belinda had a chance to response, Henry came around the corner of the house and turned the hose on. He directed the stream of water at the goats but ended up spraying Sylvia instead.

"Yikes, that's cold!" Sylvia raced up the back steps and took shelter on the porch.

"Oops, sorry about that." Henry aimed the hose at the goats once more, and this time Belinda ended up getting wet.

"For goodness' sake, Henry, please watch what you're doing!" Belinda was tempted to grab the hose from his hand and give him a good dousing. If she hadn't been so angry at the goats for ruining one section of the garden, Belinda might have thought the whole thing had been funny.

When the feisty animals kept kicking up their heels and frolicking about, she grabbed the hose from Henry and shouted, "Let Blackie out of his pen. I'm almost certain he will chase those crazy critters out of the yard."

Henry handed the hose to Belinda and hurried across the lawn. Soon the dog was out of his pen, leading the goats on a merry chase. A few trips around the yard with Blackie barking and nipping at their heels, and every one of the goats made a hasty exit from Belinda's property.

Still holding the hose, and with the water turned on, she shot a little spray in Henry's direction.

"Hey! What'd ya do that for, Mom?"

"Thought you might need to cool off." She chuckled. "This day is starting off to be rather warm."

"It ain't funny." He leaped onto the porch and stepped behind Sylvia.

Belinda let loose with another laugh, only this one more boisterous. "At least that cold water got our blood pumping this morning, jah?"

"What about the poor garden?" Sylvia pointed to the trampled plants. "What those *gees* did to it pretty much puts the kibosh to us canning the last of the tomatoes."

Belinda turned off the water and joined Henry and Sylvia on the porch. "It's okay. With your wedding coming up in two weeks, we really don't have time to do much more canning."

Sylvia sighed. "Even so, it would have been nice to have the tomatoes and other produce to eat. Our neighbors down the road who own those goats should make an effort to keep them penned up."

"Some gees can be pretty crafty," Henry interjected. "They're good at figuring their way out, even when they're fenced in."

Belinda nodded. "Which is why we don't own any goats. They'd just be one more thing to worry about."

Sylvia opened the front door. "Guess we'd better go inside and get breakfast started. Allen and Rachel will be up soon, and before you know it, Henry will need to take them over to Lenore's so we can open the greenhouse."

A short while after Belinda entered the greenhouse, she spotted a beautiful Monarch butterfly hovering over one of the flowering bushes. She stood watching for several minutes, almost mesmerized by the flying insect's gorgeous colors and delicate, fluttering wings.

Belinda moved on down the row, pausing to pluck some dead leaves off a rust-colored dahlia plant. *People plant flowers for different reasons,* she thought. *Some enjoy the beauty of the blossoms, while others like the sweet fragrance that many flowering plants give off. Then there are people who plant flowers for the fun of simply watching them grow.*

She placed one hand on her chest. *And I plant* blumme *for all of those reasons.*

Belinda couldn't imagine not owning this greenhouse, with so much floral beauty around her each day. After she and Herschel were married, she would miss the joy of working with her hands and watching things grow before putting them on the shelves to offer her customers. If only there was some way she could continue to run the greenhouse after they became husband and wife. But that would be a challenge, since Herschel's home was in Gordonville, which would mean a commute every day. Besides, if she moved to her new husband's place, she'd have to sell her own home, and whoever bought the house might also want the greenhouse. This was an issue she should have talked with Herschel about before agreeing to marry him or at the very least soon after they became engaged.

Belinda turned and reached the front counter as the front door opened. She was surprised when Herschel entered the building. Normally, he came by later in the day and then stayed for supper.

"Guder mariye," she said with a smile. "I wasn't expecting to see you here at this time of day."

"Good morning to you too." He moved over to stand beside her. "I hope you're not disappointed."

"Of course not." Her face warmed. "I'm always pleased to see you." It was silly and made Belinda feel like a schoolgirl, but sometimes merely looking at her intended caused her to blush.

"I came to talk to you about something, and I thought if I got here early enough, you might not have any customers yet."

"You're right. Henry and Sylvia aren't even here yet, although I do expect they'll be along soon."

"Well good, then no one will be embarrassed when I do this." Herschel embraced Belinda and kissed her gently on the lips. Now she felt like a giddy teenager.

When they pulled apart, he smiled and said. "There's something we haven't talked about that needs to be discussed."

"Oh, what's that?"

"Our living arrangements once we are married."

"It's funny you should bring that topic up because I was thinking about that very thing before you arrived."

Herschel cleared his throat. "I was wondering what you would think of the idea of me selling my business in Gordonville and helping you run the greenhouse after we're married. Would it bother you to live in the same home with me that you once shared with Vernon?"

Belinda felt an unexpected release of all tension as she slowly shook her head. "I wouldn't have a problem with that at all."

Herschel grinned and gave her a second kiss. "That's what I was hoping to hear."

Belinda felt such a sense of exhilaration it was hard to keep from bouncing on her toes. She'd never expected Herschel would want to be part of the greenhouse or that he'd be willing to sell the bulk-food store and move here to Strasburg. Her only concern was how Henry would react to the arrangement. He still hadn't accepted the idea of Belinda marrying Herschel, and what if he never did?

Virginia picked up the cell phone and dialed her friend's number. Stella answered on the second ring. "Hi, Stella. How's it going?"

"Good. How are things with you?"

"Pretty much the same—except for one thing."

"What's that?"

"We got an invitation to the wedding of Belinda's oldest daughter, and I figured you might want to come here for a visit and go to the event with us."

"Sounds like fun. When will it take place?"

"Two weeks from today, at nine o'clock in the morning."

There was a brief pause before Stella responded. "Sorry, Virginia, but I won't be able to make it."

"How come?" Virginia couldn't hide her disappointment.

"Joe and I already have plans on that day as well as the weekend that follows."

"Can't you change them? It's a pretty big deal to be invited to an Amish wedding, and it sure would be nice if you could be there with me."

"I'd like to attend, but our trip to the shore was planned some time ago, and we'd lose money if we cancelled the reservations we made to rent a house that is practically on the sandy beach."

"Yeah, okay, I understand." Virginia gave a frustrated shake of her head. *So my friend gets to spend time at the beach, and Earl and I probably won't make it there this year—especially since he spent a good chunk of the money we were saving on a big-screen TV.*

"I'd like to talk more, Virginia, but I have a dental appointment in an hour and I can't be late. We'll catch up again after my mini-vacation, and you can tell me all about the Amish wedding."

"Okay, sure. Bye, Stella." Virginia clicked off the phone and lowered her head. She wasn't that enthused about attending Sylvia's wedding, but if she and Earl went, at least she'd have something interesting to share with Stella. Maybe it would even entice her friend to come back to Strasburg for another visit.

Virginia sagged against her chair. *At least I can hope for that.*

She felt Goldie's soft fur against her leg and reached down to pet her. Virginia was rewarded with a soft *meow* and some gentle purring. How thankful she was for the cat, because there were times like now when Virginia felt like she didn't have a friend in the world. Tears sprang to her eyes. *I have no family except Earl and no friends who live close by. Maybe I deserve the situation I find myself in, because I've made so many bad choices in my life.*

Chapter 40

"I can't believe we are about to attend an Amish wedding," Virginia commented to Earl as they were ushered into Belinda King's barn through tall double doors.

He nudged her arm. "Please keep your voice down. I feel conspicuous, and some people are already looking at us."

"Stop it, Earl," Virginia whispered. "They're looking because we're not one of them."

"Yeah, okay, whatever you say."

Virginia felt relieved when they were invited to take seats on folding chairs in an area where three other non-Amish couples sat. *At least Earl and I aren't the only ones not wearing Plain clothes.*

Virginia looked down at her own attire. With Earl's help she had chosen a pair of bright blue slacks that blended well with a coral-and-blue-patterned blouse. Her gold-and-blue jewelry was bold and bright, to accentuate the outfit. Virginia had also recolored her hair a few days ago, and the red was most vibrant.

As other people arrived and took their seats, Virginia studied the large building. The wooden walls were rustic and rough-looking. Behind her, she noticed a ladder leading up to a loft. How odd it seemed to have a big wedding inside of a barn.

Virginia sniffed. Despite all the cleaning and clearing away of the animals this barn would normally house, she detected the faint aroma of horseflesh and manure. It seemed that no amount of scrubbing could completely dispel such putrid odors.

Virginia fiddled with her wedding ring, wondering when things would get started. She hoped the service wouldn't take long, because the metal chairs that she and Earl sat upon were hard and unyielding. She couldn't imagine how the Amish people sitting on backless wooden benches might feel by the end of a wedding, funeral, or church service. Virginia's back, and even her bum leg, would probably be stiff and sore from sitting more than thirty minutes on one of those benches.

"Look, Earl, here comes the bride and groom." Virginia bumped Earl's arm with her elbow as Sylvia and Dennis entered the barn and took seats in chairs facing each other near the center of the room. Two other couples had walked in behind them. The women sat on either side of the bride and the two young men did the same with the groom. Sylvia's sister, Amy, was one of the women, but Virginia didn't recognize the other young woman. Virginia presumed she might be a friend of Sylvia's, or maybe a cousin. She knew Sylvia's teenage brother, who had accompanied Dennis, but Virginia couldn't remember having met the young man sitting on the other side of Dennis. Maybe he too was a relative or friend.

Virginia noticed Belinda sitting behind Sylvia and her attendants. She held a baby in her arms. After talking to Belinda at the mailbox a few weeks ago, Virginia had learned that Amy had given birth to a baby boy. No doubt the infant Belinda held belonged to Amy and her husband, Jared.

Next to Belinda sat a young Amish woman with auburn hair. She held a small boy in her lap, and a little girl sat beside her. Virginia had not seen this woman before, and wondered if she too might be related to the King family. From what Virginia had heard, the Amish liked big families, so there was no telling how many people in this barn were related to either the bride or groom.

Virginia nudged Earl when some chant-like singing began, but she didn't understand any of the words, since they were sung in a foreign language. She had heard this type of singing with no musical instruments, before, when the Kings had church at their place and during Amy's wedding. But she'd never been seated in the midst of it all.

Earl nudged Virginia right back and leaned close to her ear. "This is sure different than any wedding I've ever been to. I wonder what's next." He kept his voice down, and with the singing going on, Virginia felt sure no one had heard him.

She yawned and glanced at her watch. *Wish I'd thought to bring a pen and tablet with me. I could have taken notes so I could remember all the details of this unusual wedding to tell Stella about.*

As Belinda listened to the bishop preach, her thoughts went to Herschel. In another two months they would be sitting in this barn again, only this time the preacher's message would be meant for them.

The thought of marrying Herschel brought a smile to Belinda's lips. She still could not believe that he'd agreed to move to Strasburg and help her run the greenhouse once they were married.

Two things still bothered Belinda. One was concern over whether more vandalism or threats would occur. The other was Henry's attitude toward Herschel. If she went through with her plans to marry Herschel, how would it affect her relationship with her son? Henry had never come to grips with the loss of his father and brother, and he'd made it adamantly clear that he would not accept Herschel as his stepfather. Surely that would all change once she and Herschel were married. Belinda's new husband would prove to her son that he not only cared about her welfare but Henry's as well.

Belinda's thoughts changed direction as she looked down at the precious grandchild she held, noting his slow, even breathing. The sleeping baby was so sweet and innocent, with not a care in the world. *If only such innocence could last forever. It's a shame every baby that's born must grow up and endure life's hurdles.*

Belinda reflected on a verse of scripture she'd read during her devotional time the other day. *"I will say of the Lord, He is my refuge and my fortress: my God; in him will I trust."* Indeed that was what everyone who followed Christ needed to do. *We need to trust.*

She touched the infant's tiny hand and stroked it gently. *I wonder what lies ahead for this special child. Will Amy and Jared be blessed with more children? I'm sure they will be good parents to this little one and any brothers or sisters he may have.*

Sylvia sat across from her groom, listening to the preacher's message and preparing to stand before the bishop and recite her vows to Dennis.

She remembered the day she and Toby had said the same vows. In some ways it seemed like only yesterday, but in other ways it felt like a long time ago. Although Sylvia would never forget what she and Toby once had, she felt ready to marry Dennis and be the best wife she could.

Sylvia thought about her children. They'd both been so young when their daddy died. Although it was possible for Allen to have some vague memories of Toby, Rachel was only a baby when her father had been taken from her, and she would have no memory of him whatsoever. The only father her children would ever really know was Dennis. Sylvia felt certain her new husband would be a good daddy to Rachel, Allen, and any future children they may have.

Although she was supposed to concentrate on the bishop's message, Sylvia's thoughts continued on—this time to her mother. She was glad Mom had found a man she loved and hoped that she and Herschel would have many good years together. Sylvia was also pleased that Herschel would be moving to Mom's home after they were married and was willing to help out in the greenhouse. It would be hard for her mother to sell her home and the greenhouse and have to move to another Amish community, even if it was within commuting distance. With a grown man living in Mom's home, perhaps the person responsible for the vandalism, threatening notes, and phone calls, would give up and leave them alone. If the things had been done by the man who owned the greenhouse on the other side of town, surely he was smart enough to realize that Mom's business was no threat to him. From what Sylvia had heard, the new greenhouse was doing a good business, so there really was no competition.

Sylvia glanced at Henry, sitting beside Dennis. Her brother looked so grown-up today, dressed in his church clothes and sitting so straight and tall. She was glad Dennis had asked Henry to be one of his witnesses. He and Henry had become close and had a lot in common, with their interest in birds as well as their dogs. She hoped someday in the future Henry would find the happiness in life that he deserved. It had been hard on him, losing both Dad and Abe, and then taking on so many extra duties and chores that he didn't enjoy. Perhaps once Herschel began helping Mom in the greenhouse and doing other chores around the place, Henry would have more freedom to enjoy life. And some day, a few years down the road, her younger brother would settle down, find a wife, and start a family of his own.

Sylvia pushed her thoughts aside when the bishop called her and Dennis to stand before him. It was finally time to say their vows.

Herschel gave his full attention to the bride and groom as they rose from their seats and took their place in front of the bishop. Dennis and Sylvia were still in the prime of life and Lord willing would have many years together. With Herschel and Belinda being an older couple, their time as husband and wife would likely be shorter. But it didn't matter. Herschel would live each day to its fullest and try to never take his spouse for granted. With God's help and guidance he would do his best to be a good husband. Herschel hoped he could form a lasting bond with all of Belinda's family—especially Henry, who still seemed aloof whenever Herschel was around.

Seated on the men's side of the room, Herschel could only see the back of Henry's head as he sat straight and tall. Like the others here today, he was about to witness his sister and Dennis respond to the bishop's questions and state their vows.

Herschel rested his hands in his lap and listened.

The bishop looked at Dennis. "Can you confess, brother, that you accept this, our sister, as your wife, and that you will not leave her until death separates you? And do you believe that this is from the Lord and that you have come thus far by your faith and prayers?"

Dennis answered, "Yes."

Then it was Sylvia's turn to respond after the bishop asked her a similar question. She too answered, "Yes."

The minister continued by asking the bride and groom another pertinent question. Once they'd both replied affirmatively, he took Sylvia's right hand and placed it in Dennis's right hand, putting his own hands above and beneath their hands. He then continued with a blessing. Following that, all three of them bent their knees in a partial bow.

"Go forth in the name of the Lord," the minister directed. "You are now man and wife."

Sylvia and Dennis seemed to radiate a blissful glow as they returned to their seats.

Herschel felt a thickening form in his throat. He was eager to answer those same questions when he and Belinda stood before their bishop in December.

Virginia couldn't believe she had made it through the entire wedding service without falling asleep or getting out of her chair. Although it had been uncomfortable to sit for three hours and listen to the singing and preaching in another language, she'd been fascinated with the whole procedure. She had waited for the preacher to pronounce the bride and groom as man and wife, followed by them sealing it with a kiss, but that moment never came. No walking up or down an aisle, as in a traditional English wedding; no musical instruments; and no hand-holding or kiss. Strange but interesting nonetheless.

After everyone left the barn, most of the people gathered in groups to visit while they waited for the first meal of the day that would be served inside the white tents that had been erected in the yard.

Virginia and Earl stood off by themselves until Jared and Amy came up to them.

"I'm glad you could be at my sister's wedding." Amy smiled. "It was too bad you weren't able to make it to ours."

"What are you talking about?" Virginia's brows squished together. "We didn't come because we never got an invitation to your wedding."

"I'm so sorry. You were on our list, and I thought your invitation had been sent." Amy placed her hand on Virginia's arm. "Please accept my apologies. It certainly wasn't intentional."

"It's all right," Earl spoke up. "Mail gets lost sometimes, and at least we got to be here for your sister's wedding."

Jared and Amy both nodded.

"Your mother told me that you had a baby recently." Virginia's comment was directed at Amy. "Was that the infant she held during the wedding?"

"Yes. Jared and I are pleased that God gave us a healthy little boy."

Virginia wasn't surprised to hear a mention of God, since the Amish were quite religious. She, however, had no interest in God, because He had done nothing for her. Most of Virginia's life had been a struggle, and as far as she knew, no prayer she'd ever uttered had been answered—at least not in the way she wanted.

"Where is your baby?" Virginia questioned. "Does your mom still have him?"

Amy shook her head. "Jared's mother is holding him now, and no doubt, he'll be passed to other family members as the day goes on." She laughed. "The only time I'll probably get to hold Dewayne is when he wants to be fed or is in need of a diaper change." She looked to her right. "And speaking of relatives, here comes Mom with my oldest brother and his family."

Virginia watched as Belinda approached. A tall, bearded man walked with her, along with an auburn-haired Amish woman and two children. The young girl was next to her mother, but the Amish man held the little boy in his arms.

"Virginia and Earl, I'd like you to meet my son Ezekiel. He's the one I told you lives in New York." Belinda gestured to the young woman beside him. "This is his wife, Michelle, and their children, Angela Mary and Vernon."

Ezekiel reached out and shook Earl's hand. "Nice to meet you."

Earl responded, "Same here."

It dawned on Virginia that Ezekiel's wife must be the daughter-in-law Belinda had told her used to be English. There was something familiar about the woman's pretty blue eyes, auburn hair, and creamy complexion. Virginia wondered if she may have seen her somewhere—perhaps on some occasion when Ezekiel's family had been visiting their family here and gone out shopping.

Virginia extended her hand to the woman. "Michelle is a pretty name. I knew a little girl by that name once. In fact, she was—"

Michelle's face paled, and she blinked multiple times. "Ma...mama?" She swayed slightly, as though she might faint. "No, it can't be. I'm just feeling *verhuddelt*."

Chapter 41

"What's going on, Michelle? Why are you confused?" Ezekiel put his hand on the small of his wife's back.

With a shaky hand, Michelle pointed at Virginia. "Is–is your name Ginny Taylor?"

Virginia bit down on her lower lip until she tasted blood. "It used to be."

"I knew it!" Michelle looked up at Ezekiel, then back at Virginia. "This woman is my mother. I haven't seen her since I was a young girl, and she's older-looking now, but I'd recognize her face and that bright red hair anywhere."

Virginia's eyes widened and she grabbed Earl's arm for support. "Oh, my word. . . Can this really be true?"

"I don't know how, but I believe it is." Michelle drew in a breath and blew it out quickly. "How'd you know I was here? Have you been tracking me somehow?"

Virginia shook her head. "How could I have known? When Child Protective Services took you and your brothers, I thought I'd never see you again."

Everyone began talking at once until Belinda held up her hand. "We won't start eating for another half hour or so. Why don't we all go into the house so we can talk privately and figure out what's going on?"

Michelle shook her head vigorously. "I don't want to talk to this woman. She's a child abuser, and I don't want her anywhere near our children." She stood in front of the little girl as though the child needed protection.

"I'm so sorry. I never meant to hurt you." Virginia reached out her hand toward Michelle, but the wide-eyed young woman took another step back. *Michelle doesn't want to talk to me. She must be harboring anger for the way I treated her as a child. I can't blame her for hating me. Oh my—I can't believe I'm standing here talking to my very own daughter who I never thought I would see again.*

"Let's do as Mom suggested and go inside." Ezekiel guided Michelle toward the house but paused when she stopped walking.

Michelle looked over at Amy. "Would you and Jared please take the kinner for a while? I don't want to upset them."

"Of course." Jared took the baby from him, and Amy said something in Pennsylvania Dutch before motioning for the little girl to come with her.

When Ezekiel, Michelle, Earl, and Virginia entered the house behind Belinda, she asked them to all take a seat in the living room.

Virginia's mouth felt so dry she could barely swallow, and her leg had begun to throb, so it was a relief to sit on the couch.

Belinda sat next to Virginia, with Earl on the other side of her, while Michelle and Ezekiel seated themselves in two chairs facing them.

Michelle massaged her forehead as she stared at Virginia with her head cocked to one side. "Where's my dad? Did you finally get fed up with him and file for divorce?"

"No, I remained faithful to him until he passed away several years ago." She reached over and took Earl's hand. The warmth of it and the gentle squeeze he gave her fingers helped Virginia find the courage to say more. "Earl's my husband now, and he's a good man. It's because of a job change for him that we ended up moving here," she added.

"I see." Michelle's voice was barely above a whisper, and she kept glancing at Belinda, as if needing encouragement or reassurance.

Virginia studied her daughter's face. Michelle had grown into a beautiful woman, even without makeup and fancy clothes. It didn't seem possible that she had become Amish. And what were the odds that Michelle would be related to Virginia and Earl's neighbor? It all seemed like a dream, or maybe it was a miracle. After all these years of wondering where her children could be, did God have a hand in bringing Virginia and Michelle together? Would they be able to work things out and have some sort of relationship?

Pausing to answer questions, Michelle gave her mother a brief explanation of where all she had been from the time she and her brothers were taken from home and what had lead up to her joining the Amish church and marrying Ezekiel.

"That's incredible." Virginia looked at her husband. "Don't you think so, Earl?"

"Yep. Never heard a story quite like that one. It almost seems impossible."

"It's all true," Michelle assured him. "I faced some dark, depressing days until I met Ezekiel and his family. I'm ever so thankful God led me to them."

Virginia tilted her body toward Michelle. "Do you know where your brothers are?"

"Yes, I do, but I'm not sure they would want to see you. It was hard for Ernie and Jack to be separated from me, and we've only been reunited for a few years."

"So they're both doing all right?"

Yes, but no thanks to you. Michelle managed to nod as she struggled with her pent-up emotions.

"Maybe you could call Jack and Ernie," Ezekiel suggested, looking at Michelle. "At least let them know you and your mother have been reunited, and see if they'd be willing to talk with her."

Michelle looked down at her hands, now folded in her lap. "I don't know."

"You did try to contact your parents once, remember?" Ezekiel responded.

"Yes," she admitted quietly. After accepting Christ as her Savior, Michelle had wanted to let her mom and dad know that she'd forgiven them for their ill treatment toward herself, Ernie, and Jack. But now, with her mother sitting a few feet away, Michelle found it difficult not to let bitterness and resentment resurface. It wasn't the Amish way to refuse to forgive someone who had hurt them, and it certainly wasn't what God expected of her either.

The words of Matthew 6:14 popped into Michelle's head: *"For if ye forgive men their trespasses, your heavenly Father will also forgive you."*

I forgave my mom once, but she didn't know it, so now I need to do it again and mean it.

Michelle got up and asked her mother-in-law if she could take her place on the couch. When Belinda stood, Michelle sat next to Virginia. Feeling a sense of peace that had suddenly come over her, she turned to the woman who had given birth to her, and said, "I forgive you, Mama, and I promise to let Jack and Ernie know that we have been reunited." Gulping back a sob, Michelle hugged her mother.

"Are you as hallich as I am right now?" Dennis asked, leaning close to Sylvia as they sat at their corner table during the wedding meal.

"Jah, I'm very happy. Everyone else seems to be having a good time. Just look at the smiles on their faces."

He chuckled. "It must be all the good food they've helped themselves to as the bowls and platters have been brought to the table and passed around."

Sylvia motioned with her head toward the table where Ezekiel sat with his family. Virginia and Earl sat across from them, and there seemed to be quite a conversation going on. "Looks like my bruder and Michelle are getting acquainted with our neighbors from across the street."

"Have they met them before, or is this the first time?"

"I don't believe Virginia or her husband have been over here when Ezekiel and Michelle have come for a visit."

"They certainly seem to be getting along well, and that Earl's eating enough food for three people."

Sylvia gave Dennis's arm a poke. "Now don't be critical. This is only our first meal of the day. By the time it's all been said and done, you and I will probably need wheelbarrows to carry us out of the tent."

Dennis leaned closer. "You're so cute when you tease. Do you know how hard it is for me to keep from kissing you right now?"

Sylvia's cheeks warmed. "That will have to wait until later, when there aren't so many people watching us."

"I bet most folks aren't paying any attention to us. They're too busy eating and talking with the people around them."

"That could be." Sylvia took a sip from her glass of fruit punch, while she thought about the nice card and note she'd received from Toby's parents earlier this week. In addition to congratulating Sylvia on her upcoming marriage, the Beilers had given her their blessing. The note stated that they were happy Sylvia had found love again, and they felt sure their son would want her to be happy. It meant a lot to Sylvia to have received her previous in-laws' approval.

She looked over at the table where Dennis's mother; his brother, Gerald; and his three older sisters, Marla, Dorcas, and Hannah sat with their families. How nice it was that they could all come down from Dauphin County for the wedding. She hadn't always felt this way, but from the warm greeting she'd received from them when they'd arrived last evening, she felt sure that they too approved of her marrying Dennis.

Next Sylvia's gaze came to rest on the table where her mother sat beside Herschel. She smiled. *Only two months to go, and then it'll be Mr. and Mrs. Herschel Fisher sharing a meal with their wedding guests.*

That evening after all the visitors had gone home, Belinda sat on the porch swing beside Herschel.

"It was a good day, jah?" Herschel took hold of her hand.

"Yes, a very good day—for Sylvia and Dennis as well as for Michelle and Virginia." A few minutes ago, Belinda had filled Herschel in on what had transpired before the first wedding meal of the day.

"Sure amazes me sometimes how God works things out in a person's life—often in ways least expected."

"You're right about that." Belinda leaned her head against his shoulder. "I never would have dreamed I could fall in love again or find a man as kind and gentle as you."

Virginia took off her bedroom slippers and curled up on the couch with Goldie. Earl had one of his favorite TV shows on and seemed totally absorbed in watching it.

When the movie paused and an advertisement came on, she asked if he wanted something to eat or drink.

Earl angled his body so he was looking at her. "I'm still full from all that food we had after the wedding today, but a glass of cold cider would sure hit the spot."

"Okay."

Virginia got off the couch and headed to the kitchen. When she returned a few minutes later, Earl's eyes were closed, so she figured he may have fallen asleep.

She set the glass of cider on the small table beside his chair and was about to head back to the couch, when Earl called out to her. "Hey, where are ya going? Why don't you sit in the other recliner and we can watch the rest of the show together."

Virginia had no desire to watch a movie that was half over, but she did as he asked.

"Today was certainly full of surprises, wasn't it?"

"Yep."

"I never thought I'd reconnect with my daughter, let alone that she'd be related to those Plain folks across the street."

"Does that mean you're gonna change your attitude about them?" He took another drink from his glass.

"I don't know, Earl. It does put a different light on things." Virginia hit the lever on the recliner and leaned back for a more comfortable position. "Michelle wants to visit with me again tomorrow. We have a lot of catching up to do."

"Won't she and her family be going back to their home in New York?"

"Not for a few more days." Virginia gave a deep, gratifying sigh. "I still can't believe she was willing to forgive me for all the years of abuse I put her through."

Earl frowned. "I never knew till today that you had mistreated your children. I can't even picture it in my head."

"I never meant to be a bad mother, and I wasn't at first. But when Herb began beating on me, I became so angry I ended up taking it out on the children." Her eyes grew hot with the need to cry, and her throat ached when she swallowed. "After the kids were taken from us, Herb continued to abuse me." She lifted her bum leg. "He did this to me when he got drunk one night and was in a rage."

"Why didn't you leave him? You had every right to."

"I tried several times, but he always came after me, promising never to do it again." She sniffed as tears sprang to her eyes. "I wanted to get the kids back, but I didn't have a job and couldn't have provided for them if I'd struck out on my own."

"You shoulda got away from him. You shoulda got some help."

"I know that now, but it's too late to go back and do things over." Virginia paused to collect herself. "You know what?"

"What?"

"This is the happiest I've been in years. I not only found my daughter today, but I discovered two grandchildren I didn't know about. And with any luck, I may get to see my boys soon too."

Chapter 42

Clymer

Excitement combined with nervousness welled in Virginia's chest as they followed Earl's GPS to Ezekiel and Michelle's house. They'd been invited for Thanksgiving dinner, and Jack and Ernie would be there too. *My sons must want to see me,* Virginia told herself. *Otherwise, they wouldn't have agreed for us to meet at Michelle and Ezekiel's house.*

She fiddled with her dangly earrings and blew out a quick breath. *I hope I don't say or do anything wrong while we're there. I don't want to mess up our reunion and lose contact with my sons yet again.*

"Stop fidgeting and try to relax." Earl bumped Virginia's arm with his elbow. "We're almost there."

"I can't help it. The closer we get, the more nervous I become."

"If you're that nervous, then maybe we should have stayed home."

She shook her head. "No way! I've spent too many years wishing I could see my children again, and I won't miss this opportunity no matter how it turns out."

"Which I'm sure will be fine. Look how nice your daughter was about accepting you back into her life."

Virginia pulled a tissue out of her purse and blew her nose. "True, and she even said she's forgiven me for the way I treated her in the past."

"So there you go. . . If she forgave you, then her brothers probably will too. That's how it is with those Amish folks."

"But Ernie and Jack are not Amish. They may not even be religious."

"Then you oughta get along with them just fine, since you're not religious either."

Virginia clasped her hands together in her lap. When she and

Michelle had gotten together the day after Sylvia's wedding, they'd spent part of the time talking about God and what a difference it had made in Michelle's life when she'd become a Christian. Michelle had shared several scriptures with Virginia, and even written them down. The following week, Virginia went out and purchased a Bible. Ever since then she'd read a few passages from God's Word each day.

I wonder what Earl would say if he knew that. He had told Virginia several times since they got married that he had no need of a religious crutch and thought people who needed it were weak.

Virginia picked at a hangnail on her thumb. *Guess that makes me weak, because I've come to the conclusion that I need a personal relationship with Christ, and I'm hoping Michelle can tell me what I need to do.*

Strasburg

As Belinda and her daughters prepared their Thanksgiving meal, which they would be sharing with Herschel and his parents, she decided to ask them a question that had been weighing on her mind the past two weeks.

She joined them at the counter where they were peeling potatoes. "I'm concerned about something, and I need your opinions."

Amy's brows furrowed. "You look so serious. What is it, Mom?"

"Henry has still not accepted the idea of me marrying Herschel, and I'm wondering if it would be best if I called off the wedding."

Sylvia shook her head vigorously. "No, that would not be best—for you, for Herschel, or even for Henry."

"Why do you say that?" Belinda felt a tightening in her chest. "Don't your brother's feelings count for anything?"

"Of course they do," Amy interjected, "but Henry is being selfish and unreasonable about your relationship with Herschel."

"That's right," Sylvia agreed. "If he cared about anyone other than himself, he would quit moping around and be as happy for you as we both are."

"I've known for some time that you and Herschel were meant for each other." Amy put the potato peeler down and placed one hand on the small of Belinda's back. "Herschel is a wonderful man, and he loves you very much. If you don't marry him, I'm afraid you'll regret it for the rest of your life."

"I agree with my sister." Sylvia touched Belinda's arm and gave it a few pats. "And remember this—Henry will not be living at home with your forever. Eventually he'll be old enough to move out and start a life of his own—maybe even with a wife."

Belinda breathed in and out, lightly clasping her hands together as she reflected on all that her daughters had said. The words they'd spoken made sense, but she would need to do some serious praying before reaching a final decision.

Clymer

"This meal you fixed for all of us is sure good, Michelle. Thanks for inviting Earl and me to join you and your family today." Virginia looked over at her two grandchildren. They were both so sweet and well-behaved.

Michelle smiled. "You're welcome. I'm glad you could come, Mama. And you too, Earl."

He smiled and helped himself to another piece of turkey.

Virginia looked across the table to where Ernie and Jack sat with their wives. "And thank you for agreeing to see me, and for listening to my apology for not being the kind of mother you needed and deserved."

Jack looked straight at her. "It's in the past, so there'd be no point in me holding a grudge. Besides, Ernie and I had foster parents who treated us well."

Ernie nodded but made no comment. Virginia wasn't sure if he'd forgiven her, but at least he had been cordial since she and Earl had arrived. No doubt it would take some time for Virginia to gain her children's trust, and she would do everything in her power to make it happen. How good it was to know that Michelle, Jack, and Ernie were doing well and had moved on with their lives, in spite of their terrible childhood. Things could have turned out much differently for them if they'd stayed with Virginia and Herb.

Virginia felt a dull pain throughout her body and struggled to keep her tears from falling. *I was a horrible mother and I have a lot to make up for, but I don't see how God could forgive me.* She looked over at Michelle. "After dinner, I'll help you with the dishes and clean up the kitchen. It'll give us some time to talk, because I have some questions about the Bible I'd like to ask you about."

Michelle smiled. "Of course, Mama. I'd be happy to answer any of your questions. And since Ezekiel is a minister in our church district here, I'm sure he would too."

Ezekiel agreed.

Although Virginia still didn't understand why Michelle had decided to give up modern things for the Plain life, she had obviously chosen well when she married Ezekiel. In the short time Virginia had known him, she'd become certain that he loved her daughter and would always treat her and their children well.

Strasburg

After their meal, Henry excused himself, saying he wanted to go out to the barn to check on the animals. Herschel had a feeling that Belinda's son just wanted to be alone and perhaps away from him.

The women began clearing the table, suggesting that the men go to the living room to visit. Herschel waited about fifteen minutes and then he told his dad, along with Jared and Dennis, that he was going outside for some fresh air.

"Sure, go ahead," Jared said. "When you come back in, maybe we can get a board game going."

"Okay." Herschel put his jacket and hat on, then left the house and headed straight for the barn. He figured it was about time he and Henry had a serious talk.

Upon entering the barn and seeing no sign of the young man, Herschel climbed the ladder up to the loft. Sure enough, Henry sat crossed-legged in front of the large open window, staring out at the yard.

"What are ya up to?" Herschel asked, taking a seat beside him.

"Just doin' some thinking and watchin' for birds." Henry sat quietly for several minutes, and then he turned to face Herschel. "You may as well know this right now—you ain't never gonna be my daed."

Herschel put his hand on Henry's shoulder. "I don't expect to be your dad, but I would like to be your friend. For your mother's sake, if nothing else, are you willing to give me a chance?"

Henry shrugged. "We'll see."

"All right. For now at least, that's good enough." Herschel wished there was something he could say or do to win Henry's favor, but he couldn't think of a thing other than to continue praying about it. The problem was, he and Belinda would be getting married in two weeks. If Henry didn't show some acceptance of him soon, Herschel might feel compelled to call off the wedding. As much as he loved Belinda and wanted to be her husband, he didn't see how they could make it work if her son kept his negative attitude and did not accept him.

"What kind of birds are you watching for?"

"Nothin' in particular. Just whatever birds come to the feeders in our yard." Henry glanced at Herschel and then looked away. "I keep a journal of all the birds I see, and sometimes if one of them is kinda rare or a bird not seen too often around here, I call the birding hotline and leave a message. That way, others, who are also bird-watchers, can keep an eye out for that particular bird."

"Sounds like an interesting hobby."

"Yeah. It helps to take my mind off all the problems we've had around here since my daed, brother, and brother-in-law died."

"I understand about that. I hurt really bad when my wife passed away, and it was hard for me not to dwell on it." Herschel laid a hand against his breastbone. "For the longest while I visited Mattie's grave almost every day. Even put flowers on the plot of dirt where she was buried, even though it wasn't something our church leaders approved of."

"Guess we all do some things others don't like." Henry groaned. "I've been trying to figure out who's done all the vandalism to our place, but Mom and my sisters think I'm wasting my time." His shoulders slumped. "I've been the only man in this family since Dad died, and I haven't done a good job of protecting Mom or my sisters."

"No one's been physically hurt though, right?"

"Nope, but every act of vandalism and threatening note has left them—and me—nervous and wondering when the next nasty thing will be done." Henry rubbed his forehead. "I have several suspects in mind, but so far, I've found no proof that any of them are guilty."

"Maybe the two of us can put our thinking caps on and come up with some answers together," Herschel offered. "Would that be okay with you?"

Henry hesitated but finally answered, "I guess so."

Herschel gave Henry's shoulder a light squeeze. "Remember the old saying. Two heads are better than one."

As they approached their own home late that night, Virginia felt the need to tell her husband what had transpired when she was in the kitchen with Michelle after their meal.

"You know something, Earl?"

"What's that?"

"As glad as I am about having found my three children, I'm even happier now, because I found Jesus today."

"Is that so? I didn't know He was missing."

"That's not funny, Earl. What I meant was, I accepted Jesus as my Savior and asked Him to forgive my sins. Michelle helped me recite the sinner's prayer."

Earl gave a piglike snort but said nothing.

Virginia couldn't help but wonder what he was thinking. Did Earl believe she'd become a religious fanatic, or might he too be interested in learning about Jesus? *I wonder how he would respond if I shared a few Bible verses with him.* She pursed her lips. *I may as well try, so here goes. . .*

"Two of those passages of scripture Michelle read to me are found in John 3:16 and 17. Would like to hear them?"

"Not particularly."

Ignoring his response, Virginia reached into her purse and pulled out a slip of paper, along with the small flashlight she kept in there. "Here's what verse 16 says, Earl: 'For God so loved the world, that he gave his only begotten Son, that whosoever believeth in him should not perish, but have everlasting life.'"

Virginia paused to see if Earl would comment, but when he said nothing, she continued. "Verse 17 of that same chapter says: 'For God sent not his Son into the world to condemn the world; but that the world though him might be saved.'"

"Super."

Virginia tried to ignore her husband's sarcastic tone and read him another verse she had written down today. "And 1 John 1:9 says: 'If we confess our sins, [God] is faithful and just to forgive us our sins, and to cleanse us from all unrighteousness.'"

"I don't need a sermon, Virginia. And if you don't mind, I'd like to change the subject. Better yet, let's listen to some music." Earl turned on the radio and upped the volume.

Virginia leaned heavily against the seat and closed her eyes. *Guess I shouldn't have said anything to him right now. Maybe some other time if I bring up the topic he'll be more receptive. If I become the person God wants me to be, Earl might realize that he needs the Lord too.*

Chapter 43

With just a week before the wedding, Belinda knew she had to make a decision. She'd prayed about it, talked it over with her girls, and asked herself many times if marrying Herschel was the right thing to do.

I need to speak with Henry again, Belinda told herself as she looked out the kitchen window and saw him walking toward the house.

She went to the back door and opened it for him, since his hands were holding a box.

"We won't be going to the greenhouse this morning," Henry announced when he stepped inside. "Someone broke in, and the place is a mess. I brought in the few jars of honey that hadn't been broken."

Belinda's thoughts went blank, as if her brain had stopped working. She stood staring at the box he held.

"Mom, did ya hear what I said? The place is trashed. Gift items we were hoping people would buy for Christmas gifts are ruined; all the Christmas cactus and poinsettias were knocked on the floor, and it looks like someone trampled on 'em." Henry shook his head. "There ain't much left that we can salvage."

Belinda's brain started working again, and her spine stiffened. "Whoever left that last threatening message on our answering machine has finally made good on their promise because I haven't sold our home or the greenhouse." She paused long enough to rub her forehead and instructed Henry to put the box on the kitchen table. "What are we going to do, Son? If the person responsible for this attack can do something so mean and destructive, there's no telling what else he or she might do if we don't sell our place and move." Belinda sucked in some air. "I think it's time to call the sheriff."

"Not yet, Mom. Whoever did this dropped something, and I believe I know who it belongs to." Henry set the box on the table, reached into his pocket, and pulled out a small knife. "I found this outside the greenhouse by the door that was broken into."

Belinda twisted her head-covering ties around her fingers. "Then we need to call the sheriff and tell him you think you know who's behind all the vandalism."

"If it's who I think it is, I wanna take care of it by myself."

"You believe it's Monroe, don't you, Son?"

"I can't say for sure till I've confronted the person, and I'm gonna do that right now." He turned toward the door.

Belinda's pulse quickened as she reached out and clasped her son's arm. "Wait, Henry. You can't go alone. What if the person you accuse is innocent? Or worse yet, what if they're guilty and see your accusation as a threat." She gripped his arm tighter. "They could become angry and your life might be in danger."

Henry shook his head with a determined expression. "I don't care. I wanna look this person in the face and ask why they would do such horrible things to us. After they admit their guilt, then you can call the sheriff." Henry pulled away and dashed out the door.

Belinda was right behind him. "Henry, wait!"

He'd only made it halfway across the lawn when a horse and buggy came into the yard. When it pulled up to the hitching rail and Herschel got out, Belinda breathed a sigh of relief.

Rubbing her arms against the cold, she ran out to meet him. "Someone broke into the greenhouse during the night, and they ruined all the plants, flowers, and gift items." She paused to draw a quick breath. "Henry thinks he knows who did it, and he wants to go after the person by himself."

Herschel's brows knit together, and he pulled Belinda into his arms. "It's cold out here, and you're shaking. You need to go inside and put a jacket on."

Despite holding her arms across her chest, Belinda continued to tremble. "Didn't you hear what I said? My son is about to put himself in what could be a dangerous situation."

"Yes, I understand, and I'll go with him. Just please, go into the house."

Belinda wasn't sure whether to do as he said or insist on going along. But her teeth had begun to chatter, and she felt as though she might pass out from the cold.

She touched her forehead. *Or maybe it's fear that's making me feel lightheaded. Fear for the safety of my son and the man I've come to love.*

After Belinda went inside, Herschel walked over to Henry, who was taking his dog out of the pen. "Your mamm told me what happened in the greenhouse last night. I'm sure sorry to hear it."

Henry's fist tightened around Blackie's collar as he turned to face Herschel. "Yeah, and I think I know who did it." He clipped a leash onto the dog's collar. "I'm goin' to confront the person, and I'm takin' my hund along in case there's trouble."

"I'm sure your dog would offer protection, but it might be a good idea if I go with you."

Henry angled his head toward Herschel. "You'd do that for me?"

"Of course. I not only care about your mother's welfare, but yours as well."

"Really?" Henry spoke in a disbelieving tone.

"Definitely."

Belinda's son gave Herschel a hint of a smile before reaching into his jacket pocket and pulling out a pocketknife. "See this?"

"Yes."

"I think it belongs to the person who broke into the greenhouse and trashed the place." He held it up higher. "Have you ever seen it before?"

Herschel shook his head. "I don't believe so."

"Well, I have, so it's to that person's house I think we oughta go."

"All right. Should we take my horse and buggy?"

"No need for that. He's headed this way right now."

When Henry pointed at the man walking up the driveway, Herschel's mouth dropped open. "Henry, are you sure about that? We shouldn't make any accusations until we have some proof."

Henry held out the knife in his hand. "Here's the proof."

Walking beside Henry and his dog, Herschel made his way down the driveway, meeting the man coming toward them halfway.

"Good morning, Henry," Earl said. "I came over to talk to your mother."

"She's in the house, but I'd like to talk to you."

Henry spoke with an assurance that surprised Herschel. He figured the boy might be shaking in his boots. Herschel wanted to ask Belinda's neighbor a few questions himself, but figured he'd let Henry speak first.

"I don't have time for your questions." Earl moved past Henry and Herschel, and made his way up the driveway at a fast pace.

Herschel looked at Henry, noticing the determined set of his jaw. "We'd better go in with him. You can ask your questions when we're in the house."

Belinda was surprised when she heard a knock on the door—actually, it sounded more like pounding. Thinking it might be Herschel coming to check on her before he left with Henry, she quickly opened the door. She was equally surprised when she saw Earl on the porch, with Henry, Herschel, and Blackie coming up behind him.

"What's going on?" Her gaze traveled from Earl, to Herschel, and then to her son.

"Herschel and I saw Earl coming up our driveway, and when I said there were some questions I wanted to ask him, he said he needed to talk to you."

"Come inside, all of you, and warm yourselves." When they entered the house and followed Belinda to the living room, she gestured to the fire crackling in the fireplace.

Earl hesitated at first, but then took the chair closest to the fire.

Henry wasted no time in stepping in front of him. "Is this yours?" He held the knife out to Earl.

"Yes, it is. Guess I must have dropped it when—" A red blotch erupted on Earl's cheeks as he looked over at Belinda. "I came here this morning to apologize, because I have a confession to make."

"What kind of confession?"

"I'm the person responsible for all of the nasty things that have been done to your place."

Henry snapped his fingers. "I knew it! As soon as I found that pocketknife, which I saw you fiddling with before we all sat down to eat after Sylvia and Dennis's wedding, I realized it must have been you who'd done all the vandalism." Henry's eyes narrowed. "How could you do all those things? Haven't we been good neighbors?"

When Belinda saw her son's nostrils flare, she felt it was time to take over. "Yes, Earl, please explain why you would want to hurt us."

Earl's chin practically dropped to his chest as his posture slumped. "I did it for my wife."

"What?" Belinda's voice cracked. "Are you saying that Virginia asked you to do all those things?"

He looked up and shook his head.

"Then please explain," Herschel interjected.

Earl moaned. "From the time we first moved here, all Virginia did was complain about the noise from the traffic and the smell from the horses on the road that separates our homes. She blamed it on the fact that your place of business brought in so many people who might otherwise not have traveled our road. I figured if I scared you bad enough, you'd sell out and move, and then there'd finally be some peace in my home."

Belinda lowered herself into the rocking chair at the shock of what he'd said. At one time she'd felt Virginia didn't care for her, but lately, the woman had seemed more friendly—especially after learning that her long-lost daughter was married to Belinda's son. "Did your wife know you were doing all those things to us?" she asked.

"Virginia had no idea." Earl dropped his gaze again. "After she was reunited with Michelle, Virginia stopped complaining about the traffic, noise, and smell. But then something I never expected happened."

"What was it?" Henry and his dog had taken a seat on the floor, but he never stopped looking at Earl.

"She got religious."

Herschel took the chair beside Belinda and placed his hand on her arm. "Is that a bad thing, Earl?"

"It was to me. She kept quoting Bible verses, and I began to panic."

"How come?" Belinda spoke in a gentle tone. In spite of all that he'd done to them, she felt compassion for this poor, confused man.

"I panicked because I didn't want to acknowledge that I'm a sinner. Last night, after Virginia went to bed, I snuck out of the house, came over here, and broke into your greenhouse. In a rage, I shouted at God for turning Virginia into a different person and trying to change me. I went ballistic and wrecked nearly everything in the building."

Belinda sat quietly, unsure of what to say, but Earl continued before she was able to formulate a response.

"This morning, after getting little or no sleep last night, I got up before Virginia did and went out to the living room, where I picked up her Bible. I found John 3:16–17, which were two of the verses she had quoted to me on our ride home from Clymer on Thanksgiving." Earl put both hands against his red cheeks. "I sat there with tears running down my face and acknowledged Jesus as the Son of God, and I asked Him to forgive me of all my sins." He folded his hands, sighing deeply. "I'm ashamed of what I did, and I came here to confess and ask your forgiveness, which I clearly don't deserve." Tears welled in the man's eyes. "I'll do anything in my power to make it up to you."

Belinda got up from her chair and walked over to stand beside him. Reaching out to touch Earl's arm, she said: "Your apology is accepted. I forgive you."

"Thank you for being so gracious." Earl reached into his pocket and pulled out a hanky, which he used to dry his damp cheeks. "I'm supposed to be at work in half an hour, but when I get home this evening, I'll be over to clean up the mess I made. I will also pay for the damage I've caused since that first act of vandalism, even if I have to use all of my savings." He rose from his chair. "Thank you for listening to me this morning and for your forgiving spirit. I'll see you later in the day." Earl said goodbye and hurried out the door.

"Wow, that was sure somethin' I never expected." Henry pushed his bangs out of his face. "Do you believe him, Mom? Do you think Earl will be over after work to clean up the mess he made?"

"I have no reason not to believe him. He seemed sincere in his apology, Son."

"Speaking of apologies, I owe you and Herschel one."

Belinda angled her body toward Henry. "Oh?"

"I'm sorry for not accepting your decision to get married. It's obvious that you both love each other, and I was wrong for trying to come between you." Henry looked over at Herschel. "I appreciate you wanting to go with me when I said I was going to confront the person who had done the vandalism. It proved how much you care about all of us."

Herschel moved his head slowly up and down. "I care very much, Henry. And I promise to be your friend and not act like a daed, because no one can replace your father."

"Thank you." Henry moved toward the door with Blackie. "Guess I'd better feed this fellow before I put him back in his pen. I'll leave you two alone now to talk about your wedding, 'cause it'll be taking place soon."

When Henry went out the door, Herschel pulled Belinda gently to her feet and wrapped his arms around her. "Any doubts about marrying me?" he whispered against her ear.

"Absolutely none." Belinda smiled up at him. "Next week at this time, I'll become Mrs. Herschel Fisher."

Epilogue

Four months later

With a cup of coffee in her hand, Belinda stepped out the front door and handed it to her husband.

"Danki." Herschel smiled as she took a seat on the porch swing beside him. It was a pleasant morning, and she savored these moments before it was time to open the greenhouse.

"Would you look at all the robins out there on the lawn, searching for worms." Herschel pointed.

She smiled. "It's that time of the year again."

He grinned back at her. "Henry gave me a lesson the other day on those red-breasted birds."

"Oh did he now? Are you ready to join him in his bird-watching endeavors?"

"I doubt I'll ever be as serious about it as your son is, but he can still teach me a lot."

Belinda leaned her head against his shoulder. "I'm glad you and Henry have been getting along so well since our marriage."

"Same here. Although I know he'll never think of me as his father, Henry is the son I never had."

"He sees you as a friend he can look up to and learn from. That should count for something."

"It does." Herschel laughed when Blackie ran across the lawn near the porch, in pursuit of the stick Henry had thrown for him. "Living here with you and Henry and being involved in your greenhouse business makes me happy. I don't miss working at the bulk-food store one bit."

She clasped his hand. "I'm happy and contented having you here too. I can't imagine my life without you."

"That goes double for me." Herschel lifted Belinda's hand and kissed her fingers.

Belinda spotted her neighbor walk across the road to get her mail and waved. Virginia waved back. Since Virginia and Earl had become Christians, they'd started going to church every Sunday. Virginia had told Belinda the other day that she and Earl were studying the Bible together.

Last night as Belinda and Herschel had held their devotions together before going to bed, they'd read the second verse in Psalm 91, and it spoke to her heart. *I will say of the Lord, He is my refuge and my fortress: my God; in him will I trust.*

Belinda thought about Monroe. He'd moved to the Amish settlement near Harrisburg three months ago to run his new business. Last week she'd received a letter from him, wishing her and Herschel well and giving them an update on how things were going for him. Recently Monroe had begun courting a woman in her late forties who had never been married. They got along well, and Monroe felt in time there could be talk of marriage. Belinda wished him well.

Smiling, her gaze went to the greenhouse, and the second building they had added last month. Their business was doing well, and Belinda no longer had to worry about anyone vandalizing their place or trying to get them to move. Her grown children were happy, and their marriages were strong. The grandchildren were growing, and soon another little one would come along, as Sylvia and Dennis were expecting their first child together this fall. Michelle and Ezekiel came to visit often, and they spent part of their time with Virginia and Earl.

What more could I ask for? Belinda closed her eyes and lifted a silent prayer. *Heavenly Father, I thank You for Your goodness to us and for Your watchful eye. I have sensed Your presence through the good times as well as the bad. My greatest desire is to bless others the way You have blessed me.*

Belinda opened her eyes and smiled when she saw Maude at the mailbox, talking to Virginia. Although the elderly woman had a nice cozy cabin to live in year round, Belinda had continued to give her things in order to help out.

Belinda leaned closer to her husband and released a contented sigh. Even though it had been a difficult couple of years following the death of three special people in their family, God had always been at their side, helping them through each trial. This spring and, Lord willing, for a good many more years together, Belinda and Herschel could relax and enjoy the cheerful sound of the robin's greeting.

Belinda's Savory Baked Beans

1 pound dry navy beans
2 bay leaves
¾ cup ketchup
½ cup brown sugar
¼ cup molasses

1 tablespoon dry mustard
1 medium onion, chopped
1½ cups cut-up cooked ham
   or ham lunch meat

Combine navy beans and bay leaves in large bowl. Cover with water and let soak overnight. Drain and place in large kettle, cover with water, and boil. Cook 45 minutes or until tender. Drain beans, reserving liquid. In a bowl combine ketchup, brown sugar, molasses, dry mustard, onion, and ham. Place beans in uncovered roasting pan, stir ketchup mix in and add reserved liquid. Bake at 350 degrees for 3 hours. Add more liquid if contents in roasting pan become too dry.

Discussion Questions

1. Virginia felt uncomfortable around her Amish neighbors because their way of living was different from hers. Is it possible to have a friendship with someone whose lifestyle is not the same as yours? How should we treat our neighbors?

2. After Belinda's husband died, she never expected to fall in love again or to be courted by two very different men. Do you think it was right for her to see both men socially? How did it help her decide which one to choose?

3. Belinda's son Henry was determined to find out who was behind the vandalism and threatening messages his family had received since his father, brother, and brother-in-law died. Do you think his motive for wanting to do this was only because he was concerned for the safety of his family? Or did Henry believe that if he could learn the person's identity, it would prove to his mother and siblings that, although still a teenager, he could behave as a responsible adult?

4. Amy tried her hand at matchmaking because she was convinced that Herschel was the best man for her mother. Have you ever become a matchmaker? If so, how did it turn out?

5. Sylvia postponed her wedding to Dennis for a few months in order to help her mother in the greenhouse. Do you think it was necessary for her to do that, or should Belinda have insisted that her daughter keep her original plans? Have you ever set an important plan or event aside to help someone else? If so, how did it make you feel?

6. Monroe had been interested in Belinda since they were teenagers and was disappointed when she married someone else. When Belinda became a widow, Monroe felt he was given a second chance. Do you think Monroe did the right thing by pressuring Belinda to marry him? Have you ever been in a similar situation? If so, what did you do about it?

7. Herschel had been a widower for some time and spent many years pining for his wife. Until he met Belinda, he never thought he would fall in love again. But Herschel felt inferior to Belinda's other suitor because he was less successful than Monroe in material things. Should a person ever let their lack of success keep them from establishing a relationship with someone they love? How can we rise beyond our insecurities when others are more successful?

8. Belinda was kindhearted and giving, even to an elderly woman who had stolen things from her. What verses in the Bible teach us how we should respond to people who have been unkind or used us? How are we supposed to treat widows and those who are poor?

9. Virginia had kept her past hidden from others because she felt ashamed of how she had treated her children. Is there something in your past that you have shared with only a few people, or perhaps no one, because you were afraid of people's reactions? Is it important to share past mistakes with others, or would it be better to keep quiet about our mistakes, even if someone could benefit from knowing?

10. When Michelle met her mother for the first time after many years, did she respond the way most people would? Was Michelle's willingness to forgive her mother something she had to force herself to do, or did it come naturally because of her faith in God? What does the Bible say about forgiveness?

11. When the truth was revealed about who had been doing the vandalism to the Kings' property, how did you feel about the way Belinda reacted? Should she have let the sheriff know, even though the one who'd done it apologized? How would you have dealt with such a situation?

12. How did forgiveness play into this story? Does forgiveness mean we don't have to hold people accountable for their actions?

13. Why are some people able to forgive someone who has wronged them, while others harbor anger and resentment toward those who have hurt them or their loved ones? How can we learn from Christ's example to forgive others?

14. Henry loved his father very much and became upset when his mother decided to marry another man. He was worried that her new husband might try to act as though he was his father. Were Henry's fears legitimate? Did the man Belinda planned to marry handle things well with Henry? Have you or someone you know faced a similar situation—either as a child whose parent decided to remarry, or as the parent who felt concerned about the children when he or she decided to marry again? What can a parent say to a child who feels anxious about a new person coming into their lives?

15. By reading this book, did you learn anything about the Amish way of life that you didn't already know? Did it help you understand why the Plain people adhere to their traditions?

16. Were there any scriptures mentioned in this book that spoke to your heart or helped you in some way?

About the Author

New York Times bestselling and award-winning author **Wanda E. Brunstetter** is one of the founders of the Amish fiction genre. She has written more than 100 books translated into four languages. With over 11 million copies sold, Wanda's stories consistently earn spots on the nation's most prestigious bestseller lists and have received numerous awards.

Wanda's ancestors were part of the Anabaptist faith, and her novels are based on personal research intended to accurately portray the Amish way of life. Her books are well-read and trusted by many Amish, who credit her for giving readers a deeper understanding of the people and their customs.

When Wanda visits her Amish friends, she finds herself drawn to their peaceful lifestyle, sincerity, and close family ties. Wanda enjoys photography, ventriloquism, gardening, bird-watching, beachcombing, and spending time with her family. She and her husband, Richard, have been blessed with two grown children, six grandchildren, and two great-grandchildren.

Check out Wanda's website at www.wandabrunstetter.com.

More from Wanda!

Wanda E. Brunstetter's Amish Friends
Healthy Options Cookbook (Coming May 2021)

Loaded with dozens of Amish recipes for the health conscious.

Everyone wants to feel healthy, right? Food can be one of our best
medicines, and many Amish are known for seeking ways for health to
begin in the kitchen.

Brand new, from *New York Times* bestselling author of Amish
fiction, Wanda E. Brunstetter, is a helpful cookbook from Amish and
Mennonite cooks who offer healthy recipe options. Over 200 recipes
are divided into traditional categories from main dishes and sides to
desserts and snacks with labels for gluten free, dairy free, sugar free, etc.
Also included are health tips and remedies.

Encased in a lay-flat binding and presented in full-color, home
cooks of all ages will be eager to add this cookbook to their collections.

Comb Bound / 978-1-64352-925-7 / $16.99